JACK MURPHY
DIRECT ACTION

Also by Jack Murphy:

The PROMIS series:

PROMIS: Vietnam

PROMIS: Rhodesia

PROMIS: South Africa

PROMIS: Lebanon (forthcoming)

The Deckard series:

Reflexive Fire

Target Deck

Direct Action

Non-Fiction

US Special Forces: Weapons Report Card

Benghazi: The Definitive Report

Direct Action is a work of fiction. Names, places, and incidents either are products of the author's imagination or are used fictitiously.

Printed in the United States of America

http://reflexivefire.com

First Edition

Author's Note:

The plot of this novel is a work of fiction which ties a series of events together into a story, however, most of the individual situations, scenarios, and conversations in this book depict and describe factual events. The author was told by numerous people in the Special Operations and Intelligence Community that he would be murdered for investigating these subjects.

Prologue:

Afghanistan, 2005:

Navy Chief David McAtee was alive when the jihadists moved in. They were Chechens. Foreign fighters who had over run the hide site he had occupied. With three teammates, he had tried to escape and evade down the side of the mountain. There were simply too many of them for him and his recon team to successfully break contact and escape.

Chief McAtee was alive when the enemy started picking over his body, beginning to strip him of his weapons and equipment to divide amongst themselves. Shot through one lung, both legs, and through his cheek, he was in no condition to defend himself. His arm was limp; he couldn't even feel any sensation in it as one of the Chechens undid the clasp on his wrist watch and then let his arm flop to the ground.

Chief McAtee was alive when the Chechens cut the gear off his body and yanked away his M4 rifle off by its sling. He struggled to breath. His three comrades were dead, that much he knew for sure. He had watched them die one by one. Now, he knew that they were better off.

Chief McAtee was alive when the knives came out and they began the cutting.

Wind howled down the side of the mountain. Snow-streaked crags of rock poked up from beneath the white ground, forcing the team to negotiate their way around them. The windswept mountain was an even bigger obstacle than the enemy, the terrain slowing them as they moved uphill through knee-deep snow.

Master Chief Bill Geddes saw the world through a green-tinted lens. The PVS-14 Night Optical Device limited both his depth perception and his field of vision but he was walking point and needed to be able to see the enemy before they saw him. Although the wind was blowing snow drifts off the side of the mountain, the night was clear with a full moon hanging over their heads. The added illumination would make it easier for the Master Chief to spot the enemy, but it would also make it easier for the enemy to see his team.

For what seemed like the hundredth time, he wiped snow off the lens of his NODs so that he could see.

The word to describe their current mission was anger. As members of Naval Special Warfare Development Group, commonly known as SEAL Team Six, they had been assigned to lay up in a hide site over a valley and watch for suspected enemy activity. Intelligence indicated that large numbers of foreign fighters were moving from Pakistan to Afghanistan through the valley, and the brass up at the Joint Operations Center in Bagram wanted a heads-up as to what was coming their way.

A second reconnaissance team, led by Chief McAtee, had occupied another overwatch position where they had a vantage point over a section of the road running through the valley that Bill's team couldn't cover. Four hours ago, McAtee's hide site had been compromised. From what they could gather from the radio transmissions, the team had been on the run ever since. Two hours ago, they had lost radio contact with McAtee's team altogether. Bagram couldn't get them on comms and neither could Bill.

A Troops in Contact call had been sent over the net, but higher said it was a no-go. There was a storm moving in and they could not risk flying in close air support or the SEAL platoon that had been standing by as a Quick Reaction Force. Last month a CH-47 filled with Rangers had been shot out of the sky by the Taliban. It had turned into a big fiasco on the news networks back home and now the commanders were risk adverse about sending in helicopters on another rescue mission.

They could write off a small four-man recce team, but another downed CH-47 could cost some Colonel his star.

Pissed. That was another adjective that described how he felt, Bill thought to himself.

Since the cavalry wasn't coming and they had no overhead surveillance, Bill decided to take the initiative. His four man recce team abandoned their hide side and began trudging through the snow towards the last known location of McAtee's team.

Bill and his men had hardly slept since occupying the hide site several days prior. Now they were dehydrated from snaking their way up the side of the mountain. Most of them were big guys, weight lifters with a lot of upper body strength. Now they were paying the price as those large muscles required a lot of oxygen during exertion, oxygen that wasn't available at high altitudes. They were exhausted, but Bill knew that as SEALs, there was no way they would turn around, no way they would quit, not without bringing their comrades home with them.

His legs dragging trails behind him, Bill was perhaps the most tired of all as he was up front breaking through the thick snow and making their route selection. Time seemed to standstill in the night, their faces having gone numb from the cold wind, their heads beginning to hang as sleep deprivation set in. Maybe it was another forty five minutes, maybe an hour and a half. During the after action review, Bill was unable to recall with any clarity when he saw the four silhouettes in the night.

The Master Chief could see them clearly through his PVS-14s from several hundred meters out. They wore thick jackets and Afghan *pakol* caps on their heads. The four of them had AK-47 rifles slung over their backs as they squatted, huddled around something. There was no camp fire. Adjusting the focus on his night-vision monocle, Bill could see their long ratty beards blowing in the wind.

The firefight was nothing spectacular. The SEAL Team Six operator had his men get on line and they opened fire as one, cutting down the four enemy fighters in half a second. No fancy tactics were going to be applied with the men exhausted and in such difficult terrain, and none were needed. Their M4 rifles cracked through the night. Two of the jihadists dropped like marionettes that had their strings suddenly cut. Another was struck in the shoulder, then tried to get back up and run until Bill emptied the rest of his magazine into the jihadist's back. The last fell face-first into the snow. At first he tried to push himself back up, then thought better of it, laid back down, and promptly died.

Bill dropped his expended magazine, inserted a full one, and dropped the bolt on his M4 to chamber the first round. The other three SEALs on his team did the same.

Moving forward, the mountain planed out into a small ledge. As they grew closer, the SEALs put a few insurance shots into the Chechens just to make sure they were well and truly dead. Closing on the bodies, the SEALs were able to see what the enemy had been crouching around. Bill slung his rifle and ran to the prostrate form. Laying face down, the snow around Chief McAtee had been stained a dark shade of crimson.

The seam down the back of McAtee's fatigues had been sliced open with a knife. His ass was bloody where the enemy had been sodomizing him. Bill took a knee and rolled his friend over on to his back. Reilly, the team medic, dropped his aid bag and began digging through its contents.

As Bill rolled McAtee onto his back, his blood ran colder than the wind blasting down the side of the mountain. McAtee convulsed in his arms, in a deep state of shock. He was not conscious but still technically alive. When Bill cradled his friend in his arms, the SEAL's head hinged backwards with a jagged second mouth opening at the neck. McAtee was shaking in his arms.

Reilly crouched over him with bandages, but there was nothing he could do. He was a Special Operations trained medic, but felt utterly useless as his comrade's condition was beyond anything he could begin to treat in an emergency room much less on the side of a mountain during a blizzard. They could hear McAtee gurgling as he struggled to breath.

Finally, the ravaged SEAL convulsed for the last time and lay dead in Bill's arms. The four SEALs stared at the ground in shock. Each of them was a veteran of countless battles. Ship seizures in the Persian Gulf, covert operations in Somalia, targeted killings in Colombia, and direct action raids in Afghanistan, but none of them had ever experienced anything like this. This was different. This was crossing a line from which they could not return.

Bill laid McAtee down in the snow. Digging into his kit he found a space blanket that he used to cover the remains with. He then began camouflaging the body under snow with the other

SEALs joining in. Reilly got out his GPS and wrote down a ten-digit grid location, marking where the body was cached. A snow storm was quickly blowing in from the west.

Getting to his feet, Bill slung his rifle in front of him and looked up the side of the mountain. They had three more SEALs to recover. They were up there, somewhere. With the Chechens.

Bill looked over his shoulder at his recce team. His gaze cut right through them.

"From this day forward," he shouted over the wind. "It is an eye for an eye."

The SEALs nodded.

"Every single day. For McAtee and the rest."

Master Chief Bill Geddes ground his teeth and stepped off in search of the others.

"Its blood for blood," he yelled up the mountain at anyone who would listen.

Three SEALs followed close behind their team leader, walking in the footprints he made in the snow.

Soon, the four operators disappeared into the snow storm.

1

Present Day

Deckard fell towards the earth, nearly going end over end as he struggled to maintain a positive body position. Glancing at his altimeter, he waved off at 6,000 feet, looked back at his altimeter and then reached for his ripcord at 4,500 feet. When he gave it a yank, his head snapped to the side. He had been pulling on the tube running from his oxygen mask to the bottled O2 strapped under his MC-5 parachute. Making another attempt, he reached in and snatched his ripcord. He pulled it but nothing happened; the metal grip separated from the steel cable which would have pulled the pins and released his parachute.

He didn't bother to look back at his altimeter, but knew he was burning altitude fast. Tracing the main lift web on his parachute harness, he grabbed the floating cable and pulled as hard as he could. He was pins-out somewhere around 2,000 feet. The pilot chute was out, but caught in a wind bubble on his back where it bounced around but failed to catch in the air and deploy his main parachute.

Then, the CYPRES system detected the barometric pressure at low altitude, indicating that something was wrong. The computer was a fail safe in case the jumper was knocked unconscious. To his horror, the reserve parachute deployed just as the pilot chute finally pulled his main parachute out of its deployment bag.

Two parachutes, both with forward drive, were now over his head, his reserve and main parachute snaking around each other and becoming intertwined. With two canopies over his head, cutting away and pulling his reserve was out of the question. All he had was a main and a reserve and they were both deployed already.

Deckard reached up and grabbed the suspension lines of the reserve parachute, desperately trying to prevent it from entangling itself around the main parachute. If his main chute was collapsed by the reserve there was no recourse or corrective measure which could save him. His biceps were burning as he pulled and separated the suspension lines, but the reserve chute was still trying to drive forward. Since it was anchored to the parachute harness, and to Deckard, it kept trying to make a U-turn back into his main chute.

As the main parachute began to collapse, Deckard felt weightless, the ground rushing up to reach him. Somehow he managed to survive the landing. Shrugging out of his parachute harness he put his M4 rifle into operation and moved out.

The enemy was quickly advancing. Joined by his teammates, Deckard opened fire. A single round fired from the rifle before it jammed. Deckard executed the malfunction drill by muscle memory without consciously thinking through the steps. Slapping the magazine, he racked the bolt and tapped the forward assist. Pulling the buttstock back into the pocket of his shoulder, he aimed down the sights and squeezed the trigger on the first enemy he spotted. The hammer dropped on the firing pin but the rifle did not discharge.

Now his teammates had to pick up their rate of fire to compensate for Deckard's weapon being out of action. He performed the malfunction drill again. Slap, rack, but no bang. The man to Deckard's left went down under a hail of gunfire. Slap, rack, but nothing. Deckard dropped the magazine, pulled the bolt to the rear and inspected the chamber. It looked clear. Loading a fresh magazine he attempted to shoot again. Nothing.

His other teammate on his right side collapsed like an empty coat. Deckard slapped the magazine, racked the bolt, and squeezed the trigger but the weapon still would not fire. The enemy was right on top of him. He was still attempting to get his rifle back online when the terrorists swarmed in on him.

That was when Deckard woke up.

His chest heaved as he tried to catch his breath, his mind taking a few moments to recognize his surroundings. He was in an apartment in Las Vegas, a temporary safe house where he was waiting out a different kind of storm. Forty-eight hours ago, Deckard and his crew had smashed through a conspiracy that stretched from Mexican drug cartels to a Private Military Company that had been training Iranian terrorists in the Nevada desert. Since clearing out of Area 14 on a Department of Energy training site, Deckard and his teammates from Samruk International had been in hiding. No casinos for them, not while half the world was wondering what the hell had happened out in the Nevada desert.

He stretched his back while he lay on the couch and felt his back pop.

Deckard and Samruk International were what had happened. They had taken on the cartels and their puppet masters. They walked away from that fight, the enemy didn't. But they had walked away with something else as well. While busting into a top-secret facility, a special activities center for the G3 Communications Corporation, they had retrieved several bags worth of sensitive documents.

Pat had made a phone call to an old girlfriend in town and secured them a place to stay until some of the heat died down. After spending an entire day sleeping and eating, Deckard, Pat, Aghassi, Nikita, and Kurt began moving around the apartment. With little else to do, they sat around the coffee table poring over the intelligence material they had collected while Nikita busied himself cleaning his HK 417 sniper rifle.

Sitting up on the couch, Deckard felt the soreness deep in his muscles and joints. He had run himself ragged during the campaign in Mexico until he literally collapsed. After getting a few bags of saline solution by intravenous drip, he went right back into the fight. When they first got to the apartment, he collapsed onto the couch. It was less like sleep and more like a coma. When he woke up he was dehydrated and his tongue was stuck to the roof of his mouth.

But after a few solid meals, sleep, and drinking lots of water, he was starting to feel a lot better, even though his body was still recovering from the wounds and abrasions he had taken along the way. Meanwhile, the rest of his Private Military

Company, Samruk International, had been flown back to Kazakhstan. Having left Frank and Sergeant Major Korgan in charge of the two platoons, they had paid the men and then put them on leave for some much needed R&R.

Deckard looked at the files and folders strewn across the table.

The CEO of G3 Communications was still out there. Deckard would attend to him, but at a time and place of his choosing. Right now, the CEO was no doubt prepared for him after learning about Samruk's hit on Area 14. The documents they had recovered pointed in other directions. G3 was not just running illegal operations in Latin America but also in the Gulf States. One document in particular caught Deckard's interest. It was a company roster for a G3 subsidiary registered in the United Arab Emirates.

The roster listed over a 150 employees by name along with their place of birth, passport number, phone number, blood type, and their duty position within the company. Interestingly they were all coded into the roster under the number 11. When looking at the index for the roster, number 11 listed that position as "maintenance." Deckard had a hard time believing that employees from the Ukraine, South Africa, Pakistan, and England were all hired and flown to the UAE simply to be janitors.

More curious, there was a small cell isolated within the roster. They were not listed by name but rather an alphanumeric designation ranging from O-1 to O-7. The cell name was Liquid Sky. No passport numbers were listed but they were all Americans, aside from one of them whose place of birth was listed as Sri Lanka despite being a US citizen. They were the only Americans working within the entire company in fact.

Deckard sat alone in the early morning light, unable to fall asleep after the nightmares. What he had uncovered in the documents thus far was grinding at him.

There was also a target deck within one of the binders of people who appeared to have been eliminated by Liquid Sky. Pat's gal pal was a nurse and still at work, so Deckard logged into her computer and downloaded some software that would allow him to search the web anonymously. He started tracking down the names in the target deck. Many of them did not come up in any of his searches which was to be expected if they were third-world terrorists or, for that matter, intelligence professionals who didn't want to be found in life or death. Some names did produce search results.

One was a Saudi prince who disappeared and was found a week later in the desert with a bullet in the back of his head. It was written off in the media as an inter-familial feud within the royal family. Another was a Somalian warlord who had been reported by the Associated Press as being killed by a Predator drone strike, but according to the logs in the target deck, he had actually been killed two weeks prior. A third target was an Al Qaeda terrorist emir in Yemen. They were bad guys, or at least baddish, until he got halfway down the list.

The turning point seemed to be in 2011, when the targets shifted from being exclusively Islamic extremists and corrupt Arabs to pro-democracy demonstrators, protest leaders, and human-rights advocates in the UAE, Yemen, Tunisia, Libya, Egypt, Saudi Arabia, Syria, and throughout the Arab world. Just as the Arab Spring picked up momentum, it seemed that Liquid Sky had received new taskings. The client had to be the leaders of the Gulf States who wanted both Islamic extremists and anti-monarchist, anti-dictatorship protestors off their backs.

The fat cats in the Gulf States were content to rake in oil money and bang Russian hookers but needed American expertise to maintain their position in society. American Special Operations expertise. Who was holding down the pro-democracy movement in the Middle East? Who was helping to keep the Arab world a dictatorship and a breeding ground for terrorism? It looked like one arm of that apparatus was called Liquid Sky, a group of renegade military contractors.

There was one name listed in the target deck that had not reached his expiration date. One that was scheduled in for service within a weeks time. Would Liquid Sky be alerted that their OPSEC was blown when Area 14 had been set ablaze? Deckard scratched the stubble on his face.

Liquid Sky's next target was currently located in a hospital in Karachi, Pakistan.

He was the last name on the list.

2

One week later:

Karachi, Pakistan

Deckard crouched next to the body of a dead Pakistani doctor.

His white jacket was stained red as blood leaked into a pool beneath him. Ripping a few buttons on his shirt, Deckard could easily spot the entry wounds. A veteran of countless firefights, he quickly identified them as being from 9mm bullets. Two shots, each with impeccable round placement. The shooter had used the doctor's collar as a point of reference when aligning his sights.

Aim small, miss small.

The entry wounds were almost touching each other.

Leaving the corpse behind, he strode up the steps, taking them three at a time to the front door of the hospital. The door had been locked so the shooters had used an explosive charge to breach and make entry into the structure. Deckard had heard the detonation as he drove towards the hospital. He was just a minute behind them. One critical minute.

The door looked like it had been sliced in half. They used a cutting charge, probably explosive cutting tape which used RDX explosive and a metal filament to blast through obstacles. With the building's exterior lights turned on, he saw a tangle of clear wire laying in a heap next to the door. It was the remnants of the shock tube that had been used to detonate the cutting charge.

The sharp scent of the explosives hung in the air as Deckard stepped inside. Deeper in the hospital, he could hear the sound of gunfire. The Liquid Sky team was clearing a path to their target.

With his Kimber 1911 pistol leading the way, Deckard picked up the pace. Jogging halfway down the hall, he slipped and nearly fell on a slick of blood. Two Pakistani policemen had been slaughtered before they could even draw their weapons. The Paks had put security on their man, but not very good security. At a glance, Deckard could tell they had both been shot numerous times in the torso with added shots following up as the shooters moved towards the policemen to make sure they were really dead. One shot looked like it had flayed the skin right off one of the policemen's neck.

Aghassi and Jager were right behind him and grabbed him under the elbows before he could topple over. Leaving a trail of bloody footprints behind him, they kept moving.

"This is Shooter-One," the earbud connected to his cellphone crackled. "In position."

"Roger," Deckard replied into the mic.

Nikita had taken an overwatch position outside where he could cover the front of the hospital while Pat stayed with their vehicle.

The Samruk International mercenaries had a week to get themselves to Pakistan and conduct mission planning to intercept the Liquid Sky team. Considering the *ad hoc* nature of the mission, everything had come together fairly well and they were confident that they could catch the Liquid Sky shooters, whoever they really were, in an ambush before they even got near their target.

Then someone had set a fire in the basement of the Joint Forces hospital on the Naval Base and the patients had to be moved across town to the Aga Khan university hospital instead. It seemed that Liquid Sky had been conducting their own surveillance and didn't like what they saw, so they induced a situation in which their target had to be moved to a location where the conditions would be more favorable to the assassins.

It worked. Deckard's plans were tossed out the window and now they were improvising on the fly.

What else was new?

Expended brass casings littered the floor.

A Pakistani policemen, this time with tactical gear, including body armor and an assault vest, was sprawled on his back. The shooters had fired center mass, and when the bullets failed to penetrate the body armor, they walked their shots up into his face and fired until he went down. It was known as a failure drill. Put the first two shots center mass and then shoot into the skull until the target is no longer a threat.

Deckard rounded the corner with his two comrades and continued in the direction of the sound of gunfire.

Now he knew beyond a shadow of a doubt. ECT on the door, failure drills, and the information contained in the roster they had recovered in Nevada. These guys were Americans and not any ordinary Americans.

These were the type of Americans that Deckard had worked with for years, trained with, conducted combat operations with. These guys were Special Operations; it was just a question of which tribe they had come from.

Following the trail of destruction, the trio took another turn and bounded up a flight of stairs. They stepped over several more corpses in tactical gear. It looked like some kind of police para-military unit had been assigned to guard Liquid Sky's target.

Only one of the bodies was interesting. Deckard paused for half a second, noting the deep cuts on the face, neck, and forearms of the body. They were made by a short defensive blade as the Pakistani had tried to defend himself. Someone who knew what they were doing and had made quick work of their opponent, taking him apart like a chicken.

Racing down the hall, they passed under a broken florescent light, the adjacent lights blinking on and off due to a flash bang grenade that had exploded. The door of the target's hospital room was ajar. Several sets of bloody boot prints trailed out and back down the hall. Deckard stood in the doorway.

Abdulkarim Al-Khalifa lay in his hospital bed, one arm hanging lifelessly over the side as blood ran down it and softly pattered onto the floor. He had been a social organizer and protest leader in the country of Bahrain. Al-Khalifa had been so successful in organizing pro-democracy movements that he had to flee the country with state security services nipping at his heels. Eventually he found his way to India where the Pakistani intelligence service, ISI, had kidnapped him. It was to be a for profit operation for ISI.

The Pakistanis had been in the final stages of negotiating a ransom with the Kingdom of Bahrain. Al-Khalifa had continued to be a thorn in the government's side by utilizing social media websites to communicate with the opposition groups. Bahrain wanted him back so that he could be imprisoned, and eventually, permanently silenced. But the ISI was driving a hard bargain, so somebody decided to take matters into their own hands.

A third party called Liquid Sky.

Gunfire sounded back on the ground floor, the staccato bursts rattling the windows. The mercenaries could distinguish between the initial shots, from Nikita's sniper rifle, and the return fire that came a moment later.

"Fuck," Nikita cursed as he hot mic'ed the radio. "Shit!"

"I'm on it," Pat's voice came over the net. His PKM machine gun was now shaking up the party.

"These guys are good," Nikita transmitted. "I took down the first one and the others immediately hit the ground. One deployed a smoke grenade and the others returned fire on my position."

The full auto gunfire broke off into stunted bursts and the Liquid Sky gunfighters returned fire one more time.

"They're breaking contact," Pat reported. "Flushing them back in your direction."

Deckard took a final look into the hospital room.

Al-Khalifa's wife lay sprawled out on the bed on top of him. She had been trying to protect him from the onslaught of gunfire and had died alongside her husband.

Deckard keyed his radio.

"We're moving."

The team followed him back down to the ground floor. Liquid Sky had tried to bail out a side exit to make their escape, but Nikita had that angle in his field of fire. They retreated back into the hospital, but now it was a question of whether they would hard-point it and wait for extraction or attempt another breakthrough and escape. Deckard could hear the shouting just ahead of them.

Women were screaming. Somewhere in the fray, a man's voice could be heard.

"Get the fuck outta the way!" the voice echoed.

Bursting into the burn ward, Deckard shot a glance over the front sight of his 1911 and caught a flash of the enemy as the Liquid Sky member moved into the next room. Sprinting between occupied beds, several patients turned to look at him. Others were in no state to do anything other than let a machine breath for them. Rear security hadn't spotted Deckard yet, and he pushed into the next room.

Seeing a moving shadow with a rifle in its hands, Deckard's shot blasted through a hanging IV bag, spraying the fluid into the air. The .45 caliber round ricocheted off the metal pole that had held up the bag, saving his target from growing a third eye. The shooter ducked and dived through a doorway after his comrades.

A flashbang grenade rolled into the room and spun across the floor towards Deckard's feet. Without hesitating, Deckard kicked it back. The distraction device made it halfway back to the door before it went off. Even though he knew enough to turn away, the flash was momentarily blinding. The bang was enough to rattle all three of the mercenaries for a few seconds.

Blinking away the spots in his vision, the three mercenaries ran through the orthopedic department and out into the courtyard just in time to see the last Liquid Sky member slip over the wall and out onto the street on the back side of the building. Their blind spot where Nikita and Pat had no coverage.

"Shooter-One, Gunner-One," Deckard called out Nikita and Pat's callsigns. "Secure the body you made and get to the extraction site. We are going to pursue."

Without waiting for a response, Deckard ran at full speed towards the high wall. Leaping into the air, he planted a foot on the wall and pushed off it, vaulting himself up onto the lip of the wall where he grabbed hold. Pulling himself over the top, he stayed low as he slid over the wall and dropped down into the dirt and trash on the ground.

Five shadows moved down the street ahead of him. The third-world stench was thick in the air as burning trash, body odor, and diesel exhaust combined with the stifling heat. The shadows were in a mad dash, no doubt having shifted their extraction point by radio. Kurt and Aghassi dropped down alongside him as they came over the wall.

Staying in the shadows, the Samruk mercenaries chased after Liquid Sky. They didn't get far before a white van blasted around the corner up ahead and screeched to a halt. Red brake lights blinked as the van rocked forward before settling into place. The sliding door opened and the five shooters piled inside.

Deckard stepped out into the street, leveling his pistol. With Aghassi and Kurt, the three of them unloaded their handguns into the van. Bullets pockmarked the metal siding, one taking out a rear light as the van sped away but none of them seemed to strike the driver of the getaway vehicle. Now under fire, the van took the first right-hand turn to escape the killzone.

Cutting up another side street, Deckard's lungs felt like they were about to collapse on him. He still wasn't fully recovered from his previous mission. Although a week and a half had done a lot to help him heal up, he still wasn't at a hundred percent. For a moment, it seemed futile. Back on the main boulevard, he turned his head. Sweat stinging his eyes, he spotted a single brake light. The van was caught in traffic.

Kurt Jager moved to the nearest car as the driver slowed. Tearing open the door, he grabbed the mustached Pakistani by the head and tossed him out of the vehicle. The mercenaries got in and slammed the doors. Seeing the firepower they were carrying, the driver decided to leave well enough alone.

As Kurt took the wheel, Deckard keyed his radio again.

"We're heading west," he announced. Towards the port.

As Kurt began nudging cars out of the way and driving up on the shoulder to get ahead, the driver of the van noticed that they were still being pursued and did the same. Spinning the wheel, the driver took them onto another side street, finding an alternate route to the port of Karachi. By now they were less than a mile away from the coast. The van driver now slammed on the brakes, slowing down enough to prevent the vehicle from spinning out as the paved road turned to dirt.

Kurt Jager downshifted. Experienced in rally racing, Kurt got everything he possibly could out of the third-world jalopy. It wasn't much. Deckard held on to the door to prevent himself from being thrown around the back seat. They were gaining on the van, but now the plume of dust kicked up in its wake was obscuring Kurt's vision. He was forced onto the shoulder of the road; otherwise he would be driving faster than he could see.

As the dust cleared, Kurt immediately yanked the steering wheel to the left to avoid a giant crane the size of the tractor trailer parked on the side of the road.

The van driver realized he had an accidental weapon on his hands and began swerving back and forth to kick up an even bigger dust cloud. Leaning into the next turn, Kurt was forced to slow down or risk slamming into another crane or pallet of bricks.

Deckard gritted his teeth, the dust coming through the window sticking to his lips. His suspicions had been confirmed in triplicate. Liquid Sky was the real deal, and they were about to slip outside his grasp for good.

Kurt veered left with the road and the dust finally cleared. Looking at a parallel running road, they could see that they had missed a turn. The van was racing towards the end of the port, and now there was a set of train tracks between them and their target.

The port was lit up in a golden glow at night, the shadows wavering through the sedan as Kurt struggled to stay on their query. Tanker ships bobbed in the dark waters, the golden flow from their deck lights bouncing gently on the waves. Connex containers and oil containers flashed between them and the van as they ran parallel paths.

The former GSG-9 commando finally found a passage over the tracks and cut the wheel. The van was doing the same, nosing towards the towering cranes that indicated a commercial shipping yard. The vehicles shot through the connex container storage area and out onto the loading docks. The van stopped near the first crane and the five shadows spilled out. The driver jumped out as well for a total of six.

Anticipating their next move, Kurt put a small administrative building between themselves and Liquid Sky. Gunfire chased them until they reached their cover. Bullets continued to streak through the thin sheet metal walls and shatter windows. To their flank, Deckard heard the roar of a high-powered boat engine gassing towards the dock. The long, slick craft passed them and slowed down alongside the dock. The mercenaries kicked open the car doors before they had even slowed to a stop.

Taking a knee, Deckard broke cover from behind the structure and returned fire. At forty meters, it was a long shot with his .45 caliber pistol but at least it gave some maneuver room for Kurt and Aghassi to move.

The motorboat pulled up alongside the dock and one by one the Liquid Sky shooters dropped down into it. When the entire team was aboard, the boat peeled off. The mercenaries ran for the edge of the dock, firing after the boat but it was too late. The boat powered off into the night, leaving them behind.

Deckard stood with his pistol in slide lock, trying to catch his breath while reloading.

That was when the van exploded.

The sides of the van bulged outwards, tearing at the seams to let an orange fireball escape from inside. The fire curled into the air and became black smoke. Deckard groaned as he pulled himself to his feet. He was sweating profusely, and now dust was stuck to every inch of exposed skin. He could feel the heat from the fire on his face.

A black SUV pulled up behind them, no doubt vectored in by the giant fireball which gave away their position. Pat got out of the driver's side, hefting his PKM machine gun out with him. Nikita got out of the passenger side with his HK 417 sniper rifle.

"We lost them," Aghassi said shaking his head. He wasn't accustomed to losing his targets. As a Special Operations soldier he had lived as a nomad in Afghanistan where he watched terrorists for weeks and months, living like a local. He was once placed in a Pakistani prison in order to eavesdrop on imprisoned Al Qaeda operatives in an attempt to locate Osama Bin Laden. Everyone knew that Aghassi was someone who got the job done when it came to human intelligence. He had proven it to Deckard in Mexico.

"We lost them," he repeated. They all knew they didn't have any other leads. They were on the trail of a black ops team that specialized in two things, killing and not being found.

Deckard slammed home a fresh magazine and thumbed the slide release. He said nothing as he holstered the weapon.

"Take a look," Nikita said to him, reverting back to his native Russian language. Deckard was still learning that one but understood what the sniper meant.

Nikita opened the SUVs rear door. Inside was the body of the Liquid Sky shooter he had killed when they had initially exited the hospital. The 7.62 round had smashed his face pretty good, enough to leave it unrecognizable in a photograph.

On the other side of the wharf, red and blue police lights were flashing.

"Get us out of here," he told Pat. The entire Samruk International team got inside with Deckard crawling into the back. As they began driving, he pulled out a small LED red light to look over the body. He was a big dude, Caucasian, definitely lifted weights.

Underneath his clothes, the shooter wore concealable body armor. Over it was a locally procured chest rig that held

22

magazines for the MP5 sub-machine gun he had been carrying. It looked like the tags had been cut from his clothing and kit. The team had gone in sterile.

Deckard suddenly realized that he might have known this man in another life. Was he rifling through the body of a guy he had gone to selection with? Could he be an old Ranger buddy? Was this a former teammate who had gone over to the other side? He pushed the thought away.

As the police lights closed in, Pat positioned the SUV between two connex containers and cut the headlights. A half dozen police cars screamed by towards the scene of the explosion. Once they had passed, Pat crept back onto the road, turned on the headlights, and began driving towards their safe house.

The corpse also had tattoos. A red crusader cross on the forearm. SPQR tattooed on the shoulder. Stripping off the chest rig and body armor, Deckard located a black rectangle on the ribcage. It was where Nazi soldiers would get their dog tag information tattooed during World War Two. Many modern-day soldiers, including Americans, had adopted the practice. This soldier had gone back to a tattoo studio to have that information blacked out rather than pay for a laser removal.

He had nothing. Maybe dental records if he could get access to military databases but even that seemed doubtful.

Deckard leaned back against the side of the SUV as Pat navigated the back roads of Karachi. Cold sweat trickled down his neck and seeped into his clothes. It hit him like sucker punch.

He was trying to analyze what he had to find a lead where there was none. What he did have was a body. What he did know for a fact was that Liquid Sky had just had a member killed in action. What he had was an opportunity: an opportunity to entice Liquid Sky into finding him.

Come tomorrow morning, Liquid Sky would be looking for a new operator.

Deckard grinned.

He knew just what name to drop in the hat.

23

3

Washington DC:

This is the dumbest fucking idea you've ever had.

Deckard thought over Pat's words to him before he had stepped on the airplane. The passenger plane had just touched down in the bizarre city where every other jerk off had a graduate degree and a plan to save the world.

It wasn't that Deckard disagreed with what Pat was saying, he just didn't see any other option. With no trails to follow, the only path left was to put one of their names out there into the netherworld as seeking employment and see who called. Both of them began making phone calls to certain former Special Operations and intelligence professionals who served as personnel feeders for various black projects.

Pat insisted that it should be him going in, not Deckard. Deckard was the CEO and leader of Samruk International, and he wouldn't be leading anything while working undercover. Deckard insisted. There was a big difference between Pat and him. Pat was something of a legend in the Special Operations community. He retired out of Delta Force as a Master Sergeant. He was a rock star operator who was loved and respected by the community.

Deckard on the other hand, was completely disgraced. When shit got ugly between him and the CIA, they had completely disavowed him. Today he was considered *persona non grata* in many circles by people who were pissed at him. Some were angry over things he actually did, others were angry over baseless rumors they had heard. Still others were just angry.

They were trying to infiltrate a rogue group of para-military contractors. Bad ass operators like Pat with sterling reputations wouldn't cut it. Not on this op. Liquid Sky would never even consider someone like that. They would want someone who was already on the fringes, maybe someone who was already guilty of something. They both knew that Deckard was the right man for this job.

You always had one foot in the grave and the other on a

banana peel, Pat had reminded him as he boarded the plane.

Deckard unbuckled his safety belt as the flight attendants opened the doors, and he made his way down the aisle. He didn't have any bags with him. It was another one of those trips.

After floating his name out there as a freelancer looking for work, Deckard received a phone call in less than twenty-four hours. He had no idea if it was Liquid Sky or some other group that was trying to recruit him. He just knew that Liquid Sky would be looking for a warm body and threw the dice.

Some times you just have to let them bitches roll.

His instructions, received via email, were to report to a nondescript building near Embassy Row for processing, whatever that meant. Pushing through the glass doors, he spoke briefly with the receptionist before she took his photo with a webcam and printed off a black and white photo building pass for him.

"You want to go up to Jorge Bio-Medico on the 5th floor," she instructed him.

Getting on the elevator, Deckard punched the button for the 5th floor.

When the elevator doors opened, Deckard walked to the door with the Jorge Bio-Medico logo on it and hit the buzzer. "Please look directly into the camera," a female voice instructed through the speaker system.

Looking up, he saw the CCTV camera mounted in the corner of the hallway and looked into it. After a moment the door buzzed to allow him in.

A stunning redhead rounded the corner and came to meet

him at the door. Deckard was flustered for a moment and at a loss for words. She wore a tight dress that left little to the imagination as to her profile, along with a collared shirt with the top buttons undone. Her smile lit up the room, her features framed by flowing red hair.

"Hi Mr. Deckard," she extended her hand. Deckard held it a little longer than he should have. "My name is Sarah."

"Nice to meet you," he said with a grin that he hoped didn't betray him.

"Just this way," she said, still smiling as she spun around and led him to an office.

A bank of computer terminals was set up along with a series of different electronic scanners.

"What's this?" he asked.

"I just need to take some biometrics."

Sarah instructed him to place his hands down on a glass scanner which read his finger and palm prints. She sat down at her desk and followed the computer prompts to save Deckard's bio-metric data.

"Now please stand up against the wall Mr. Deckard."

There was a large white sheet tacked to the wall, like where passport photos taken. He stood right in front of it. A camera mounted into a ball-shaped casing rotated up and down on a pivot mount until it focused in on Deckard. He could see the shutter move across the lens as it took his picture.

It seemed like the entire office was empty except for him and Sarah. What was this place?

"Okay, now we need to get voice. Please state your full name."

"What is all this about?" Deckard asked.

"We are just gathering your biometrics Mr. Deckard."

"You don't already have all this stuff on file somewhere?"

"We are a private firm, Mr. Deckard. Various entities contract us and we have no access to your military or other service records," Sarah explained politely. "Can you say your last name please?"

"Deckard."

"First name?"

Deckard opened his mouth to speak but was interrupted.

"Never mind. It was recording the entire time and it

looks like the system has enough of your vocals on file now."

"Great."

Biometrics was a game-changing technology that measured various biological characteristics. Fingerprints had been used by law enforcement for years, but today advanced sensors could also measure other unique details from person to person such as the distance between a person's eyeballs, his gait, the shape of his face, conduct voice spectrum analysis, or match DNA samples. The technology could help the government and corporations secure their property by ensuring that only authorized people were given access, but biometrics also carried with it a lot of historical baggage.

The Nazis had used eugenics, racial hygiene, and other types of junk science to catalog human beings for extermination. Another holocaust, this time in an era of advanced biometrics, would make the extermination of the Jews in Nazi Germany pale by comparison. Big brother was watching, and even professional spies were feeling the heat. In a few years the technology would be so pervasive around the world that it would be impossible for the CIA to plant covert operatives into foreign countries.

While Sarah continued to work on another camera to record his specifications, Deckard just had to grin and bear it. It was a high-tech cavity search, painless until it wasn't.

Grabbing a pen and a piece of paper, she wrote something down, folded the paper, and walked towards Deckard with her heels clacking across the floor. She slipped the paper into his shirt pocket and smiled again, her blue eyes showing interest.

"There is a Greek restaurant not far from here," she whispered. "I wrote the address down. Meet me there in three hours."

"I'll be there."

She held the door for him on the way out.

"See you soon!" she beamed.

Deckard walked to the elevator wondering what had just happened.

It was a beautiful sunny day in Washington D.C., but Deckard decided to show some discretion and chose a table in the back of the restaurant rather than sit outside. He had no pressing need to get all spooky, but if Liquid Sky had people watching and assessing him, they would lose respect for him for meeting with Sarah while using sloppy tradecraft.

He ordered a beer and told the waiter that his friend would be along shortly.

Taking a sip from his Heineken, he looked up as Sarah slipped into the chair across from him with a sigh. She tossed her hair back and smiled.

"Hi."

"Howzit?"

He felt like an idiot for reverting back to slang from the place where he was born. Nobody talked like that, including himself.

"Good," Sarah said handing him a manila envelope. "I think you are all set."

Deckard popped open the envelope and slid a handful of documents into his hand, a blue U.S. passport staring up at him. It was a full identity package, and on short notice too. Flipping open the passport, he noted his picture alongside the name Sebastian Rothrock.

"Hell of a name," he commented with a frown.

Sarah shrugged.

"Not my decision. Let's get something to eat."

Deckard ordered the lamb souvlaki and Sarah had a Greek salad. Before slipping the false identification documents away, he noted the plane ticket. He was already electronically signed in for a flight later that day. He was going to Kabul, Afghanistan.

They talked while waiting for the food to arrive. Sarah asked a lot of questions about Deckard's background. Much of it he lied about or was otherwise evasive. She picked up on something and steered the conversation in another direction. Deckard asked her similar questions and found out that she had a degree from Georgetown and a Masters from the London School of Economics. She had spent a lot of time in Iraq and Afghanistan using her biometrics background to help intelligence agencies and Special Operations units locate enemy fighters.

"You know," Sarah said as she finished her salad. "I see guys like you come through here every so often. Usually a lot of spooks, people who need covert or clandestine covers, but sometimes former Special Operations guys, which I assume you are, heading to one place or another."

"We're all looking for work these days."

"I never know where you are coming from," she continued. "Usually I don't know where you are going either. I just process the paperwork and never see you again."

"Sounds like you are getting sentimental about the job," Deckard said with a smile.

"Maybe," Sarah said as she rested her head in her hand, with her elbow on the table.

"If it makes you feel any better, we usually don't know what the hell is going on ourselves."

"But you make it sound so romantic."

"Trust me," Deckard laughed. "The honeymoon ends fairly quickly."

"Then why keep doing the job?"

"Everyone has their reasons. Most people will tell you it is patriotism, and yeah, there is a little of that, but mostly they do it for the money. There are lots of jobs you can do as a patriot that don't involve thousand-dollar-a-day paychecks sitting behind a computer in some third-world shithole, jobs that pay better too. But there is a certain amount of path dependency; soldiering or spying is the only life they've really known."

"But not you?"

"I don't need the money if that is what you are asking, and I don't hide behind the American flag. I do this job because I like it. Even when I don't like it, I choose my own missions, take the jobs that are personally important to me."

"Like this one?"

Deckard wondered if she was trying to draw him out. Maybe she already had. He was going after his own kind this time around. Rogue operators assassinating democracy advocates around the world. This may not have been the most important mission he had ever committed too, but he knew it would be the most challenging mission of his entire career. And the most personal.

"Like this one."

"You're an interesting guy Deckard."

Sarah pulled out her business card, clicked a pen, and wrote a phone number on the back of it before sliding the card across the table to him.

"That's my personal number," she told him. "Give me a call when you get back."

Deckard watched her as she turned around and headed for the door. Her hips rocked gently as she put on her sunglasses and walked out into the sunlight. She looked over her shoulder and smiled at him one last time before turning back towards her office.

Damn.

4

Deckard touched down in Kabul where he was met by a minder, a bored-looking private security contractor who escorted him to a waiting area where he sat quietly until his name was called. Boarding a CASA C-212, the aircraft took off down the runway like a shot, forcing Deckard to hold on to the fuselage to avoid being thrown out of his seat. No one bothered to tell him what their destination was. There were several pallets of supplies on board, probably destined for some remote combat outpost in the hinterlands somewhere. Deckard was just a strap-hanger hitching a ride.

Drifting off to sleep, he woke with a start as the landing gear bounced off a dirt runway. The CASA spun around at the end of the landing strip as the loadmaster lowered the ramp. Hooking a thumb out into the dusty runway, he indicated to Deckard that it was time for him to unass himself from their bird so they could head to their final destination.

Stepping off the ramp, Deckard moved to the side to avoid the CASA as it powered back down the runway and soared off into the air. He soon oriented himself, recognizing where he was by identifying the aircraft graveyard to the side of the runway. There were old Russian planes and helicopters that sat collecting rust and dust under the Afghan sun.

He was at FOB Chapman in Southern Afghanistan. He had passed through the base several times back when he used to do work for Ground Branch.

Left to his own devices, Deckard walked alongside the runway. He spotted a few contractors milling about in the distance around some of the buildings, but there was no one waiting for him or even acknowledging his presence. Heat coming up off the ground created a mirage, making the buildings ahead of him seem to ripple in the morning light.

It was a long walk, so Deckard undid a couple buttons on his North Face shirt to try to get some air. By the time he walked up to the camp, a pickup truck had come through the gate and cruised up alongside him. The driver wore a pair of sunglasses and sported a half assed beard and mustache. His skin was dark, Filipino maybe.

"You Deckard?" the driver asked.

"Yeah."

The driver got out and patted Deckard down. All he had in his pockets was his alias passport, a credit card, and the other documents that Sarah had issued him in DC.

"Get in."

Deckard did as he was told, slamming the door as he jumped into the passenger seat. Spinning the wheel, the driver took them back out through the gate. Several Afghan guards and a CIA Global Response Staff contractor opened the gate for them. Outside, they drove onto a dirt road, up the side of a dry stream bed and onto a paved road heading south.

His escort wasn't the talkative type, apparently and didn't even give a name. Deckard noted the Glock 19 strapped to the driver's hip and the AK sitting on the backseat. Deckard was unarmed. If shit went sideways, he'd go for the AK and it would be a mad minute. Whatever happened, happened.

He sniffed at the familiar scent that hung in the air as the pickup truck kicked up a long plume of dust in its wake. Large patches of poorly farmed plots of land zipped by on both sides, small blotches of green showing where the Afghans had managed to irrigate the soil. Large, walled compounds that housed entire families sat amid the open fields.

Holding on to the handle on the door, Deckard bounced as the driver launched them down the side of an embankment, going off-road. They were rumbling across the Khowst bowl. The flat, lunar landscape stretched across the earth in all directions until the heat mirage blended it into the distant snow-capped mountains. Those mountains could leave men dead in seconds, Deckard knew from first-hand experience. He had last been in Afghanistan less than six months ago with Samruk International when they cleared out an Afghan drug lord's enclave from his mountain redoubt.

They drove through the morning. Deckard squinted in the sunlight but the driver wore his dark sunglasses and remained stoic, unphased by the passing terrain or his passenger. Deckard tried to place him.

Of the four words he had muttered, the accent was clearly American. He wore Solomon cross-trainers, blue jeans, and an Afghanistan soccer jersey. Even sitting down, Deckard could tell that the driver was short, maybe five foot five. His skin was brown and had probably darkened since he had been in country. Most likely of Filipino descent. There were Filipino-Americans who served in US Special Operations Forces, but it could also be possible that he was a veteran of the Filipino Naval Special Operations Group which did extensive training and exchange programs from his home country to the U.S. Navy SEALs.

Time would tell.

The driver reached behind Deckard's seat and grabbed a couple bottles of water. He tossed one to his passenger while unscrewing the cap on the other, locking the wheel by holding it between his knees.

"Drink up."

It was early afternoon by the time they rolled up on their destination, a lone compound near a spur coming off the mountains. Clicking a handheld radio, the driver announced their arrival and someone inside opened the gate for them. Pulling inside the thick earthen walls, the driver parked alongside the mud and stone structure in the center of the compound. There was one other pickup truck and a large Afghan janga truck inside the compound.

Covered from top to bottom with colorful murals, ribbons, blue and yellow sashes, and hanging chimes, the trucks were used by locals for transporting materials, the outside of the vehicles painted up and decorated for good luck.

"Wait here," the driver instructed as they stepped out of the pickup and slammed the doors. The Filipino disappeared inside the stone hut while the gate guard who had let them in strode towards him. His eyes were slits as he stared at Deckard with contempt. He wasn't just sizing up the newcomer. There was something more. He looked at him like he was a piece of steak on a table. The gate guard wore dusty civilian clothes with an AK-47 slung over his back. He readjusted it on his shoulder as he blew past Deckard and followed the driver inside.

Leaning up against the pickup, Deckard felt that everything inside the compound had gotten a little too quiet. In the cab of the truck, he could see the rifle that the driver had left behind. It put him somewhat at ease. A loaded rifle would not have been left there if they were planning to kill him. It wouldn't have been a bad plan from their point of view. If this really was Liquid Sky, they could run a counter-intelligence operation by luring in potential infiltrators and then killing them. It would send a hell of a message to anyone else who might have been thinking along the same lines. Who was really laying a trap for whom?

A hulking figure emerged from inside the stone building. He was built like a linebacker with arms and legs like tree trunks. Coming in around six foot three, he was almost as wide as he was tall. As he approached Deckard, his eyes drilled holes into the newcomer.

"You're Deckard?" he asked as if his driver may have picked up the wrong person. "Tell me a story," he said as he ran a hand over his goatee.

"What kind of story?" Deckard said with a frown.

"A Deckard story. One of the good ones. The kind I hear are so outlandish, so fucking bizarre, I don't know what to think. I've seen some shit in my day but the stuff I hear about you makes me wonder."

"What have you heard? I will tell you if its real or not."

"Heard you are some kind of rogue operator. Deckard: used to be shit hot in Army Special Operations, got picked up by the Agency, and then you fucked up so they PNG'ed you."

"True story."

"Vigilante Dirty Harry shit, assassinating terrorists. Working as a singleton to rescue a Delta team in Colombia."

"Maybe."

"Rumors going around that you almost started a war with the Chinese in Burma, cleaning out one of these Hodji drug lords from his mountain fortress," the man motioned to the Hindu Kush mountains that towered above them. "Even heard you were involved with para-military operations in Mexico."

"Some of those stories are exaggerated."

"What about this tale people whisper in hushed tones about some cruise liner in the Pacific Ocean. The one that sank with all hands on board, the ship packed with high level shot callers in government and business. You involved in that?"

"They call it one of the world's largest public safety accidents."

"Public safety accident?"

"That's what they say. Like the Hindenburg."

"Like the Hindenburg?"

"Fucking Nazi zeppelin."

"And I suppose that story is just a tall tale."

"Must be. Can't believe every conspiracy theory you hear."

"You can call me Bill," he told Deckard while reaching into his pocket and pulling out his Oakley sunglasses. "I run this outfit. Here is the deal. You check out as legit, some ugly shit in your past but that is the name of the game. We've only had a day to prepare for a mission that is probably going to go down tonight. You are tagging along. Probationary status only. You kit up, go where you are told, do what you are told. No questions. My team does the op. You just pull security and make sure we don't get our asses shot off. Got it?"

"Got it."

"Come with me."

Bill led him inside the stone building which served as their operations center. The conditions were spartan inside. Some gear and weapons were stacked up against one wall. A couple desks had been improvised by laying plywood on top of stacked cinder blocks.

Deckard's driver sat at one of the desks, looking at an open laptop that displayed satellite photography. He had an Iridium satellite phone pressed to his ear, a wire from it leading out a window to an uplink antennae on the roof. His shirt was pulled up a little, revealing the handle of a Filipino karambit fighting knife.

"You've met Ramon," Bill informed him. Now he had a name to go with the face. Deckard was taking it all in. Who was Ramon on the phone with? Someone back in Kabul? Someone in the field? As Bill had pointed out, it wasn't his place to ask questions.

"This is the team you'll be working with."

Bill waved towards the men lounging around the room. "Your gear is in the corner over there. We go in like Indig. This is a low-vis operation, so everyone will be sterile when we leave the wire. If you die, we will try to recover your body, not because we like you, but in order to protect our OPSEC. If you get left out there for the enemy to pick over, you will be presumed to be a white mercenary, as you will have no identification papers on you and no American weapons or gear."

Bill sat down in front of another computer and opened his email.

"Get your kit together. We are standby to launch at 2230."

The three other operators on the team stared at Deckard. They were sizing him up like a piece of meat. There were no handshakes or high fives. It wasn't just a professional distrust that stemmed from them not having any past experiences together. Deckard felt like he had just walked into a meeting with the mafia. There was no brotherhood, just a nest of vipers who could turn on him at any moment.

He had expected nothing less, but the question remained, was this Liquid Sky?

Recognizing one of the team members as the guy who had opened the gate for them, Deckard tried to piece together who these guys were. This one had long, slicked back hair, looked like he was well manicured even out in the field. He was the pretty boy on the team. He had a mobile game console fired up and was engrossed in shooting up space aliens or something, not even bothering to look up at Deckard again. The other two were built like Bill and looked like they had been drafted from an NFL lineup. One of them snorted at Deckard before going back to flipping through a magazine. The other was busy cleaning his Glock pistol.

Deckard went to the pile of gear that Bill had pointed him towards as being his for the mission. There was a locally made man dress, the *dishdasha* that Afghan men wore. There was also some el cheapo concealable body armor made in Latin America, a Glock with locally procured cloth holster, an AK-47, a Chinese chest rig for spare magazines and a few other odds and ends. It wasn't much to work with. If their mission was to be completely denied, then they had to use local weapons and kit. No high tech on this mission.

It got him thinking again. Why the need for deniability? U.S. Special Operations Forces were still conducting counter-terrorism missions in Afghanistan on a regular basis. With Conventional Forces withdrawing, it was left to Special Operations to perform maintenance on any Islamist fools who went past a certain threshold. Once a terrorist started acting up too much, they would send in shooters to sort him out. Or a drone strike. It had become such a sport that Delta Force was even sending their students from the Operator Training Course to Afghanistan for their final exam, a live combat operation.

So what was the need for this team and their plausible deniability?

Deckard spent an hour and a half squaring his kit away. He had a small commercial radio which he made sure was charged up with a full battery. He loaded up five AK-47 magazines from a box of loose ammunition before loading up his Glock magazines as well. Then, he field-stripped both weapons and conducted functions checks. He was careful and deliberate about this final task; it was possible that Bill had his weapons rendered inert by messing with the trigger mechanism or filing down the firing pins, but both weapons were good to go.

After getting his kit together the way he wanted it, he went off and found a cardboard box full of bottled water. Twisting off the cap, he downed half a bottle in one gulp. He needed to be hydrated if they were going to be out all night cruising through 'vills and scaling ridgelines.

As he sipped the rest of the water he tried to place Bill and his team. It seemed that his intuition had been correct about the team he was after being former U.S. Special Operations, but which unit did they come from?

Each unit had their own culture, their own bravado, and their own way of doing things. Rangers were typically younger guys. Hard-charging, door-kicking muldoons who took no shit from no one. Special Forces guys were usually older. Often with age they brought some more maturity to the table and the ability to operate in small teams. Most of them were pretty laid back dudes, a character trait needed when conducting their primary missions, unconventional warfare and foreign internal defense. The Ranger mentality didn't exactly lend itself to training foreign third-world soldiers. While the team sized up Deckard, he had sized them up as well. These guys were not former Rangers or Special Forces.

The other Army Special Operations unit was Delta Force, and that was a whole other animal. Trained for counter-terrorist operations ranging from direct action raids to aircraft take-downs, Delta drew talent from both Special Forces and Rangers and then polished their combat skills to ridiculously high levels. Delta was known for being the military's most professional unit. The team he was with now seemed a little too nonchalant, like they had an expectation of victory. A sense of entitlement.

The Marines had Recon, Force Recon, and their new Special Operations component, MARSOC. Marines were brought up the right way, starting at boot camp at Paris Island. The Recon and MARSOC shooters in the Marine Corps were clean-cut, belt-fed, straight shooters who knew how to take the fight to the enemy. Their sense of tradition, *esprit de corps*, and, along with their infantry background placed them closer to Rangers than Special Forces. Deckard frowned. You could pick a single Marine out of a crowd of a hundred people and none of these people were one of them.

Then, you had the Navy. He already suspected that Ramon was a U.S. or Filipino Navy SEAL. Deckard had worked with and respected many men on the teams but had to wonder. The linebacker body types that most of them had came from an obsession that many SEALs had with jacking steel in the gym. There was one particular squadron within SEAL Team Six, the Navy's equivalent to Delta Force, that was known to specifically recruit the biggest guys out of Green Platoon. It wasn't much to go on though. Finishing his bottle of water, Deckard knew he'd have to wait and see, develop the situation, and see what shook out of the woodwork.

Hopefully he wouldn't die in the meantime.

"So you're here to pick up the slack for Henderson?" A voice said from behind.

Deckard turned to face him, thinking fast. It was the dude with the slicked back hair who had been playing video games.

"Henderson?"

"Made a non-verbal withdraw from the course on our last op. Ate one to the facepiece."

"Sorry to hear that."

"Why?" he asked with a shrug of his shoulder. "Fuck do you care."

"Just saying. I didn't know him."

"Just try to hang with us tonight and don't step on your crank with golf cleats. If you fuck us, we'll leave your sorry ass out there."

"I understand."

"What the fuck ever," he said as if there was a period after each word. "I heard the RUMINT on you and I don't fucking buy it. I think you're just a shithead Army fuck who bolo'ed his ops. You don't even belong here. You're not one of us."

"You mean because I wasn't in the teams?" Deckard dropped it, intentionally trying to elicit information.

"Fuck the teams. That's vanilla shit. We operate on a whole different level, even before we left the Navy."

Gotcha, Deckard thought.

"Hey!" Ramon interrupted from across the room. He was on the satellite phone again.

"We a go?" Bill asked as he looked up from his computer.

"Overwatch has eyes on the target. He just arrived at the objective. This should be his bed-down site unless overwatch reports him leaving."

"That's a green light," Bill confirmed. "Everyone kit up; we roll in ten."

Deckard's antagonist with the pretty hair swung back around to confront him one more time.

"You stay on me while we are out there cheese dick. You're going to pull black-side security on the objective and make sure Hodji doesn't skull fuck us while our backs are turned. I'll release you once we get close to the target compound."

"Okay."

"Grab your shit and let's go."

"What's your callsign on the net?"

"What the fuck is this callsign shit? Just call me Rick."

Deckard ditched his civilian clothes and slipped into the *dishdasha*, then shrugged into his chest rig, holstered the Glock, slung his AK-47, and clipped his radio inside his collar. Ramon was already taking all of the documents and maps from the operations center and dumping them into a burn barrel outside. Lighting a match, it all went up in a golden glow that burned in the early evening light.

Deckard headed outside.

Now he was convinced.

It was going to be another one of those nights.

Deckard was now rolling with Liquid Sky.

5

Yellow flames were still licking out of the top of the burn barrel as they loaded up into the back of the janga truck.

Bill, Ramon, Rick, and the two other team members had kitted up. Deckard had been listening to them banter back and forth about who would get more kills on this mission and picked up the names of the final two team members, they were Zach and Paul. With Deckard now filling the void left by Henderson, a void created by Nikita's sniper rifle in Pakistan, they had a six man assault element.

A young kid, maybe eighteen or nineteen, had been warming chai tea over a small fire in the courtyard. Bill spoke to him and the kid responded in broken English. He would be their indigenous driver for the mission. It was a simple but ingenious infiltration method. With a local driving the janga truck, the Americans would be hiding in a secret compartment in the back. The Trojan Horse was alive and well.

After a few words with Bill, the Afghan went and opened the gate, then fired up the truck. The hidden compartment was a large metal box that had bags of rice thrown on top of it to give the truck the appearance of hauling a full load. The door to the compartment was disguised to look like the side of a crate. The Liquid Sky members took turns searching each other over to make sure none of them unwittingly brought any non-local items. The video games and Maxim magazines had to go into the burn barrel before they left. Once out on patrol, they had to be completely sterile.

Deckard handed Rick his alias passport and other false documents. The former SEAL Team Six operator tossed them in the burn barrel and then patted him down just to make sure he didn't have anything squirreled away. He didn't. If Deckard died on this mission it was unlikely that Pat and the others back at Samruk International would ever discover what had happened to him. They had no idea where he was or what he was doing. His body would be quickly buried by the locals who would not want to be discovered with a body, especially a white one by other Afghans or Coalition Forces.

Deckard climbed into the janga truck with the team, and

then Bill got inside and shut the door behind him. They would leave the compound unattended. The operations center had been sterilized and they would not be reoccupying their forward staging area after the mission.

Bill talked into his radio, "Check the bug light."

The driver hit a button under the dashboard, and a red light flickered on and off inside the hidden compartment. It was a non-vocal warning in case something was wrong. From inside their hiding place, the team had zero situational awareness of what was going on around them and would be relying on the driver for a heads up.

"Punch it out of here," Bill radioed the driver.

With a squeal of metal on metal, the janga truck lurched out of the compound and rumbled down the dirt road. Where they were heading, Deckard had no idea. Wherever they were going, he was happy that the team at least had the foresight to add some air holes and install a fan inside their compartment. It was brutally hot, and they had loaded an entire case of water bottles inside with them to stay hydrated.

They rode in silence, the compartment occasionally lit up as someone flipped on a pen light to check a watch or to make last minute adjustments to their gear. For the first hour, Deckard just leaned up against the metal wall while sitting. By the second hour he was starting to feel rattled due to the worn slat shocks on the truck's suspension banging up and down on the rough Afghan roads. By the third hour he was getting motion sickness. He felt like a bug sealed up inside a tin can which was then shaken vigorously by a small child.

He was attempting some breathing exercises to help maintain his composure when the bug light went off. It was a relief to say the least.

Bill broke squealch on his radio.

"What is it?"

White noise hissed over the net before the driver answered. "Taliban check point. They make me to stop."

"Got it."

In the darkness, Deckard heard the guy sitting next to him grunt out several curse words. It was Rick.

"This is all you," Rick then told Deckard.

"Huh?"

"What the fuck Deckard!" Bill's words bellowed through

the cramped compartment. "Rick just told you to take care of this shit so take care of it!"

"No problem."

"No problem my ass," Bill snarled. "Rick, take this fucker's guns."

"What-" Deckard exclaimed.

"Hand 'em over," Rick ordered. "Let's see what you're made of."

"How many of them are out there?"

"No idea," Bill answered. "For your sake I hope it is less than a dozen!"

"Fuck me," Deckard groaned.

The driver stopped on non-existent brake pads. The entire team lurched forward and then back in the opposite direction as the truck screamed to a halt. Rick reached over, undid a latch and threw open the door. He then relieved Deckard of his AK-47 and Glock pistol.

"Good luck bro," he said as Deckard slid out into the night. "And thanks for the extra ammo."

Climbing out of the hatch, Deckard readjusted the *pakol* cap on his head and crept along the back of the truck to peer ahead. At first he had to steady himself by holding on to the side of the truck, the motion sickness fading off after a couple seconds. They were on one of the perilous mountain roads that snaked around the spurs and draws as it wound deeper into Indian country. The side of the road terminated in a sheer cliff that went nearly vertical for several hundred feet. Deckard heard rushing water down below and could just make out the reflection of moonlight off the surface of the river. There were only a few feet between the truck and edge of the road. The Taliban had stopped them at a perfect choke point.

Deckard rounded the side of the truck, sticking to the shadows cast by the moonlight. There were three of them. Wearing *dishdashas* and black head wraps, the three men at the checkpoint each had long Wahhabi beards, the type that blow up under your armpit when you are running from AC-130 gunships at top speed. One reached over and pulled open the driver's side door while another was saying something to their Afghan driver.

Three bad guys, three AK-47's. He would have to act fast.

Deckard crept forward, his heart in his throat. They

were distracted as they tried to shake down the driver for some kind of Taliban Value-Added Tax. They needed extra money to buy acid to splash in schoolgirl's faces or something. Deckard just hoped he wasn't spotted until he was on top of them. Inching forward, he saw the driver becoming more distraught. He began flashing money, but glancing back over his shoulder, Deckard could see several dark silhouettes back at the rear of the truck. Some of the Liquid Sky men had hopped out to watch him work.

Grabbing the nearest terrorist, Deckard flung him right off the edge of the road. The terrorist's arms were pinwheeling as he stumbled and went over the edge. Deckard didn't have time to listen to his screams. The other two checkpoint guards turned to face Deckard, the driver's jaw was hung open as he could only watch in horror.

The closest of the two tried to bring his AK into play. Deckard pivoted away from barrel to clear the line of fire while simultaneously reaching out and grabbing the barrel with his hand. Using his other hand, he swatted away the terrorist's support hand on the foregrip of the rifle. In one final blur of motion, Deckard swung the rifle barrel straight up where it smacked into the terrorist's face. Temporarily stunned, Deckard relieved him of the AK and slammed the buttstock into the face of the remaining terrorist.

With the wooden AK buttstock blasting into the side of his face, the terrorist rocked backwards and ran into the side of the truck. Deckard gave him another buttstroke for good measure and the terrorists knees began to turn to jelly before he headed for a faceplant in the dusty road. Transitioning the AK into one hand, Deckard grabbed the terrorist by the collar and flung him down the cliff to take a magic carpet ride with his buddy.

The remaining terrorist recovered enough by this point to charge at Deckard. The American grabbed him by the wrist and elbow, then shifted and dumped the terrorist over his hip in a simple judo throw. The terrorist coughed and tried to get back to his feet. Deckard placed a shoe on his forehead and pushed him down the cliff.

He could hear the terrorist scream impacted the nearly vertical slope below and began somersaulting the rest of the way down to the river below.

Deckard was hardly breathing heavy, but truth be told, his leg burned like hell from an injury he had received on his previous mission to Mexico. He went from one job to the next and hadn't had enough time to heal.

That was when someone initiated a slow clap. There was one at every party. Deckard looked back. It was Bill.

The entire team was gathered at the back of the truck. Rick stood with his arms crossed. Zach and Paul, both with their Taliban starter beards had taken advantage of the pit stop to smoke cigarettes. Bill finished clapping and scratched his goatee.

"Not bad Deckard, but I gotta know. Why didn't you just kill those fuckheads outright?"

"I did. None of these dumbasses even knows how to swim. If they manage to survive the fall, they will sink right to the bottom of that river down there."

Bill frowned. His face looked like worn leather, his biceps and shoulders threatening to tear the man dress he wore open at the seams.

"Next time use a bullet. A bullet is always the right choice."

"I didn't want to compromise our mission in case there are other enemy positions in the area."

"This is Afghanistan," Rick lectured. "No one will notice a few gunshots and besides, what's a little stray gunfire between friends?"

"Get back in the cab," Bill motioned the driver who was still gathering his wits. "Let's load up and get rolling. We have hard times to hit."

Deckard walked back to the rear of the truck, forcing himself not to favor his bum leg.

Rick glared at Deckard as he reclaimed his AK and Glock before pulling himself back inside the hidden compartment.

It was another couple hours in the stifling heat of the closed compartment, bouncing around in the back of the janga truck before the driver stopped again. Liquid Sky disembarked the truck and Bill had a few more words with the driver, both of them taking turns pointing to a ridgeline silhouetted against the starry night sky. Afghanistan had no light pollution, and unlike the Western world, you could see an entire universe of stars out in the badlands of Central Asia.

Bill slapped the driver on the shoulder and returned to the team.

"This is our VDO," he said, announcing their vehicle drop off point. "We will rendezvous with the driver at the exfil point early in the morning."

Deckard checked the knock off Rolex watch that had been a part of his issued kit. It was almost midnight and he had a feeling that they would have a long walk ahead of them. Each Liquid Sky member grabbed a couple bottles of water on the way out and shoved them into their pockets. Bill had an old Soviet map in hand and led the patrol up into the mountains.

The approach to the mountains was hazardous to say the least, and suicidal at worst. They couldn't use flashlights because the light would compromise the patrol, and night-vision goggles were too high tech for a sterile mission that could have no hint of American involvement, mercenary or otherwise. There was enough ambient light for them to slowly feel their way up the side of the mountain, but they still slipped and slid on the soft rock that broke away under their feet. Slowly but surely, Liquid Sky gained in elevation as they climbed towards the ridge above that bumped across the night sky, looking like the broken spine of a dragon.

Within half an hour of climbing, they were all covered in sweat, their man-dresses soaked through. They drank water while on the move. The former SEALs chugged water and then tossed the water bottles on the rocks. It was bad form to leave any sign of your presence behind, but clearly these guys didn't care. They were on a one-way trip and their only real concern was getting to the target that night and doing the dirty deed. Deckard downed his first bottle of water and followed suit, dropping the plastic bottle behind him.

Their VDO had left them about a third of the way up the mountain to begin with and now they were climbing higher and higher. At some points it was so steep that they were able to reach out and grab the terrain right in front of them. Bill led the patrol, taking them in winding switchbacks that inched up the ridge when the going got too steep.

There was nothing technical about their climb, it was good old-fashion LPC's, leather personnel carriers. That and a lot of sweat. Still, they were doing it like the locals, traveling with the bare essentials in weapons and equipment. They were not nearly as weighted down as American soldiers were in body armor and other equipment, so at least they had that going for them.

The Liquid Sky team took a short five-minute break after climbing the wind-swept rock for another hour. They sipped on what water they had left and tried to let their legs rest as they sat facing downhill. Steam was coming off their overworked bodies in the cool night air. Bill was the first to stand and start the final push to the top of the ridge.

Forty-five minutes later, the team huffed and grunted over the ridge. Deckard's leg was throbbing, the cut on his thigh was hot to the touch with inflammation. The rest of the team was also hunched over, grabbing their knees as they tried to catch their breath. They were in good shape and no one complained, but between the altitude and the demanding climb, they were all winded.

"That's it," Bill said pointing down into the valley.

Below them was a small archipelago of walled compounds. Pinpricks of light could be seen in the darkness from morning fires being lit in the courtyards. Bill was pointing to the nearest compound at the base of the mountain. That was their target.

"Let's get down there and clean the place out," he ordered.

Liquid Sky scrambled down the side of the mountain for the better part of two hours, the way down actually being more strenuous than the way up. It was almost four in the morning by the time they bottomed out in the valley and walked along the edge of a dry river bed. It was a wide, rocky gouge in the earth that looked like it hadn't seen water since the Triassic Period, but when the rains came in once a year, water would come rushing down the riverbed like a deluge and sweep away anything in its path.

Bill picked up the pace as they moved out in a single file. They had to make up some time to get into position, hit the compound, and move out before the sun came up. Moving from the riverbed, they crawled over a rock wall and walked through a terraced field. Finally, they were within a hundred meters of the target compound.

"Listen up," Rick whispered to Deckard. "You are our

black-side security, so that means you need to position yourself where you can see the back of the compound."

Deckard knew what black-side security was, and merely nodded his head.

"Find a good field of fire so you can waste anyone who tries to go over the high walls and escape."

"Got it."

"We will be preparing to breach. Radio us when you are in position."

"Will do."

Deckard skirted around the edge of the compound, weaving between scraggly trees that barely clung to life. It only took a few minutes for him to find a shallow depression that he could lay in where he would have an open lane of fire on the back side of the compound with his AK-47. He pressed on the push to talk button on his radio.

"This is Deck. I'm set."

"Okay dude," it sounded like Rick.

They would not be explosively breaching the compound's gate. That would give away the American's presence. Deckard didn't see any mechanical breaching equipment like battering rams or hoolie tools, none of them would want to have carried that crap up the side of the mountain anyway. He did see Zach with a locally procured double-barrel shotgun over one shoulder, so he knew it would be a ballistic breach.

The radio crackled and hissed, so Deckard turned the volume down a little bit more.

"Standby," came the call.

Two shotgun blasts punctured the night. Deckard tucked the stock of his AK into the pocket of his shoulder and waited. There was a long silence as the Liquid Sky mercenaries began clearing the compound. Then came the gunfire, first in spurts and then full auto blasts. It was a one-sided firefight, Liquid Sky no doubt catching the enemy stumbling out of bed in the night. More auto fire sounded, then silence, then a few single shots here and there. Finally, everything went quiet again.

Then, an Afghan dropped down off the back wall and crumbled to the ground.

Show time.

Deckard confirmed a pistol in the Afghan's fist as he

attempted to run away out into the fields. Pushing the selector lever one click down, he aimed low at the runner's legs and triggered a full auto burst of gunfire. Three of the five rounds he let off spun the Afghan around and sent him staggering to the ground.

As he lay in the prone, he began to get cold. The last few hours before dawn are usually the coldest, and his soaked-through clothes were only adding to the problem. Fifteen minutes went by before he heard anything over the radio.

"Black-side security," It sounded like Bill. "You got anything?"

"One down crow," Deckard reported.

"Nice."

A few minutes later, Rick radioed that he was coming out to meet Deckard. He stood up and whistled to Rick when he heard him getting close.

"Where is he?" Rick asked.

"Over here," Deckard said leading him over to the body. Rick fired a couple more shots into the body. It never hurt to make sure corpses were still corpses but then Rick loaded a full magazine. Taking a step back, he aimed at the dead body and fired at the Afghan's head on full auto. His gunfire blasted the top of the terrorist's skull clean off and splattered his brains in the dirt. The Liquid Sky member held the trigger down until the rifle cycled through the entire thirty-round magazine.

It was a completely unnecessary and unprofessional gesture. Rick had effectively turned the top of the Afghan's skull into a canoe.

"What was that for?" Deckard asked absently.

"Sending a fucking message," Rick scolded him. He then patted the body down and pocketed some cash he found in one of the pockets.

"Let's get the fuck out of here."

Deckard followed Rick back around the compound to the breach point. Zach was outside smoking a cigarette. His man dress was splattered with blood, his AK slung over one shoulder. Paul came walking out of the compound with two floppy pancakes in his hands. It took Deckard a moment to realize that the pancakes had hair. Paul had been inside collecting scalps.

"I got two," he told Zach with a smile.

"Just the woman," Zach replied, motioning to the clump

of long hair and congealing blood at his feet.

Deckard had no illusions about who he was dealing with. They were out murdering democracy advocates and helping to suppress the Arab Spring, but this was off the charts. Even among those who went off the reservation, this was pretty much unheard of. He was shocked, and would not have believed it if someone had described the scene to him in a bar.

Bill came out with another scalp in his hand and a bloody hatchet in the other.

"Fucking savages never had a chance," he grinned.

Deckard still couldn't believe what he was seeing.

Ramon came out carrying a plastic bag filled with documents and computer hard drives he had collected on the objective.

"Get rid of that shit," Bill told him. "Sterile means nothing goes on the objective and nothing comes off. Zero evidence that we were ever here."

"This was a major command and control node for the network," Ramon insisted. "We can ball up the entire network based on what these guys have here."

"Not our problem," Bill said. "Let the fucking knuckle-draggers in Big Army sort this bullshit third-world country out. We work contract to contract."

Ramon looked pissed, but walked back into the compound with the bag of sensitive materials he had collected. Rick followed him in and returned back with a couple scalps of his own which he dropped at Zach's feet.

"There is my two."

Bending over, he wiped the blood off his hatchet on Deckard's man dress.

"Thanks bro. Gotta make sure this bad boy is ready to go for next time," Rick informed him.

"We got a pickup inside the compound," Ramon said as he walked back out.

"Good, that will save us some time," Bill replied. "Deckard, go hotwire that fucker and get us out of here."

Deckard nodded.

"Wait a second," Paul said stopping him. "Let me give you a hand."

Reaching into his pocket, Paul pulled out a dismembered hand and threw it at Deckard. It bounced off his chest and thumped between his feet in a cloud of dust. The Liquid Sky team burst out laughing at the look of disgust on his face.

Deckard walked back inside the compound trying to process what had just happened. These guys were so far gone that there was no turning back for any of them. His plan had always been to infiltrate and then destroy. Now it didn't matter what his plan was. He was all out of choices. These were former Special Operations men like himself and so many others who served.

It was his responsibility to clean up this mess. There was no need for him to justify this to himself, it justified itself. It was time to choose the hard right over the easy wrong. Finding the pickup truck in the corner of the compound, he threw open the door and went to work on the ignition.

As he began to pry the ignition cylinder out with a piece of metal he found laying around, Deckard felt completely disgusted with what he had involved himself in. Even if they were terrorists, this wasn't how soldiers carried themselves. It wasn't just about disrespecting the enemy dead, more importantly, it was about the discipline and self-respect that the soldier had for himself. Once the rot of war crimes infected a military organization, it would spread throughout the unit like a plague and destroy everything that they had once stood for. They would be no different than Al Qaeda and the other human savages that they fought. At that point, the war was already lost.

Just as he hotwired the truck, Deckard knew he would have to be slow and deliberate. He couldn't allow his emotions to control him like the Liquid Sky team. One slip up and he was a dead man. He needed to play along, maybe no matter how dark this road he was heading down got. When the time was right, at a place and time of his choosing, he would drop the hammer and be done with this.

The pickup truck rumbled to life. Deckard got behind the wheel and worked the stick shift, driving out of the compound. Outside, the five other Liquid Sky operators piled into the truck, several sitting in the back. Bill got in the passenger seat and told Deckard he could flip on the headlights and white light it down the road. They just needed to make a quick exit from the target area before daylight and the risk of an ambush was fairly low. He gave him directions on where to go as they drove towards their extraction site. After driving for half an hour, the sun was starting to crest above the horizon.

Bill ordered everyone out of the truck. Deckard put it in neutral and they pushed the vehicle into a creek bed where it rolled over on its side. At least it would be out of sight to any passersby. Then it was back up the mountain. They had done an off-set infil, first traveling by Trojan janga truck and then moving by foot to the objective to maintain the element of surprise and absolute secrecy prior to their assault. It was sound planning, but now they had to walk all the way back to the exfil site where their janga truck driver would pick them up along a different spot on the road.

By the time they were halfway up the ridge, it was full daylight. The good thing was that they were far enough away from the road below and their objective that it was unlikely anyone would spot them. They could see the smattering of compounds below, but without optics, no one was going to see a few ants climbing the side of the mountain.

By eight in the morning they again crested the ridge. Everyone was out of water. It was a short-duration mission with one specific task: hunting and killing with zero American involvement as far as anyone could prove. They took five up on top of the ridge, everyone having a seat on the rocks and admiring the view. Afghanistan was really the prettiest part of hell. It would have been a nice place to visit if not for the jihadist crazies. And the occasional rogue mercenary.

Zach and Rick got into a blow-by-blow about who killed who and how it had all gone down.

"They were Al Qaeda?" Deckard asked Ramon.

"Naw man," he answered. "Those were Karzai's guys."

"Huh?"

"Yeah, they were tied into the President of Afghanistan. Running a huge drug-trafficking network for him. Completely untouchable by U.S. Special Operations for political reasons. That's why we got called in."

"Shit."

"No kidding. They let him get away with it for a long time but I guess he is starting to lean away from America and more towards China these days so someone wanted to give him a gut check. That's my take on it anyway."

"Its a good thing we took them out."

Ramon turned to him and whispered, "Look, you did

good today. Just keep your head down and they will offer you a full-time job. We do a lot of killing and make good money at it. Its just harder for us Army guys to get an in with them."

"I got it."

But Deckard didn't get it. He had completely misread Ramon by thinking he was a SEAL.

They picked it up and started their descent. It was a long haul through the morning as they suffered in the heat and slipped down through the dirt and debris. A few times they had to cling to the sides of cliffs and move hand over hand until they could find a wider path down the mountain. Bill was up front again and he began talking into his radio when the road came into view. There was no sign of their ride home, but he was talking to someone.

They walked down a spur-coming off the mountain overlooking the road and halted. Bill signaled them to stay low as they gathered around a rocky outcropping that looked like something that belonged on the set of Conan the Barbarian.

At this point, they were only a few hundred meters above the road. Down below was a village with a stream running alongside the road. Terraced fields were dug into the opposite side of the valley with houses and huts propped up against the sides of the cliffs at impossible angles. People lived where the water was, no matter how ridiculous the terrain might be. They learned to live there.

In the stream next to the road, a woman in a blue burka stood in the water up to her ankles, washing dishes, pots, and pans that she laid next to her one by one as she scrubbed them out.

"Where is our GI Joe Army guy?" Bill asked. "Deckard, get your ass up here."

Deckard high-crawled over to Bill and watched the scene below.

"You see that Hodji twat down there?"

"Yeah."

"This is our extraction point and that fucking cunt is in the way. She'll compromise us. You're disguised as a local, so I want you to get close to her and cut her fucking throat. Think you can do it?"

"Yeah," Deckard said without hesitation.

"You got a knife?"

"No, just the kit you issued me."

"Here," Bill said handing him a rusty butcher knife. Another local purchase. "Make it happen. Once it is done we will come down and I'll call in our driver."

"Piece of cake."

"Yeah," Bill said dryly. "We'll find out in a few minutes, won't we?"

"Do that bitch Deckard," Rick told him. "God only knows how many puppies she will squeeze out that will become Allah lovin' terrorists."

Deckard looked down at the road for a moment and plotted his route down to the stream. He figured it out in a few seconds and then dropped down below the crest of the spur, keeping the terrain feature between himself and the woman below. He stepped very carefully now so not to give away his position. Stepping from heel to toe, he slowly maneuvered his way down to the road. The small stones still ground beneath his footsteps but that couldn't be helped.

Moving slowly, he made it down to the road, then crossed it out of sight of the woman. With any luck, she would have finished her task and have walked back home by the time he got there. Another reason why he was in no rush.

There was no way that Deckard was going to murder a civilian in cold blood. The game was over before he had even gotten started. Bill had called his bluff. They wanted to see if he was one of them, ensure that he was a war criminal and just as guilty as the rest of the group. No doubt, the entire Liquid Sky team would have their rifles pointed at him and the woman, ready to open fire on them both if he failed to complete his task.

Crouching in a thicket of bushes, he checked his AK-47 and Glock pistol to make sure he had rounds chambered and ready to go. Once he closed on the woman, he would drag her across the stream and behind a stone wall a few meters further back. From there he would have to escape and evade, run as hard as he could, ambush the Liquid Sky team when and where he could to slow them down, and eventually find a vehicle and make his way back to Kabul. Truth be told, he'd be lucky if he lasted five seconds into that plan and he knew it.

He was a dead man walking, killed by his own self-restraint.

Silently, Deckard moved through the thicket in a crouch.

He cursed as he saw the blue burka through the twigs and leaves of the bushes. She could have saved her own life, if she had only known. Now they were both dead.

Deckard was on the opposite bank of the stream from her, but the stream was only a few feet wide. Once he closed the distance he would be right on top of her. He could jump out of the bushes, grab her, and make a run for it. Maybe. A big maybe.

The Afghan woman bent down to wash another one of the pots. He was almost within striking distance now. The American commando readjusted the sling on his shoulder and prepared to move. He had the butcher knife in his hand up until this point, but now he stuck it in his belt.

He took a deep breath. It was now or never. His muscles tensed, prepared for what was about to happen. He was ready to execute.

Suddenly, the woman stood straight up and turned towards him.

Deckard froze.

"What the fuck do you think you are fucking doing you stupid cocksucker?" she asked him.

His jaw hit the ground.

"Get your dick beaters in the air where I can see them. What the fuck are you doing over there?" The voice coming through the burka didn't match anything Deckard had expected, to say the least, but it was a woman's voice. "Hey fucker, I'm talking to you."

Suddenly the crackle of a radio sounded under the burka.

"Got you good this time," Bill's voice said over the radio. Laughter could be heard coming over the net.

"Very funny asshole," the burka clad woman said. "Who is this needle dick you sent down here to hide in the bushes?"

"He's the new guy," Bill answered. "Whatever."

Deckard was pissed.

"Who the fuck are you?" he asked the woman.

"Who the fuck *am I?*" she answered as if she was insulted. "I'm the one who has been pulling overwatch on your fucking objective for twenty-four hours, dick face. I confirmed that Muhammad what-ever-the-fuck was bedding down there. Then I walked through the night to secure your fucking extraction," she practically screamed. "That's who I fucking am, so who the fuck are you?"

"Just a trigger puller told to do a job," he answered honestly.

"And like a true meathead you proved to be very good at following orders. Good for you. Just squat there in the bushes and try not to piss me off any more than you have already."

"Yes ma'am," Deckard said as he rolled his eyes. This was getting stupid.

Exhausted, Deckard sat on the edge of the stream with his feet in the water. The woman kicked the pots into the water and cursed at him some more. They sat silently for a few minutes, Deckard unable to discern anything about her through the mesh eye window in the burka. A few minutes later the rest of the team arrived and sat down alongside the stream. The tactically correct answer was to push into the thicket and maintain a security perimeter but that didn't seem to concern Liquid Sky.

"What the fuck was that?" the woman asked.

"C'mon Nadeesha, it was just a joke," Rick laughed.

"And how far would you have let that joke go before that pussy sunk a knife into my back?"

She was pissed, balling up the burka and throwing it into the stream. Underneath, she wore spandex shorts and a loose t-shirt. That and a MP-5k sub-machine gun. Deckard's eyes went wide. Her skin was dark like someone from southern India, but she had almost Caucasian features and large brown eyes. The woman, Nadeesha, busted him too, seeing the look in his eyes as she swung around to point at him in her fury. She paused for a split second, also surprised by the expression on his face.

She was beautiful and none of it made sense to him.

"Fuck all you guys," Nadeesha spat. "I quit."

"Bullshit," Zach laughed.

"Yeah, that is like the fifth time you've quit," Paul said.

"We pay you way too much for you to quit," Bill reminded her. "Speaking of which, where the fuck is our extract."

"He should be here any minute," she said shaking her head. "Where did you find this peckerwood?" Nadeesha asked while cocking her chin towards Deckard.

"Craigs List," Bill said.

"What the fuck."

Just then, the janga truck pulled up, the driver wearing a big, toothy grin. Another successful mission and another big pay day for him. One by one, Liquid Sky crammed back into the secret compartment in the back. Nadeesha scowled at Deckard as there was limited space inside and she had to sit next to him. The truck started to move, and while the door was still cracked open, Rick passed out the remaining bottles of water, then locked the door shut.

Five hours later they arrived back on FOB Chapman where they discreetly unloaded and jumped on an awaiting CASA airplane heading to Kabul. Bill had paid the janga truck driver in cash, which he happily accepted. The plane touched down in Kabul, and an hour later the entire six-man and one-woman team flew out on an international flight.

Meanwhile, in southern Afghanistan, the drug trafficking organization they had hit during the night decided to retaliate. Tied into the Taliban, they called in fighters from all over the province, as well as insurgents from as far as Pakistan.

For the next few weeks they set up ambushes and IEDs alongside the main roads that weaved through their territory. Without any suspects in the hit on the drug lords' compound, and the murder of him and his entire family, the Taliban simply assumed that the Americans were involved and struck back against whatever Americans they could find.

Within six days their IED's and ambushes had killed four American soldiers. Private First Class Nelson, Specialist Rodriguez, Private First Class Thomas, and First Sergeant Harper were all returned to the United States in flag-draped caskets. A dozen others were flown to Ramstein Air Force base and then to Walter Reed with critical injuries.

6

      The entire Liquid Sky element was passed out as they flew commercial air to Germany, and then on to Italy. They had changed out of their mission clothes and into civilians provided by the staff at FOB Chapman. The team was still bleary eyed as they boarded a private aircraft in Milan to their final destination. Deckard tried to discern where they were going, but found no indication and no one was telling him. Rick, Zach, and Paul bought some hard liquor in the duty free shop before taking off, pounded a couple shooters of vodka or whiskey and passed right back out. The others just gave Deckard the cold shoulder. Ramon watched an in-flight movie for a few minutes before falling back asleep. Nadeesha looked at Deckard like he was lower than dog shit before she drifted off to sleep.

      Tough crowd, Deckard thought to himself. Before long, he fell asleep as well. They were all exhausted from the operation and Deckard was especially jet lagged from bouncing between time zones.

      He came awake to the sound of laughing and screaming. After their cat nap, the Liquid Sky team had taken to watching another in-flight movie in their Gulfstream aircraft. It looked like the comedy movie, *Superbad* was keeping them entertained. Zach and Rick were giggling like school girls. Paul recited the movie line for line in a never-ending stream of commentary. Nadeesha kept to herself, flipping through a copy of *Flashbang* magazine.

      Uninterested in the movie, Deckard wished he had a book to read, but he had always been someone who was comfortable with his own thoughts, if restless in his actions. Sitting around with nothing to do over long periods of time made him uncomfortable, but he knew how to manage it. There was an onboard refrigerator, so he helped himself to a bottle of water.

      Deckard watched out the window as they landed several hours later. The terrain was fairly flat with low-laying vegetation and blacktop roads crisscrossing throughout. Disoriented, Deckard had no idea where they were. They landed at a substantial modern airport with a large terminal complex. The private jet taxied off towards the private hangers where a white van was waiting for them. Everyone piled in. If this was another operation, it didn't feel like it.

They exited from the private aircraft area's gate and out into the countryside. The road was surrounded on both sides by green rolling hills, sugarcane coming right up to the edge of the pavement and pressing out into the street. Palm trees also dotted the landscape. As they drove through the outskirts of a city, Deckard spotted a Hindu temple and knew he must be somewhere in India. Then he saw a Christian church and finally a Muslim mosque.

Now, he was really confused.

Further inland were green-covered mountains stretching up to touch the blue sky. Deep into the stalks of sugarcane he also saw a few abandoned factories and other structures. It wasn't until he saw a billboard in French for a cellphone service that he figured it out. They were in Mauritius, an island in the Indian Ocean.

The van swerved through an intersection and passed the entrance to several four-star hotels. They got dropped off right alongside the ocean. Waves broke against the shore and the sun was already sinking into a blue and purple sky. The smell of salt carried on the breeze. It was a residential area with bungalows lining the beach.

"Party is at my place tonight," Bill announced. "See you then."

The team bombshelled in both directions down the street.

"You come with me Deckard," Bill said to the new guy on the team. "I have to give you the key to Henderson's old place."

Bill led him on a stone path to his beach house. The Liquid Sky team leader was so tall that he had to duck under the roof on the back deck. Deckard spotted a security guard roaming the premises. Punching a number into the keypad on the door, Bill led him inside. Like the other bungalows, it was a one-story deal, but spread out with plenty of interior space. The kitchen and living room was wide open. He had pool tables and an indoor bar. Through the sliding glass doors, Deckard could see an extensive gym out on the front deck, which was littered with kettlebells and 45-pound bumper plates.

Opening a drawer under the kitchen counter, Bill

shuffled through some odds and ends until he found a key ring and handed it to Deckard.

"You are two houses down, between Rick and Zach. We own this whole row of eight houses on the shore. Whatever Henderson had stowed away inside the house is yours I guess. No one back in the States gave a shit about him. Keep it or throw it in the trash; I don't care. He traveled light anyway so it won't be much."

"All right."

"Our rules here are pretty basic. We work hard; we play hard. Mandatory team party tonight just like after every op we do. PT is on your own, but we usually work out together. When our optempo slows down you can catch a plane to wherever you want until I recall you, but I'm not sure when that will be. Shit has been picking up the last month with no sign of slowing down."

"It's a dangerous world."

"And they need us to stop it from all coming apart at the seams. We'll work on getting you set up with a bank account here on the island later on so you can get direct deposits. Mauritius is a tax haven and we got a good set up here."

"I like the sound of that."

"Go do what you have to do and I'll see you in a few hours."

As Deckard turned away, Bill had one final item to add.

"Deckard, remember that you are still on probationary status until I decide if I have any use for you or not. There are some pipe hitters out there that just don't have what it takes to be on a team like this. We'll see if you got it or not. In the meantime, we practice strict OPSEC. Say what you need to say inside our team areas. I have this place under 24-hour guard, and our houses are routinely swept for bugs. Ramon will hook you up with a secure cell phone tomorrow. Aside from that, nothing gets said outside these walls. Do nothing that will draw excess attention to our operation here."

"Goes without saying."

"I hope so."

Deckard shut the screen door behind him on his way out and walked over to his new crash pad. As he continued to scope out the area, he had to admit to himself that he could have done much worse. In fact, he *had* done much worse. Sleeping in rundown safehouses in Lebanon, crapping in plastic bags in a spider hole on the Iranian border, or sleeping in a jungle hammock in Colombia had almost became a way of life for him. This seaside secret agent stuff was a whole new world. There were some things that these former SEALs were definitely getting right.

Turning the key in the knob, Deckard stepped inside his bungalow. It wasn't as big as Bill's place, but there was more than enough living space for several people inside. It was furnished with chairs, couches, a flat-screen TV, and everything else a guy would want at a beach house. There was a full bathroom and another shower stall outside with a hose for washing the sand off before coming back inside after a swim.

Henderson.

The Liquid Sky member that Nikita had killed in Pakistan.

The operator whose corpse Deckard had picked over in the back of a van looking for intelligence information. Now he was in the dude's house, literally filling his shoes on the team. The other team members seemed resentful of Deckard, not because they took exception to him replacing their former team mate. They actually seemed completely ambivalent about Henderson's death. Liquid Sky was just pissed that they had to break in a new guy and didn't trust him any farther than they could throw him.

It was still a surreal moment.

Deckard found Henderson's iPod on the counter, where it had been laying with the headphones attached since he left on a one-way flight to Karachi. It was loaded with heavy-metal music like Slayer, Cannibal Corpse, and Megadeth. They were all sterile missions apparently. He had left everything behind. Deckard continued to walk around and examine the layout of the house, conscious of the fact that Liquid Sky probably had hidden cameras installed so they could keep tabs on their newest recruit.

In the bathroom, Henderson's toothbrush leaned diagonally in a glass. The toothpaste tube was squeezed in the middle, the inconsiderate bastard. At least the cabinet was stocked with toilet paper. In the bed room there were some dress shirts. Deckard was still wearing the Walmart clothes that Liquid Sky had waiting for them on their way back through FOB Chapman. He found a shirt which was probably small on Henderson to show off his beach muscles, but would fit Deckard normally.

Going through the dresser to find a pair of cargo shorts, Deckard found an envelope full of pictures. Inside was a whole roll of photographs of Henderson with a blonde. It looked like they were on the shore, maybe Virginia Beach. They were self-shot pictures, close-ups of the two of them kissing and smiling.

Who the hell was this guy?

Henderson, Bill, all these other guys aside from Ramon and obviously Nadeesha, had served in the SEALs as far as Deckard could discern. They were the Navy's most elite commandos. How had they drifted so far? Throwing the pair of shorts on the bed, Deckard shut the dresser drawer.

Then the more important question.

Who were they working for?

He knew from the records he and his Samruk International mercenaries had seized that Liquid Sky were in business with G3 Communications somehow, but the full picture remained obscured. It would take time to uncover. Time he may not have.

Undressing, Deckard stepped into the shower and began to scrub away days of sweat and grim. He didn't have a lot of time, because as he infiltrated Liquid Sky, they were also co-opting him and using his talent for their own agenda, to cure their own contracts, one by one. Sure, they would take him on a couple of righteous kills. Do some terrorists or narco-traffickers. First they warm him up, then they take him out on the real work, killing people like Al-Khalifa, and those who got in their way, like Al-Khalifa's wife.

Toweling himself dry, he slipped into the cargo shorts and began buttoning the blue and white striped shirt over his chest. Deckard caught a glance of himself in the mirror. His eyes were open, even more focused than usual. Hyper vigilant. He put on a pair of Henderson's sandals. He was slowly transforming himself into one of them.

Deckard's priorities of work were simple. Get away from Liquid Sky and beat their surveillance long enough to get a message out to Aghassi and Pat. Let them know he was alive, where he was located, and what he knew about Liquid Sky thus far so they could begin working on the problem sets. It was unlikely that he would be able to take out Liquid Sky by himself. He would need some backup when the time came.

Next, before walking Samruk International into the target, he had to get to the bottom of who Bill was taking his marching orders from. Where were the contracts coming from exactly? Who were the puppetmasters behind the scenes? Only when that question was answered could they cut this head off the hydra and move on to the CEO of G3 Communications and whoever else Liquid Sky was in league with.

As he headed out the door to attend Bill's post-mission beach party, he found he had another reason to be glad he had insisted on doing this mission himself, and not sending Pat, Aghassi, or one of the others. He was heading down a dark road. He was wearing a dead man's clothes and working for a kill team.

Some people might find they liked this life. Some might not want to come home.

7

Zach was mixing the jungle juice.

"Don't look at it," Paul explained as Zach upended a handle of vodka into the pot. "If you don't look at it, then it is okay, it can't get you drunk!"

Once he drained it, Zach dropped the glass bottle in the trash and began stirring his concoction of hard liquor and juice. They were in Bill's place for the team party. Mandatory fun in Deckard's eyes, but the alcohol would be flowing and would help him get a bead on the other guys. He stood off to the side drinking the local brew, Phoenix beer.

Bill had to take a call outside. Of course Deckard wanted to eavesdrop, but he had to play it cool. Rick showed up with a fresh batch of hair gel in to keep his hair slicked back. Ramon walked in a few minutes later. No sign of Nadeesha.

"Drink this, Deckard," Zach said handing him a mug of the jungle juice. He was about six-foot-two with sandy blonde hair. Deckard took the drink.

"Thanks dude."

Zach could have been a stand-in for a kid in an Abercrombie ad or the Hitler Youth. Paul had been right, he realized as he took a sip. If you didn't know there was alcohol in the drink, you'd never know what it was.

"Nice shirt," Zach commented. "Fucking Henderson was all into that Malibu Barbie shit."

"So you were in Army Special Operations?" Rick started in. "What's up with that?"

"I got around," Deckard answered.

"My thing with the Army is that all you guys know that BUD/S is the graduate-level program, and everything else you guys have going is just vanilla."

"You guys were with Dev?"

"Yeah, in the same squadron together."

"TACDEVRON-what?"

"Fuck do you care?"

Deckard decided to back off. Rick suddenly got defensive when he asked which squadron he had been in. But he had confirmed that they were in SEAL Team Six, also known as

Dev Group depending on which way the wind was blowing that day. Meanwhile, Bill walked back inside and picked up a pool cue. He had a couple billiard tables in the living area. Must be a hobby, Deckard thought.

"I don't think you've got what it takes to be on this team. I don't care who you were back in the Army."

It was Deckard's post-Army career where things got really froggy but he didn't feel the need to mention that. Bill had before and knew bits and pieces. Nobody knew the full story of what really happened out there. Not even Deckard if he was to be honest with himself.

"Give me some work. Anybody can put bullets in a muldoon jumping over the wall on the black side of an objective."

"You might get your wish sooner than you think."

"Have to ask you."

"Another question..."

"A woman on the team."

"Not my decision."

"Wouldn't you love to splat a map of Hawaii on her forehead?" Zach yelled from the other side of the room. Paul spun up the stereo system.

"Look," Rick said. "It's not for any lack of trying."

Bill was racking the billiard balls and was about to break.

"I would do things to her that I wouldn't do to farm animals," Paul confirmed.

"She's a bitch," Rick continued. "A woman has no business on this team other than getting passed around the team room."

"You think she likes to scissor with girls?" Deckard said playing along. "Lez it out?"

"Who the fuck knows? Maybe Uncle Bad Touch fingered her no-no place and now she's got some kind of fucking complex." Rick rolled his eyes. "She just does intel shit for us, can go places and suck dicks that we can't. Bill recruited her and ordered us to leave her the fuck alone, so it is what it is."

"I understand. I was just wondering. We didn't have them anyplace that I worked in the Army."

"What?" Zach said. "Split-tailed females?"

"Yeah, except when they got passed around our team

houses."

Zach, Rick, and Paul laughed this time.

"Yeah, well," Zach said, "you would have better luck getting inside Margaret Thatcher's pussy. If you want to fuck Nadeesha you better slip her a Roofie-Colada."

"If this jungle juice doesn't do me in first."

"Man up," Rick sneered. "PT tomorrow unless you're too pussy."

Rick was a hard sell. Didn't like Deckard because he wasn't from the right tribe. Ramon was on the other side of the room having a drink and messing with the TV.

"You from the PI?" Deckard asked as he approached.

"Born and bred," Ramon answered in a matter-of-fact manner. Deckard was hoping he had built a little rapport with him up on the ridgeline.

"You were there in 2006?"

"Why?"

"Because that is when JSOC had their target killing program going on over there."

"You got it all wrong man, I was a Warrant Officer in 1st Group. You?"

"The Legion."

Ramon laughed as he flicked channels until he found a soccer game on one of the satellite channels. "Yeah, I was an intel guy for the CIF."

"How did you get tied in with these frogmen, then?"

"Bill brought me on for a specific mission in a country where I had a lot of local experience and connections. I helped stand up Group 14 after I left the CIF. Ever been to Cambodia?"

"Yeah."

"When you were with GB? The Agency funded all that."

"No. It was a commercial endeavor."

"If you say so. I don't know what to make of you, man. No offense, but people say some weird things about you."

"Some of them are probably even true."

That was when the door opened and Nadeesha walked in like she owned the place. She had changed into a spaghetti-string top and a pair of jeans that clung to her body in all the right places. Deckard found it impossible to avert his gaze as her hips gently swayed. She blew all of them off and walked straight over to Bill.

Over by the billiard tables she started talking to Bill, her hands flying through the air.

"That girl is something else," Ramon said as he sank into the couch. "Maybe you should ask her about the PI. She was part of The Harem, or so I'm told. What do I know? I was just a Wobbly One straight out of the WOC."

Deckard noticed Bill nod his head towards him. Whatever he was talking about with Nadeesha involved him somehow. She didn't look happy. She had both palms up in the air and was having words with Bill. Despite the hardass SEAL persona that he ruled over Liquid Sky with, Bill seemed to take Nadeesha in stride. He never lost his cool with her and Deckard noted it. Bill was a thinker, he could think several steps ahead. He knew how to manage personalities and play the long game. He was a step above Rick and the others. That was probably why he was in charge.

"It took you guys a while to get into the fight didn't it?" Deckard asked Ramon while pretending his didn't notice the conversation about him.

"Yeah, it did. We finally got the CIF in-country and doing some good work. We had some other teams up north in Kurdistan, too."

He kept things going until he heard Bill call out for him.

"Get over here, Deckard!"

Setting down his drink, Deckard walked over to the pair.

"You're going to Dubai," Bill told him.

"I don't fucking need him there," Nadeesha cursed. "He will just get in the way."

"We are being hunted. We got hit hard in Pakistan. I'm not letting you go alone."

"This is my op."

"And it is my decision."

Nadeesha brushed her long dark hair over her shoulder as she shook her head and then crossed her arms under her breasts.

"When can he be ready?" Nadeesha said looking at Bill.

"I'm ready now," Deckard interjected.

"Good," Bill responded. "This is Nadeesha's op. She leads, you follow. Got it?"

"Got it."

"Not this guy," Nadeesha pleaded. "Why not Ramon?"

"I need him for mission prep in the PI. Only he can do that job. All of my boys are assaulters, they are no good for Dubai and you know that as well as I do."

The female intelligence operative sighed. Deckard again wondered what her story was.

"I have several other identity packages for Deckard that Sarah sent us from DC. That is good enough to get both of you to Germany. I will make a call tonight and have her overnight a new package for the two of you with the same surname to pick up once you arrive in Berlin. Your cover will be husband and wife. It's only for twenty-four hours and should hold up fine."

"What do you need me to do?" Deckard asked.

"Watch my ass," Nadeesha explained.

Deckard's eyebrows shot up.

"Oh?"

Nadeesha simply turned and stormed out of the house. She was pissed at being forced to drag Deckard into an operation that she was going to run as a singleton.

"I just want an overwatch element in case she gets into trouble," Bill said. "On our last mission before we picked you up in Afghanistan, we got some unexpected resistance. That is how we lost Henderson. Whoever they were, they were good. I'm just sending you as a precaution. She should be able to handle the operational aspects of the mission on her own. You are just there to get her out of trouble if shit really hits the fan."

"I'll be there."

"Finish your drink and then get to bed. Meet Nadeesha here at seven in the morning and I'll have flight confirmations for you to Germany, and then on to Dubai."

"See you then."

Finishing his drink and bullshitting with Zach for a few more minutes, Deckard realized that he would have no opportunity to break away and get a message out to Pat and Aghassi, not without breaking his cover and sneaking out in the middle of the night. It was doable, but if he got caught, his infiltration would be compromised. He'd be killed or on the run and be no closer to understanding who the power brokers behind Liquid Sky were.

Shit.

He was heading back into the fray.

8

Deckard and Nadeesha touched down in Berlin twenty-four hours later, met a courier outside the terminal who handed off their new passports, then rented a car and drove to Hamburg. Deckard made several attempts to ask his companion what their mission was and what would be expected of him, but she blew him off and made him drive while she worked from her iPad in the passenger seat.

They were flying out of Hamburg because it would raise too many suspicions if they showed up at the Berlin International Airport again five minutes later with new names and passports. Nadeesha also seemed to know that the security in Hamburg was not utilizing biometric sensors, at least not today. Otherwise, they would get popped as they went through security. If their biometrics were recorded in Berlin, put onto a computer database, and then their fingerprints or facial features were again read in Hamburg but attached to different names, it was safe to say they would both be spending the night, and many others, in a German prison.

Deckard drove through the cold overcast weather and drizzling rain until they neared the Hamburg airport.

"What are you doing?" Nadeesha asked him.

"Hold on," Deckard said as he parked in front of a convenience store. A few minutes later he came back with a couple of disposable cameras. Getting back in the car, he shut the door and began tearing open the packages.

"We can buy a camera in the airport or once we land in Dubai," Nadeesha said, thinking he wanted one as a part of their cover as tourists on their honeymoon.

"We have to zap the RFID chips in our old passports. We can keep them hidden in our luggage, but if a scanner in the airport or anywhere else picks up a second set of passports, we are screwed."

Deckard tore up the camera's plastic housing and yanked out the chip the camera's flash device was mounted to. In a few minutes, he had pulled some other wires out of the cameras, stripped them, used some tack he had bought in the store to create a short across the leads from the battery, and held them up to the RFID chip mounted in the covers of their old passports. One by one, he zapped them, making the chips inside unreadable. They would still work as valid passports, and they could simply shrug their shoulders at customs if someone asked why the RFID wasn't working. They could have been magnetized. Or something.

Nadeesha watched Deckard intently, the rain having matted down the hair on his head as he worked with his improvised tools.

"You learned how to do that in the ONI's OPB course?" She asked.

"I learned how to do that from being on the run with no one else to rely on."

With his task completed, Deckard got back outside, threw the remains of the disposable cameras in the trash and drove to the airport. They turned in the rental car, stashed away the old passports, pocketed the new ones, and then went to the ticket counter. One of Bill's Liquid Sky cutouts, a shell company in Singapore, had already purchased their tickets with their new aliases.

Flying Emirates Airlines made any American airline company look like a dive bar with a blinking neon light, in the window where all you could order was warm cans of Budweiser beer. There was plenty of room to spread out, even when flying in the economy class. The service and the food were first-rate, unlike the soggy sandwiches you get on American Airlines or Delta.

Nadeesha continued working on her tablet before reading a newspaper, an Arabic language newspaper. Deckard had some suspicions about what she did when she was in the Army, but he couldn't ask here and she wouldn't answer him anyway. He heard about a cell of female intelligence operatives within JSOC. Ramon had mentioned The Harem to him at the party.

She read Arabic, but didn't look it. More likely she was from Southern India. Her skin was the darkest brown except for her pink lips. By contrast the white around her large brown eyes stood out even more, made her even more beautiful, if that were possible. She stood as tall as Deckard's shoulders. Lithe and fit, Deckard had not a single doubt that as an intelligence operative, she was able to elicit any information from any man on the planet.

He would give her his M4 and his MC-5 parachute any day, all she had to do was ask.

She knew English and Arabic, probably Hindi too. With her ethnic background she was able to blend in with a multitude of different cultures. She had a mouth on her too. That came from field work, from working around people like Deckard, and probably from getting treated like shit by far too many of them.

They ate their food in silence. Nadeesha then put her headphones on, crossed her arms, and watched an in-flight movie on the screen mounted to the seat in front of her. Deckard pulled out a book he had bought in the airport in Hamburg. He tried to read, but had trouble concentrating.

He couldn't stop thinking about what he could be walking into in Dubai.

Sometime during the flight they both drifted off to sleep and only woke up when the flight attendants turned the cabin lights on as they prepared to land. Looking out the window, Deckard could see the city lit up in blue and gold in the night. As the Emirates Airlines jet pulled up to the terminal, Deckard and Nadeesha grabbed their carry-ons. The terminal was ultra-modern with slick chromed metal everywhere, mirrors on the ceilings, and artificial palm trees lining the courseway.

They paid no mind to the shops or roped-off Ferraris parked in the middle of the terminal. Although neither of them knew it of each other, both had been through this airport and operated in Dubai previously.

After clearing customs with their man and wife matching

passports, they rented another car. This time Nadeesha took the wheel. It was her mission and she was going to be running it. Good thing they were not in Saudi Arabia, Deckard recalled. Otherwise, she wouldn't have been allowed to drive even if she wanted to due to the strict Sharia law in place.

Hitting the road, it was only a twenty-minute drive to their hotel. They checked in and got a room with a single king-sized bed to stick with their cover. It was a five-star hotel, not far from the Burj Khalifa, the world's tallest building. Deckard sat down on the bed and flipped on the television. He was starting to get used to the idea that he was just along for the ride and would have to react to whatever his teammate threw at him.

"I have to get ready," she said as she opened her suitcase. "He will be here in a few hours."

"Who will?"

For once she didn't blow him off.

"The target. He stays in this hotel whenever he flies in to Dubai for business. He is a financier for some bad people who do bad things in this part of the world."

"I'm used to improvising on the fly, but I should tell you that, like anyone else, I can perform better when I know what my task and purpose is ahead of time."

"You are my overwatch element," she said as she swept her black hair over her shoulders. "Our information is that he stays here every time and that he likes to indulge in things that are *hareem* back in his home country."

"Russian hookers."

"And alcohol, but if I throw myself at him he will forget all about the hookers."

"I imagine."

"You just keep tabs on me downstairs in the bar or wherever he wants to take me. I need you to go out and run some errands before he gets here. Buy a couple cell phones, SIM cards, and then gas them up with phone cards. I need a way to alert you if something is wrong."

Deckard nodded and took his passport and some local currency with him. Driving to the nearest shopping mall, he parked and walked through the sliding doors. It was absolutely freezing inside. Apparently the royal family wanted to show off to the rest of the world that, despite living in the desert, they had the best air conditioning that money could buy.

71

He found an electronics store and picked up a couple of cellular phones, installed the SIM cards, and then bought a bunch of phone cards. Back at the hotel he plugged both phones into the electrical outlets to make sure they had a charge.

The bathroom door opened and Nadeesha walked out with a towel wrapped around her body. She had just gotten out of the shower. A red cocktail dress hung in the closet on a hanger.

"If you need to take a shower, do it now because I need time to get ready."

She wasn't kidding. A makeup kit was laid out on the bed.

Deckard figured she was trying to drop a hint on him, and so he took a shower and changed into some fresh clothes. Henderson had made a postmortem clothing donation, Diesel jeans, another button-down shirt, and black shoes. When he came out of the bathroom, still drying his hair, Nadeesha was standing over her makeup case. She had somehow fit herself into the impossibly tight dress. The shoulder straps were undone and hung off her brown shoulders. Her chest looked like it was about to burst out of the dress at any moment.

"Come here," she said as she turned around.

All business, Deckard told himself as he zipped up her dress.

"Take one of the cell phones. I programmed each phone's number into the other. There is an app on the phone that you can press with one tap and it will bring up a distress message on the other phone. There is also a geo-location feature in case you lose track of me."

Then, she turned her head to look back at him out of the corner of her eye.

"Don't lose me," she stated flatly.

"I won't."

"Good. Now go find something to do, and be ready for me in the bar downstairs in forty-five minutes. I have to take care of a few things."

"Which of us is going to take this guy out, or both?"

"I handle that. I will call you when its done and for a pickup."

Deckard grabbed one of the cell phones and pulled out the charger. Nadeesha tugged at the top of her dress to try to get comfortable in it. She did sexy amazingly well, but clearly she felt more comfortable doing shorts, a t-shirt, and a sub-machine gun. He didn't blame her.

"Later," he said as he closed the door behind him.

Outside, Deckard returned to their rental. Inside, he quickly rolled down the windows and blasted the air conditioning.

He did have something to do before they got started. While at the shopping mall he had also picked up an 11-piece steak knife cutting set. Using some duct tape he gotten at the hardware store, he cut pieces of cardboard and made improvised sheathes by folding the cardboard back on itself.

Then, he rolled back his sleeves, put the steak knives in their sheaths, and pressed them under his forearms while ringing rolls of duct tape over the cardboard and around his forearms. Once both knives were in place he rolled his sleeves back down. He would have to be careful. The improvised weapons would be concealed better if he was wearing a jacket, which he would if they ended up in another venue with mega air conditioning but otherwise it would just look out of place in the desert heat.

Even at night, the temperature would only drop from about 110 during the day down to about 95 degrees. It still felt like staring into a blow dryer, and it was almost 11pm. Locking up the car, he made his way back into the hotel and took a seat at the end of the bar.

His cell phone began to vibrate. It was Nadeesha texting him to announce that she would be down in a few minutes. Deckard walked into the bar and sat at a table where he could keep an eye on the entrance, the bar itself, and most of the tables. When the waitress arrived, he ordered a beer. Drinking was permissible for non-Muslims.

As he sipped the beer, his mind staggered for a moment as he wondered who was mean-mugging him across the bar. He didn't even recognize his reflection in the mirror anymore. Although he was still in his thirties, he had grown old, gone through several more life cycles than most people do. He was bitter. Restless.

War was the only time the world made sense to him. Putting boots to asses was the only satisfaction he really had. It was something he was good at and something he kept doing because he enjoyed it. There were a lot of assholes in this world and he liked putting them out of business.

His self-reflection was thankfully broken as Nadeesha walked through the door. With her hair and makeup done up she could have graced the cover of any magazine she chose. Whoever this Arab financier was, he didn't stand a chance. She'd probably murder him and then Deckard in their sleep before the night was over.

Nadeesha slid onto a stool at the bar with her back to him. She ordered a drink and shot down two men before it even arrived. They were fat Arabs, but not the right fat Arab.

Ten minutes later, he showed up. The Arab financier had the physique of a hippopotamus and a head shaped like a perfect egg. He wore a blue trainer outfit and tennis shoes. He clearly didn't do much training, but this was the fashion in some parts of the world. Deckard pegged him as Lebanese. Probably Hezbollah.

As the bartender brought him a Martini, Nadeesha slid off her seat and approached him.

That was when a British expat decided to introduce herself to Deckard.

"Hi, I'm Audrey."

Deckard reached out and shook her hand, smiling back at her.

"Jon," he said, using the alias name on his passport. "Would you like to have a seat?"

"I thought I might trouble you for a light, but yes I would." She sat down across from him.

Deckard didn't mind, he kind of stood out sitting by

himself.

They made small talk while he occasionally eyeballed Nadeesha and her prey. Audrey was in Dubai to spend a semester teaching English in a girls school. Technically she was doing her fellowship for her PhD back in the UK, but she needed to pick up some scratch in the meantime. Deckard offered vague details about himself, gave his cover without mentioning that he was "married" to the woman across the bar for obvious reasons.

Twenty minutes later found Nadeesha and the target walking out, arm in arm. Deckard sincerely hoped that this was a wham, bam, thank you ma'am type deal because he didn't want to chase the would-be lovebirds all over town. No need to wine and dine.

"Be right back love, have to find the rest room."

"Oh, see you soon!" Audrey said.

Yeah, right.

Deckard was relieved when he saw the couple heading for the elevators. He watched the digital readout above the elevator tick up and stop at the 21st floor. She was keeping this easy by making sure she took him to their room. He had the key card so if it got ugly he would be inside the room in seconds.

Jumping in the second elevator he hit the button for the 21st floor. The doors opened and Deckard stepped into the hall just in time to hear the door to their room slam shut. He hung out by a vending machine, pretending to try to jam a bill in it whenever someone walked by. He kept his keycard under the Dirham bill. He kept the ruse up for ten minutes, alternating between pretending to look at his cell phone and playing with the vending machine.

Then the cell phone vibrated. Deckard looked at the screen which displayed a single word

Red.

In a half-dozen long strides, he was at the door and shoving the key card in the reader. The LED on the door flashed green and Deckard flung the door open.

The Arab was stripped naked and had Nadeesha pinned against the wall, holding her by the neck. The woman's brown arms and legs struggled against his weight as he pressed her into the wall. Deckard used the edge of his shoe in a downward strike that nearly separated the Arab's calf muscle.

Nadeesha fell to the ground. She wore only a black

thong, apparently well into the game of seducing the Arab.

Deckard didn't notice as he fixated on his target, knocking him to the ground. With both hands, the American commando reached for his inner wrists and seized the knives by their handles. Tearing both free from their sheaths, he held the steak knives in a reverse grip. The Arab struggled to his feet, favoring his uninjured leg, both hands clutching his chest.

Deckard assumed a boxer's stance. He was about to go to work.

"Wait!" Nadeesha shouted at him. "The Stux is starting to take effect."

"The what?"

The financier staggered back to the ground. He looked as he was having a heart attack.

"Succinylcholine," Nadeesha informed him as she picked up an empty syringe from the floor.

As their target squirmed on the carpet, Deckard looked back and noticed her nakedness. He pretended not to note that she was perfectly endowed in all the right places.

"It is a paralytic, but he wasn't about to sit still for me to stick him in a vein so I had to put it in the muscle. The drug takes longer to kick in that way."

Finally, the Arab went still. The room suddenly began to stink.

"Son of a bitch," Deckard cursed. "He had a jumper in the door."

Deckard looked back, making sure he looked her in the eye. For just a moment, he saw it. The hard case was gone and he saw what she looked like when she was scared. It had been a close call.

"Pack your shit," Deckard ordered. "We can peel out of here tonight. It will take the authorities a while to put this together if they do at all."

"Okay."

The female operative didn't bother with a bra and threw on a white button down and then a pair of black slacks from her suitcase. Deckard just tossed whatever was laying around into their bags. Her make up, her hair dryer, his deodorant, he didn't care what ended up in what suitcase. They were packed in five minutes and out the door. They left the corpse in place, resting in his own filth. Nadeesha made sure she policed up the empty syringe though.

They left the hotel without checking out. Halfway to the airport, Deckard zeroed out both of their cell phones and dumped them into the trash along with the syringe. He winced as he tore the cardboard sheaths off his forearms and chucked them into the garbage with the knives. Nadeesha got on her tablet and made sure their reservations were confirmed for their flight out. She checked them both in before they dumped the rental car and walked into the airport.

Two hours later they were in the air, catching the red eye out of Dubai. Landing in Italy, they split up and took separate evasion routes. Nadeesha bounced around for a few days in Africa. Deckard flew to Bangkok and went overland into Cambodia where he dumped his married passport and reverted to his single passport. From there, he caught a flight to Indonesia, and then on to Madagascar. Finally he booked a flight back to Mauritius. Nadeesha got a flight from Kenya and landed on the island the morning that the news broke in major international television outlets that someone had been assassinated in a hotel in Dubai.

The suspects were still at large and Dubai was cooperating with Interpol and other international organizations to compile evidence. A week later it was clear that the trail had run cold in Europe.

9

Physical training with Liquid Sky put Deckard in a world of shit. He was a hybrid athlete as necessitated by his lifestyle. As the leader of a para-military mercenary unit, Deckard led from the front, often doing body weight routines and kettlebell workouts with the Kazakh mercenaries in the gym, ruck marches with fifty pound packs, and five-mile runs in full combat equipment.

Liquid Sky took masochism to a whole new level.

At dawn they dived into the ocean for a swim. Deckard was a strong swimmer, but the former SEALs were like fish as they cut through waves that knocked him back and forth in the water. Bill took them out past the breakers and then turned around to head back to shore. Deckard was the last one to the beach. Even Ramon, their former Special Forces member, was out in front of him.

Washing up on shore, Deckard jogged across the beach and up to Bill's bungalow to catch up. They were already spotting each other as they cycled through on the bench press.

"You're up," Rick told him just as he climbed up onto the deck. Soaking wet, he knocked out five repetitions on the bench. He was tired from the swim but could hang in there. Coming from the Army side, he was a runner and ruck marcher more than a swimmer.

Next they did Renegade Man Makers with 25-pound dumbbells. A weight was held in each hand while hitting the ground and doing a push up, then you shifted your weight and executed a row, bringing the weight level with the chest, then repeating it on the other side. Next, you got to your feet with the weights and pressed them above your head. That was one repetition. They did five reps.

Next came five box jumps. From a standing position, you had to jump on top of a wooden box that was two feet high. Also for five reps. Then came five reps on the dip bars. After that came five Goblet Squats which were done holding a 25-pound kettlebell. Then, they did 25-meter sprints down the beach to shake it out. That was one set. There were four more to go.

Deckard was sucking. Most of the other guys were on steroids and were blowing through the exercises at first. Rick was actually the first one to puke. The entire workout was done for time and now it was starting to catch up to them. Ramon puked off the edge of the deck during their third time through the Renegade Man Makers. Deckard puked third, this time during the sprints. Zach got it on the last set, barfing into the ocean as he staggered away after the box jumps.

After the fifth and last set they all lay around panting. Except for Bill. He was a human wrecking ball. Deckard saw that he was covered in sweat but didn't even seem to be breathing that hard. The Liquid Sky leader picked up a water bottle, swished the water around in his mouth, spat it out in the sand and walked inside.

"Fuck me," Deckard said to himself.

When he finally managed to get to his feet and walk back to his beach house he was just in time to see Nadeesha glide out of the waves and stride up the beach in a blue bikini. She was on her own PT program and the guys simply left her to her own devices. She made eye contact with him for a split second before turning and walking down the beach to her place, not even acknowledging his existence.

Deckard stood in the cool morning air for another minute before going inside and taking a shower. Most of the food in the refrigerator had gone bad and had to be thrown out but Deckard downed some cereal he found in the pantry. His body was starving and he'd have to make sure he got some more food in his system soon to help recover from the workout. He also drank several more glasses of water.

After he got dressed, Deckard locked the door and walked a few blocks to the main street. He was on his own time until the team party tonight. It was time to get to work.

Hailing a cab, he told the driver that he wanted to hit up the market in Port Louis, the island's capital located about twenty minutes away from where he was on the northern tip of Mauritius. The cab driver nodded. Almost everyone seemed to speak English here.

On the way into the city, Deckard observed the port. It really was a multicultural island with many faiths and people living on top of one another without any real problems. It wasn't just the churches, mosques, and temples, but even the port was filled with run-of-the-mill fishing vessels and Chinese junks. There were also naval ships, which looked to be retrofitted with stealth characteristics.

Paying the cab driver, he walked into the center of the city. Port Louis was second world, but perfectly comfortable and the people very friendly. Still, he couldn't help but notice that like most countries he traveled too, the tallest buildings in town were the ones reserved for the banks and private financial institutions. Like Malta, Mauritius was an off shore finance nexus.

Deckard walked a long surveillance-detection route, winding his way through the city blocks and stopping several times. He had to make absolutely sure he wasn't being followed.

The market was a large two-story building in the city center. Produce filled baskets in every stall with bright orange, green, red, and yellow fruits, along with various nuts, stalks, and roots. Looking through the breezeway up to the second story, Deckard could see clothing and other household goods for sale. Climbing the stairs, he pretended to look at a few stalls before stopping at a stall that sold electronics.

He bought a Samsung cellphone with cash and picked up a SIM card while he was there. Outside, he found a vender selling phone cards and bought several from him. Deckard again took a long meandering route that would allow him to see if he was being followed. Finding a pizzeria, he ducked inside and asked the waiter to be seated in the back of the restaurant.

Ordering a pizza and a drink, he went to work as soon as the waiter walked away. Slipping in the SIM card, he inserted the battery into the phone and found that he had a half charge. Good enough. Scratching off the code bars on the back of the phone cards, he typed them in and put minutes on his phone.

Furiously, Deckard began hammering out an intel report with his thumbs.

Pat sat up in his chair as his cell phone vibrated across the table.

Samruk International was still working out of a hangar at the airport in Astana, Kazakhstan. Frank and Sergeant Major Koran had flown in with the Kazakhs from Mexico and made sure they were paid for services rendered before putting them on two weeks of leave. Now the troops were filtering back from across the country. The problem was, Samruk International didn't have a new contract for them yet. The Kazakh mercenaries were re-fitting, and Korgan was drawing up a training plan, but they still needed to find work.

Now that Frank was back to his old self and walking around without crutches, he was setting up business meetings with the Kazakh government to bid on a counter-narcotics contract. Something local would be nice for a change.

Snatching the phone off his desk, Pat typed in his PIN and saw that he had a new text message. As the former Delta Force operator began to read, he immediately knew what he was looking at.

"Aghassi!" He called across the hangar. His voice echoed through the open space. A massive An-125 Russian cargo jet sat in the middle of the hangar, its twin brother was outside on the tarmac. They were expensive as hell to operate, but necessary for a highly mobile private military company.

"Get over here!"

Aghassi and Nikita were currently tasked with training-up a six-man recce cell but this was critical. They had a man in the field. Under and alone.

Pat scrolled through the message:

81

Operating out of Mauritius
Seven operators incl/ me
Last tgt in dubai told he was money for terr org
Previous tgt in afghan said they ran dope for karzai
guy in Pak named Henderson girl back home?
others, Bill, Paul, Zach, and Rick. Former SEALs. Bill
1IC

Ramon. former 1st sfg CIF
Nadeesha. not sure, jsoc intel maybe
nasty group, witness war crimes in afghan.
still on probation w/ tm

"Ho-ly shit," Pat said. "Fucking Deckard. He did it."

The assassination in Dubai was all over the news. Fingers were getting pointed everywhere, but mostly at Mossad. No one could prove anything, of course.

"I'm catching the first flight out tonight," Aghassi said. He was now reading the message over Pat's shoulder.

"Got it. I'll get in touch with Cody back in the States for the electronic piece."

Cody was a hacker that Samruk had contracted previously for the Mexico operation.

The next text message was an address to the place where Deckard was staying on the island. Aghassi wrote it down and then opened one of the laptops sitting at their *ad hoc* command post and began making arrangements. The phone vibrated one more time.

There is a # in my kit. pocket on plate carrier i used in
MX
Remember the two NSW guys we ran into down there
Call them. find out who these guys are
want to know what the fuck happened to them.

Pat texted him back to acknowledge the message. He didn't hear back. Deckard was probably already throwing the cell phone into the ocean. The last text referred to two SEAL Team Six operators that they had crossed paths with while they were sniffing out an arms trafficking pipeline in Mexico. The two Spanish speaking SEALs were acting as advisers to the

Mexican forces battling it out with the cartels. Tearing through Deckard's combat gear in the corner of the hangar, Pat found the piece of paper with their numbers on it. Dusty and Flakjacket were their nicknames.

The last two weeks had been spent waiting for Deckard's corpse to turn up somewhere, in which case they would be lucky because it was far more likely that he just disappeared into the ether never to be seen or heard from again. Now that they had an inside man, it was time to start getting inside the enemy's decision-making cycle. Pat sat back down and starting making some calls.

Deckard erased the phone's memory, then removed the battery. He devoured the pizza, his body still starved from the morning workout. Paying the bill, he made his way back towards the port and tossed his cell phone over the railing and into the Indian Ocean. The city's main shopping mall was right across the bay so Deckard walked over and bought some food and other household items he needed for the duration of his stay. However long that might be.

Taking a cab back to his pad, Deckard put away the groceries. He had to be careful not to get comfortable here. It was an island oasis that Europeans flocked to on vacation, but for him it was Bad Guy country. It didn't even have to be his mistake. A few phone calls to the wrong people in the United States for instance. If certain information began to fall into Bill's hands, Liquid Sky would start to get suspicious. Suspicion would quickly give way to paranoia. You could never be too careful in this line of work. That paranoia would lead immediately to Deckard being executed. He could never let his guard down here. He was always operational, even when not on an operation.

He continued to wonder if his entire house wasn't wired for sound and video with someone playing voyeur as they watched him on a closed-circuit television screen. If that paranoia did set in with Liquid Sky, he would never see it coming once they decided to do him in. He could improvise some weapons like in Dubai, or better yet, secure a gun somewhere on the island, but for now, secrecy was his security.

Back at his bungalow, he took a long nap on the couch with the television muted. Late into the afternoon, he woke as someone banged on the screen door that faced out to the ocean.

"Hey," Zach said, "team meeting before the party. Let's go."

"Sure," Deckard said as he rubbed his eyes. "Be right there."

Deckard opened the screen door and stepped outside.

Mauritius was a relatively tiny island in the middle of nowhere. Isolated, it was tucked away from all the distractions and complications found elsewhere. The waves broke on the shore, pulling the beach out with it as the tides changed. It felt like he was standing on the edge of the world.

Walking down the beach, he crossed Bill's workout area on the deck and stepped inside. Zach and Paul were shooting the shit about some French tourists they had banged the night before.

"This island is a pussy buffet, bro," Paul laughed.

"Fucking Euro girls don't lube up right when they're drunk though. Gotta help 'em out a little," Zach complained.

"Give them a break," Rick cut in. "I'm sure she did fine with what little she had to work with."

The Liquid Sky men roared with laughter as Rick high-fived Paul. Everyone went quiet as Nadeesha entered and sat down in a chair in the corner. Bill was sitting on his couch with his laptop open.

"Now that everyone is here," Bill said as he eyeballed Nadeesha, "we can get started."

Deckard noticed that Ramon was missing.

"I know everyone has been nervous about the client. Recent events back in the States scared him off and his company decided to abandon a number of classified projects including some indig proxy force they were training out in Nevada. After we got hung out to dry, I had to find us employment elsewhere. Pakistan was for a Prince in Bahrain. Afghanistan was a one-off paid for by some ex-Agency guy working a private network in Pakistan. Then, Dubai was for the Yids.

"We had a couple interested parties who were going to pick us up on a permanent basis like G3 Communications did, but some of those fell through. A lot of the players had experience with BW, and the executives over there left a lot of scorched ground between the decision makers and the contractors. I almost set us up working directly for a group of princes in the Gulf States, but now I think I got something better.

"A retired American General is going to pick up Liquid Sky and his 'leadership academy' or what-the-fuck-ever will sponsor us covertly. This way, his group acts as the middle man between the princes who have plenty of work for us to do. This Arab Spring thing is really fucking up their jive. That's where we come in. Between them and these Wahhabi sand niggers they got their hands full and a bunch of inept A-rab soldiers in their military who sleep most of the day and spend the rest fucking their boyfriends. So we won't be hurting for work."

"So what are we looking at?" Rick asked.

"They've got something for us to start on now. Ramon finished his pre-mission prep and has already moved into the target country to begin operational preparation of the battlespace. Tomorrow, the rest of us move out to the staging area. The targeted individual has already had five assassination attempts on him in the last two years, so he is paranoid as fuck and is prepared. He knows someone will try again and will be waiting for us. This is going to take some brass balls to pull off, but what the fuck else is new.

"Don't worry about that shit now. Party it up tonight. Tomorrow we fly out to begin training and it is back to business."

A couple whoops went up and the boys began dragging out a keg that they had on ice. The next time Deckard turned around, Nadeesha had already disappeared. Bill tapped the keg and started passing out beers. Paul got a few dozen shot glasses and lined them up on the kitchen table. The other guys were making phone calls to some of the expat girls they knew on the island.

Zach shotgunned four shots back-to-back and the party was started. Deckard was pretty drunk by the time a half dozen women showed up. Four were from France, one from Switzerland, and another from Germany. They brought drugs with them, too.

Bill did a couple lines of a blow off one of his billiard tables. Deckard was starting to get nervous. Former operators filled with booze and coke and haunted by the wars they fought in was not exactly a great combination.

Sitting down with a fresh beer, one of the French girls came over and sat down on his lap. Deckard had no idea what the blond was saying to him and he cared even less. Across the room, one of her girlfriends was grabbing Zach's crotch as they took turns downing shots. She frowned at her and then went back to Deckard, kissing him on the lips. They seemed to be in competition with each other.

Rick fired up a couple lines of coke between vodka shots.

Now the French chick had pulled out Rick's cock. It was Deckard's turn to frown. The Prince Albert piercing had to hurt. Getting down on her knees, the blonde girl's friend went to work, deep throating Rick right there in the middle of the party. The European girls cheered, a few offering advice on how to improve her technique.

The blonde was clearly pissed over something and jumped off Deckard's lap to go use the bathroom. When she came back, her pupils were huge, dilated from whatever pills she had swallowed.

By then, Bill had bent the big-titted German girl over a billiard table, dropped trou and was drilling her, the moans drowned out by the loud deathmetal music blasting over the stereo.

Jesus Christ, Deckard thought. When he was a young soldier they used to have Squad parties. He recalled his Squad Leader doing keg stands all night, throwing the keg off his back deck, and then doing donuts around his house in a beat-up Toyota pickup truck. All of that seemed pretty mild compared to this cocaine-fueled orgy.

Once Bill finished with the German, the blond pillhead let her jean shorts fall around her ankles and bent over the pool table to wait her turn. Soon, her finger nails were tearing up the billiard table's upholstery.

Deckard could take a hint, if he stuck around much longer there was a good chance that one of these nymphos was going to handcuff him to a radiator and shock his balls with a couple wires attached to a car battery. He made a hasty exit as Paul and Zach swapped girls and were going for their second round.

Later on, he couldn't remember stumbling back to his beach house. He woke up in the early morning hours, still wearing his clothes while laying in the bathtub with the shower on, soaking wet.

"What. The. Fuck."

10

Deckard launched himself off the ramp of the airplane and into the darkness. He still had trouble stabilizing as he exited the aircraft and rocked from side to side for a few moments as he rode the hill of air down through the sky, his body riding along with the forward throw of the plane on exit. Seconds seemed to stretch on forever, but he finally got stable in the air and assumed a position called a high lift track position in normal parachuting, that is, with his arms extended but swept back and his legs extended all the way out.

Unlike a HALO jump in the military, he was wearing a wing suit which would provide additional lift and therefore, more forward-glide during freefall. The sheets of material stretched between his legs and out from his arms. An ancient dream was now achievable: human flight.

Turning his head slightly, he could make out the sleek forms of four other Liquid Sky members flying behind him in the moonlit night.

Pivoting his hips and shifting his legs, Deckard was able to steer by using the wing suit like a giant rudder. Splotches of gold floated beneath him as he soared over the city. Manila.

He got on azimuth, heading west, over the city and pointed towards the ocean beyond. He was dumping altitude, dropping a meter for every couple of meters that he traveled forward. The wind howled in his ears as the cityscape below him shot by.

Angling himself downward, he picked up speed as he flew towards his target. Through the wind goggles he wore, Deckard could now make out the outline of the Aquino Building. He was moving at nearly a hundred and twenty miles an hour, and the rooftop was the smallest dropzone he had ever had to hit in his career.

It was coming up fast.

The other Liquid Sky members floated alongside him, each maneuvering slightly away from each other to clear their airspace. In the night they looked like giant flying squirrels in their wing suits. One operator dropped his hips to try to adjust his trajectory. At this point they were all trying to make small adjustments to get on the right track before deploying their parachutes.

To his right, one of the wingsuit parachutists peeled away from the formation. He was too far off the required fight path and was having trouble getting stable. He would have to deploy his parachute and land safely at a secondary landing zone on the ground. Deckard didn't notice, he was completely fixated on his target.

The leading edge of the target building was coming up. Deckard reached back and deployed his pilot chute. The drogue caught in the air and yanked out his main parachute. Everything was a blur of motion as Deckard's world swayed, his parachute opening above him. He was looking down into the lights inside the rooftop swimming pool.

He was too low.

Deckard reached up to grab his toggles to try to steer while he still had some space to maneuver. Below him, he saw another jumper slam right into the side of the building and through the plate glass windows. His parachute never had a chance to deploy at all.

Deckard reached out but the edge of the roof was still a good ten feet away. He sunk beneath the lip of the roof and was staring at his reflection in the windows. His heart was in his throat as he made impact.

The scene froze in front of his eyes.

Feeling his boots make contact with the floor, he stood up. The harness had lowered on its pulley system at the end of the scenario. The blinking word RESET flashed in his goggles. He flipped the visor up on his forehead and looked across the dark room. Everyone was quiet. It was their tenth time through the same scenario and none of them were getting any better.

He squinted as the lights came back on.

"Not a single person made it on to the rooftop," Bill scolded them. "Take it from the top."

Deckard stretched his neck, his arms, and legs as he was still secured in his parachute harness and couldn't start walking around while tethered into the metal frame.

Each of them wore a parachute and black S-Bird wing suits made by TonySuit. Following the Special Operations adage, train as you fight, they used the same gear in the simulator that they would use on target. The S-Bird wing suit would allow them the forward glide they needed to jump from an airplane, fly into the restricted airspace over the city of Manila, and then land on their objective. This model wing suit also came equipped with escape sleeves. Normally the wings of the suit had to be unzipped manually after the jumper deployed his parachute so that he could reach up and grab the parachute's toggles in order to steer it. There would be no time for that on this gig, they would be right on top of the objective by the time they got silk over their heads.

Later, they would add their combat equipment to their rigs. At the moment the kit loadout was still being finalized as Ramon collected intelligence on the target in the Philippines. As it stood, it didn't really matter what kit they carried on objective if none of them could even get there in the first place.

A gray-haired technician sat in the corner of the warehouse. He was behind a computer, clicking away with his mouse as he began to reset the training scenario.

The simulator and the software were created by a company called ParaSim. The scaffolding structures were lined up next to each other, five in a row for the Liquid Sky operators. Nadeesha was working intel and logistics for them at their staging area and would not be going on target.

At the top of the scaffolding was a series of electronic pulleys and servos that moved the suspension lines that each parachutist hung from during the simulation. The suspension lines would reel themselves in and out and reposition the jumper's body based on what was going on in the simulator. It would even release and drop the jumper down to the floor when he landed on the ground in the simulation.

Sensors were hooked up to the parachute ripcord and toggles so that the jumpers actually used their gear in physical reality, and got real time feed back inside the virtual reality simulator. A modified flip-down night vision goggle headset was worn on the helmet of each jumper but the normal night vision goggles were replaced with a virtual reality screen. The simulator could replicate all sorts of different scenarios based on the inputs added by the technician behind the computer.

Windspeed, jump altitude, weather conditions, and much more could be adjusted on the software side to give the most realistic experience possible. In this case they had the sub-contractor, where they were now located in Australia that ran the staging site, and programmed the exact scenario they had in mind for their mission. It was constantly being updated based on the feedback sent from Ramon who was already watching the building in Manila.

They were still working out what their jump altitude should be, what their pull altitude should be, and what their angle of attack should be as they came in on the objective building. Beyond that, they were all still having trouble controlling their wing suits.

"Come up five hundred feet on the jump altitude," Bill told the technician.

"Got it, resetting now," the technician announced.

Deckard flipped down his VR goggles as the suspension lines began to retract and pull him up into a freefall position.

"Don't fuck it up," he heard Bill say, his voice echoing in the warehouse.

Then they were jumping out of the back of an airplane over Manila and blasting over the city again. Deckard overshot the target and slammed into another building.

Everybody else died too.

Rick pushed a piece of plywood into position and held it for Deckard. While holding a half dozen nails in his mouth, Deckard began nailing the plywood into the wooden frame that they had spent the day constructing. Each of the Liquid Sky members were covered in sweat, their clothes soaked through while they labored in the Australian heat.

Nadeesha weaved her way through the mock-up they were building with a clipboard in her hand.

"When you finish with that I need you two to help Paul frame out the dining room."

Rick and Deckard looked at each other as she walked off. She was taking her role as foreman a little too seriously. Using the pictures that Ramon was taking of the objective area, they were building a scale model of the rooftop apartment they were going to raid. Once they finished building it, they would run through it, training with guns that shot paint pellets.

Nadeesha kept pushing them to work faster. They still had a mission brief to do and then it was back into the simulator until they didn't suck anymore.

Deckard finished nailing the plywood in place, and then went to go find Paul.

Back in the warehouse, everyone was relieved to be able to sit in the air conditioning for a while. Nadeesha had just gotten off the phone with Ramon and was now ready to start the brief. A map was laid out on the table alongside some overhead satellite photography taken from Google Earth. The next step would be to make a three-dimensional model of the city to help conduct talk-throughs of the mission.

Bill turned on a tablet and passed it around. It showed a thirty-something Filipino with a goatee and eyeglasses.

"This is our target, Kanor De Jesus. He runs a finance network for the moose limbs. Some of them are targeting the royal families in the Gulf States, so the client wants this guy out of the picture. The problem is that various players, including JSOC, have already tried to kill him. Five botched assassination attempts in the last two years. These days he doesn't ever leave his rooftop apartment. The building is locked down with security from top to bottom. It would take a battalion of soldiers to fight their way up to the top. He knows there will be another assassination attempt and has taken precautions."

"For some reason De Jesus just doesn't sound like a Muslim name," Zach remarked.

"It isn't. This guy is a businessman; not a moose limb. His MO is providing financing to individuals and small cells that conduct terrorist attacks back in their home countries. Yemen, Saudi Arabia, Jordan, UAE, Kuwait, Iraq, and so on. He has a network that goes out and buys pre-paid cards. You have to show identification to buy the cards, but not to reload them. So De Jesus has some local patsies buy the cards, then he has his men reload them with cash, all the way up to 10,000 dollars which is more than enough to get into the Middle East and run a small-scale terrorist operation. Sometimes he will hand out multiple cards anyway.

"The thing is, these attacks he is funding are becoming so frequent that each country's intelligence services are having a hard time countering them. He is using swarming tactics. Remember those anus bombs?"

"Butt bombs?" Paul asked.

"A couple moose limbs stuck HME," Bill said, referring to home made explosives, "along with a cell-phone detonator right up their poop chute."

"Sounds painful."

"These fuckers have lots of practice playing butt darts so I'm sure it wasn't that big a deal. They almost killed the intelligence minister of Jordan a few months ago with one of those attacks. The other went off and killed a bunch of people in Riyadh during Ramadan."

"Killing their own people," Zach remarked. "Fucking savages."

Deckard said nothing. He wasn't at all surprised. That was how groups like Al Qaeda operated. Muslim or not, you, your wife, and your kids were going to be turned into corpses if you didn't believe in AQ's bronze-age worldview.

"The thing about these pre-paid cards is that they are an easy way to transport large sums of money across international borders, and they are completely untraceable. It allows terrorists to access funds in ways that would set off trip wires otherwise.

If they were moving cash around in some other manner it would get picked up by banking software and red-flagged by American and foreign agencies.

"There was also an IED that injured a Saudi prince a couple months back. The scale of the attacks is increasing while the duration between them is decreasing. De Jesus is handing out these pre-paid cards to moose limb motherfuckers like it is going out of style. But this is what really has the client freaked out," Bill said as he grabbed the tablet and flipped to a new picture.

"This guy works for the People's Liberation Army with the General Staff Development's Third Department."

"The what?" Rick asked.

"Uh, it's like China's version of the NSA."

"Not really," Nadeesha chimed in.

"Well, then tell us knuckle draggers what the fuck this guy represents."

"He goes by the name Dai Kexue, a mid-level executive with a state-owned manufacturing consortium. His real name is Major Shen Banggen."

"And what does he do for Red China?" Rick asked again.

"He facilitates certain programs and projects, only a few of which we know anything about. We do know that the Third Department is invested in securing China's cyber infrastructure and protecting its national security, but it isn't anything like the NSA. The Third Department takes a more holistic approach to national security called *informatization*. This means that their cyber security initiatives work in tandem with China's efforts to secure its place in the global marketplace, continue its economic growth, and compete commercially."

"What the hell does that mean?" Paul asked, clearly frustrated.

Deckard leaned forward and began to speak.

"It means that Major Banggen is tasked with ensuring that China has total information dominance for political, economic, and military purposes. Baggen is clearly working with De Jesus as part of a Chinese shaping operation. They are facilitating outcomes in the Middle East that they feel are favorable to China and unfavorable to the United States."

"I still don't get it," Paul said rolling his eyes.

Nadeesha blew air through her teeth.

"It means we have to kill De Jesus," Deckard said.

"You should have just said that in the first place."

"You guys can go bone-to-bone and see who is bigger later on," Bill told them. "Nadeesha has been compiling the intel that Ramon has gathered so far and will brief you on the general layout of what you will find on the rooftop of the Aquino building when, and if, you make it there."

They slept in cots in the warehouse. The team was cut off from the rest of the world and kept in isolation. The technician who ran the simulator would bring them food in the morning and other odds and ends they requested.

Bill woke the team at nine in the morning. Using replica M4 rifles that shot paintball pellets, they began clearing the mock up that they had begun constructing the previous day. Most of De Jesus' apartment was framed out, but it still needed some work. Still, they were just familiarizing themselves with the floor plan. Bill only set up a few paper targets inside for them to shoot at.

Deckard had to give it to Bill, as unprofessional an outfit as it was, Liquid Sky had a pretty squared away training plan for this mission. He was using the crawl, walk, run method to train up the team and prepare them for their mission in the PI. The simulator, the mock up, using the kit they would have on the mission, it all made sense and greatly increased their probability of success.

After a few hours in the mock up, Bill called them back to the warehouse before they got burned out and lazy running through the wooden structure again and again. The human mind reached the point of diminishing returns after a while.

Then it was right back into the simulator.

Bill was the first one to stick the landing on the rooftop. Deckard was the second but was still hit or miss. Then Paul made it in the next couple simulations. Zach made the landing once, but just barely. Rick still had a big goose egg for a score in the simulator that night. It was early in the morning when Bill decided they were done for the night.

They were getting better.

Slowly.

At least they had a high degree of confidence that their target wasn't going anywhere.

After lunch they drove out to a nearby airfield with their parachutes and wingsuits. A small prop plane would take them up. It was basic familiarization with their equipment. Some of them, like Deckard, had hundreds if not thousands of jumps but had never used a wingsuit before. It wasn't exactly standard issue after all.

As they waited for the plane to spin up, Deckard heard Zach and Paul talking about how they wished Nadeesha was coming along so they could sabotage her parachute and be done with her once and for all. Liquid Sky wasn't like a military unit. It wasn't a brotherhood. It was like the mafia. Everyone was guilty and that guilt was the only thing that bonded them together. That and fulfilling their own self-satisfaction, be it for drugs, for money, for pussy, or whatever it was.

Finally, the pilot indicated that he was ready for the first lift. They set their altimeters and got onboard. They quickly rose to 12,000 feet. When Bill opened the door, the air that rushed in was damn cold. They would have to glide to their drop zone.

Tucking his limbs in, Deckard dived out the door of the plane then, extended his arms and legs to begin tracking forward. With his arms swept back and his legs fully extended, he could feel the lift being generated by the wing suit. He was tracking several meters forward for every meter that he dropped. With the rest of the Liquid Sky team, he glided towards the drop zone.

As they dropped in altitude, it really became possible to see how fast they were moving in relation to the terrain below. With a wing suit, a jumper could get going up to a hundred and twenty miles per hour. That became apparent as the shrubs and desert of the Australian outback below blasted by. At four thousand feet, they deployed their parachutes.

These were much smaller parachutes than the military used. The T-10C static-line parachute and MC-5 HALO parachute had to be able to carry two entangled jumpers to the ground, with all of their combat equipment. By contrast, civilian parachutes did not have any such requirements and were true sport parachutes. They deployed faster and dumped altitude faster. The margins for error were also much smaller.

A MC-5 had 370 square feet of material in the parachute. Their civilian parachutes had about 150 square feet of canopy.

The reality was, they would be deploying their chutes about 500 feet above the target. That wasn't a small margin of error, it was no margin of error. They knew this. There were no high fives or woots when they touched down on their drop zone. Everyone knew that this jump had been child's play and didn't even begin to compare to the insert they would be attempting in Manila.

That night was spent diving through Manila in the simulator.

They had perfected the variables at this point. The jump altitude was finalized, the approach path was on target, now they just had to learn to compensate for the variables that they couldn't control, like wind speed. They also had to have split second timing when it came to deploying and steering parachutes. They only had about ten seconds from the time they pulled to the time they were hitting the deck on top of the

Aquino building.

Bill was hitting the rooftop about half of the time. Deckard was hitting it about the third of the time, but he was quickly getting used to the wingsuit's aerodynamics. Zach and Paul were still hit or miss. Rick hadn't stuck a single landing.

It was the eleventh simulation that night. Deckard zoomed over metro Manila, letting the gold-lit buildings guide his way. He had every landmark, every hit point memorized by now. Crossing the river was his first heads-up; then the oval-shaped Rockwell East Tower told him he was getting closer.

The ground was coming up to meet him. He was gliding and dropping at the same time. Running out of air, running out of time. It had to be perfect.

He cruised over the helipad on the top of the Roxas building, just a hundred meters over the roof. The Petron Mega-Plaza passed on his right flank. He shifted his legs to steer left. Next he blasted right between the Four Seasons and the Grand Soko Makati. Suddenly he was over Velasquez Park.

This was it. Reaching back, he yanked out his pilot chute and released it into the wind. The parachute deployed, the pulleys on the simulator lowering him from a freefall position to a vertical position as if he were really under canopy. The Aquino Building was right at the tip of his feet.

Only under canopy for a few seconds, he steered as close to the center of the building as he could with his toggles and yanked down on them at the last moment to brake. The suspension lines on the simulator suddenly went slack, dropping Deckard to the warehouse floor to simulate a real landing.

The screen froze.

Chalk up another touchdown. In the virtual reality goggles, the other jumpers were listed as they hit their assigned dropzone. Bill, Zach, and Paul all made it to the top of the building. Rick was still shitting the bed.

"Rick," Bill bellowed in the empty warehouse. "Unclip from the simulator and de-kit. You're done."

"What do you mean *I'm done?*"

Deckard could hear the voices talk back and forth before he flipped up his goggles.

"Exactly what it sounds like. You are not hitting the dropzone. You're done."

"That's fucking bullshit."

"What's bullshit is that the most cherry fuck on this team is hitting his targets and you aren't," Bill said referring to Deckard. "I said, fucking de-kit!"

Deckard flipped up his goggles in time to see Rick unclip from the simulator and unceremoniously drop his goggles and parachute on the cement floor. Tearing off the wingsuit he tossed it and stormed outside, the heavy metal door slamming shut behind him.

"Nadeesha!" Bill yelled. "Kit up and get in the simulator. The rest of you are done for the night."

Nadeesha looked up from the folding table where she had been going over intel reports and working on the layout of the objective.

"You waiting for a second invitation, sweet pea? Kit the fuck up. You're in for an all-nighter."

"What the hell is this," Zach said in shock. "You're taking Rick off the team for some squall?"

"I need pipe hitters on my objective, but that pipe hitter can't even get to the objective. If Nadeesha can get her piss flaps to the top of the fucking building, then a squall trigger-puller is better than no trigger-puller."

"She does intel and logistics, not operations," Zach said as if Bill needed reminding.

"She only has to be operational for all of five minutes on target and I don't have time to find someone new. Ramon has the remote devices on batteries to watch the target, but now he is busy working logistics for our infil and exfil."

Apparently Nadeesha didn't need to be told twice. By the time Deckard had unclipped from the suspension lines and shrugged out of his parachute, Nadeesha was already set to go in what had been Rick's simulator station.

"So, since you don't think she is up to it," Bill told Zach. "I want you to brew a fresh pot of coffee for her."

Then he turned to the technician working the computer.

"Feed her a cup after every five simulations once she starts getting tired. I want her going all night. She has a lot of catching up to do to get up to speed with the rest of us."

Deckard unzipped his wing suit and set it down next to the parachute. Nadeesha was being pulled up by the pulleys into the freefall position. The VR goggles were down over her eyes. The wing suit was going to need some further adjustments for her smaller frame, but they would work that out later. Rick wasn't that tall to begin with.

Fuck that dude anyway.

11

Liquid Sky explosively breached the mockup with a flex linear charge. The explosion sent wood splinters everywhere as the door burst into six or seven pieces. They put Deckard up front as the first man through the door, reminding him that as the new guy on the team, he was really nothing more than cannon fodder to them.

Ramon had called back to the staging area to tell them that he had secured Ingram MAC-10's with suppressors for the mission from the Philippines' extensive black market. They would just have to make do in training with the M4 paintball guns. It was an imperfect world.

Deckard stepped over the broken door and cleared the first corner. It was a wide open living space, framed out by bare plywood walls. Second-hand furniture had also been placed inside the mockup. Ramon's intel was that De Jesus routinely hired hookers from Manila's most famous upscale whore house, Air Force One. Regularly attended by Ambassadors and Generals, Air Force One was where you went to score some "Tier One ass" as Bill had put it.

Deckard also noticed that, although they were expecting civilians on target, all of their targetry in the mockup were shoot targets. None of the silhouettes were no-shoot targets. Everyone in the apartment was being marked for death.

Point shooting the first target, Deckard put two blue paint rounds center mass. He and Zach then cleared the kitchen area, taking down another two targets. Practicing a form of room clearing known as free flow, they had the entire apartment cleared in seconds.

The worst part was that they had to clear the entire objective while still wearing their wing suits. There would be no time to take them off, only to unzip a slit between the legs so they could walk and escape from the wings by rolling back the sleeves. Once they hit the rooftop, they would release their main parachute via a cutaway pillow and begin the killing. How the MAC-10 and spare magazines would be arranged on their kit was something that was still being worked out.

Then, once the apartment was covered in blood and

spent brass they had to exfil with their reserve parachute, a stunt chute designed for base jumpers in this case. The entire mission was Hollywood as hell in Deckard's opinion. The only reason why it would work was because no one would be expecting it.

Liquid Sky hit the training objective five more times. Nadeesha had her jet-black hair pulled back, and was now covered in sweat like the rest of them. So far, she was keeping up on target. No one was talking to her though; she was considered an outsider to the assault element.

After dropping their kit, the team guzzled bottled water from a cooler they had brought along and piled into a van to head back to the warehouse. They ate an early lunch and then went into the simulator. Ramon had left remote devices in two rented offices in buildings near the Aquino building. They knew the target was on site. Meanwhile, Ramon had secured their weapons and was building up their logistical infrastructure for the operation.

They were making progress in the simulator. Everyone was itching to do the hit.

Deckard bailed off the ramp of the virtual reality airplane and into the night for what seemed like the thousandth time.

He counted off the numbers.

River.

Rockwell building.

Petron Mega-Plaza.

Thread the needle between Four Seasons and the Grand Soko Makati.

Velasquez Park.

Pull!

Deckard's body screamed into the target as his parachute joltingly interrupted his descent and he crashed onto the rooftop.

This time the entire team made it to the rooftop. It was the decisive point of the entire operation. If they successfully infiltrated to the objective, then the breach and room clearing aspects would be fairly straightforward by comparison. Then there was the exfil.

That could go either way.

"Deckard, come with me," Bill said. They were just finishing dinner. "Grab your kit."

Tossing his paper plate and Styrofoam cup into the trash, Deckard shouldered his parachute and wing suit. Bill had his gear as well and opened the back doors to the 10 pax van they had outside. They both dumped their kit inside and Bill got behind the wheel.

"Where are we going?" Deckard asked as he took the passenger seat.

"Practice jump."

"Just us?"

"Yeah, you are the most switched on, so you're coming with me. Consider this a feasibility study."

"You still don't think jumping with night vision goggles will work?" Deckard asked him as they pulled off down the dirt road towards the airstrip.

"Too many lights in the metropolitan areas of the city. If your night vision whites out for even a second, that second is more than enough to kill you."

"There should be enough cultural lighting to find our way to the objective," Deckard agreed.

"Let's find out."

Bill stopped the van. The Twin Otter turbo prop was spun up and waiting for them on the airfield. The pilot opened the window and waved them forward. Picking up their gear, Bill and Deckard climbed aboard and set their altimeters. It was pitch dark in the desert when the pilot lifted off. The two Liquid Sky operators began donning their wing suits and parachutes.

Bill seemed huge inside the aircraft, as if the plane had

been built for midgets. He got bigger just by looking at weights. Deckard knew he must have been going crazy without being able to hit the gym and drink a steady stream of protein shakes. As the plane leveled out, he leaned in close so that Deckard could hear him over the noise of the turbo props.

"What do you think the chances are of us actually pulling this off?" he asked.

"It all depends on whether or not we can get to the objective. If so, I would say 95 percent," Deckard answered.

"What do you think are the odds of getting to the objective then?"

Deckard shrugged.

"50-50."

"Fair enough. Let's find out."

Bill turned and sat down, taking up two seats.

Deckard sat down and checked his equipment over. He started getting nervous when he realized they were heading north. They were flying towards Darwin, one of Australia's northernmost cities. By plane, it was about an hour away.

They sat in the dimly lit cabin, the plane vibrating beneath their feet. Finally, Bill went up and said something to the pilot. Coming back into the cabin he leaned in to yell into Deckard's ear.

"I found a building in Darwin that is about the same dimensions as the Aquino Building. It is the Marrakai apartment building. Just follow me. We're going to prove that this can be done tonight. Illum is bright so we should be good to go."

Should be.

"Roger."

To say that Deckard had reservations was the understatement of the century. He had learned to control his wing suit very well but didn't know any of the landmarks in Darwin. All he could do was follow Bill and hope for the best. If he missed the target building he would have to deploy his chute and land in the street or something, hopefully avoiding any electrical lines.

Bill opened the door on the side of the aircraft. Cold air rushed in, an old familiar feeling.

Deckard put on his helmet, strapping it under his chin. Then he reached up to swing down his virtual reality goggles.

He was glad that Bill didn't see him make that subconscious mistake. There was nothing virtual about this run. Just the ghosts of muscle memory, like a puppeteer pulling his strings.

Bill placed his feet at the edge of the door and carefully leaned out to spot for their jump. Looking at the lights of Darwin in the distance, he motioned Deckard forward. Deckard looked at the back of Bill's neck, right where his spinal cord connected to his skull. He wished he could kill him now and get it over with but he had to find out who Bill was working for. Otherwise, his handlers would just spin up another team after Liquid Sky had been eliminated. A minute later, Bill leaned in and gave him the thumbs up.

Stepping forward, Bill jumped out into the darkness and disappeared.

Deckard took a deep breath and followed him out.

A rush of wind took him out into the night sky. He saw the moon wobble in front of him for a moment and, then he got stable in the air. Assuming the correct body position, he began gliding. It took a moment for him to spot Bill in the moonlight. He was just a black splotch floating through the sky. Deckard maneuvered behind him as they nosed over the harbor towards the city.

Deckard began to relax a little. Everything was quiet and peaceful as he floated over the harbor. They had about ten miles to fly before they reached their drop zone. Down below, he spied the lights of a few oil tankers heading into port. Up ahead, Bill began adjusting his angle of attack. Darwin was coming up fast.

They soared over the port, coming in low. The cityscape all looked the same, low-lying structures and houses everywhere except for two towers straight ahead. One was the Holiday Inn. The other was their target building. Deckard shifted his position to the left, offset of Bill. Getting caught in each other's canopies was a serious concern.

The two jumpers were nearly side by side when they deployed their parachutes. The pilot chute pulled out their main parachutes, ribbons of suspension lines going taut above their heads. Reaching up and grabbing his toggles, Deckard made final adjustments. The roof of the building was dark, but the apartments below had their lights on, providing a perfect outline of the top of the building for them.

Bill and Deckard's canopies were nearly touching as they landed parallel to each other. They touched down on the roof feeling feather light for once, both landing on their feet. The parachutes collapsed next to them as they quickly reeled in one brake line to make sure it didn't get caught in the soft sea breeze.

"That's it," Bill said as he scooped up his parachute. "This can be done. My guys are just mind-fucking themselves at this point. They've got enough training. It is what it is."

"It is doable," Deckard agreed as he policed up his own chute.

"Find us an exit," Bill ordered him. "Then you hot wire a vehicle for us. Consider it urban escape and evasion training."

"I'll see what I can do."

Deckard took off his parachute harness, rolled up the chute like a sleeping bag and shoved it into its deployment bag. He could repack it later.

"When we get back I'm telling Ramon that we are coming in tomorrow for the hit. We jump and whoever makes it makes it. Whoever dies, dies. Its not like this is my first crew."

"This isn't your first team?"

"Fuck no. I had a few others but broke all of them."

Deckard tried not to dwell on that as he looked for a way to bypass the lock on the rooftop door.

12

The Twin Otter lifted off in the morning with six passengers on board. Rick had extra hair gel applied today and his ear plugs in, listening to music and not talking to anyone. He was still bitter about being bumped from the mission and moved to the support role.

The pilot, the one who had flown for their training jumps, was a drug runner who routinely made illegal flights from the South China Sea to Darwin and knew the routes in and out of the area well. The Liquid Sky members had their wing suits and parachutes with them. In the unlikely event that they were stopped along the way, they would appear as nothing more than sport jumpers.

Deckard leaned back and watched fluffy white clouds float by the window. Was he scared? Scared of what? Jumping out of a blacked-out aircraft over a major metropolitan city, gliding between buildings while wearing combat equipment, deploying a parachute at the very last second, landing on the smallest drop zone imaginable, then explosively breaching a door, and getting into a shootout with dozens of goons, killing a terrorist financier, all before parachuting off the roof down to the streets? What was there to be scared of?

At least a couple of them were going to die on this mission according to Deckard's calculations. Bill didn't seem very conflicted about that fact after basically admitting it to him. Who was he kidding, they were all going to die on this mission. Deckard closed his eyes and tried to get some sleep. He had been there before.

They landed at a remote airfield in Indonesia to refuel before continuing on to the Philippines. Some of the guys slept, others watched movies on their tablets.

It was late at night when they landed at the Barradas airfield, a dusty airstrip not far outside of Manila. Under the cover of darkness, the team policed up their gear and walked to a waiting van. As they approached, Ramon got out from behind the wheel and shook hands with Bill.

"I have the team house set up and ready to go," Ramon told him.

"Where?"

"About a hundred meters away from the airfield, just a short drive around the block."

"What about our weps," Zach asked.

"Good to go," Ramon assured him. "Test fired all of them myself last week."

It took the pilot half an hour to get the Twin Otter into the small hangar on the airfield and power down, but then they all crammed into the van and drove off. True to Ramon's word, the team house he had secured was all of three minutes away. It was a one story house and had a garden around it that was well attended to.

Each of them had a simple cot to sleep on, and Ramon showed them where the food was so they could cook themselves some dinner while he went over preparations with Bill.

"We're on a reverse sleep schedule from here on out," Bill told them. "Do all your preparations for the op tonight and sleep during the day."

The hit was laid on for the following night.

Wood boxes were filled with the combat gear they would need for the mission. There was a Ingram MAC-10 sub-machine gun for each of them. Chambered for the .45 caliber round, each gun came with a threaded barrel for screwing on the suppressor. They had three 30-round magazines each. The sub guns and the cans for them were in "pre-owned" condition, but Ramon said he tested them himself. Deckard picked one up and racked the charging handle on the top of the box-shaped weapon. On inspection, it looked clean. He then conducted a functions check: so far so good. He would have liked to have fired it himself prior to the mission though.

Nadeesha reached for a box of ammo and started jamming magazines. The others sat down on their cots and did the same. Their next course of action was to rig up in their wing suits and parachutes and figure out how to run their combat load with it. They had small chest rigs that they could wear under the parachute harness but slinging the MAC-10 was problematic.

Among the supplies lying around the team house, Deckard found an elastic bungee cord that he hooked around the wire shoulder stock of the sub-machine gun. The other end of the bungee he looped around the chest strap on his parachute. Next, he screwed the suppressor on the MAC-10 and routed a

108

rubber band under his waist strap, looping it over the suppressor to hold the MAC-10 in place diagonally across his body.

This kept the weapon secured while being able to quickly bring it into play when he hit the ground simply by snapping the rubber band when he yanked on the gun. The others saw what he did and began rigging their weapons in a similar manner. Even Rick was kitting up on orders from Bill. If one of them got hurt, got sick, or got dead between now and the hit time, then Rick would be taken off the bench and put back into the game.

Meanwhile, Bill and Ramon sat in front of an open laptop. Ramon's remote devices were still running off batteries and would be for the duration of the mission as they kept an unblinking eye on overwatch on their objective.

The apartment was situated in the middle of the rooftop, a penthouse that included a pool and party area outside. Sometimes De Jesus' security people patrolled the pool area, but usually, they stayed inside unless they came out to have a smoke. A couple times a week De Jesus would send a few body guards down to Air Force One to pick up some girls, and they would throw a massive rooftop party. Bill was adamant that they not infil on one of those nights, it just added to the number of things that could go wrong.

The good news was, from spying through the glass windows in the apartment from two separate angles, it did not appear that De Jesus had a safe room. Liquid Sky would bring explosives anyway, just in case.

One by one, they found their way to the kitchen to find something to eat. The preparations went on deep into the night. With Bill's permission, they each went outside and popped off a few suppressed rounds through their MAC-10's into a dirt mound to make sure everything was kosher.

Zach dug into the explosives cache that Ramon had secured for them. It was mostly industrial explosives that had probably been stolen from a mining site before they turned up on the black market. That was sketchy as hell. He could test the time fuse, but they were too close to civilization to do a test shot of the detonation cord and plastic explosives. Worst case, they would shoot through the windows and enter the apartment that way. They also had a half dozen hand grenades that they could use to breach if need be.

As they laid their kit out one last time before donning it the following night, the Liquid Sky members joked with each other, pretending they weren't scared of smashing into a building at 120 miles per hour.

"Shit dude, we could be the biggest bugs on the world's largest windshield if we fuck this up," Paul said, his respectable-sized Taliban beard shaking as he chuckled to himself.

"Unfortunately, this mission doesn't come with any fringe benefits," Zach complained.

"Oh, you mean like that pile of pirate's treasure we pulled out of Abottabad?" Paul asked.

"Right now I think Rick has the pirate's treasure," Paul joked while curling his shoulders in. "The sunken chest!"

"Don't forget to lick my balls while you're down there," Rick said as he got red in the face.

"What do you think, Nadeesha?" Zach asked. She hadn't said a word all night.

"Suck my dick."

The room exploded with laughter until Bill told them to shut up.

Deckard saw his opening.

"You guys were on the Abbottabad mission?" he asked.

"Yeah," Zach answered. "Got a large haul off that one."

"Intel?"

"Fuck no. The Agency has been playing that angle up. We hardly got anything. Old boy hadn't been operational in years. We got a big haul of gold though," Paul told him.

"He had a stockpile of gold?"

"Yeah. Spanish, French, and Italian intelligence services had been paying the Taliban in bullion for years and years not to attack their troops, so there was an influx of gold bullion in Afghanistan, which eventually filters into Pakistan."

"The Europeans pay off the enemy because casualties would upset their shaky coalition governments, and you rake up the fruits when you hit the targets."

"Fucking A," Zach answered. "The CIA has been paying their Taliban informants with blue pills, unfortunately, so they are not helping us out at all."

"How do you get all that gold back?"

"Teeny Weeny Airlines. Dev has their own aircraft."

"Shit, sounds like a good deal. And old boy goes into

the ocean on the flight home, huh?"

Zach smiled.

"You really think we just dumped his body in the ocean, dude?"

Deckard frowned.

"Then where is it?"

"Somewhere in the United States."

They lay down as the sun was coming up, and got up eight hours later. No one had slept particularly well.

Their pilot pounded down some chow, threw on his sunglasses, and walked over to the airfield to start preparing the Twin Otter for the night's flight. The others loaded all their gear into the van. Ramon and Bill made some last-minute inspections of the objective using the remote cameras. Ramon would be able to access the cameras via a 3G connection on his tablet, so he could update Bill in real time as they made their infil.

The sky was turning a hazy yellow. It was time.

Liquid Sky boarded the van and drove back to the airfield. They spent over an hour just kitting up and getting their gear exactly where they wanted it, then checked each other over just to make sure. Each team member going on the objective carried a half brick of C4 and an initiation system.

Rick and Ramon would be securing the second drop zone down on the ground, their exfil point. When Ramon walked into the hangar with his concealable plate carrier on and MAC-10 slung over his shoulder, Deckard noticed a curved knife the former Special Forces soldier had sheathed on his belt. It was the same Filipino karambit fighting knife he had seen him with in Afghanistan.

Images from Pakistan flickered in front of his eyes. One of the Pakistanis he had seen in the hospital in Karachi had a series of deep, defensive knife wounds on his body. Now he knew that he had witnessed Ramon's work.

They didn't bother rehearsing actions in the air. After the training jumps and unending hours in the simulator, they either knew their shit at this point or they didn't. They took off their helmets and propped them behind their parachutes to lean back on as they sat on the floor of the hangar.

Ramon and Rick got in the van and drove off to the exfil site where they would be waiting to pick up the Liquid Sky team.

The wait began. They drank bottled water and waddled off occasionally to take a piss in the grass.

Deckard turned and caught Nadeesha's eye for just a moment. She had her hair pulled back in a ponytail. Her trigger hand lay over the MAC-10 tied down across her chest. She turned away from him, breaking eye contact.

Ramon called Bill on an encrypted cell phone. They were in place in Manila and had their tablet up, watching the camera feeds. They had positively identified De Jesus when he stepped outside to make a phone call by the pool. It was almost ten at night. Bill stood.

It was their green light.

The pilot fired up the Twin Otter and Liquid Sky filed through the door.

Deckard felt oddly relaxed as the aircraft lifted off and he clipped his pro-tec helmet on under his chin. He had decided that he was going to make it to the rooftop.

They gained altitude as the pilot took them north, over the lagoon towards Manila. Bill opened the door and began spotting for their jump. It would be a short trip, as the pilot flew on a flight plan that took them just east of the city. Zach, Deckard, Paul, and Nadeesha stood up to be on standby for the jump. The airplane rocked under their feet, forcing them to hold on to the seats for balance.

Sweat rolled down Deckard's face as he steadied himself, burdened under all of his equipment. The wing suit, the parachute, the weapons, explosives, and helmet made it awkward to move around to say the least. Without thinking about it, the jumpers began closing on each other, getting nut to butt as they inched towards the door.

As they flew along the edge of the city, Deckard saw that Manila was lit up as brilliantly as any other major metropolitan city with hues of gold, blue, and yellow. They would have no problem identifying landmarks as they navigated around the city. The only problem was that, unlike land navigation, there was no doubling back.

Bill had his head stuck out the door looking for their release point. It was a flood gate on the outskirts of the city. The Liquid Sky team leader turned to look inside the aircraft. He held one finger in the air telling them that they were one minute out. Then he turned to look back outside.

The other four jumpers were now right on top of each other, almost as if they were going to push Bill out the door if he didn't get out of the way. Bill leaned inside again, holding his thumb and pointer finger about an inch apart. Thirty seconds out.

Deckard swallowed. Everything seemed surreal, he could hardly hear anything with the turbo props going and his helmet covering his ears.

Finally, Bill gave a follow-me motion and dived out of the door. One by one, Zach, Paul, Deckard, and Nadeesha spilled out into the night.

Following Bill's lead, they glided behind him heading west, into the city. Settling into position, Deckard noted the golf course passing on his left as they continued towards the river. They had six miles to cover before reaching their target. Manila looked like a painting from their vantage point, pin pricks of gold light shone through windows, larger street lamps and signs made big blotches of star shaped light. Wind whistled in Deckard's ears as Liquid Sky glided deeper into the city.

Their next landmark was coming up, the river that weaved through the center of Manila. Bill adjusted his attack angle slightly, shifting left and pointing directly into the metro area where buildings jutted into the night sky like jagged teeth. The rest of Liquid Sky followed his lead as they assumed a file formation, one jumper after the other. Bill was first in line, Deckard second. The other three were stacked up behind him.

It didn't look like it did in the simulator, but close enough. As he dumped altitude, Deckard could make out more details on the ground and see cars driving on the streets, the pedestrians below completely oblivious to what was happening above them.

Deckard soared over the Rockwell building and knew he was getting close. He could see the soles of Bill's boots has he shifted his weight again, trying to acquire the perfect angle. Deckard ignored what was going on below and focused straight ahead. He flew silently over seven more city blocks and then cleared the top of the Roxas building. It seemed like he was picking up speed, but the reality was, he had just gotten lower to the ground and his eyes could now judge how fast he was really going.

He steered carefully, making minute corrections as he blasted through the city. The Petron Mega-Plaza towered over him on his right flank.

Steady.

He held his position and shot between the two buildings. He lost track of Bill, fixating completely on his target. The Aquino building was dead in his sights. Then, he was over Velasquez Park. Deckard pulled his chute.

He had walked through the maneuvers so many times that, by now, it was impossible for him not to do it right. The parachute caught in the air. Deckard swept in and landed alongside the rooftop pool, touching down on both feet.

A Filipino security guard wearing a black polo shirt turned to Deckard as his parachute collapsed behind him. A Glock pistol was holstered on his hip and an unlit cigarette dangled from his lips. Deckard shrugged out of the wing suit sleeves, slapped for the MAC-10 hanging from his chest, snapped the rubber band, and leveled the sub-machine gun. Flicking the safety off, Deckard zapped the guard with a suppressed burst that tore across his chest. The security guard was dead before he hit the ground.

Just then, someone splashed into the pool like an elephant. Nadeesha hit the roof right behind Deckard and stumbled into him as he was unzipping his legs from the wing suit flap.

Deckard pulled his cutaway pillow to jettison his main parachute. He stepped over the guard's body, heading straight for the pent house door. Bill was on the other side of the pool where he had put down. He took long strides, heading for the same doorway.

Zach had cut away his chute and was clawing his way out of the pool. No sign of Paul. He hadn't made it.

They were ready to blow the door, but Bill wisely tried the knob first. He turned to Deckard and nodded. It was unlocked. He was up.

Bill flung the door open and Deckard stepped through. A half dozen guards sat at the dining room table playing cards. Deckard had the wire stock of the MAC-10 extended and tucked into his shoulder as he walked his bursts from left to right across the security crew. Bill was at his side a second later, working them from right to left. They met somewhere in the middle as the corpses slid to the floor.

That was when the other heavies rushed in from a side room. Bill and Deckard dove to the ground as pistol and submachine gun fire tore up the living room. A flashbang exploded, shattering one of the windows. Deckard rolled behind a couch that would offer concealment if not cover. Bill got behind a billiard table. It was one large open party space for De Jesus to entertain his guests with a dining area, hot tub, pool tables, and couches around a wide-screen TV. Zach knelt down next to Bill. Nadeesha fired a few suppressive bursts as she slid in next to Deckard.

9mm bullets zipped through the couch and ricocheted off the tile floor. De Jesus' security detachment had better cover from behind the bar on the other side of the room. Deckard had the whole rest of his life to figure this one out. That gave him about half a second.

One of the card players at the dining room table had slipped out of his chair and sprawled out on the floor. He had been sitting on an office chair with roller wheels on the bottom. Out of the corner of his eye he saw Bill and Zach try to pop up and return fire only to be driven back down as the gunmen sprayed them down with autofire.

They were pinned down with nowhere to break contact to and were about to be shot to pieces in the blink of an eye.

Deckard broke cover and jumped onto the chair, rolling across the tile floor towards the bar. Holding down the trigger on the MAC-10, he fired right into the faces of the security guards as he raced up to meet them. They were so stunned by the unexpected move that the Filipinos were unable to react fast enough. He walked a line of .45 caliber rounds across them until

115

the back of his chair collided with the far wall.

Dropping his empty magazine, Deckard rammed a fresh stick into the pistol grip to reload. The gunfire had ceased for the moment, gun smoke lingering in the air. Five security guards lay behind the bar, dead or dying. Deckard fired several mercy shots.

Bill ran for the bedroom and kicked in the door. Zach and Nadeesha were on his heels.

Deckard heard several stunted suppressed shots as he entered the bedroom.

De Jesus lay on his shag carpet, bleeding out.

His chest heaved as the terrorist financier struggled to breath. Bill's shots had collapsed his lungs. Zach stepped up and fired a couple bullets into his crotch, causing him to shake and moan as blood bubbled around his lips.

Straight-arming his MAC-10, Bill fired on full auto. He cycled through the entire magazine, blowing off the top of their target's skull and splattering his brains all over the carpet.

"Cocksucker," someone in the group remarked.

Bill reloaded his MAC-10.

"Let's get the fuck out of here."

Back in the living area, Deckard saw numbers on the display next to the penthouse elevator, ticking up.

"We're about to have company," Deckard warned.

"Stay here and slow them down," Bill ordered. "Nadeesha, you cover him. I don't want these assholes shooting us on the way down to the park."

"Got it."

Bill and Zach walked out onto the patio next to the pool and continued to the edge of the building. Deckard reached for a frag grenade in his kit and yanked the pin out while holding the spoon down. He looked to Nedeesha.

"You shoot, I'll frag."

"All right," she said as she shouldered the sub-machine gun.

When the elevator doors pinged open, she raked the inside of the elevator with .45 caliber fire. Security personnel backed up into the back of the elevator, trying to hide from the gunfire. Deckard overhanded the grenade. It bounced once, then rolled into the elevator and detonated as the two Liquid Sky commandos hit the ground.

The elevator bulged out on the sides from the overpressure. Flaming pieces of insulation or foam tiling floated through the air. It was a slaughterhouse of torn limbs and torsos. The stench of burned flesh stung their noses.

Nadeesha stumbled over some debris. Deckard took her by the elbow and led her towards the door. Just as he was about to step outside he heard some banging behind him. Even over the ringing in his ears he could hear shouts and then gunshots. Looking over his shoulder, he saw a metal door near the elevator shake as security guards on the other side fired their guns right through it.

The door shook as the guards began kicking it in, the lock barely holding.

"Shit," Nadeesha cursed.

Deckard turned back around just in time to see Bill and Zach jump off the roof and disappear below the lip the building.

"They left us," she said, exasperated.

He pushed Nadeesha outside as the door was kicked in. Deckard leaned back and fired one handed. The chatter box rattled in his hand as the bolt slid back and forth. The suppressor slowed the already low-velocity rounds as he serviced the first target that bolted through the door. This was the security quick reaction force. They wore black uniforms and carried M4 rifles.

"I'm black!" Deckard yelled as he ran onto the patio and took cover behind a concrete planter.

Nadeesha picked up the rate of fire from a kneeling position next to him.

Deckard loaded his last magazine. They were only carrying enough gear to last them for a five-minute surgical operation. Now they were in combat and running low on ammo fast. Letting the Ingram MAC-10 hang by the elastic bungee cord, he went back into his kit and quick-attached the initiation system to the half block of C4 he carried. Pulling the time fuse, he stuck the charge in the planter.

Sixty seconds of time fuse.

It was to be used in case De Jesus retreated into a safe room they had missed during recon. Now, the charge would cover their withdrawal.

Nadeesha went empty on her sub gun. Now it was Deckard's turn to fire.

"Bound back," he ordered Nadeesha between bursts.

117

The return fire was getting intense as a couple dozen guns for hire wearing full SWAT team get ups stormed the pent house. 5.56 rounds zinged and popped around him, many chipping into the planter he was taking cover behind. The kitchen windows exploded outwards as gunmen inside found new firing positions.

Nadeesha reloaded on the move and took a position next to a large heating and air conditioning unit on the roof near the pool. Deckard threw his last hand grenade at the open door as a couple of security guards attempted a break out. Ducking behind the planter, the explosion stopped them dead in their tracks. At least for a few more seconds. As Nadeesha fired, Deckard ran back to her position.

"Jump!" He yelled in her ear over the gunfire. "I'll cover you."

She looked up at him with wide eyes.

"Okay."

Deckard popped around the corner of the HVAC unit and took single well-placed shots with the MAC-10. He was almost out of the ammo and by his estimation, only 30 seconds of time fuse remained. He caught another muzzle flash in the kitchen window so he fired a shot there and the muzzle flash went away.

Nadeesha turned to run for the edge of the building. She let out a scream as enemy gunfire hit her from behind. She stumbled and fell to the ground alongside the pool. Sensing wounded prey, the gunmen inside the penthouse fired on her, bullets chiseling the tile next to her and making splashes of water in the pool to her flank.

Deckard ran out into the open and laid down suppressive fire with what he had left in the MAC-10. The gun cycled empty and Deckard dropped it in the pool. Without slowing down, he scooped Nadeesha up and dragged her forward. He propelled both of them back behind another concrete planter. It was their last piece of cover; they were all out of building. A few feet away was a fifty-five story fall to the streets below.

He tore her MAC-10 off her kit and shot a burst over the planter without sighting in on anyone specific. The guards were bounding out of the doorway and moving towards them. He could hear them trying to coordinate their movements in Tagalog.

Deckard looked over his partner. The rounds had torn

apart her second parachute, the reserve she would need to get off the building.

"Fuck," he cursed.

"Go," she mumbled. "Just go."

It was time to go.

Deckard grabbed her hands and put them around the main lift web on his own parachute.

"Don't let go for anything."

Wrapping an arm around her, he dropped the MAC-10 and grabbed the ball on his parachute that pulled free the pilot chute.

He heard the enemy shouts as he stood up. Two steps forward and he was off the ledge and into the night.

Nadeesha's scream died in her throat.

Deckard released the pilot chute as they fell.

The C4 detonated as his parachute caught in the wind, clearing off the top of the Aquino building. The parachute popped open while they flashed by still-lit offices in the building under the penthouse. Nadeesha hung on to his parachute harness, her legs kicking in the empty air.

"Don't let go!" she screamed.

"I have to!"

They were tracking forward and were seconds away from impacting the adjacent building. Deckard could see the desks and swivel chairs inside the offices as they were about to slam into the window.

Releasing his hold around Nadeesha, he reached up and grabbed the parachute toggles while she clung to the parachute harness. Yanking down hard on his right toggle, they cut a hard turn. The two of them dangling under the parachute, they nearly brushed up against the office building.

Nadeesha looked like she was about to panic. She pulled herself up as she held on to the harness and wrapped her legs around him.

Deckard knew they were burning altitude fast. The street lights below swirled like a kaleidoscope as he twisted and turned the parachute, angling towards the Ayala Gardens.

A military parachute was designed to safely carry two entangled jumpers and their equipment to the ground. This wasn't a military parachute.

They were coming in hard, their feet passing just a

couple meters above the Paseo Center before they cleared it and went out over the gardens. Deckard wanted to make an adjustment to keep them out of the trees but nothing he did mattered at this point.

The ground came up to meet them. Deckard grunted as he made impact and slid on the wet grass. Rolling, his vision redded out for a second when the back of his head hit something. He felt a weight on his chest as the parachute collapsed on top of him.

He opened his eyes to see Nadeesha almost nose to nose with him. Her pink lips were next to his as they both took short ragged breaths. It was dark underneath the parachute, everything forgotten for a moment.

Nadeesha buried her face in Deckard's neck as she held on to him.

"Ho-ly she-it," a low-pitched voice said.

"Did they come in on one chute?" another asked.

"That was some gangster-ass shit."

Deckard tried to sit up with Nadeesha on top of him.

Bill and Ramon tore the parachute off of them. The accidental tandem jumpers were now hopelessly entangled in their parachute and the suspension lines.

"Fucking hell," Rick said as he ran up to them. "It was like the entire rooftop blew up as you fell off."

Zach came up and joined Bill and Ramon who were using their knives to cut through the suspension lines. Deckard sat up with Nadeesha on his lap.

"Thanks for covering our withdrawal," Deckard said dryly.

That snapped Nadeesha back into the zone.

"Yeah, thanks for nothing you assholes."

"I thought you were covering our withdrawal," Zach insisted.

"We did, and were hoping you might do the same."

"Whatever," Bill said cutting in. "Stop complaining. You're alive."

Nadeesha shook her way out of the suspension lines and stormed off. Deckard undid the buckles on his harness and dropped it. Police sirens were approaching in the distance. Paul was at the dropzone as well. He missed landing on the building but obviously had managed to make it down to the ground in one piece.

"Time to boogey," Ramon said.

Deckard left the tangled parachute as they ran for the van. They didn't have time to police it up, and none of the gear could be traced back to them anyway. As the first red and blue lights came flashing up to the park, Ramon fired a burst into the hood of the police car. The cops got the message and did not pursue, opting to call for back up instead.

Liquid Sky piled into the back of the van. Ramon took the wheel and began navigating through the Manila streets as they left the gardens.

The police had already thrown up one road block heading out of the metropolitan area. Ramon threw a light jacket on over his kit. The others stayed in the back of the windowless van so they would not be seen.

"*Konting pabuya para sayo bossing,*" Ramon told the cop in Tagalog as he handed him a folded bill.

"*Salamat at magingat po kayo sir,*" the policemen said with a smile.

13

"It happened again."

Admiral Corbett looked up from his desk and set his reading glasses down so he could see his J3 officer. The Admiral always left his door open, a literal open-door policy. Where he worked, he needed a team more than he needed a hierarchy.

"You're kidding me," Corbett said as he sat back in his chair. "Again?"

"I'm afraid so, sir."

"Who the hell is doing this?"

"We're about to sit down in the SCIF and try to hammer that out right now."

Admiral Corbett left his desk and followed his right hand man down the hallway. A vault door was open which led into the Sensitive Compartmentalized Information Facility. This was where sensitive operations and intelligence were discussed and records stored. At JSOC, practically everything was sensitive.

"Where?" Corbett asked.

An assistant J2 intelligence officer turned to his commander.

"Manila. It was Kanor De Jesus."

"I remember the name. He was on the SIGMA-11 target deck."

"Yes, sir," the intel officer confirmed. "Two TF Green attempts, one TF Blue, and local competitors tried to bump him off a couple times as well."

"What happened?"

"We're still trying to piece it together. We have someone from The Activity on the ground working with local authorities. The police found a parachute in the park nearby which explains how the killers got off target, but no one knows how they got there to begin with. We've had the special entry troop working this problem set for months. The building is a fortress."

"What the hell is going on? This is our third target that someone else took out in nearly as many weeks. First those guys working for Karzai that the bed-wetters in Washington wouldn't let us touch, then Hezbollah's main money man gets whacked in Dubai. Now this?"

"It has happened before. De Jesus had hits put out on him by both the NPA and Abu Sayaf. Whenever these guys carve out a piece of the local black market for themselves, there is always a competitor who wants that slice of pie for himself."

"Too many coincidences," the Admiral stated. "And the hits are too precise, too well-planned. The Israelis are good but they don't have this kind of reach. Besides, they wouldn't play in our backyard without a courtesy call."

"What about Langley?" the J3 said as he rolled his eyes.

"They are ready for a tele-conference right now," the J2 said.

"Put them on," the Admiral said as he sat down at the long table in front of a projection screen.

The screen came on showing a bald headed CIA officer in a suit sitting next to a Army Officer in his Class A uniform, a Special Forces liaison officer detached to Central Intelligence.

"Hey Russ," the CIA officer said, addressing the JSOC Admiral by his first name. Technically, they were of equivalent ranks but they also had a working relationship stretching back to the first days of the War on Terror.

"Francis, I need some help here."

"I heard. Someone is working your target deck."

"Talk to me."

Francis shook his head. The Special Forces officer clasped his hands in front of him on the table.

"It's not us, brother."

"You know I don't believe in coincidences."

Admiral Russ Corbett sat back in his chair. He didn't ask questions that he didn't already have the answers to. He knew Francis was telling him the truth because the CIA had hired dozens of former JSOC operators to do their dirty work. Those operators had loyalty to the home team and kept JSOC informed of everything the agency was up to around the world. He was simply hoping that Francis could help him unravel this puzzle.

"I hate to say it Russ, but do you think someone over there is saying some things they shouldn't to some people they shouldn't be talking to?"

"SIGMA-11 is locked down. We can do an informal 15-6 just to snoop around but the CI around that program is air tight."

"I hope so," the CIA officer said. "Because I agree with

your assessment. Someone is working your target deck and for both our sakes, we better find out who it is fast before this shit blows up in both our faces. You know how this works. Our fingerprints are on SIGMA, so we'll take the fall for whoever these chuckleheads kill."

"It could jeopardize other programs as well."

They both knew what programs he was referencing. Collection and sabotage in a country whose name started with an I and ended with a ran.

"Get this done, Russ. I'll let my people know to help you however they can."

"Thanks Francis, I appreciate it."

The screen blacked out as the teleconference ended.

The Admiral took a deep breath.

Someone was working their target deck, but it wasn't Special Operations, the CIA, or even an allied country. It was time for the Admiral to make a phone call to an old colleague. He had been his predecessor as the commander of JSOC. A General who had been publicly disgraced and removed after a series of revelations in the newspapers. It was known to those in the know that the General could get more done on the outside through his commercial endeavors than he ever could as military officer.

It was time to call General McCoy and see what he was up to these days.

14

The exfil was more like an all expenses paid vacation. Liquid Sky quickly forgot that they were still on a mission, relaxing on the pump boats that ferried them south. All of their kit had been sunk to the bottom of the ocean the moment the opportunity presented itself. Their pilot had headed for the South China Sea, where he could hide out for a while. The assault team took a separate route, using a ratline that Ramon had established prior to them arriving in the Philippines.

They were called *banka* boats, and were used for fishing and as water taxis between the various islands in the Philippines. The Liquid Sky mercenaries sipped on beer and worked on their tan while they were transported in a lazy, winding path that took them generally south. Unlike air travel or even vehicle traffic, maritime transportation was the least monitored, and allowed for low-visibility movements over long distances.

After a week of cruising alongside some of the most beautiful beaches in the world, they island-hopped over to Sabah in Malaysia, where their pilot met them on an airfield in his Twin Otter. From there, they flew back to Darwin, Australia.

Back at the staging site, Bill ordered his two non-performers to tear apart the mock-up of the objective. Rick for failing in the simulator and Paul for failing to make it to the target during the mission. They grudgingly went about their task. The others prepared for an epic beer blast. The pilot and the technician who ran the simulator for them were both invited.

That night all the wood from the mockup was piled up and set ablaze.

The technician was coerced into drinking a bottle of vodka. Zach was less successful in coercing Nadeesha to give the tech a lap dance but eventually she relented. Cheers went up as she began grinding on his crotch. The beer and liquor was flowing, and everyone was finally relaxing for the first time in weeks. The technician promptly stood up as Nadeesha was rubbing his face in her cleavage. She fell into the grass as the gentlemen stood with a big dumb smile on his face and projectile vomited a half gallon of vodka into the bonfire.

That got even more cheers than the lap dance.

Their pilot was buzzed out of his mind from smoking marijuana and could only muster a half-assed applause.

"Deckard, I need to talk to you," Bill said as he walked up to him.

They walked off to the outer edge of the fire while the party continued. Bill snorted through his nose and spat a snot ball onto the ground. When he turned to Deckard, his face was half concealed by the dark, the flickering light of the fire lighting the other half of their faces.

"I didn't want to talk to you about operational details until we were back to safe ground. That was some ballsy shit you did back there."

"Which part?"

"All of it. Sticking the landing for one. Then jumping onto a chair while sliding across the room firing on full auto. That was some Bruce Willis shit. I can't believe you pulled it off."

"We ran out of options, that's all."

"The only reason why I left you on that rooftop was to make sure you could survive when you were really in a tight spot."

"And Nadeesha?"

"I didn't know the girl's parachute was going to get shot the fuck up, obviously. Again, pretty ballsy getting her off the roof like that. I'm shocked that you two are alive, or at least not rocking a full-body cast."

"I'm hard to kill."

Bill held out his hand. Deckard took it.

"Welcome to the team."

"Thanks, I-"

"250,000 dollars will be deposited in a Mauritius bank account for you. Payment for the three ops you've done for us. Don't let me see you sober again tonight."

With that, Bill walked off to find another beer.

Deckard stood by the fire, his eyes getting lost in it for a moment.

"Don't let it go to your head, Deckard."

He turned and to no surprise, he found Rick lecturing him. He was obviously half in the bag, already shaky on his feet and slurring some of his words.

"What's that?"

126

"Your amazing one combat operation with us. That other bullshit doesn't even count."

"Whatever man."

"Yeah, whatever man. That's all you got? I know you, Deckard. I've seen your type and you are not prepared to go all the way."

"Obviously you missed my crash landing. Two jumpers, one chute, C4 burning down on the way out."

"You don't have the balls to do everything that is necessary. My old unit has been fighting this war for a long time. That's why all the SEALs on this team know how it is done. We know how to show those savages who is the alpha dog. Killing is the only language that makes sense to them. That's why we take scalps. It's about sending a message."

"I thought it was a hobby."

"Its about establishing street cred. Simple as that. We don't believe in target discrimination. If you're brown, you're down. We go over the high walls, we blast down the doors, everyone inside dies. Period."

"Everyone?"

"Everyone. We cleared out entire compounds in Afghanistan on the reg. Standard Operating Procedure. Men, women, and children. They're all terrorists. We start clearing rooms, and we really clear fucking rooms. The kids make for smaller targets. Its funny, because they don't understand that they've been shot. Just like a dog or something, they will try to get back up so you have to shoot them again."

"They're all going to grow up to be terrorists, huh?" Deckard remarked, trying to see how much more Rick would divulge. He was drunk, angry, and suffering from small-dick syndrome after their last mission.

"Americans don't want to know what we do, they just want us to do it," Rick informed him. "We get shit done. Cleanse the earth of these savages. Dump the kids and there are no future terrorists. Tell the entire family to go back inside; everything will be fine. Then, drop a five-hundred pounder on their fucking heads. Babies too. You know why?"

"Why?"

"Because fuck you, that's why."

"You've still got a lot to learn in this outfit, and I still don't think you have what it takes."

Rick stumbled off, tiring of not getting the responses he wanted out of Deckard.

Fucking Nazis, Deckard thought to himself. *How the hell did this happen?*

Special Operations soldiers were not choir boys by any stretch of the imagination, but these ex-SEAL Team Six guys were completely out of control. Deckard knew that something like this didn't just happen overnight. It had to be a long-standing cultural issue within the unit, a pervasive attitude that allowed these war crimes to occur.

Deckard looked back into the fire, remembering Bill's words.

Welcome to the team.

15

Deckard walked under a sign that stretched across the road on two posts at either end of the street. It announced that he was entering China Town. China Town in Port Louis. He walked his surveillance detection route through the city, visiting a number of shops along the way. They had only finished breaking down the staging area in Australia and landed back in Mauritius a few hours prior. By the time he got to the third shop, he realized he had picked up a tail.

Stopping at a fruit stand, Deckard picked a kiwi out of a basket and tossed it into the air several times. The person tailing him stopped alongside and picked up a mango.

"How long have you been in country?" Deckard asked.

"Long enough, brother," Aghassi responded. "Long enough."

They walked into a nearby Chinese restaurant and immediately sat down at the table they wanted without waiting for a server to seat them.

"You look beat, dude."

"I'm hanging in there."

"This is starting to come together. You won't have to do this much longer. I've done the forward reconnaissance of the address you gave me and scoped out all those bungalows. We can get a platoon from Samruk in here within a week and clean this nest of vipers out. Pat is already talking to people in Madagascar about it."

"No," Deckard said. "Not happening. It's not enough."

"What do you mean?"

"We need to effect an enterprise takedown."

Aghassi nodded. They had recently conducted one in Mexico. One particularly nasty cartel was giving them a hard time in the Mexican province of Oaxaca. However, once they got their hands on a source, the cartel's money man, they had racked and stacked the entire organization in a night. Jimenez, the cartel boss, still held out in his fortress and had to be dealt with, but the cartel itself was functionally dead after that one night of non-stop raids by Samruk International mercenaries.

"We've been here before. After we took down Jimenez,

we followed the flow of guns upstream. The problem is that we thought we were dealing with one rogue operation. We didn't realize that the weapons trafficking into Mexico was but one of many programs run by G3 Communications. We shut down the weapons pipeline and killed their MEK terrorist proxies in Nevada, but at that time we didn't know about the other arm of that enterprise."

"Liquid Sky."

"Right. I've confirmed that they are no longer working for G3, their CEO cut sling load on Liquid Sky after we hit Area 14 in Nevada in order to distance himself. Now they are working contracts that are coming out of the Gulf States, with a retired American General acting as a cut out, proxy, and pay agent."

"Who is he?"

"I don't know yet. I was only taken off probationary status after this last mission. Maybe now I can dig a little deeper, but if we bring Samruk in now and clean out Liquid Sky, we will never find out who the puppet masters are."

"Once we know that, then we take down the entire enterprise," Aghassi finished for him.

"With pleasure," Deckard told him. "I don't want to be here any longer than I have to be. Speaking of which, what did you find out about these dirtbags?"

"Shit," Aghassi said. "How much time have you got?"

"Start at the beginning."

"Pat and I have been making phone calls. Cody has been digging through the net as well. We found the phone number in your kit and have called Dusty and Flakjacket but haven't heard back from them yet."

"Probably still deployed off the coast of Somalia."

"Here is what we do know. In 2007, the U.S. Navy commissioned a study on retention rates within Naval Special Warfare Development Group AKA SEAL Team Six. Guys were popping smoke left and right, not re-upping even if they were only a few years away from retirement. The study concluded that it was because of a ramping up of private-sector contracts."

"They were getting out to do private security contracting. That was happening long before 2007, though."

"Yeah, but this is what the report didn't uncover: A former SEAL Officer who was running a private military company at that time was offering big money to SEAL Team Six operators who came to work for him. He was pitching individual operators in person at one point. He would pay them three times their normal salary, plus the equivalent of their military benefits and pension after they got to a combined twenty years between the military and contracting."

"No wonder why they were leaving for greener pastures."

"You said in your text that the leader of Liquid Sky is named Bill?"

"Yeah."

Aghassi took out his smartphone and brought up a picture to show to Deckard.

"This him?"

It was Bill's Department of the Navy photo from the military.

"That's him."

"He was one of the first to take that offer and jump to the commercial side. Bill Geddes. A rock star operator in Dev Group. Got into some real nasty shit in Afghanistan when another recce team had their OP overrun. Both elements were denied air support and their Quick Reaction Force because of some political bullshit going on at the time."

"They got hung out to dry."

"Oh yeah. Bill got out as a Master Chief with 18 years of service in the SEALs, nine of it with Dev. After that, he went to work with that one former SEAL but they had some falling out over a botched operation in Liberia. He jumped between contracts but it gets difficult to track him as these programs are hidden behind both corporate proprietary as well as levels of classification. Who knows what the fuck he was doing."

"He mentioned that Liquid Sky was not his first team, that he burned through his other guys."

"That seems to fit his personality."

"Who else?"

The former ISA operator brought up another picture on his phone.

"Zach?"

Deckard looked at it for a second. He was a little younger in the picture but still a good-looking blonde kid who could have jumped off the cover of a surfing magazine.

"Yup."

"Zach Larson. I talked to a teammate of his. He wasn't a SEAL, actually, but a Navy EOD guy," Aghassi said referring to Explosives Ordinance Disposal. "They are allowed to apply so he got picked up, went through Green Platoon and spent ten years in Dev."

"He take the same offer as Bill?"

"Nope, they kicked him out. Remember when all those Dev Group guys got the boot because they were consulting with a video game company while still active duty?"

"I've been a little out of the loop."

"Well, it was a breach of military ethics at the minimum, if not completely illegal. They were giving this video game company sensitive Dev Group tactics to use in their game, putting on capability demonstrations for them, all kinds of shit. Zach was one of those guys, but also took it a step farther and was doing public speaking engagements. He did one in Las Vegas just a few months after getting back from the Bin Laden raid, the speech itself being about the raid. It was for the Forbes 100 set and was supposed to be about leadership, but he divulged all kinds of classified information. That was the final straw, so they kicked him out of Dev. He could have gone to the regular SEAL teams, but with your reputation ruined like that, not too many guys want to face being ostracized by their team mates. He separated from the Navy and went to work with Bill."

"Interesting."

Aghassi brought up another picture and showed it to him.

"Rick."

"Rick Teague. A half dozen DUI's. Got pulled over with automatic weapons out of the armory and C4 explosives in one case. Naval Special Warfare swept it all under the rug. I talked to one of his teammates as well. Rick went through a messy divorce. For years he was on the outs with her. He kept volunteering for deployments because he thought it would save his marriage by giving him and his wife some time apart."

"He never struck me as the type. He is the most narcissistic of the bunch."

"Not always. He tried hard to save his marriage, but of course he was trapped in a vicious cycle. Deploying in a misguided attempt to save his marriage, going back to the 'stan over and over again. Loaded up with PTSD, the only one of them in this Liquid Sky group who actually sought help at one point, there was no hope for him. His wife took their kids and bailed. He left the Navy with fifteen years in and found work with GRS."

GRS or Global Response Staff, was the CIA's para-military force that acted as a security detachment for their case officers and targeting officers. They also did static security and occasionally worked operations.

"That gig ended for him when he was speeding around Kurdistan in an up-armored SUV and ran over a kid. No one knows for sure if he was drunk or not. GRS tried to cover it up, but the case officer dropped dime and got him booted. Bill must have picked him up sometime after that."

"God damn," Deckard said shaking his head. "These guys were a train wreck before they even left the military."

"Big time. That guy Nikita whacked in Pakistan-"

"Henderson."

"Yeah, him."

"I'm wearing his clothes right now."

"Well, that's special."

"Isn't it." It was a statement rather than a question.

"Henderson was on meth, coke, and hard liquor pretty much every day from what I understand. Suspected of stealing weapons from the unit a few times, but that got covered up as well."

"Of course. He had a girl?"

"Back at Virginia Beach. She doesn't know where the fuck he is."

"And she never will."

They had dumped the body into the Indian Ocean.

"Next up," Aghassi said, changing the subject back to the living. "Paul."

Aghassi showed him the picture he had.

"That's him, but without the Taliban beard he has now."

"Guess he really liked Leonidas in 300, huh?"

Deckard rubbed his forehead urging Aghassi to continue.

"Okay, so his name is Paul Paul."

"Paul Paul?"

"For sure."

"Who the fuck were his parents?"

"Mormon missionaries, actually. He was holy roller back in the day. That's actually how he got his job in Dev. The commanding officer of one of the squadrons in Dev was also a holy roller, into all that crusader shit. He hand picked Paul from Green Platoon because they were both taking Jesus pills."

"What happened?"

"Don't know when he fell off the wagon. It sounds like greed got the best of him, though. He ordered a lot of individual components for night vision goggles while he was overseas and then legally brought them back to Dam Neck with him. Once back in America, he had all the parts, but they were not on the property books because they were not assembled and had no serial numbers. He put them together and was selling them for 500 bucks a pop. He was also suspected of shipping captured Taliban weapons home in ISU-90 shipping containers. The real kicker is the gold."

"They told me a little about that."

"Yeah, they had it down to a science, apparently, from raiding so many compounds. Put a gun to the wife's head and make her open the safe. They would get the shit back to Kabul on their own private airline. From there they would convert the gold into U.S. dollars and deposit the money into overseas bank accounts. The bank accounts then fed into mutual funds managed by brokerage firms on Wall Street. Firms where former SEALs are employed. They have a cute cover story within Dev that the money was a black ops slush fund, but that's bullshit. It is war loot, plain and simple.

"But some red flags started going up when these guys came home from overseas and started buying brand new Land Cruisers and in-ground swimming pools in the backyard for their kids. They asked him to leave before someone initiated an investigation."

"What the hell was going on in that unit?"

"Here is the thing, Deck, all these guys served in the same squadron in SEAL Team Six. That is how they all know each other and why Bill brought all of them on board. It is the other members where things start to get really interesting."

"Yeah, I was wondering how Bill got a girl on the team."

Aghassi pulled up the picture.

"That's her."

"Hotter than a pistol."

"I don't have to be told."

"Nadeesha Senevirathne," Aghassi said pronouncing the last name syllable by syllable. "She came into the Army with very high test scores and got brought into Counter Intelligence. She worked in a couple different top secret programs in Iraq, most of them I'm familiar with because I had to liaison with these guys when I was with ISA. She did real work. Ten deployments to Iraq and Kurdistan, two to Colombia, one to Bangkok, one to Egypt. She was assigned to a special cell of female intelligence operatives within JSOC who would be drawn from as needed. Sometimes that cell of women is known by a nickname: The Harem."

"She's pretty young to have that many deployments. She must have been drawn out every day."

"Thirty one years old actually, and you're right. They run roughshod over these women because there are so few of them. When I called my buddies back at Ft. Meade they told me that she was for real, pulled her weight operationally, did her job. I don't know why, but she separated from the Army on her own. Probably, it was just burn-out from being deployed so often without time to decompress."

"Happens more often than anyone wants to admit."

"The connection to Bill comes from a counter-terrorism operation that SEAL Team Six ran in Colombia. Bill was the team leader and Nadeesha was attached to them to run intel. That must be where they first met."

"What happened to her?"

"Don't know, but her test scores are off the chart. It freaked the people out at the JFK Special Warfare Center. She almost maxed out their IQ test. Speaks like a half dozen languages."

"And she is of the right ethnicity. She can blend in with dozens of cultures. No wonder why JSOC jumped all over her."

"It is this last guy that really bothers me."

"Ramon?"

"Yeah, Ramon Pascua."

"He is the most solid of any of them. They sent him forward to prepare the battle space. He's a former 1st Special Forces Group guy from what he told me."

"That's true. After growing up in the Philippines, he came to the United States with his father. He was a Warrant

Officer in 1st Special Forces Group and deployed with the CIF Team to Baghdad. He was a good operator by all accounts. Aside from running direct action missions with the CIF, he did low-vis work all over Southeast Asia."

"So what is the concern?"

"That he appears squeaky clean. A guy like that would never work with a team like Liquid Sky. Are they blackmailing him or something?"

"No idea."

"It is bizarre because the only other thing I can think of is that whatever he fucked up, wherever he stepped out of line, it had to be so bad and so sick that the entire chain of command buried it and simply asked him to leave for the sake of all their careers. I can't find shit for dirt on this dude, but he is black-balled in the contracting world. No one will touch him."

"I will probe the wire a little more. I have good rapport with him."

"Do that, because this creeps me out. Nadeesha should be working for DARPA or JPL, but I get why she is here after being abused by her command for so long. Ramon doesn't make sense to me at all."

"I'll get another burner phone and text you whatever I find out. Keep Samruk on standby. If you can pre-stage in Madagascar that is great, but no further than that. Not yet."

"I'll let Pat know. But there is one other member of Liquid Sky we haven't covered yet."

"Oh?"

Aghassi looked across the table at him as their Chinese food arrived.

"So what's your deal?"

16

Morning PT crushed the entire team. To warm up, the team ran barefoot two miles down the beachfront and then back. It was a slow, comfortable pace, but everyone knew what was coming next. With a barbell they took turns doing three repetitions of the power snatch which involved lifting the weight above your head and squatting it. They increased the weight every three reps until failure.

Then they did the same for the power clean, which was a similar exercise, but the barbell was only brought up to under the chin with a reverse grip. The power jerk was done for the same repetitions and was also similar, but from under the chin, the barbell was then snapped above the head in one popping motion. Next was the clean pull. From the squatting position, the lifter snapped up with the bar held in an overhand grip until he was standing on his toes, and then lowered the bar back to the ground.

Repetitions were increased to five for the front squat. Again, more plates were added after each repetition. Holding the barbell under the chin, they did five squats for one set. Last but not least was Bill's favorite, the bench press. About half of the Liquid Sky team puked this time around. Deckard managed to hold it down but had to wonder what the point was. They could probably take turns kicking each other in the balls and get the same result. They wrapped up with a two-mile cool-down run. Most of them took water bottles and tried to rehydrate as they jogged up and down the beach.

After dragging ass back to his pad, Deckard took a shower, tried to pound down some more water and stretch out. He found it funny that Liquid Sky was so careful about their operational security, but six physically fit men running and swimming around a residential area was a signature in of itself. Apparently the guys just told the locals that they participated in adventure racing around the world, sponsored by some jockstrap company or something.

Sitting down on the couch, Deckard began to plan his next move. He didn't have any time to waste. Bill had mentioned during PT that he would be reviewing a series of new contracts to bid on that afternoon. A comment like that made Deckard wonder how many other teams might actually be out there. He would have his hands full taking this enterprise down as it was.

Deckard had to hand it to Liquid Sky. These guys were not fighting some one-sided firefight against chicken-shit terrorists in Tikrit or Ballad. They were skating the edge, almost for the sport of it. And they were winning. They were good, but the lack of discipline would catch up with them. Back to the operational security again. The war crimes were not just unprofessional, they also violated OPSEC by creating a signature. If they were scalping or canoeing bodies on every objective, then eventually someone would put two and two together and realize it was the same team conducting these hits all over the world.

He knew that more than likely, some intel agency somewhere had already done just that and had Liquid Sky on their radar because of it.

The next phase of Deckard's operation was to find out who this retired General was that Bill was getting his contracts from. Once he had that name, he could call in the cavalry and get this job over with. In the meantime, he tried to kick back and relax. Making the hard sell didn't work in human intelligence operations. If he came off as over eager and overplayed his hand, then Bill would figure out what his game was. He had to take his time, build rapport with each member of the team, and slowly gather each piece of the puzzle. It was frustrating, but necessary. Their odds of taking Bill alive in a direct confrontation and forcing the information out of him were slim to say the least.

Deckard just hoped he could run this charade long enough, because sooner or later, this whole house of cards was going to come crumbling down.

"Come here," Bill said with a smile on his face.

Night had come, and with it there would of course be another party. The girls were on their way, and then everyone was going to go out dancing at some disco somewhere on the island.

"You know why you are still here, Deckard?" Bill asked him. "It is because you understand something about combat that very few even in elite units seem to get. Combat isn't just about being technically and tactically proficient. It isn't even a game of luck. You know what our game is?"

"What's that?"

"Making the biggest grandstand play. That's what you did in Manila. Threw your balls on the table and made it happen. I respect that."

"I'm just happy to be on a team that knows how to get work done," Deckard said playing up the bravado.

Just then the girls showed up at the front door. They all took a couple of cabs out to a night club set up inside a nearby hotel. The boys were cutting some rugs on the dance floor and everyone took turns going to the bathroom to blow lines of coke. Deckard agreed to partake, but brushed the cocaine he was given onto the floor when no one was looking.

He was getting pretty drunk on rum though. As the partying continued deep into the night, he quietly slipped out knowing that he wasn't going to get any further intel off the guys this night. He had no desire to hang out with any of them if he didn't have to.

Hailing a cab, he had the driver take him back to his bungalow on the coast. He paid the driver and went inside.

Sitting down on his couch he began to feel something deep inside of him, something bubbling to the surface. He pushed it down.

Henderson had kept a sizable liquor cabinet above the sink. Deckard dug around until he found what he was looking for in a green bottle. Laphroaig whiskey, aged 18 years. He poured a glass and sipped it. The whiskey tasted like a burning church. He stood over the counter with his hands bracing himself over the bottle. He finished the glass and poured another one.

Before Liquid Sky, that last mission in Mexico had been rough. Deckard had been to some dark places, darker than he ever imagined existed, but Jimenez had pushed him somewhere he had never been before. When Deckard and Samruk International started putting pressure on his cartel someone struck back in the most flamboyant way possible to try to get a reaction out of Deckard, to try to get him to make mistakes. They executed an entire Christian mission, murdering the priest, the nurses, recovering drug addicts, and large number of mentally handicapped patients in cold blood.

Deckard struck back and picked apart the cartel, and later another player called The Arab. But when he caught up to Jimenez, things got ugly. Deckard not only killed him, but hacked his head off and displayed it to the surviving members of the cartel. He didn't do it for pleasure. It served a purpose. It made for no doubt in the cartel member's minds that their war was over and Deckard had won. They got the message and retreated.

His act might have been justified, he might have been able to explain it to himself, but it was still in the same league as the war crimes that Liquid Sky committed on a daily basis to satisfy their own petty emotional needs.

Deckard finished the glass and poured a third. Holding the whiskey bottle in his fist, he slammed it down on the counter.

"Motherfucker," he cursed under his breath.

They were all wrapped up in this conspiracy in some way or another. He had heard the stories about SEAL Team Six back in the day when he was a para-military contractor in Afghanistan, but didn't really know what to make of them. There was no way that he ever could have suspected that some of them were this far gone. Everyone hits that burn-out point.

Scientists had found it in Special Operations soldiers, astronauts, and Olympic athletes but Deckard didn't accept PTSD as the rationale behind the war crimes. There was more to it than that. A decision had been made, by all of them.

Deckard took the glass and walked out onto his back deck. He stood looking at the horizon for a moment.

He was no saint. He was nobody's role model, but he had to be the one who stopped this insanity. This cancer had to be destroyed. He would burn every bridge he had, do whatever it took to make that happen. He wasn't saving anything for the next mission. This was it.

That was when he noticed a lone form standing on the beach in front of the crashing waves. A small sarong on her hips blew in the wind. Deckard took another sip of the whiskey before setting it down and walking towards her.

"Out here all alone," he said as came up behind her.

"You too," Nadeesha said without moving an inch and keeping her back to him.

"Got tired of the party."

"I'm surprised it took so long."

"Yeah."

"From what I hear, you are a card-carrying member of the team now."

"So they say."

"You saved my life. Up there on the building."

"That is what we do."

"Actually it isn't. You saw how Bill and Zach bailed. Any of the others would have left me to die. *That* is what we do."

"That isn't what I do."

Nadeesha turned to face him, her hair blowing in the wind.

"And that's why I hate you."

"I thought I was the loveable rogue on this team," Deckard tried to joke.

Nadeesha closed her eyes as she shook her head, ignoring his comment.

"Fuck you. You are the worst out of any of them. I've seen enough of you. You've been to some shitty places but managed to hold it together. Not like me. Not like them."

"You're saying I'm not on the same page?"

141

"Not even close. You're still a soldier. Where the fuck did you come from? Who are you?"

"Like you said, a soldier."

"You don't belong here. Going back for teammates like that." She said it like a curse. "I saw the look in your eyes in Dubai. You came through the door to save me, not to eliminate the target. You're not one of us. You're a fucking boy scout."

"I do my job. I thought that was all that mattered."

"You can't fake the funk forever. You're disgusted by all this bullshit. Taking scalps, mutilating bodies, you haven't even seen how bad it gets yet. This is nothing."

"So I've heard."

"Why are you here?" She repeated.

"For a fucking paycheck. What do you care?"

"Bullshit!"

Nadeesha pulled away, kicking sand with each of her footsteps. Deckard saw an opening. It was a long shot but he took it.

"It isn't just that it is morally wrong," he told her. "It's unprofessional. That isn't soldiering."

Nadeesha spun towards him with her teeth bared.

"Unprofessional? Are you fucking kidding me Deckard? Listen to yourself. You've seen the same shit we have."

"What shit?"

Nadeesha stabbed a finger right into his chest.

"Fuck. You. When I ran intel for JSOC I used to be like you. I woke up. I was running a source, a village elder in Afghanistan. He married off his eight year old daughter to another village elder. On their wedding night he wanted to fuck her but a god damn eight year old doesn't know shit about sex. I found out all about it after the fact."

"Nadeesha, I-"

"She cried for hours as he tried to shove his dick in because her pussy was too small. You know what he did? He took a knife and slit up her pussy down to her asshole and up into her stomach, then fucked the bloody hole. The girl went into shock and bled out, dead the next morning with her hands clenched in front of her from saying her fucking death prayer.

"That is what we are fucking dealing with so who gives a *fuck* how many scalps these assholes take? Who gives a fucking shit how many heads they cut off, how many people they execute, how many dicks they cut off. With these fucking savages, nothing we do can even begin to compare!"

"Nadeesha-"

"Fuck you," she snarled. "You're the worst of all because you know better."

She stormed off to her bungalow, leaving Deckard alone with the tide and the wind off the sea.

He stood there for a long time, just watching the waves come in and then wash back out into the ocean.

She was right. In some ways he was the worst of any of them. He had options; he could go in other directions in life. This was the life he had chosen and he would not apologize for it. He had a mission and he would complete it.

Unless he never heard the retaliation when it came.

Footsteps.

Deckard clenched his teeth. He didn't expect to hear it. Adrenaline surged through his system. It was going to be a fight.

Pivoting in the sand with one foot in front of the other, he brought his fists up in front of him but not fast enough.

Nadeesha's arms circled around the back of his head as she pressed her lips to his. Her tongue went into his mouth as they kissed deeply. She let out a soft moan as he lifted her up and they both fell onto the sand.

Deckard tore the knot that held the sarong in place, then untied the laces that held the bikini in place on her hip as they kissed. Her hands tore at his pants and opened them. She reached inside and grabbed him. As he pulled her bikini bottom to the side her legs wrapped around him. They were both already short of breath.

With her heels on his hips, she drove him into her.

Deckard climaxed immediately. He could see the veins in her neck go taut as she began to shake in his arms. So had she.

He pulled away slightly and tore away her bikini top, grabbing her chest with one hand and her hair with the other. Slowly, he began grinding his hips into her. After a few moments, she was able to speak again.

"Holy shit," she whispered. "Deckard. I'm not used to someone this big."

She had another orgasm and her body shook again. Her arms and legs got shaky as she laid her head back in the sand. The waves were at their feet when they came together again a third time.

As the tide came in, he picked her up in his arms and carried her inside.

<u>17</u>

Deckard woke up as he felt someone grabbing him. He turned around in bed and found Nadeesha smiling. She rolled on top and straddled him. Her perfect hips bulged slightly as she sat down on top of him. She was soaking wet already.

That was when her cell phone began to vibrate on the bed stand. Reaching over, she snatched it up and looked at the number.

"What the hell," she cursed before answering the phone.

Deckard popped his hips, bouncing her several inches into the air.

"Oh!" she screamed with the phone held to her ear. "I mean, hello."

He tried not to laugh as she had a brief conversation.

"And you," she said as she hung up the phone. "We're flying to Egypt. Everyone needs to be standing by to drive to the airport in twenty minutes. Sounds like some kind of an emergency."

"How big an emergency?"

Nadeesha rocked gently on his lap and placed his hands on her hips.

"Nothing that can't be put off for another nineteen minutes."

Liquid Sky boarded a Gulfstream private jet that morning and was soon wheels up, flying to Jordan. They carried their cover identity passports and no weapons. There was no time to plan a more complicated clandestine entry. This was a crash mission, thrown together on an *ad hoc* basis in response to an emergency.

Nadeesha sat a few seats in front of Deckard. She looked back and smiled at him before turning away. They both preferred to keep their recent...situation, private.

"What's the story boss?" Zach finally spoke up.

"We're all going in as NGO workers," Bill said as he stood in front of them. "Half of you will be going in with a cover as working for some feed-the-kids bullshit and the other half will go in as human-rights observers. We'll take separate flights out of Jordan so that we stagger our arrival into Cairo. It's sloppy, but our timetable is extremely tight."

"What's the job?" Paul asked.

"Nothing special. Just a no-notice hostage rescue in a city besieged by fucking savages protesting the other savages running their country which is on the brink of civil war with a follow-on asset recovery mission for some classified tech that fell into the hands of the Egyptian military."

"Oh, that's all," Ramon laughed.

"We need to procure weapons on the ground," Bill told them.

This got better and better.

"Then, the main element will strike the prison where these three kids are being held. They are frat boys back in the United States, and apparently one of them is the son of somebody which gives this mission added priority."

"And what is this device?" Rick asked.

"Some high-speed tech dreamed up in a DARPA lab I guess. It causes blackouts and allows one to penetrate computer networks. I don't know, I didn't ask for information I don't need to complete the mission but the three college kids were using it when they got popped by the Egyptians. Now which of you went to the SEAL sniper course?"

Paul threw his hand up.

"I've been to SOTIC," Ramon offered. The Special Operations Target Interdiction Course was the Special Forces sniper school at Ft. Bragg.

"Okay fine. Ramon, you take Deckard with you. He is still the cherry on this team, so you make him go in and snatch the device. I made some phone calls about where we can find weapons, and we will get something for you to pull overwatch with."

"Got it," Ramon confirmed. With so little information, there wasn't much to discuss. They were making this up as they went along.

"The rest of us have the prison. Its going to be a shit show one way or the other."

"That's why they are using us," Rick said. "Delta or Dev specialize in missions like this. Why not use them?"

"Because we're expendable," Nadeesha finished.

"You got that right," Bill said. "I'm not here to blow smoke up your ass. Some of us might even survive. I'll have an exfil point worked out by the time we do our hits, which will have to be executed simultaneously. Probably a boat that can get us into international waters but right now we need to take it one step at a time. First you need to clear customs, then we hit a weapons armory I've located."

Three college students and a mysterious device.

Deckard realized that the reason why U.S. counter-terrorist units were not being sent in for this mission wasn't just because of the political ramifications of sending U.S. troops into Egypt, but because of the target itself. What were the three kids doing with the device in Egypt in the middle of the Arab Spring?

The team split up and flew commercial air into Cairo with their false passports. Thankfully, their covers were backstopped. They could provide some official looking NGO paperwork and phone numbers that had someone on the other end sitting on a phone and ready to pick up. Deckard wondered if it wasn't Sarah, the girl he met in Washington D.C. prior to joining up with Liquid Sky, who was standing by to back up their cover. They got asked a few questions in customs, but pretty much breezed through.

Bill hit up a Western Union booth and came back with wads of cash that he immediately divided up between the team. It was their op fund, but also money to escape and evade in case they got compromised. They rented two vehicles and began driving southeast to the port of El-Sokhna. Bill was on the phone pretty much the entire trip through the desert, trying to get a handle on the mission parameters and logistics. Ramon was making calls as well.

It was dark by the time they arrived on the coast of the Red Sea. Bill had both of their vehicles pulled off to the side of the road for some bare bones mission planning before they went in to secure the weapons for their mission.

"I contacted some people who work the maritime security circuit to get the lowdown on this place," Bill told his team. "They have an armory at the port where Egyptian authorities secure the weapons of maritime security contractors."

Deckard knew some guys in that line of work as well, mostly former military. Armed security on civilian vessels was still kind of a mess, and existed in a constant legal gray area. Technically, security guards in international waters could be armed to defend against piracy, but many of the countries where the ships docked were places where such weapons were illegal.

As commercial ships loaded with oil or connex containers traveled through the Suez Canal and headed south, they faced the presence of pirates off the coast of Somalia. The pirates were known to board the commercial ships and ransom back the crew and the ship for big payout from the insurance companies in London. Some even believed that the pirates had an insider racket going with the insurance companies, as the pirates had intel on where ships would be and when with just a little too much accuracy at times. The pirates also knew exactly what the most amount of money was that they could extort from the insurance companies, making some wonder if there were not some kind of kickbacks involved.

The presence of armed security guards on the ships almost always scared the pirates off. The pirates had a system down; it was a business model for them and they had no desire to have a shootout with armed security. They would go find a less protected ship to capture. When they did, that was when Deckard's friends in SEAL Team Six would raid the ships, kill the pirates, and free the crew. In fact, that was what Dusty and Flakjacket were doing right then several hundred miles to the south.

But when the armed security guards came into port with their ships, they had to have a deal with the local government, otherwise their guns would have to be thrown off the side of the ship and into the ocean while still in international waters. In Egypt an agreement had eventually been worked out that the Egyptian police would take control of the weapons in port and hold them in a secure facility until the ship was heading back out to sea.

The arrangement worked pretty well, other than the odd security contractor getting detained by crooked policemen and shaken down for bribe money.

Bill blasted through how the armory at port worked with the maritime security contractors in a couple seconds before detailing the information he had just gotten from some contractors who recently passed through the port. They knew where the armory was, and they knew that there were weapons there because several ships were at port having cargo loaded and waiting for their respective security teams to show up.

The seven of them would rush in, overwhelm the two Egyptian policemen standing guard, and bust open the armory. There would be very little finesse involved in this approach. The team huddle broke, and they drove for the port.

The Egyptian police officer looked over his desk with a cigarette burning between his fingers as the door opened and then slammed shut. He stood up as the newcomer approached him and looked through the metal grate that separated the armory and office from the waiting area. The guard wore a black police uniform and perhaps the most half-assed beret in history, bad enough to make a French painter's beret look professional by comparison.

"Hey, how goes it?" the Westerner asked. He had a long, bushy beard like many of the American contractors that passed through the port. The policemen often thought that it was funny that they seemed to mimic the Wahhabi beards of Islamic extremists. Just then, he noticed that another man had also entered the building, a small, Filipino-looking guy. It wasn't uncommon for maritime security teams to be composed of one British or American leader who supervised a team of Filipinos.

"We're here to pick up our guns," the bearded one said.

The policemen looked down at his clipboard.

"I don't see any scheduled-" he began to say in broken English.

The bearded guy leaned closer to the grate.

"I'm sorry, I can't hear you?"

The Egyptian leaned closer.

"I do not have any-"

Reaching through the shoebox-sized opening in the grate, the American grabbed the policemen by the neck in an iron grip and slammed him forward into the metal crosshatch. He screamed something in Arabic as his black beret fell to the floor.

The Filipino sprung forward, reached through the grate and wiggled his arm down to the holster at the policeman's side. Tearing the Beretta out of the holster, the Filipino racked the slide just as the second policemen came running from the other room where he had been watching television news footage of the protests in the Tahrir Square in Cairo.

Ramon fired a single shot through the grate. The second policemen's hands went to his neck as blood leaked from between his fingers. He staggered back towards the break room, then collapsed.

"Where are the keys?" Paul demanded. "Where are your keys?"

The guard was shaking as he reached into his pocket and handed them to the American.

Paul tossed the key ring to Ramon. The former Special Forces soldier first opened the front door and waved the rest of the team in before going and unlocking the door that led to the offices and armory. The other five Liquid Sky members walked in while Ramon secured the policeman.

Deckard looked down at the dead policeman who had been shot in the neck. Paul and Ramon went in unarmed. He had no idea they were going to start killing cops who were just doing their jobs. Deckard knew he had to take control of the situation before it spun further out of control.

He grabbed the Beretta 9mm pistol from the holster of the dead policeman and strode across the room to secure the other cop from Ramon.

"Go get the armory open," he told Ramon. "I'll take care of this fucker out back."

"Have at it," Ramon said with a shrug, letting the prisoner go.

With the policeman still shaking, Deckard man-handled him out the front door and along the side of the building until they were behind a connex container.

"Please, please, please," the policemen begged. He was mumbling and could barely get the words out.

Deckard bent down and picked up a large rock. Kicking the policemen down on his knees, he slammed the rock over the back of the cop's head, knocking him out cold. Chambering a round in the Beretta pistol, Deckard leaned in close and fired a single shot.

He blew off the top half of the cop's left ear. If any of the Liquid Sky members walked by, they needed to see some blood near the body or they would investigate further. The fleshy part of the ear exploded and sprayed blood into the gravel next to him. There was a pretty good drip going from where the ear had been severed, but nothing that would cause him to bleed out and die.

The cop would wake up in a world of shit, but at least he would wake up.

Back inside, Deckard found that Liquid Sky had already opened the vault door and were inside the armory. The paint-chipped weapons racks were pretty empty, most literally covered in dust. Maritime security companies were cutting every corner they could in order to turn a profit, so they were not going to find any Heckler and Koch 416 rifles in the armory, just cheap M4 knockoffs with iron sights. After a little digging around, Ramon did find what he was looking for.

There were a few American companies that did issue their security teams with the hardware needed to repel a determined attack. Ramon flipped open the latches on the case and cracked open the lid. Inside was a Barrett .50 caliber anti-material rifle with a 10-power scope and several loaded magazines.

"Gotcha," the Filipino said with a smile.

Deckard found a Norinco AR-15 in the racks and claimed it for himself. He would have to fashion a sling for it using a backpack strap or something later on. It was bare bones, with a carrying handle and rear iron sight. No frills, that was the reality of military contracting for most folks. He slipped several loaded 5.56 magazines into his pockets. He would have to make it work.

On the way out, no one took a second glance at the policeman sprawled out in the gravel. Deckard was glad, for both their sakes that he didn't wake up while they were loading up the vehicles.

It was a long ride back to Cairo.

18

Bill turned around in the passenger seat to face Deckard as he terminated a call on his cell phone.

"I've got a geo on a dead drop you guys are going to need. One of the technical guys at the U.S. embassy stashed it a while back in case something like this came up."

"Surprising amount of forethought on their part," Deckard said.

"Yeah, no shit. Almost like they anticipated this situation, huh? Most of those guys couldn't find pussy in a Mexican whorehouse."

Bill sent a text to Deckard's cell phone. They all carried encrypted cell phones that Ramon had set up for them back in Mauritius.

"That is the lat-long for the dead drop," Bill told him. "Pick it up and I will get back to you with a grid to wherever the device is being stored. I don't have it yet, but the client should get it to me soon."

"He better if he wants it back."

"Just do your job and let me worry about that."

It was four in the morning when they arrived back in Cairo. The streets were a cluttered maze of brown buildings covered with satellite dishes. The streets were relatively quiet with light traffic as it was early morning. Riots could still break out at any time. Egypt had descended into its own French Revolution where Generals replaced the President; then, the next revolution saw the Muslim Brotherhood take charge. Then, the military came back into power and Colonels replaced Generals. What happened in the next stage no one knew, which managed to scare everyone, including the West.

Ramon and Deckard were dropped off while the rest of the team drove off to begin their own recon. A mission like this would usually take weeks of planning, and Deckard was all too aware that they were simply flying by the seat of their pants. Liquid Sky was half-assing it because somebody's ass was on the line, that same ass unwilling to risk actual American soldiers to unfuck their problem because if they got compromised, it could make things even worse back in the U.S.

Ramon carried the black case as they found a building that looked to provide an overwatch position of their dead drop. Deckard had his AR-15 broken down and hidden under his shirt. Again, half assing it. At least the streets were pretty dead at this time of night. They walked a few blocks until they located a building with an external staircase that spiraled up seven stories to the top. The mercenaries had to hop a wall, but then were inside the apartment complex. Deckard snatched a bed sheet off a clothesline on their way.

Sweat was pouring off their bodies as they reached the rooftop. Both men went about assembling their weapons. Deckard's M4 was simple to snap together with take down pins as he attached the upper and lower receiver. Ramon extended the .50 cal rifle's barrel and slid the recoil spring into place. Then, he made sure the bolt and buffer spring were in place as he held the charging handle slightly back and attached the barrel to the butt stock and trigger mechanism, pinning it in place. They each loaded magazines.

"The sun is going to be up in an hour," Ramon said to no one in particular.

"We should recover the dead drop before then."

"I agree."

"What is it?" Deckard asked.

"The dead drop? Specialized ammunition that we are going to need to penetrate the secure compound the device is being held in."

"What, like API or Raufoss rounds?"

"No, not like that. Come on, let's get eyes on before sending you down there."

Deckard spread the bed sheet over Ramon and the Barrett rifle once he got into position. It would give him some concealment in case low-flying aircraft flew by, which they would be as they monitored protests and riots.

"There it is," the Filipino mercenary said as he looked through the Leupold scope. From their vantage point, they had a good view of the sprawling neighborhood below. Down the street was a concrete bridge that crossed over a shallow depression. "The dead drop is under that bridge."

It looked like there were just a few feet of clearance under the bridge, enough room to scoot through if you hunched over.

"You can see that narrow opening between the ground and the bottom of the bridge," Ramon said as he scanned. "That is your FRP for this cache according to the data Bill sent me."

The FRP or final reference point was a fixed position which could easily be found by the person uncovering a cache. From there, he would have precise measurements to follow to locate the cache itself.

"Take a look," Ramon said while pushing the Barrett over to Deckard so he could recon the site with the ten-power scope.

Deckard settled in behind the rifle.

"What the fuck?" he cursed.

"What is it?"

"The cache site is compromised."

Through the scope, Deckard saw an Egyptian man wearing khaki pants and a brown button down shirt squeeze out from under the bridge. He walked up the embankment and onto the street. Deckard passed the rifle back to Ramon so that he could see for himself.

"Holy shit," the Filipino said as he looked through the scope. "Another one just came out from under the bridge. It's like a fucking clown car down there. This one is zipping up his pants on the way out. I guess that was what was going on. He was squaring his buddy away with *creme of some young guy*."

"What idiot placed this cache?"

"Too late now. Get your ass down there to that underground homo den and see if the cache is still there. It's up under the bridge, a small case resting on the lip of the fifth I-beam in from the entrance."

"Looks like I'm drawing the short straw again."

"Here," Ramon said as he reached for something on his belt. "That AR is too big for confined spaces anyway. I smuggled this through the airport."

Ramon handed him his karambit knife. It was curved like the claw on the hind leg of a velociraptor.

"Take care of business and get that package. The sooner you do, the sooner we can get the fuck out of here."

Deckard left his AR-15 with Ramon and started back down the stairs to the streets below. He held the karambit close to his body with his pinky finger through the hole at the end of the blade's handle. Walking down the street, he shuffled down the embankment to the opening under the bridge. Looking over his shoulder, he knew Ramon would be watching from his crow's nest above, but Deckard would have no backup once he went inside.

Deckard could hear something shuffling around in the dark.

Holding the karambit in his fist, he stepped into the darkness.

Ramon lay in the prone, motionless, as he watched the scene unfold below. Observing through the sniper scope, he saw Deckard look back at him over his shoulder then turn and duck under the bridge. His partner was an odd cat, but Ramon had to admit that he was squared away and generally fearless.

Scanning the surroundings for a few minutes, he hoped that Deckard made it fast. Dawn was already approaching.

"Uh oh," Ramon said under his breath.

He spotted one of the men they saw exiting the cache site walking down the street, heading back towards the bridge. Ramon had no way to contact Deckard since he would not be able to get cell phone coverage under the bridge.

The Filipino mercenary smiled to himself.

It would be interesting to see how Deckard handled this.

Deckard squatted in the darkness, giving his eyes time to adjust. Something was definitely moving inside the urban cave.

"Who is there?"

It was a women's voice, asking him in Arabic.

"Who is that?"

She had also sensed that she was no longer alone. Deckard heard metal drag on metal as her feet kicked through the dust as she tried to move. Reaching into a pocket, Deckard turned on a small pen light. The white light cut through the darkness like a knife.

What he saw turned his stomach. A homeless woman wearing rags was chained to a piece of rebar sticking out of the dirt. He could only imagine why.

"How long have you been here," he asked her in Arabic.

"How could I know? They chained me up down here. He charges men in the neighborhood for them to come down here and rape me."

The American had seen some demented things in his travels. Unfortunately, he wasn't surprised in the least that such activities occurred, just surprised that he encountered it in the cache site. The woman's hair was a rat's nest, her clothes covered in grim. She was barefoot, kneeling in the dirt with the handcuffs securing her to the metal bar.

"I'm going to get you out of those handcuffs."

They both froze as a third voice came from the entrance.

"*Marhaban?*"

Deckard flicked off his flashlight.

"That's him," the woman whispered in the dark.

"*Marhaban?*" This time the voice was closer.

157

The woman began talking to her slave master and pimp in their common language. Deckard palmed the karambit. The pimp thought someone else was in his dungeon and that the woman was running some kind of side business when he wasn't around.

Deckard crouched in the darkest shadows and waited for him to get closer. Edging towards the middle of the urban cave, the pimp flicked on his lighter so he could see the woman. Deckard seized the opportunity, coming up from behind and wrapping a hand around the pimp's face. With the other hand, he crossed the curved blade of the karambit along the side of his neck. Deckard then yanked both hands in opposite directions as fast as he could.

The pimp dropped to the ground like a rag doll, his body convulsing as blood streamed out of his neck like a firehose. Turning on his flashlight, Deckard wiped the blood off the knife on the soon-to-be-deceased man's pant sleeve. The woman spit in his face as the pimp struggled for one final ragged breath. Then the pimp's body shook a final time, and he died.

Going through the dead man's pockets, Deckard found a key ring, but not a handcuff key. He then searched the dead man's wallet and again came up empty. Finally, he relieved the corpse of its wrist watch and used the metal on the strap as a shim to crank open the handcuffs.

"*Shukran,*" the woman said through her tears. "God bless you."

She looked up at him and for the first time noticed that he was a foreigner.

"Thank you," she said again.

"Stay here for a moment, I have to find something. We can leave together."

Deckard didn't want her to run outside by herself and get shot by Ramon who would have no idea what was going on.

He quickly located the small plastic case he was looking for hidden up under the bridge and pulled it down. The case was about ten inches by ten inches and another ten deep, almost a perfect cube. There was no writing on it.

"Follow me," he told the woman.

Using the flashlight, he navigated his way to the entrance, then put the light back in his pocket and fished around for his cell phone. He stepped outside and called Ramon, quickly explaining the situation.

"Just get back up here; the sun is coming up," Ramon told him.

"Be right there," Deckard said before terminating the call.

The woman slipped out into the burning night air.

"If I were you," Deckard said as he looked at her. "I wouldn't want to be caught here come sun up."

She looked back at him with wide eyes.

"Good luck."

"If God wills it," he replied.

They turned and walked off in opposite directions.

19

Nadeesha walked the Cairo streets.

Having bought local clothing she tried to blend in. But with her dark skin, people probably thought she was from Southern Egypt. Men jeered at her and made obscene gestures. A few offered to purchase her for a quickie. She was used to having to work in incredibly misogynist cultures, but as one pedestrian grabbed her ass, she hoped the entire country just burned to the ground.

Having completed a close recce of the Egyptian Army compound, she sat down for morning tea near the target and watched the soldiers and officers arrive in twos and threes, wearing their puffy berets with elastic rat tails hanging from the back.

Scrolling through her cell phone, she e-mailed the pictures she had taken of the Army building to Bill and the guys. They were looking for an appropriate vehicle to steal. She was looking for an appropriate officer to steal. Time passed. Her tea grew cold.

The intel they had, she didn't ask what the source of it was, indicated that the three college students were being held inside the Army installation where prisoners were sometimes kept until they could be transferred to a larger prison. The three Americans were being kept there indefinitely so that the Army chain of command could keep an eye on them. Those kids wouldn't last long in an Egyptian prison without protection.

All they knew for certain was that the three American students had been detained while on a rooftop overlooking Tahrir Square during the latest mass protest forty-eight hours ago. Over a million Egyptians flooded back into the square in defiance of both the Muslim Brotherhood and the military dictatorship that they were slowly coming under the control of. When the Americans were detained, the military also found them with a mysterious device, but that wasn't her target.

They had to free the Americans. Conducting a surgical raid to rescue hostages was one of the most complicated missions around. They had the most bare-bones intel, no mission planning, and almost nothing for equipment. It was a mess to say the least. She didn't even know what cell they were being held in or even a confirmation that the Americans, were in fact, inside the Army compound.

Nadeesha spotted an Egyptian soldier, wearing the rank of a Colonel on his epaulettes, leaving the compound.

It was time to rectify some of their intelligence gaps. Paying for her tea, she texted Bill to let him know that she had a mark in sight and began to tail the Colonel. Bill texted back to confirm. He had her location as they were tracking each other's cellphone's using Google Latitude. The rest of Liquid Sky had hotwired a mini-van and would be pulling up behind her in a minute.

She hoped the Colonel didn't get into a car and drive off before they arrived.

Her phone rang.

"Yeah?"

"We're on your six," Bill said. "Is that him in the uniform about twenty meters in front of you?"

"That's him."

"Okay, we'll ball him up. Run to catch up and help push him in."

The gray mini-van accelerated, passed, and pulled up alongside the Colonel. Nadeesha broke into a sprint. Paul, Zach, and Rick threw open the sliding door and their hands reached out and grabbed the surprised military officer. They pulled him into the van and dropped a few fists and elbows on him before Nadeesha ran up and flung herself inside the van.

Slamming the door, Bill stepped on the gas.

It was time to get some answers.

Ramon and Deckard had reset. They bought local clothes to wear, plussed up on food and water to get them through the day, and found a new hide site which overlooked their target. The University of Cairo was spread out over several square miles to their front. Their particular target was the engineering department, the electrical engineering department specifically. That was where the device was being kept according to the intelligence information provided by the client.

Taking turns on glass, each of them alternated looking through the Barrett's sniper scope. Deckard had also bought a suitcase with rollers to transport the sniper rifle and a small backpack to hide his AR-15.

They each used the mil-dot reticule in the scope to estimate range and draw out a range card which would help both of them when Deckard made his infiltration. The electrical engineering building itself was 700 meters away from the building they decided to lay up in, which was empty and still under construction.

They had gotten into position deep inside one of the empty floors near the top of the building. They had good cover and concealment, and with the building lacking walls, just floors and concrete pillars holding them up, they also had 360-degree visibility. The team had also started building their range card early, before the heat mirage would get really bad later in the day and make range estimations difficult if not impossible with the mil-dot reticule.

Deckard had enough on his mind as he was trying to determine an approach path to break into the engineering department where the device he had to steal was being studied. At the same time, he couldn't forget that this was a Liquid Sky mission, not a Samruk International mission. He had his own objectives to complete.

"Did you know Jon Bellacruz back in 1st Group?" he asked Ramon.

"Yeah, of course. Good dude. We did Baghdad together and then Laos on a JCET back in the day."

"Just wanted to ask, if you don't mind. The last time we talked, he told me about a former colleague named Ramon who got blacklisted from contracting."

Ramon chuckled. Deckard had told him a half truth. He

had talked to Jon Bellacruz years ago, but Ramon's name had never come up. He was using Bellacruz's name to segue into the information Aghassi had given him about Ramon.

"Yeah, that's true. The major companies out there won't touch me. I pissed off some pretty powerful people."

"What happened?"

"I'll show you mine if you show me yours."

"What do you want to know?"

"About how you got blacklisted by the Agency."

It was Deckard's turn to laugh.

"I tried to kill a Case Officer in Afghanistan."

"Damn, that will do it."

"The Agency had me training a platoon of indig on the Iranian border for a contingency operation," Deckard elaborated. "I would have led them in an unconventional warfare campaign inside Iran. My normal job was going out with the Afghan paramilitary strike force, but I got tasked out for this special mission. I spent a couple months getting these guys up to speed, got pretty close to some of them. They were a good group of guys.

"Then this Case Officer flies in to our outpost on the Iranian border and tells me that I'm to send the entire para-military unit on a cross-border mission to hit an Iranian Army facility; however, I was explicitly ordered not to go with them. They cited legal reasons, covert action, plausible deniability and all that. On the surface, there was nothing wrong with that. But one kilometer into Iran using the ingress the Case Officer gave us, my guys stumble right into an ambush.

"The ambush was planned well in advance with overlapping sectors of fire, mines were used, and the terrain was well selected. The Iranians had been tipped off that my boys were coming. It was a slaughter. We only found out what happened because two of them somehow managed to break contact and E&E back to Afghanistan."

"You had a leak?"

"A controlled leak. It took some digging, but using my own sources that I had cultivated in Iran, I was able to find out that it was the CIA itself that passed on the information to the Iranians. It was a big sell out, some kind of quid pro quo on the political level. The Agency got something in return of course, but Iran wanted my para-military unit out of their way because they knew it was a threat."

"That's why you went after the Case Officer?"

"Hell yeah. I had a captured 60mm mortar. Drove right up to the firebase he was staying on during the night. I had already measured out the distances and knew where his hooch was. So I dropped a couple rounds down the tube and ran for it."

"You kill him?"

"I wish, one round was a direct hit and blew his hooch wide open. The problem was that the Case Officer was on the shitter at the time."

"Damn."

"Yeah, so anyway, the Agency puts two and two together and decides they need to make this problem go away right quick. A few hours later another Ground Branch element storms into my compound and detains me on the spot. Never even had the chance to fight back."

"That is surprisingly efficient on their part."

"Never underestimate how fast those fuckers on the 7th floor can work when they want to cover something up. Long story short, I'm shown the door and threatened to never speak of any of it again. They blacklisted me, but didn't prosecute for obvious reasons."

"In a court room the whole rest of the story would begin to leak out."

"Exactly."

"What did you do after that?"

"My own thing," Deckard smiled. "So I showed off my circumcision and all, how about you? What got you blacklisted?"

Ramon sighed.

"I destroyed Mars."

"What?"

"I was going through a divorce at the time so I transferred over to one of the National Guard Special Forces units and went over to 20th Group. While there I landed a civilian job working as a security guard with NASA and was assigned to watch the Ames Research Center in California. It wasn't a bad gig, and since I had a Top Secret clearance and was sniper qualified, I was almost pulling in six figures."

Deckard's head was spinning at this turn of events. Had he stolen classified material from the labs? Screwed up and accidentally shot a scientist leaving work late at night?

"So out in the middle of nowhere at the research center is this lone building with all the doors locked. It was just out there, no one ever went in or out, nobody ever checked on it. I talked about it with some of the other security guards and no one knew anything about it. It seemed like it was just some abandoned building.

"Anyhow, one day I decided to go and find out what it was for myself. So I grab a pair of bolt cutters and head out there. I snapped the locks off and opened the door. I felt this suction of air as I walked inside, like the place was sealed off tight. Inside was nothing, just a bunch of dirt and shit on the ground. I walked around for a little bit figuring there had to be something else inside, but it really was empty except for all the dirt on the ground.

"So I finish my shift, get changed, and drive home. That next day the shit hit the fan. Investigators for NASA and even the FBI were called in. They found my footprints in the dirt inside that building and matched them up to the boots I left sitting on top of my locker in the locker room."

"What the hell?"

"As it turns out, that so-called abandoned building was like some kind of bio-dome where they were replicating the atmosphere on Mars. It was some big science project they were doing to research the feasibility of long term space travel. The whole experiment was kept in total isolation from the outside world. So when I cut the locks and went walking around on the surface of Mars I fucked up a 23 million dollar NASA science project that had been underway for three years."

"Holy shit."

"Oh, yeah man. I was looking at some serious fucking jail time for breaking and entering as well as destruction of government property. I denied everything of course and lawyered up but they had my boots with Mars dust on the soles. I was fucked. My lawyer made a big stink to them about me being a war veteran and eventually NASA let me go but completely blackballed me. My name is shit with any major defense company in the United States. They even fucked me from taking security jobs in the UK."

"That is the most bad ass war story I've ever heard," Deckard deadpanned.

"I'm not sure. Mortaring a CIA Officer is pretty bad ass.

But anyhow, that is how we both ended up with this crew I guess. We're both damaged goods."

"I don't see any NASA or CIA pussies on this op, do you?"

"Good point," Ramon agreed.

20

Wearing black *kafiyah* head wraps, the gunmen stormed the Army detention center while firing their AR-15 and AK-47 rifles in all directions.

"Allah Akbar! Allah Akbar!" one screamed.

The two gate guards went down under a hail of gunfire. Another two Egyptian soldiers were shot dead on the front steps of the compound. Once inside, the gunmen blasted a lieutenant sitting behind a desk and headed for the stairs. An Egyptian soldier managed to pull his pistol free from his holster and fire several panicked shots over the heads of the attacking Islamic militants. The return fire splattered him against the wall.

By now shouts were heard through the Army facility as soldiers began to panic. They were under attack and no one was even remotely prepared for it.

"Allah Akbar!"

The prisoners heard the calls from inside their cells and cheered the attackers on. Taking the stairs three at a time the four gunmen reached the second floor where the prison cells were located. The soldier on guard duty tried to make a break for it and took off running down the hall until a burst of 7.62x39 caught up with him.

One of the gunmen found the keys on the corpse's belt and used them to open the rusty barred door that led into the cell block.

"Allah Akbar!" the gunmen screamed in unison.

"Allah Akbar!" the prisoners repeated. The prison was packed with Muslim Brotherhood members who had been rounded up by security forces and each cell was packed with nearly a dozen of the Islamic fundamentalists. They had been arrested for protesting, terrorism, and other acts of sedition, both real and imagined.

They lunged with outstretched arms from between the cell bars, the wild look of fanaticism in their eyes. Many had rough spots on their foreheads, a badge of honor for a member of the brotherhood. It came from prostrating themselves during their daily prayers.

"Amriki? Amriki?" the gunmen asked.

"*Nam*," the prisoners answered, pointing down towards the end of the cell block. American scum.

The gunmen swept down to the cell that the Brothers pointed to. Huddled in the corner were the three American college students, all of them on the verge of pissing their pants. One looked to weigh ninety pounds and wore glasses. That was Luke Thomas, 22. The goofy kid wearing a t-shirt with the word "singularity" was Adam Kauffmen, 19. The third was wearing his gay rights t-shirt, as if anyone in Egypt gave a shit about that issue. He was Aaron Helms, 20. Helms was the priority because his dad was somebody back in the world. Their contract covered all three, but they could kank the other two losers and dump them if shit got really tight.

The American students cringed in the corner of the cell as one of the gunmen stepped forward. He peered through the bars, squinting behind his black head wrap. He wore a white *dishdasha* and held an AK-47 at port arms. Leveling the Russian rifle, the gunmen blasted the padlock off the door and swung it open. Two other gunmen rushed in and secured the college students, grabbing them by the collars of their shirt and by their hair to drag them out into the corridor.

Then the gunmen began shooting the locks off the other cells.

"*Allllaaahh Akbbbbaaaaarrr!*"

The prison cell doors flew open and the Muslim Brotherhood members burst out into the hall screaming with their arms up in the air. They cheered as the gunmen dragged the infidels down the stairs and outside.

Outside in the courtyard, a crowd had begun to gather. The soldiers had long since disappeared, many of them dropping their rifles and beating feet as the already agitated public converged on the Army building. Now that people saw the Muslim Brotherhood members breaking free they openly cheered and chanted slogans. When the four gunmen emerged from the prison with their three American prisoners the crowd went wild with fervor, their extremist devotion overwhelming a few members who dropped to their knees.

A gray mini-van edged through the crowd.

Just then, a civilian ran up out of the gathering crowd with a black Al Qaeda flag attached to a thin metal pole. One of the gunmen grabbed the flag while the other three escorted their

168

prisoners to the van.

With his head still wrapped in the black *kafiyah*, the gunmen held the black flag proudly as he began to wave it back and forth.

"*Allllaahh Akbaaarr!*" he screamed at the top of his lungs.

"*Allah Akbar!!!*" the crowd screamed in return.

With the prisoners loaded into the back of the van, the gunmen handed the black flag back to a Muslim Brotherhood member. Jumping into the van, it lurched off as the crowd parted ways. Escaped prisoners and protestors alike praised these gunmen and their gift from god.

Ramon began downloading his Barrett magazines, sliding each cartridge out on by one and setting them down. The bullets were about the size of his finger and had enough kinetic energy even after traveling 1,000 meters to cut a man in half.

Their target building in the engineering section of the University of Cairo was only about 700 meters away, an easy shot with the .50 caliber rifle. There would be little compensating for gravity or wind at that range when firing a round with so much energy behind it. The former Special Forces sniper had no doubt that he could hit targets at that range with this rifle, even if he was a little rusty. They also had a very detailed range card that he and Deckard made copies of. Deckard could call in pre-designated target reference points to help Ramon get on target faster as well.

Flipping open the latches on the black box that Deckard had retrieved from under the bridge, Ramon began sliding the bullets under the feed lips of the magazine, which depressed the follower as the magazine filled with ten rounds. They looked like normal .50 caliber rounds except that the bullets themselves had clear plastic wrapped around them.

"Whoever set that cache was sloppy about it," Deckard complained as he watched Ramon. "What is so special about these bullets anyway?"

"Sloppy or just rushed," Ramon elaborated. "It was worth the risk of going in to retrieve the cache. These are EMP rounds."

"You've gotta be shitting me."

"Nope," Ramon said. "During the terminal phase, when the round makes contact with something, it will emit an electromagnetic pulse which will short out and destroy any electronics within five meters. This way I will be able to clear a path for you by disabling the security systems as you make your infiltration into the engineering building. It should be sealed up pretty tight, all things considered. We'll see what we can do about that. There are also a couple EMP grenades in that case for you."

"If you fire it too close to me, it will destroy my comms uplink," Deckard said as he picked up one of the box shaped EMP grenades and inspected it in his hand.

"Well, don't get too close."

Just then, Ramon's cell phone began to buzz.

Checking the text message he received, he then turned to Deckard.

"Showtime, brother."

"Oh shit, oh shit, oh shit, oh shit." Aaron Helms turned into a human chatter box as he sat in the back of the mini-van with the Al Qaeda gunmen, their eyes menacing him through the slits in their black head wraps. Aaron was just a liberal arts major who wanted to fight for human rights and got in over his head. Now he was on an express one-way trip to a made-for-youtube snuff flick starring him and his college bros in orange jump suits.

"We're so fucked," he croaked.

The van hit a bump in the road and Adam started to cry.

One of the gunmen finished texting someone on his cell phone. He had to be the biggest Arab any of them had ever seen. Probably he was texting AQ HQ back in Pakistan, Aaron figured. Meanwhile, Luke was hugging himself as he gently rocked back and forth on the floor of the van.

As the driver took them across the Nile River on one of Cairo's many bridges, the three college students were left to ponder their fate. Then, one of the gunmen turned to the other and began to talk.

"I think you were getting a little too into it, Zach," the gunmen said in English. "Waving the black flag around like that..what was that about?"

"I was just staying in character," the other gunmen responded. "I take my job seriously, unlike some of you."

Aaron and Adam looked at each other, both their faces streaked with tears.

"Both of you fucking jokers need to pull your heads out of your asses," a third gunmen said.

"Whatever Rick. You're just jealous of my method acting."

"Fuck you."

The van rocked as they crossed the bridge, then the wheels squealed as they took a tight turn.

"Women drivers: no survivors," the one they had called Rick announced.

"Eat my ass, Rick," a woman's voice said from up front, the driver not even turning to look at them.

"Don't threaten me with a good time. I'd eat the peanuts out of your shit, girl."

The others laughed until the big guy who had been

texting screamed at them.

"Knock it the fuck off," he snarled. "We're still in the middle of an operation."

Then he peeled off his head wrap. The others followed suit. The college kids looked on with slack jaws.

The guy with the beard looked over and saw their expressions.

"Did you guys really think Al Qaeda would break into a prison and free you just to execute you?" the American said.

"Uh," Aaron began. "Maybe."

Luke pursed his lips like he had just bitten into a lemon.

"Damn, you kids look like you are about to piss your pants," the blonde haired American said.

Luke took a deep breath.

"Too late."

"How you doing down there, high speed?"

Deckard heard Ramon's voice through the ear bud placed in his ear, the device connected to the cell phone in his pocket. He was walking onto the university grounds through the Giza Zoo, which ran right behind the engineering department.

"Three minutes out," he answered.

"I'm all gassed-up and ready to go."

Crouching in the bushes, Deckard watched the facility grounds for a moment. From observing most of the morning and into the afternoon, they already knew that there was not a roving guard on patrol. In fact, the campus was pretty dead because so many students were out protesting in Tahrir Square and elsewhere.

"I'm ready to go in," Deckard said into the microphone attached to the ear bud. "Hit it."

A second later, sparks flew from the transformer mounted on the telephone pole just outside the electrical engineering building. Three booms echoed out in rapid succession as the sound caught up with shots. From his sniper hide up in the empty building, Ramon's shots would be muffled, but still audible to those who knew what they were listening for.

"That's it. Put a shot into the transformer and two more into the generator up on the roof," Ramon told him.

Sure enough, Deckard didn't see any indications from his view through the windows that there was any power inside.

"Moving in."

Deckard walked up to the oblong, khaki-colored building. He squinted as he got closer to the door.

"Looks like there is a key card lock on the door, I am going to-"

His words were cut short as a hole suddenly punched through the door above the locking mechanism.

"Come down six inches," he advised Ramon.

"Roger."

This time he blasted the lock and pieces of metal scrap bounced off the door stoop. With the lock shattered, Deckard was able to shoulder open the door and step inside. Sliding his backpack off, he rapidly attached the upper and lower receiver of his AR-15 rifle, then locked and loaded a magazine.

"Inside, moving up."

"Got it, fifth floor looks clear from where I'm sitting."

Deckard carefully walked down the empty corridor to the stairwell and began walking up. It made sense that the device they were after was being kept by the Army inside the electrical engineering department of the University of Cairo. That would be the best place for them to study it since that is where the tools and expertise were already located. The Egyptian Army would not be so foolish as not to have it under guard however.

Then the interior lights came back on. Back up power. Somewhere in the basement probably.

"Hold up a minute," Ramon said over their cell connection. "Let me load my other mag so I'm shooting regular ball ammo if you come under fire."

"I've got a couple more flights of stairs to go."

"Cool," Ramon said. Then a second later, "Okay, I'm up."

Deckard walked out onto the fifth-floor hallway with sweat dripping off his forehead. He held his rifle at the low ready as he moved towards his objective. Their intel was that the device was being held in Lab C. Finding the correct door, he looked through the window pane to glance inside. Pulling back behind the wall, he spoke into the mic.

"Looks like at least two guards. Couple civilians in there, too."

"You're clear outside. You know what to do."

Rendering the device inoperable was the first priority, recovery at a close second. Deckard palmed one of the EMP grenades as he backed away from the door. The pulse would propagate outwards and right through the walls. There was no need for him to get it into the room to render the device inoperable. With the lab's door locked, he would normally have had to breach the door before lobbing it in. No need for that this time.

Pulling the pin, Deckard rolled the EMP grenade down the hall where it stopped at the foot of the lab's door. He scrambled away to make sure he was out of the blast radius. While it wouldn't physically harm him, it would kill his cell phone, and with it, his comms link to Ramon.

Five seconds from the time he pulled the pin, the grenade popped off. There was no brilliant plume of miniature bolts of lightning or anything cool like that, more like a weak firecracker. The EMP itself was of course invisible to the human eye. Hearing the pop, one of the soldiers inside opened the door to see what was going on.

Deckard was there to buttstroke him across the jaw.

Stepping inside the lab, there were rows and rows of desks with soldering irons for students to practice building microchips. On a black table towards the back, two engineers looked up from their work, both of them wearing those goofy magnifying glass goggles that made them look like they had giant Anime character eyes.

Another soldier standing by on guard duty went for the pistol on his hip.

"*La!*" Deckard ordered, thrusting his gun barrel in the

guard's direction.

The soldier put his hands in the air, realizing that the newcomer had the drop on him. Stepping towards the table, he waved the engineers back. He was looking at the device. About the size of a shoe box but only about two inches thick, the black box had a USB cable and a power cable leading out of it. The top of the device had been pried open and the electrical engineers had been poking and prodding around inside. The computers and lights inside the room had gone dark, which meant that the EMP had done its job.

Keeping his rifle leveled on the Egyptian soldier, while the other writhed on the floor behind him, Deckard unzipped his backpack.

Now he just needed to haul ass out of there.

Shen Banggen walked alongside the Egyptian Lieutenant Colonel as he was led to view the device. The Chinese operative was on assignment for the People's Third Department. It was his job to shape outcomes, and part of that position included securing foreign technology which had military or economic applications the Chinese government could reverse engineer to use for espionage, combat, or simply to turn a profit by mass producing and dumping into foreign markets.

They had just completed a meeting with an Egyptian General which had to be cut short. The military was desperate to quell the riots around the city, and the General had other obligations. Banggen assured the Egyptians that they would be properly compensated for the technology transfer.

"The device is just upstairs," the Colonel informed him

as they walked.

"I understand," Banggen replied in Arabic.

His track record with technology procurements was nearly impeccable, and his superiors knew it. He had recovered a sensitive computer system from the Taliban they had captured from a Navy SEAL team that they had killed. A few years later, he secured large pieces of a stealth helicopter which the Americans had crash landed in Pakistan. Other pieces of tech showed up here and there. In one major coup, he simply paid off a U.S. Special Forces soldier running a training mission in Thailand. He helped the soldier make it look like a hooker had drugged him and ransacked his hotel room. Banggen got the black tough box filled with sensitive radio equipment and delivered it to his superiors in China.

Suddenly, something popped on the floor above them. To Banggen it sounded like a single firecracker lit on Chinese New Year. But this was no Chinese holiday. The lights flickered and blinked off. The Chinese intelligence operative then noticed that the second hand on his watch had stopped ticking. The Egyptian Colonel looked up, as if he would see something on the ceiling.

Banggen then pulled out his cell phone. It was completely dead and would not turn on. First they had a power outage causing the back-up generators in the basement to kick on. Now this.

"Something is happening," he informed the Colonel. "We need to get to the device."

Taking off at a jog, they headed for the stairs.

In one smooth motion, Deckard swept the device and the opened cover into his bag with all the wires still attached. Cramming the cables inside, he zipped it up and threw the backpack over his shoulder on one strap, the other having been used to improvise a sling for his AR-15.

Before leaving, he relieved the soldier still on his feet of his Browning Hi-Power pistol and stuck it in his pocket. The last thing he needed was to get shot in the back on his way out the door.

"See ya later, Fletch," he told the guard.

High stepping it over the second guard who was curled in the fetal position in the doorway, Deckard headed down the hall.

"Got the package," he said into the mic. "On my way out."

"Roger that," Ramon answered. Good, the EMP hadn't taken out his comms.

Turning into the stairwell, Deckard suddenly found himself face to face with an Egyptian Army officer. The officer's eyes went wide with surprise, startled by Deckard swinging onto the landing. He held a BHP in his fist, but forgot it was there for a second too long. Deckard identified his threat faster and raised the AR-15 into the pocket of his shoulder, his knees already bent in a shooter's stance. The barrel barked twice, then several more times as Deckard fired 5.56 shots into the officer as he crumpled to the ground and rolled down the stairs.

Without hesitating, Deckard brought the rifle to bear on a second potential target. The approaching man backed up against the wall with his hands in the air.

"I'm unarmed," he said in near perfect English.

He was in his fifties, chubby around the waist and the neck, and obviously Chinese. Deckard's eyes narrowed. In an instant, Banggen realized that he had been made. The American mercenary recognized him from the picture they had been shown in the briefing for their mission to the Philippines. A Chinese influence agent heading up to a floor where a sensitive, captured American technology was being kept? Yeah, sure.

"That is a matter of opinion. Your weapon isn't guns or bombs is it?"

"I am here on official business with the People's Republic of-"

Deckard's rifle recoiled in his hands.

Banggen pitched forward and did a face plant.

Flicking the rifle's selector back to safe, Deckard bounded down the stairs.

Target of opportunity.

Ramon tossed his suitcase with the disassembled Barrett inside in the trunk while Deckard popped out the cylinder on the steering column using a screwdriver. Bypassing the lock, Deckard hit the ignition and they had their ride out of Cairo.

He took the wheel while Ramon got in the passenger seat and called up a map on his cell phone to help guide him out of the city. Bill had simply texted them a cardinal direction, basically the worst exfil plan in history. They would secure transportation out of Egypt once they got to the coast of the Red Sea.

Ramon directed him over a bridge heading east through the city. Cairo was volatile to say the least. Young people were out in the streets marching and chanting slogans. Pro-democracy protestors clashed with the Muslim Brotherhood, and they both clashed with the Egyptian military. Deckard did his best to skirt around clusters of protestors who could break into a riot at any moment.

His navigator instructed him when to make turns, and they weaved through the now-busy city streets.

"Take this left, then straight ahead."

Deckard followed Ramon's instructions and suddenly

found himself coasting across a wide boulevard littered with trash, discarded pickets, and empty tear gas canisters. To their right stood the military bearing riot shields, shotguns, and grenade launchers loaded with tear gas. To their left was a gaggle of twenty something year old kids throwing rocks at the soldiers.

A sniper's shot cracked, the bullet leaving a dimpled hole in the hood of their stolen car.

Deckard slammed down on the gas pedal and shot across the street.

Both men breathed a sigh of relief when they finally cleared the city and took the Cairo-Suez road to the coast. It was now getting late in the day and exhaustion began to set in. Liquid Sky had been running a no-notice hostage rescue and asset recovery in a hostile region with bare-bones intelligence, no equipment when they arrived in country, and no backup to speak of. Whether they wanted to admit it or not, their nerves were shot.

The terrain flattened out into desolation in all directions, an empty desert that probably didn't look much different that it did during the time of the Pharaohs. Halfway to the coast, Deckard pulled over to gas up their car while Ramon went and bought some coffee at a bus stop. Deckard could tell that his reaction time was slowed and he wasn't working at one hundred percent. Ramon came back with bottles of water and the coffee both of which they promptly drank, and then got back on the road.

Ramon got a text from Bill. The other Liquid Sky element had arrived in Suez and was looking for their exfil platform. After another hour on the road, they reached Suez just as the sun was setting. Making a phone call, Bill directed them south for a link-up. Driving by some residential neighborhoods, the low-laying mountains in the distance made for a change in terrain near the entrance to the Suez Canal. They spotted the mini-van in a parking lot next to the fishermen's docks.

Zach was leaning against the side of the van smoking a cigarette.

Deckard parked the car alongside the van and killed the engine.

"You have it?" Zach asked before Deckard had even stepped out of the car.

"Yeah."

Bill opened the van's passenger door and got out.

"Let's have it."

Deckard tossed him the backpack.

"Something else," Deckard mentioned.

"What is it?" Bill asked as he unzipped the backpack.

"Banggen was in the engineering building. He was on his way up to inspect the device as I was on my way down."

Bill looked at him blankly for a moment.

"You do him?"

"Fuck yeah," Deckard answered.

Bill nodded.

"Then it's done."

"What the fuck was he doing there?" Zach asked. "For him to be in cahoots with our previous target and then involved with this one as well, that isn't a coincidence."

"No, it isn't," Ramon said. "We talked about this a little on the drive here. It is possible that we are working the same mission profile as Chinese intelligence but from different approaches. They are working to influence world events in a manner that favors their economic policies. We're working to prevent world events from negatively influencing American foreign policy."

"Cool story bro," Zach snorted. "That or our OPSEC is fucking blown and the dinks are shadowing our moves."

"Not very well," Deckard added. "Homeboy ate a 5.56 round between his eyes from about three feet away."

"Everyone fucks up at least once in their life," Zach said, challenging Deckard and Ramon on their hypothesis.

The sliding door on the van swung open. Rick and Paul jumped down to the pavement.

"Who the fuck cares," Rick said, having overheard parts of the conversation. "We're alive and he's dead. That's all that matters."

Bill was still fishing around inside Deckard's backpack, pushing the broken-down AR-15 out of the way and palming the device.

"This is it, huh?" The Liquid Sky team leader was unimpressed to say the least.

He took it back to the van and crawled inside to show it to the three college students. They confirmed that it was the device they had used in Tahrir Square. Nadeesha got out of the driver's seat to join them. She was still wearing a head scarf over her hair.

"Okay," Bill told the Liquid Sky team. "I don't care about some fucking chink right now. We did our job, like Rick said. I got us a fisherman who is going to take us out to sea where we will board a commercial shipping vessel that the client secured passage on for us. Grab whatever kit you have and we can walk to the docks from here."

The seven Liquid Sky members and the three recently liberated hostages walked to the fishing docks and met up with the captain of a small boat that Bill and Nadeesha had gone to make arrangements with twenty minutes prior to Deckard's arrival. The client had secured them transport into international waters, but they had to get to that transport first.

As the fishing boat churned the waters and lumbered off to the commercial ship in the distance, Deckard started to get the idea. Who ran a maritime commercial shipping business that doubled as a logistics infrastructure for covert operations? There were not a whole lot of players in that arena. If it wasn't Langley, then this mission was Langley cleaning up someone else's mess.

The deck hands lowered a rope ladder and also a cargo net to haul up Ramon's suitcase. One by one they ascended to the top, the college students going up in the middle of the group. Bill paid the fishing boat captain and was the last up the ladder.

Once on board, the crew took them belowdeck and showed them to their berthing area. The captain was an American with a largely Indian crew, and showed up briefly to inform them that they could make their way to the galley and the cook would be ready to make them something. About half of the group stumbled off to grab some food, the rest fell asleep almost immediately in their bunks. Bill lay down with Deckard's backpack next to him as he slept.

Deckard went to the galley and grabbed a couple rolls before heading back to the bunks. He realized that he was alone as everyone else was already snoring in their bunks or still at the chow hall cramming down some grub. He should have remembered to take a picture of the device when he first snatched it, but he would have to act now. A third opportunity probably wouldn't present itself.

Tapping on his cell phone, Deckard slowly unzipped the backpack next to Bill's cot and took out the device. With the Egyptians having already tore it open, all the guts inside were exposed. Deckard could see the motherboard, the power source, and several other electrical components that he did not recognize. Whatever it was, the device was clearly professionally made in a modern laboratory somewhere, not just something the three college students jury rigged in their dorm.

He began snapping pictures with the camera on his phone. If he could get them to Aghassi, finding the origins of the device might help them build the big picture, and ascertain who the puppet master behind Liquid Sky was.

"What the fuck are you doing?" a voice said from the cabin door.

Deckard's head jerked up as he held the device in one hand and his camera phone in the other. It was Rick, who had just returned from chow.

"Taking some SSE photos in case we need them later," Deckard said trying to play it off. SSE stood for sensitive site exploitation, an evidence-gathering methodology that Special Operations units used to uncover intelligence information.

"SSE my fucking ass," Rick bellowed as he stepped through the door.

"What the hell," Bill grumbled as he woke from what had been a deep sleep. As team leader, he was probably the most exhausted.

"Deckard is here taking pictures of the fucking device," Rick complained. "OPSEC violating motherfucker. What the fuck do you think you're doing?"

"This is the kind of tech we might want to request for our own use on a future mission."

"Bullshit," Rick cursed. "What are you up to?"

"Deckard," Bill cut in. "Don't let me catch you going through my shit again. I don't give a fuck about this horseshit Rick. You two both need to shut the fuck up so I can get back to sleep. If this Army puke was going to steal the device for his own purposes, then I'm pretty sure he would have done it by now."

"Maybe that's just what he was up to," Rick said as he got red in the face.

"Deck is part of the team now, Rick. Learn how to steer

a fucking parachute, you fucking chump, then you can complain to me about how I run my fucking team," Bill said as he leaned up on one elbow from his cot. "Now get the fuck out of here and go catch a sea jack in the showers or something. I'm trying to rack out here."

Rick turned and stormed out. Deckard zipped the device back up in the backpack as Bill tore it out of his hands and flopped the bag down next to him on the cot.

"If you pull some shit like that again Deckard, I'll fucking kill you."

Deckard took the hint and hit the rack himself, with the cell phone tucked in his pants pocket.

Deckard was vaguely aware of the others filing into the berthing area in ones and twos as they hit the rack themselves. With adrenaline bleeding off, they all went into a post-mission coma while the captain of the ship went full power and headed for international waters.

It was a deep, dreamless sleep as their minds and bodies reset themselves. Ten hours later, the passengers began to wake. The ship had cleared the Gulf of Suez and was now in the Red Sea.

Bill was the first one up. He had confirmed with the client that they had accomplished their mission, but now he headed up to the bridge to re-establish commo and find out what was going on. Having seen things on the way out, Egypt had probably imploded on itself just as they were sailing off.

Liquid Sky and their three liberated college students cycled through the showers and had another meal before they peeled off in separate directions. Zach and Rick went up on the deck to work on their tans. Nadeesha and Paul sat around the day room watching television. Bill was working on his push ups in between the cots. Ramon fell back asleep.

Deckard was up on the deck, watching the sea pass by. It was now early in the morning. As he walked to the stern of the ship, he heard voices and muffled giggles. It was Luke, Aaron, and Adam, enjoying a pack of cigarettes they had bummed from the crew.

"Can I get a smoke?"

They turned to look at him, having thought they were alone.

"Bro, you can have whatever the fuck you want," Aaron said. "You guys saved our sweet virgin assholes from that prison."

"That we did."

Luke handed him a cigarette and held up a lighter for Deckard to get it started.

"That prison would have been Gitmo, Abu Gaireb, and Auschwitz all rolled into one for us," Luke said. "They were talking about transferring us to some dungeon somewhere at any moment. Then they would have let the guards have a go at us."

"Nah," Deckard informed them. "In Egyptian prisons they have a special technique for people like you."

The college students looked at Deckard with wide eyes.

"They would strip you naked and lock you in a small cage with a dog and its, uh, fully engorged member."

"A dog?" Adam asked in disbelief.

"Then when you gave up all the intel they wanted you would have a sudden and catastrophic drop in blood pressure."

"We owe you guys big time," Luke said. The other two nodded in agreement.

"Takes a special kind of man," Deckard said as he played it up. This was the real interrogation. The one where he got the information he wanted. He was just lining them up before he knocked them down.

"Are you like SEAL Team Six or CIA or something?" Adam asked.

"Or something. Freelance."

"A mercenary?"

"You know it."

"That's so gangster," Adam blurted.

184

Deckard took a drag on his cigarette.

"So they tell me that you three were in Tahrir Square."

"Yeah," Aaron said. "Had the best seat in the house from a nearby rooftop. Revolution in real time."

"I was the guy that had to go in and recover your toy for you."

"The Nexus Interceptor," Luke said.

"That is what that black box is called?"

"It's just a nickname we gave it. That bad boy is state of the art."

"What exactly does it do?"

"It is a hacking bypass tool. You know if you want to break into secure computer systems you can hack in through cyberspace, right?"

"Yeah."

"Well this allows you to sneak in through the back door. It creates a temporary power shortage in the targeted system, which creates an opening for you to then insinuate yourself into various networks."

"Why not just hack in the old fashion way from back in the United States?"

"The thing with social media networks is that when you post messages they have a geographical locator with them so the network you are posting from knows where you are physically located. This means that you have to have an actual presence in the vicinity of the network you are trying to spoof."

"And once you spoofed it what did you do?"

"Well, for instance you can then walk right into user accounts for e-mail and social media. That is what we were doing. So then we just start making posts as if we are those users."

"Egypt has been run by one dictator after the next," Aaron informed Deckard. "The people have been suffering under oppression at least since Sadat was assassinated. We came here to help them out."

"What do you mean? Help them how?"

"Human rights is a mainstay in American foreign policy," Luke said. "But America propped up Hosni Mubarak for decades. He was a dictator and the people were suffering. All of us agreed that he had to go and we could help change conditions."

"All of us being the three of you?"

"We were just facilitators. People were already flooding into the streets in droves."

"Pent up anger from years under the thumb of Mubarak," Adam said.

"Wait a second, what did you actually do with that device?"

"We used it as a bypass to gain control of thousands of Facebook and Twitter Accounts," Aaron said.

"Then used them to broadcast the message of revolution," Luke said.

"A mass blast that got the ball rolling," Adam finished.

"You three lit the fuse on Egypt's Arab Spring?"

"The fuse had been lit decades ago. Like Luke said, we were just facilitators."

"Holy shit," Deckard said as he leaned back against the railing on the side of the ship. "Don't you realize that someone back in America flipped Mubarak's switch from green to red?"

"What are you talking about?"

"Hold on a second." Deckard was getting pissed and was starting to break role at this point. "Who put you up to this?"

"What do you mean?" Luke asked.

"Who gave you that bypass device?"

"This NGO down in Virginia."

Deckard rubbed his forehead with both hands.

"Yeah," Aaron broke in. "They are called Global Freedom and Prosperity. They visit our college sometimes, really cool people. They really care about helping to get college students out into the world to help promote freedom. They offer workshops, training, and stuff like that."

"You know, like political advocacy type stuff," Adam said.

"Political advocacy type stuff," Deckard repeated ominously.

"What did you mean someone flipped Mubarak from green to red?"

Deckard took another drag on his cigarette and flicked it over the side of the ship.

"Nevermind."

"No man, what were you going to say?"

186

"You guys don't get it?"

"What?"

"Mubarak didn't simply fall. The United States government would not let their strongman fall if they didn't want him to. A policy decision was made in the halls of power in D.C. They decided it was time for him to go. Not you, not some grassroots revolution. An NGO in Virginia? Are you guys kidding me?"

"It isn't like you think," Adam said flippantly. "That is not how GFP works; they are out to promote democracy. America was in bed with Mubarak so why would they want him out of office?"

"Good question," Deckard answered. "Maybe it plays into Syria."

"And why would they care about Syria?"

"Because that plays into Iran."

Deckard turned and walked away, leaving the young men in stunned silence.

Meanwhile, the world continued coming apart at the seams.

21

"It's a no-go."

"What do you mean, *it's a no-go?*"

Deckard could feel blood throbbing in his temples.

"I can't do it."

He reached out and grabbed Aghassi by the arm.

"The hell you can't. We were in Egypt for a day and then it took four days to get back. I've seen you do the impossible with shorter timelines."

"This is different," Aghassi said. "They are different."

"You're literally killing me here."

Aghassi saw the look in his friend's eyes and knew he meant it. Despite trying to play it off the last time they met at the Chinese restaurant, Deckard was getting frayed around the edges. On top of the normal combat stress, he was working as a singleton. Piled on top was that, he was constantly undercover, even among his teammates. He was always on the job and could never let his guard down, not even for a second.

"I worked out the guard cycle at Bill's place, bypassed the three security systems he had, picked the lock, made entry into the house and poked around. His office is upstairs. I slipped a fiber optic camera under the door and spotted something."

"Spotted what?"

"A killswitch. If I trip the killswitch it will probably wipe all the drives and set off an alarm. Not only would we lose the data and compromise this entire mission, but it could put you under suspicion as well. The killswitch is rigged up to a motion and heat sensor. I couldn't even get into the same room as Bill's computer set up."

"What is the counter-measure? The next op they take me on is it. You go in there, get the data, and we call in the boys when we arrive back here in Mauritius."

"Listen Deck, I have to tell you. Someone with a security system this sophisticated is going to have PGP encryption on his drive at a minimum. I can mirror the drive and take it out with me but even if we had ten Cray super-computers decrypting it, they wouldn't be successful until our grand kids are applying for Medicare."

"Fuck me."

"I'll keep trying, but this might be a dead end."

"Then what?"

Aghassi shook his head.

"This might come down to old fashion human intelligence."

"One of them is already suspicious of me," Deckard told him. "Rick. He saw me taking photos of the device on the way out. Bill blew it off though."

"What device?"

Deckard showed him the pictures on his cell phone of the device he had recovered in Egypt. Aghassi flipped through them on Deckard's phone while getting a brief rundown on how it worked and why it had been in Egypt.

"Looks like a high energy radio frequency device. Where is it now? If you can get it to me, this could be our big break. We can use it to tap into their network."

"Too late. When our ship dropped us off in Djibouti there were a couple suits waiting on us. One took control of the three college kids to put on an airplane back home. Another took possession of the device."

"We're up shit creek."

"That isn't exactly comforting."

"Look, we've got one platoon from Samruk International in Madagascar. They hit the ground about twelve hours ago and are staging out of a hangar. They are arranging for contingency transportation to Mauritius by air and sea right now."

"Who is there?"

"Sergeant Major Korgan and Frank running things. About forty shooters total. We'll be able to call on them when we need them."

"When the time comes I'm not going to have days to wait on their ship or hours to wait for their plane," Deckard said. "It is anyone's guess who will still be standing when the smoke clears."

22

Deckard relaxed and let the current carry him.

Exhaling, bubbles escaped from around the air regulator he held in his mouth. The kelp was swept back, nearly horizontal with the sandy bottom in the strong current. His muscles were relaxed as he hung suspended in the clear blue water. Above him, ripples of yellow sunlight glimmered and cast shadows in the shallow water.

He swam underwater through the channel between two small islands. As the ocean forced itself through the channel, it created an extremely swift current. At times it was like being in a liquid treadmill as Deckard kicked with his fins but made no forward progress. Having SCUBA dived all the way upstream to the edge of the islands, he now relaxed and let the current carry him back.

The water between the two islands was shallow, maybe twenty five feet deep but with visibility that went out one hundred feet in any given direction. Now he was slowly sinking towards the bottom. Just beneath him, sand and shattered sea shells were blown with the current like tumbleweed in the desert. He inhaled, filling his lungs with oxygen. The added buoyancy was just enough for him to pop back up and rise above the sandy surface.

Small fish darted around looking for food but there was little to be found. They were fighting the current as Deckard had been, but were somewhat better suited for it.

The ocean blasted him back in the direction he had come, a half hour of swimming upstream was now a four-minute trip downstream as the horizons stayed neutral and the ocean bottom raced by below him.

Finally, he was alone.

Ten minutes later, he surfaced above the choppy waves. The wind was coming in strong, so Deckard kept his regulator in his mouth as he bobbed on the surface and kicked his way to the shore. Once he could touch the bottom, he took off his fins and snorkel, then walked in to the beach.

"How was the dive?" Nadeesha asked as she sat up and cupped her hands over her eyes to protect them from the sun.

"Good. Strong current down there today," Deckard answered as he set down his oxygen tank and began stripping out of his wetsuit.

Nadeesha, meanwhile, was completely naked as she had been sunning herself on the beach. The catamaran they had rented was rocking in the ocean one hundred meters out where they had anchored it. Gabriel Island was uninhabited, and being about eight miles off the coast of Mauritius, it seemed they had the entire island to themselves.

Deckard set his dive gear aside and sat down as the wind blew her hair in his face. Looking at her naked body, she was already the darkest shade of bronze imaginable.

"I don't know why you feel the need to tan, Nadeesha," he said.

"Call me Nadi. All my friends do."

"The guys on the team don't call you Nadi."

"They are not my friends."

"But I am?"

Her wide smile contrasted her dark complexion with her white teeth.

"Better than that," she said as she wrapped her arms around his neck and pulled him down on top of her. Nadi held him close, pressing her breasts into Deckard's bare chest. They kissed deeply, forgetting completely where or when they were.

When he pulled away, Nadi bit her upper lip.

"I think you're a little excited."

"Just a little."

She laughed at that.

"I wanted to ask you," Deckard began. "Southern India?"

"No," she laughed again. "Sri Lanka."

"I was afraid I would make a real ass out of myself and you would say Kansas City."

"No, I grew up in Sri Lanka. My dad owned the largest bottled water import business on the island. That, and his political connections with the Sri Lankan government, helped us immigrate to the US when I was a teenager. Eventually we got dual citizenship."

"What does he think of your career decision? I imagine he wanted you to go to college."

Her eyes turned hard as she looked up at him. They were still in each other's arms.

"Who cares what he thinks. I haven't talked to my family in years. He had decided that we would go to American schools. I was to go to med school and my brother would major in engineering."

"What happened?"

"I was recruited."

"What do you mean?"

"I was an athlete, even back then. Ran triathlons in college. Near the end of my sophomore year, someone took an interest in me because of the triathlons, but mostly because of my background and language ability. I did well on the tests the military gave, so I went into intel and then JSOC brought me in to work for them."

"The special cell they have?"

"That's the one. Not many women were qualified for the type of work we did, and of those that were, the others were white bread American girls except for me and one Puerto Rican girl. It was a very small group and we were pretty close. You know Special Operations. It's a sausage fest."

Now it was Deckard's turn to laugh.

"Yeah, we can be kind of sophomoric."

"Kind of?"

"Want to see my dive watch?"

Nadi sighed. "Is that the one where you pull your dick around your wrist and go around showing it to girls in the bar?"

"It's a classic. They were pretty hard on you?"

"Most guys we worked with were professional, but you still get the haters, the doubters, the people who resent you just for being there. That was an additional issue we had to deal with on top of our normal job. Besides that, they kept us deployed constantly. Seemed like eleven months out of the year we were overseas. Back-to-back deployments with no end in sight. We all kept going on them because we didn't want anyone to see us fail. A lot of the men already thought we were doomed to implode."

"You had something to prove."

"The same as any man in Special Operations, but some people couldn't see that. I got sent all over the world. They trained me as a marksman so I could infiltrate into areas and do overwatch. Sometimes I'd have to pretend to seduce some terrorist asshole in London or Bogota and then install some software on his computer. A lot of that type of thing."

"What happened?"

"They were right. We imploded. Not because we were incompetent, but because JSOC ran roughshod right over us. There were only a half dozen of us girls, and they would send us on back-to-back deployments without any time to decompress. They used and abused us until the inevitable happened. My best friend, Jennifer, she killed herself. Another girl was trying to have a baby with her husband, and after her third miscarriage she had a nervous breakdown and had to be hospitalized. Lauren got into drugs and alcohol. But nobody would throw in the towel or speak up because we knew what kind of political pressure our cell was under. Everyone wanted us to fail, but simultaneously needed us to go places and do things that the operators couldn't. I was the first to take the plunge. The writing was on the wall, so I got out while I still could."

"And came to work for Liquid Sky?"

A cloud passed in front of the sun and cast a shadow on the couple as they lay on the beach. Nadi was now able to open her eyes wider as she looked up at Deckard.

"I tried to go back to school, tried some other jobs, but I

just wasn't the same person as that nineteen year old girl that got cherry-picked out of college. They changed me. The war changed all of us, Deckard, even you."

"I wouldn't do this job if I didn't enjoy it."

"You enjoy your job, not theirs."

"I guess my motivations have always been kind of selfish."

"You're a fucking boy scout, Deckard, an obsolete joke that should have died storming the beaches at Normandy or some such shit."

"Maybe."

"Get real. No one gives a fuck about America anymore and the more loudly they talk about their patriotism the more full of shit they are. Why don't we do our own thing. Literally sail away in that boat right over there," Nadi said as she nodded towards the catamaran. "We could open our own intelligence consulting business. Travel around the world as a couple. I know from my previous work that the intel community has a huge market for that sort of thing. We could go places with that cover that others couldn't."

"You willing to put this whole Liquid Sky thing behind you?"

"I was ready a year ago. Now you've given me a reason."

"I'm a soldier, not a spy."

"You can't be a soldier forever," Nadi pulled him back down until her lips were just a few inches from his. "But together we could pull purse strings and puppet strings until we're eating applesauce and shitting ourselves in a nursing home somewhere."

"How romantic," Deckard said dryly.

"I think you'll warm to the idea."

Nadi smiled and kissed him again.

Deckard returned the kiss, knowing that one of them was destined to kill the other.

23

Admiral Russ Corbett scrolled through the messages on his cell phone as he waited in one of the booths at the back of his favorite restaurant in Washington, D.C. He was off the clock, wearing a polo shirt and khaki pants. The JSOC commander was a busy man. He oversaw the military's top priority Counter-Terrorism units as well as managed a number of highly classified special access projects nestled within his command.

At the moment, he was using Libya as a battlefield laboratory for JSOC's new ground-level architecture. The CIA's drone based targeted-killing program was falling out of favor with the administration due to political fallout in places like Yemen and Pakistan. Meanwhile, JSOC provided a working model of up-close and personal assassinations that slipped completely under the radar. The program was already spreading to Yemen and Jordan, but the bureaucrats were dragging their feet way too long with Syria. He needed to get his boys into the country so that they could start cutting the grass, otherwise Syria would become a straight-up terrorist stronghold.

Every study confirmed that the rebels would be defeated within another year by Assad's Hezbollah-backed regime, so the President finally made a decision. They would begin backing the Free Syrian Army, first only covertly, but now they would overtly assist. Still, no authorization for JSOC to play, just support. Like Angola during the Cold War, America's policy was not to win in Syria, but rather to deny the enemy an easy victory. If that sounded Machiavellian, that is because it was.

Corbett set his cell phone down as he saw his old friend approach.

"Jim," Russ Corbett said as he got to his feet and shook his friend's hand. "Thanks for coming."

"Anything for you, Russ."

As the two sat down the waiter came over to take their drink orders. Russ ordered a Blue Moon. Jim asked for a glass of water. The retired General was known to be a long-distance runner who kept an immaculate diet, even since separating from the military several years prior. The two Officers had first crossed paths way back when Jim McCoy had been the

195

commander of 2nd Ranger Battalion. Then, later, they'd worked together in JSOC. McCoy had the honor of being JSOC commander for an unprecedented six years. Someone liked him in that position. Really liked him.

Then, it all came crashing down and Corbett got tapped for the job.

To his credit, McCoy had taken it all in stride and admirably fell on the sword as the administration demanded his resignation.

"So what are you up to these days, Jim?" Russ began.

McCoy waited until the server had set their drinks down and left before speaking.

"Staying busy with my leadership courses that we run through the McCoy Group. Some solid contracts in Yemen and a few other places. What's up?"

"It is the *other places* that I'm interested in."

"You know me Russ. First and foremost, I'm a patriot. If there is anything I can do to help, you just have to ask."

"Well, this is the thing Jim, a number of people that my office has been looking at have been getting killed lately. It is too systematic to be random. I've talked to the Agency, talked to the Israelis, talked to all the players and they deny it. I've got private verification at this point as well. Whoever is behind taking down these targets is a pro."

"What are you saying?"

"I'm saying that these are our people."

The Naval officer lifted his glass of beer and took a drink. Jim McCoy's expression was unreadable. Blank. He said nothing. That's how Russ knew he was on the right track.

"I don't know what tribe they came out of, but these have to be our people. Separated from the service, working for some off-shore military contractor," Russ continued.

"I can see how you would arrive at that conclusion."

"So we're on the same page?"

"I'm afraid I don't see how I can be of any help in this matter."

The waiter interrupted their conversation as he came to take their food orders. Russ had his usual. McCoy ordered the Bison burger and asked the waiter to hold the fries. He would eat the burger with a fork and knife and leave the bun as he always did. Taking their menus, the waiter departed for the kitchen.

"The world is tearing itself apart," the retired General began. "This administration is compromising national security. In another few years he will be gone to go write his memoirs and tour the country doing speaking engagements before picking up a job in some think tank. Then guys like you and me will be left holding the mess that he created. We will have inherited an unworkable situation in the Middle East.

"He forced Mubarak out; clearly the wrong move. We had a good deal going with Gaddafi and many worked very hard to get him into our camp, but we did flip him. Then the President helps the militias overthrow him without the slightest understanding of the region and the complicated east, west, and south tribal conflict overlaid on top of sectarian issues."

Russ sighed. He dealt with it everyday and knew of the issues far too well.

"It isn't even him, Jim. Look at who his advisers are. The dynamic duo of Cass Sunstein and Samantha Powers are crafting foreign policy. This administration is way out of their league and they've got a bunch of amateurs running the show. Meanwhile, the President is content to deal with petty domestic issues because the racial stuff is what he is comfortable with. And what his staff is comfortable having him deal with."

"What do you expect from an inexperienced bureaucrat?" Jim said. "He had one term in the Senate and prior to that he was what? A community organizer? What the fuck does that even mean?"

"I fight this battle everyday, Jim. Trust me, I know. It has never been this bad. He has staffers on his National Security Council calling four star Generals in the Pentagon and reading them the riot act. It is unprecedented. The President has put out this bullshit message that he has a team of rivals working together but the reality is that he has a staff with zero national security experience calling the shots.

"I'm lucky that I have a good relationship with him, but others are not so fortunate. The Secretary of Defense can't even talk to him, he has to go through his staff. It is even worse for the Director of Central Intelligence. I admit that it is bad, but things will change after the next election."

"It isn't enough," Jim stated flatly. "Al Qaeda is not on the run, they are not backing down. We are. Meanwhile, the administration has been fomenting revolutions in the Middle East without knowing how to control or contain them. The way this is going, we're going to end up like Robespierre in the French Revolution. In the end, everyone gets their head cut off.

"We can't let some radical in the White House undo decades of work," Jim finished.

Now, Russ was starting to put together what this was about. Jim McCoy saw himself as holding together America's counter-terrorism strategy. After his unprecedented stint at JSOC commander, he was not willing to let it go, resignation or not.

"You have to let me fight this battle," Russ said. "We can negotiate with him. Then we contain him and stall his people until the next election."

"Do you know how much more damage he can do over the next couple years? We don't have that kind of time here. With or without him, we've got business to take care of. There is a group of us that are not content to sit by and watch this happen. You box him in and slow him down. I understand your position better than most. Let us do our part."

"This is going to blow up in our faces."

"Just hold the high ground as long as you can. Once he is out, there is a group of people waiting in the wings. Once the Muslim Brotherhood, Al Qaeda, and all these other idiots are done destroying each other and their countries, then we will move in. The next Presidency is going to take charge of this mess and clean things up. I'm talking about completely redrawing the map of the Middle East, redrawing it in a manner favorable to our national interests. Then we deal with Iran. Then China."

Russ found himself at a loss for words. Finally, he relented.

"That is acceptable."

When their food arrived the retired General and the Admiral made small talk. Jim was thinking about teaching a few classes at Harvard or Yale. He was also thinking about political office himself one day, which had been obvious to Russ. Jim McCoy had been feeling out both parties to see which one would give him a better deal. But that would be further down the line, not the next election, maybe the one after that.

Russ talked about his family, his wife and their three kids. One was already in college, the other two in High School.

They relived a few war stories from the Task Force days in Iraq back when McCoy was the JSOC commander and the Admiral worked under him. Finally, they caught up on the careers and gossip of various other Officers they knew.

When Russ asked for the bill, Jim told him he already took care of it.

They stood up to leave and made their way to the door.

"There is one other thing," Russ said. He closed the distance and spoke in Jim's ear. "The targets that I have getting killed. Their bodies are usually mutilated. In the same manner. Scalpings, top of the heads shot off, shit like that."

"Oh yeah?"

"You know anything about that?"

While not widely known, Corbett had been a Dev Group commander back when the unit was first formed. He had been kicked out of the unit after receiving a vote of no confidence from his men. The reason for the no confidence vote was because he had refused to engage in mutually compromising behavior.

"Do I want to know anything about that?" McCoy restated the question as they walked out the door and onto the sidewalk. "Listen, Russ. Sometimes you need bad people to go after other bad people. You know that."

"This is a little excessive."

"The only way to get things done in this political climate. The type of people who do this type of work are not like you and me. That is just the reality of sending people on what they know is a suicide mission. But just like the Arabs, they will continue to fight each other and all die in the process. The hell with it."

Jim patted his old friend on the back.

"It is what it is, Russ. Let me worry about these things, huh?"

"If you say so Jim."

"I do," the retired General said as he walked off. "And by the way, watch your ass around those journalists okay? They will be the death of you."

24

"Deckard!" Nadi shouted. "Deckard, wake up!"

As she shook him, Deckard bolted upright into a sitting position as he was startled awake. He was struggling to catch his breath as if he had just sprinted for a mile.

"Deckard, you're hurting me," Nadi said as she grabbed his forearm.

It was only then that Deckard realized that he had her wrist in a death grip. He had gripped her so strongly in his sleep that he had left bruises on her.

"You were having a nightmare," she whispered.

Deckard laid back down and tried to catch his breath.

"What were you dreaming about?"

"I don't know," Deckard said.

"It's okay, go back to sleep."

Nadi ran her hand down his chest.

They had several days to themselves now. Bill was talking about putting the entire team on leave for a couple weeks. Then, earlier that night they got an urgent request. A repeat customer, the Kingdom of Bahrain.

Tomorrow it was back to work.

Deckard held Nadi as she drifted off in his arms. He stared at the ceiling until the sun came up.

Liquid Sky hit the ground at Isa Air Base in Bahrain at 9:52PM local time. Two liaison officers from Nerve met them to drive the team to the company's headquarters. Nerve's CEO was the former commander of America's 160th Special Operations Aviation Regiment at Ft. Campbell, Kentucky, however the company itself was owned by the UAE. Emiratizing certain functions of private military companies was looked upon favorably by those who gave those companies mandates involving U.S. national security.

The tarmac on Isa Air base was covered with dozens of American F-16 fighter jets, backlit by the golden runway lights. The fighter jets were standing by, just in case something popped off.

The team was driven in two black SUVs heading north on King Hamad highway. Through the night they traveled up the length of the island to Manamah. The island of Bahrain had a population of only 1.2 million but only half of them were actual natives of Bahrain. In addition to hosting U.S. forces in the Isa Air Base, Bahrain was also home to the U.S. 5th Fleet. The strategic importance of the island Kingdom to the United States could not be over emphasized. Then there was the Saudi issue.

As the saying went in Saudi Arabia, "Allah does not see across the bridge." Taking the causeway across fourteen miles of ocean, Saudis would stop at the liquor stores located on the Bahrain side of the bridge before heading to the discotheques and club life on the island. In Saudi Arabia it wasn't easy for young men to find ways to spend their leisure money, but in Bahrain there was plenty of alcohol, and Russian prostitutes, to be found if you knew where to look.

The Arab Spring had taken Bahrain by storm starting in 2011 and this was a major concern to Saudi Arabia. Like Bahrain, Saudi Arabia was a kingdom, not a democracy. Like Bahrain, Saudi Arabia had a troublesome problem. The Royal family in Saudi Arabia was Sunni and had a Shia minority population on their eastern coast, one that had revolted in the past during the late 1970s and 80s. Bahrain had a Sunni Royal family that ruled over a Shia majority that made up as much as 70% of their country.

When protestors first began taking to the streets and occupying the Pearl roundabout in Manama, the Royal family of Bahrain responded with a crackdown, arresting and even shooting protestors who were demanding liberalization and increased representation in government. Unknown to much of the West, many Shia Muslims in the Middle East suffered under inequities not unlike black Americans had in the United States in the 1950's.

The killing of protestors created even larger protest movements as Shias rallied around the funerals of their dead. The demonstrations grew stronger and stronger. Various camps within the Shia movement demanded not just political reforms, but a revolution that included the removal of Bahrain's Royal family.

Saudi Arabia, perhaps the most medieval and repressive country in the Middle East, knew they had similar issues on the home front with their Shia minority, a minority that lived in squalor and poverty despite the immense oil wealth that the country produced. The Sunni fears in Saudi Arabia were that if the Kingdom of Bahrain fell to the Arab Spring, that the Saudi Royal family would be next on the chopping block.

Sure enough, the protests movement soon spread from Bahrain to the eastern villages of Saudi Arabia. The Saudi Royal family moved to secure their flank by deploying the Saudi National Guard to Bahrain. Armored personnel carriers and armed troops rolled across the causeway linking the two kingdoms to help Bahrain repress the protestors as the movement continued to gain steam.

With a strict media blackout imposed on Bahrain, and Western media intentionally not reporting on the crack downs because of American oil and defense interests in the region, things seemed to quiet down some. Then, when riot police in Bahrain shot and killed several teenage demonstrators, the entire Shia uprising kicked into high gear once again. In a country of only 600,000 it was estimated that nearly 100,000 were protesting in the streets each night.

The Royal family of Bahrain was teetering on the brink.

Shia protestors might have wanted their freedom, but Saudi Arabia was determined to control their own Shia problem and by extension that of Bahrain. The United States and Britain had geo-strategic interests which overrode the call for democracy. This pointed out the absurdity of the West supporting so-called democracy movements in Libya, Syria, and Egypt, all while suppressing them elsewhere.

This was when Liquid Sky was called in to help deal with the problem.

Their vehicles pulled into a walled compound within the city and parked. The two liaison officers from Nerve then walked them into the office. Liquid Sky knew this was another low visibility operation and wore civilian clothes, but civilian employees scooted to the edge of the hall to let them pass. The six-man and one-woman team made an impression.

The team was brought to a conference room and introduced to a lanky, tall American who wore a dress shirt with the sleeves rolled up and a blue-striped tie.

"Lance Klein, director of special activities," he said as he took turns shaking each of their hands. Bill took a seat without waiting to be told to.

"What are we looking at Lance?"

"Well, we've got quite a mess on our hands here," Lance said as he opened his laptop and brought up a map of Bahrain which was projected onto the screen behind him. "We've got belligerents flooding the streets and threatening the Royal family. Our firm has been hired to monitor and do the statistical analysis, which is easy since the belligerents are using Twitter and Facebook to organize. We also have access to private cell phone traffic with the Kingdom's consent but things are getting out of control. The Royal family is scared, which makes the Saudis scared, which makes the United States scared."

"What does that got to do with us?" Bill said, hurrying to get to the point.

"Listen," Lance said holding a hand up in front of him to stop Bill for a moment. "Don't tell me anything I don't want to know. The Royal family instructed Nerve to brief a team they have flying in on specifics about individual groups of belligerents in their country. What you do with that information is none of our business."

Deckard noted the repeated use of the word belligerent rather than protestor, much less pro-democracy protestor.

"Go on."

"There are three main camps within the belligerents who are staging this public disturbance," Lance began. Deckard rolled his eyes. "We have the leftist nationalist group Wa'ad, the Islamist group al-Wafiq, and a banned Islamist political party called Wafa. All three have now transitioned from calling for *islah*, or reform, to demanding *isqat*, the fall of the current regime."

Lance briefly walked them through the key personalities of each of the three groups and where they were located based on Nerve's targeting data, most of it based on cellular intercepts. His analysis was that all three groups were now acting as agents of, or at least under the heavy influence of, the Iranian supported terrorist organization known as Hezbollah. Deckard had no idea if this was true, or if Lance was merely telling his employer what they wanted to hear. The Royal family would no doubt like to paint the protestors as being malevolent agents working at the behest of some foreign power rather than address the real grassroots anger on display against their regime.

"The British maintain some home field advantage here," Lance continued, "since Bahrain is a former colony. They've been very good about keeping Al-Jeezera where they want them. After helping to oust Mubarak, they've been kept quiet about what is happening here in Bahrain. Much of the police force that is out every night enforcing curfew has come from another former British colony, Pakistan. The British also maintain a strong presence in Bahrain's National Security Agency and we've found that our interests align well with the Brits.

"With things looking bleak out on the streets, the Saudis are sending more of their National Guard to help control the protests, which are turning into riots. The UAE also has a battalion-sized strike team on call if the Royal family decides they need them.

"At the end of the day, we are playing a zero-sum game here. The police go out to crack down on the riots and kill some of the belligerents. This incites them even further, they rally around the funerals in outrage and then return back to the streets with renewed strength. Every one of them that the security forces kill has the effect of recruiting ten more. This cycle has to be broken, and frankly, Bahrain's security and intelligence services are not up to the challenge. They have relied on the United States and other countries for their defense for too long, and in this situation it is politically embarrassing for America to have their ally cracking down on demonstrators who claim to be pro-democracy.

"Providing direct support to Bahrain to help quell this movement is a political impossibility," Lance finished.

"I guess that is where we come in," Zach said as he cracked his knuckles.

With their in-country brief complete, Liquid Sky was led back to their vehicles and driven to a second compound somewhere within the city. They were met there by another American named Todd Perry. The compound he operated out of was a medium-sized residence that had been converted into his field headquarters. As he led the team inside, he told them how he had been the police chief of Miami until retiring a few years ago and getting hired by the Royal family as the Arab Spring picked up momentum.

"Nerve does information," he told Bill as they walked down the hall. "I'm an operations adviser to the Bahrain Defense Force Intelligence agency, Bahrain's National Security Agency, and the Ministry of the Interior's Criminal Investigations Department. Some of these guys have proper training, some don't but none of them are at the level of American Special Operations. Not by a long shot. That is why I advised that we bring in some professional outside help."

"We got a brief on the targets back at Nerve."

"Good. Now I want to emphasis that I called in technicians, specialists like you, because I want the leaders of the opposition movement brought in, but I want them brought in alive. We have several contingencies, but at this stage any fatalities will only make the situation worse. Bring them in quickly and quietly and they will disappear into a state-run prison for twenty or thirty years until things have died down. Way down the line we'll spring them as a part of some future political deal. That is how these things work. Then they get to go live in exile in Iran or some other camel-fucker country."

"No promises," Bill insisted. "If these guys are backed by Hezbollah, things could get ugly out there."

"I get that, but also understand that I have had significant bonuses approved for each of you if you complete this operation within the parameters I just described."

"How significant?" Ramon asked.

"One hundred large."

"Damn."

"Per operator. Bahrain shares an oil field with Saudi Arabia. Money is of little consequence."

Perry showed them into his arms room.

"Christmas comes early boys," the former police chief said.

He wasn't joking. Money really was no object. There was rack after rack lined with top of the line carbines and rifles. Crates of ammo lined the walls. There were grenade launchers, rocket launchers, good old fashion hand grenades. None of it was American for reasons of keeping their mission sterile.

"Load up," Bill ordered. "Looks like we're going on safari tonight."

Liquid Sky began reaching for weapons and ammunition while Perry sat down on a stool and watched.

"Yup," the former police chief said. "Reminds me of the good old days when we would have to have our batons weighed prior to going and breaking up protests in Miami. After they weighed in correctly we would go to the next room and drill them so we could drop lead rods down inside. Those were the days.

"Ha, better than my grandfather's time on the force. Back then, the cops would just handcuff niggers to fire hydrants and beat them within an inch of their life!"

Deckard grabbed an AK-47 and then started shoving full magazines into a chest rig he found in one of the boxes. He also palmed a handful of grenades and stuck them in pouches.

"Body armor is in another box down the hall," Perry informed them. "Haven't tested the plates. Don't want to."

"I'm on it," Deckard volunteered as the team continued to arm up.

He had to scrub this mission before it ever got off the ground.

Outside the armory, Deckard hurried out the front door

to the courtyard where their vehicles were parked. It was the oldest trick in the book. He pulled the pin on one of his hand grenades and then jammed it behind the tire on one of the two SUVs they had arrived in. With the spoon on the grenade held down as it was pinned between the tire and the vehicle, the grenade would remain as it was until they started driving.

He then headed back inside and went to retrieve the body armor. Locating the box in a room at the end of the hall, he first brought the ceramic trauma plates and set them down in the armory, then went back for the nylon carriers that also contained the soft body armor inside. The plates would go into pouches on the outside of the blue vests.

A few more minutes were spent squaring away their kit. Everyone had AK-47s so they would remain consistent and would be able to exchange ammunition. Everyone seemed to find a different handgun though, from Glocks to Berettas. Deckard claimed a Smith and Wesson M&P pistol for himself. With a little luck, he wouldn't have to use any of his guns this time around.

He wasn't naive. Deckard had seen enough of the Middle East to be deeply skeptical of the region's ability to join the modern world, but he also wasn't some thug for hire. It wasn't his job to suppress pro-democracy movements when people were suffering under an archaic monarchy. Now he was at the point where Liquid Sky's mission was conflicting with his own undercover operations to take down the hit team and discover who their puppet master was.

Bill had a three-ring binder with overhead imagery of the three target areas they were to hit. Opening the book, he had the team gather around for some hasty mission planning. Al-Wafiq was the first group they would target; they would expressly go after their leadership cell for a capture, and only a kill if it became necessary as per Perry's guidelines. Al-Wafiq was the group suspected to be the most deeply involved with Hezbollah and the group they would expect the most resistance from.

The al-Wafiq headquarters, their first target, was located to the south in Tabil. Then, in generally a diagonal line, target two was in Manama and target three was further north on the island of Muharraq. Bill pointed out their first target on the map. The building was not the party's official headquarters as the group had gone clandestine when the Saudi troops helped the largely Pakistani police force of Bahrain in the crackdowns. Nerve's intelligence indicated that the leadership cell of al-Wafiq was holed up in the basement *madrassa* where Shia school children were taught.

"The building is at the end of a dead-end street," Ramon said. "Choosing that location was a tactical decision. Only one way in or out."

"We will off set here," Bill pointed up the block. "Leave the vehicles and move on foot for better dispersal. We don't want to get taken out by a single RPG."

"Nerve will be feeding me intel updates in real time," Perry piped up. "I'll then keep you guys up to date. They want to use me as a cut out to relay information so those pussies can keep their hands clean."

"Whatever," Rick said as he rocked a magazine into the mag well of his AK.

"What do you have around here for manual breaching tools?" Bill asked Perry.

"A whole kit in the corner over there. Battering ram, sledge, bolt cutters, hoolie tool."

"Zach, take the battering ram. Divide the rest of it amongst yourselves and then we roll out."

Once everyone was kitted up, Perry walked them to the door.

"Have fun bashing in some skulls," he told Liquid Sky. "Wish I was coming with."

"I'll have a few of the girls scream your name so you don't feel as bad," Paul said as he walked by.

Deckard got into the back seat of the rear vehicle. The SUVs had been upgraded with an armor package that would defeat most small arms and shrapnel, but you never knew for sure.

Paul waved goodbye to Perry and got behind the driver's seat of the lead vehicle. Turning the ignition, he let the truck inch forward while one of Perry's people opened the front gate for them. No one noticed the grenade drop and Deckard made sure he kept still and didn't telegraph his knowledge.

The explosion washed out from under the lead vehicle, blowing out all four tires. A piece of flak spider-webbed the windshield on the second SUV. His ear were ringing as Deckard got out of the second vehicle and ran forward to help. Paul stumbled out of the truck followed by Bill. Ramon took one step out and tripped. Deckard ran over and helped him up.

"You okay?"

"What?" Ramon's ears were ringing too.

"Get off the X!" Bill shouted.

Deckard and Ramon ran to the open door where Perry was just picking himself up off the ground. They secured the entrance while the rest of the team flowed inside the hard point the structure. Bill was the last in and slammed the door behind him before locking it.

"We're compromised."

"What the hell?" Perry asked.

"It had to be one of your monkeys," Bill said to Perry. "You got a mole in your network."

"I've had these locals on my payroll for months now."

"That is the problem, you stopped vetting them. This operation is a fucking abortion. Over before it even got off the ground."

Bill pulled out his cell phone and made a phone call.

"Fuck this shit," Zach muttered.

Nerve picked up on the second ring.

"It's me. We need extraction back to the airport," Bill said. "We're compromised."

He paused for a minute while someone on the other end talked.

"This is non-negotiable. Perry's operation here is blown and I'm pulling my team out of the contract."

Another pause.

"Roger, just send vehicles. We'll drive ourselves out."

Liquid Sky continued to hard point inside the building while they waited. Several of Perry's Bahraini employees were unceremoniously tossed out the front door and locked out. When Nerve's second set of SUV's arrived from their corporate fleet of vehicles, Liquid Sky ran outside, hauled the drivers out and sped off towards the airport.

Deckard sat in the passenger seat of the lead vehicle while Zach drove. Nadi and Bill sat in the back seats. Zach gunned it, pushing ninety miles per hour as they sped south.

Everything was going according to plan.

They were just arriving outside Isa Air Base when Bill received another phone call. He listened to whoever was on the other end for a full minute before speaking.

"Zach," their team leader said. "Turn us around."

"What?"

"Things have changed?"

Zach slowed down and spun the wheel, rolling them over the median and then heading in the opposite direction. Deckard's hands formed fists.

Fuck.

Bill hung up the phone.

"We are not working directly for Nerve. The Royal family shat ten different kind of bricks when they found out we were canceling our contract."

"And our rates?" Zach asked.

"Tripled. They could have brought in someone else but there is no time. The bodies are stacking up around the Pearl roundabout. Three hours ago the Saudi military fired tear gas into an alleyway and a couple teenagers died of asphyxia. The protest then turned into a massive riot that scattered those weak-kneed camel fuckers from Saudi Arabia. The counterattack happened just minutes ago. 300 protestors were shot and killed. The whole fucking country is about to be on fire."

"Holy shit," Zach cursed. "You ain't kidding."

Deckard saw it, the orange glow emanating from the city ahead of them. It wasn't street lights, it was fire.

"People are finding out about the mass killing on their smart phones from social media. The Royal family is about to shut down internet access but the damage has already been done. We're up. The mission parameters just changed from capture to kill."

"Even better," Nadi remarked.

Deckard looked out the window as Bahrain went up in flames.

Things had just gotten a whole lot more complicated.

25

"The problem is, all three of our targets are united in opposition to our employer. They want us to not just take out the leadership cells, but to turn the survivors of each group against each other," Bill said. "Deckard and Nadeesha, you both know Arabic. I want you to hand jam some notes that we can stick into the pockets of the dead bodies we are about to make."

"Plant some pocket litter that will make it look like the three target groups sold each other out to the regime," Nadeesha said.

"Exactly."

Deckard looked in the glove compartment for a piece of paper.

"This is sloppy as fuck," Deckard said.

"Yeah, it is," Bill agreed. "But this little conspiracy we are creating doesn't have to hold up in court, it just has to survive long enough to get al-Wafiq, Wafa, and Wa'ad killing each other to break the momentum of this protest movement. Then the regime can shore up their base."

"But who really gives a fuck as long as we get paid," Nadi said.

"Exactly," Zach agreed.

"I guess we won't be here to deal with the aftermath anyway," Deckard said, going along with the idea.

As Zach drove them north to their first target in Tubil, the two vehicle convoy had to make a hard right to avoid the roadblock up ahead. Protestors had piled burning tires in the middle of the street, and the toxic black smoke created a haze in the air. Human forms could be seen skulking around the streets, back lit by the fires.

Using the Garmin GPS mounted to the windshield, Zach quickly found an alternate route. The orange light from the fires could be seen above the rooftops as they skirted through the narrow streets. If you were not in an area where the rioting was happening, it seemed like the roads were completely empty. Zach bumped back up to Al Quds Avenue and had to make another abrupt turn. Several dozen people were clogging both lanes of traffic. Someone was shooting a gun in the air.

Going back into a residential neighborhood, he cut a couple more turns and got them into their target neighborhood.

They parked the trucks five blocks away from the target building, locked them up, and moved out on foot. The Liquid Sky team could hear the riots in the distance, not to mention see the orange embers of the fires floating up into the night sky. The neighborhood they were in was seemingly deserted, while the island itself was going up like a Roman candle.

As they hit the target street, the team silently split up, each half of the group taking one side of the street. In this manner, they could pull cross coverage. The lead shooter in each column covered their front while those behind pointed their rifles across the street, scanning the rooftops above their teammates' heads for enemy snipers or scouts. The target building was ahead, a large compound at the end of a cul-de-sac.

Deckard scanned the rooftops as he crept down the street behind Zach, his AK sweeping from side to side, looking for threats in the shadows. The heat, the dust, the empty Arab street. It felt like a thousand other objectives in a hundred different cities in the Middle East. Or so it seemed.

Al-Wafiq was supposedly hiding in the target building. They were the resistance organization that was the closest aligned with Hezbollah, and the one that espoused the most extremist views of Islamic fundamentalism. Just because you were opposed to the Royal family didn't necessarily mean you were a good guy.

Suddenly, Zach came to a halt, his rifle pointed in an upward angle towards the target building. He squeezed off a single shot and someone screamed from the rooftop of the target building. Rather than maintain a stand off from the building, Zach took off running towards it, firing off several more shots in the process. Bill, who was the point man for the column on the other side of the street followed suit, sprinting for the objective.

Deckard tried to keep up; catching something in the corner of his eye. Movement on another rooftop to his flank, above Bill's line of sight. Deckard paused, pivoted his hips towards the movement and gained target acquisition. The man up on the roof also had an AK in his hands and was looking to get an angle of fire on Bill or Zach. He hadn't noticed Deckard in the shadows directly to his front.

Deckard fired two rounds center mass.

The shooter went limp, the rifle falling from his hands and clattering to the street below. He then pitched forward over the lip of the roof and somersaulted through the air before flopping into the street on his back.

Paul nearly bumped into Deckard as he turned and ran to catch up with Zach. His sneakers pounded the pavement as the entire street erupted with muzzle flashes, gunfire crisscrossing through the street. With bullets kicking up clouds of dust right behind him, Deckard arrived at the entrance of the target building.

Zach already had the hooligan tool stuck in the door jam. Bill had the battering ram and swung it against the hoolie tool, using it as a giant lever to blast open the door. Deckard took up a security position next to Zach and began firing over Paul's head as he ran towards them. Deckard shot just below the muzzle flashes he saw on the rooftops, knowing that people had a tendency to aim high when firing at night.

Bill took a couple of swings, and the door began to shatter. Dropping the battering ram, he added a few mule kicks and the door finally cracked open. Paul, Nadeesha, Ramon, and Rick joined the team as they pushed inside as fast as possible.

Inside, women were screaming. A shadow moved across the living room. Bill fired and the form collapsed. Gunfire blasted the team from an adjoining doorway. Ramon pulled the pin on a grenade and rolled it into the other room.

"Frag out!"

They braced themselves as the explosion shook the building. Stacking on the door, they flowed in and found two gunmen on the ground with AKs next to them. The frag grenade had nearly taken off the leg of one of them. The other's eyes bulged out of his skull.

Ramon found a door and edged up to it. He had no way of knowing if the door led up to the second floor, or down into the basement where the *madrassa* was located. Standing off to the side while opening the door proved to be a good idea. Gunfire from the basement tore up and through the wooden door when Ramon began to open it.

Priming another grenade, Ramon kicked the door the rest of the way open and tossed the grenade down the stairs. There were a few excited shouts from below in Arabic before the frag blew. The sickly sweet smell of sulfur and blood seeped up from below.

Paul and Rick were firing back into the room they had just come from as fighters began pouring in from outside and from the second floor.

"Paul, Rick, Nadeesha, stay up here and maintain a foothold. The rest of us are going downstairs."

"We'll be here," Rick promised.

Ramon took point as he descended into the basement with Bill, Deckard, and Zach on his heels. A single bare bulb swung from the ceiling, the rest of the lights had exploded from the blast. Deckard almost tripped over a corpse that lay sprawled on the floor. A few other bodies were still moaning and twitching. Bill and Zach finished them off with short, clipped bursts from their rifles.

The floor was covered with prayer rugs and a bookshelf against the wall was filled with Korans and other study material for the students of Islam who would ordinarily meet there for instruction.

Zach put a few shots into the groin of one of the bodies. Ramon did the same.

Bill started taking pictures of the faces of the four bodies with his cell phone. More gunfire sounded from above as the rest of the Liquid Sky team held their position. Thankfully, it didn't take long for Nerve to text Bill with a confirmation.

"Okay," Bill said as he kicked one of the bodies with his foot. "This one is the Wafiq leader. Deckard, start writing up some pocket litter to plant on him and at least one of the other corpses. You've got two minutes."

Deckard started scribbling with a pen on scraps of paper he had found in the SUV. His Arabic writing would not pass for a native's by any stretch of the imagination. As Bill had said, it didn't have to hold up under forensic investigation, just had to plant the seed of doubt in the al-Wafiq followers for a day or two.

He wrote two notes, both of them in Arabic. Both saying that al-Wafiq was being set up along with the other opposition groups and not to fall for the trap the Royal family had laid for them. Deckard didn't much care for some Hezbollah-linked Islamist group, but he would still undermine the overall anti-democracy mission anyway he could. One note was shoved into the pocket of the al-Wafiq leader, the other went into the pocket of one of the other dead men.

"You done?" Bill asked.

"Good to go," Deckard answered.

Running the gauntlet again through the street was out of the question for Liquid Sky.

Joining Nadeesha, Paul, and Rick on the ground floor, the team knew that they had completed their objective and now had the more difficult task of escaping the death trap they had walked into. Paul and Rick recovered their breaching equipment from the entrance while the others cleared the rest of the structure. The security team left on the ground floor had made a lot of dead bodies while Deckard was downstairs scribbling notes.

There was an alley between the compound and the adjacent house that looked like it led to a side street. Zach noticed it, but Bill shot the idea down. He didn't relish the thought of scooting through a one-foot-wide alley while the enemy was above them on the rooftops. One burst of auto-fire or a single grenade and the entire team would be toast.

Instead, Bill had them clear upstairs. At the top of the stairs, Deckard caught one Wafiq gunman trying to come in through a window after jumping over from the building next door. He put a burst of 7.62 into his chest and the fighter was flung back out of the window. Moving to the window, Deckard placed himself along the wall and took a glance outside, exposing as little of himself as possible.

A few dark figures bolted across the street about fifty meters away. There was some shouting back and forth but not much incoming fire. The enemy was slowly probing them while they waited for reinforcements to show up. Liquid Sky didn't want to be there when that happened.

Using the window the gunman had tried to enter from, Deckard showed Bill a way out onto the adjacent rooftop. One by one they ledged out and onto the rooftop while there was a lull in fire. The enemy was simply trying to box them in and hold out until they could call in an entire al-Wafiq mob on them. Once the team made it to the next door neighbor's roof, they leaped from rooftop to rooftop and then down onto the next street over.

Moving quickly into a single file line, they squeezed through another alley to put another block of houses between them and the al-Wafiq compound as fast as possible. Jogging over to the SUVs, everyone got inside and gently eased the doors shut.

"Holy shit," Paul said he as looked over his shoulder. Behind them was an entire mob, hundreds of rioters holding up banners and pickets with Arabic writing. The crowd was illuminated by the torches they carried. The mob shouted Islamist chants in unison.

"Time to get the fuck out of Dodge," Zach said as he started the engine.

The two SUVs raced off with the riot nipping at their heels.

26

What should have been a twenty-minute drive to Manama took almost an hour as their drivers had to take so many back roads to avoid the riots. Several times, they almost got caught by an approaching crowd only to speed away just as flying rocks and the occasional gunshot was sent their way. After detouring around the highway several times, Bill instructed the two drivers to just jump the curb and take side streets the rest of the way to the next target building.

From the passenger seat, Bill leaned back and showed them an overhead satellite picture of their target. The location was from the latest cell phone lock reported from Nerve; the map was simple commercial imagery.

"This is the next target," Bill told them. "Wa'ad."

The old school leftist political group still around from during the 1980's.

"We will pull up on the target street this time and head right down to the front door, situation dependent of course."

Deckard took one look at the objective area as Zach drove over a dead body laying in the street.

"There is a clear egress route out the back heading down the street to the west," Deckard pointed out. "I'll cut off the escape route."

"Fine. Take Zach with you."

Zach nodded as they continued to drive, "We're just a few minutes out."

The blacked-out sports utility vehicles pulled to the side of the road and stopped as they closed on the target. They were in the middle class neighborhood of sand-colored two and three story homes. Satellite dishes were on nearly every rooftop. Dark pools of brown water fermented along the side of the street.

Zach and Deckard jogged down an alleyway, dodging the air conditioner units that stuck out from windows as they moved to cover on the back side of the objective building. They arrived at the side street after having broken a sweat. Gunfire was popping off somewhere in the distance.

Pulling out his cell phone, Zach called Bill.

"We're in position."

Bill would now be moving his element with the other four Liquid Sky shooters down the street to breach the objective and kill the Wa'ad members inside.

Deckard pointed his AK-47 up at one of the rooftops and squeezed off two shots in rapid succession. Zach cringed as the shots caught him off guard.

"Saw a guy up there with a gun," Deckard told him.

It was a blatant lie. He had just fired off a few warning shots to whoever was home, deliberately compromising their objective and costing them the element of surprise. He could hear Bill screaming over the cell phone at Zach.

"We just took someone out," Zach told Bill, knowing better than to mention names. "Someone squirting off the objective."

The line went dead and Zach pocketed the phone. The former Navy SEAL looked back at Deckard with his blond hair plastered against his forehead due to perspiration.

"Got a bad feeling about this one."

"Me too," Deckard said knowing that he was pushing the envelope harder than he ever had before. It was unlikely that he would get away with it.

The staccato bursts of gunfire rattled windows throughout the neighborhood. It was coming from the opposite side of the objective. Liquid Sky had made contact. Their Kalashnikov rifles answered in kind.

Seconds later, footsteps came beating down the side street towards Zach. The two mercenaries had both taken a knee next to the walls of houses alongside the narrow street.

"Here they come," Zach said as he flipped the selector on his AK-47 from safe to semi.

Deckard did the same, then oriented the weapon away from the Wa'ad members heading towards them. Aiming down the rifle's rear sight, he lined it up with the front sight post. His hands shook as he pulled the trigger.

The single shot blasted into the back of Zach's head and immediately dropped him. He was dead before his body hit the ground.

The Wa'ad members stumbled as they tried to slow down and stop as the gunshot rang out right in front of them.

"You're safe," Deckard said in Arabic. "You are not in danger from me."

Six Arabs moved forward carefully as Deckard emerged from the shadows. All of them were carrying rifles or pistols. One of them stepped forward to confront Deckard. He was perhaps sixty years old and had a thick bushy mustache.

"Who are you?"

"I just saved your life," Deckard pointed towards Zach's body. The head wound had gushed blood all over the street.

"You are American?"

"Yes," Deckard answered. "Part of a team hired to kill you and your group."

"So why are we talking?"

"I've had a change of allegiance."

More gunfire rattled out from the objective building. Liquid Sky was still being engaged by other Wa'ad members in the area.

"We don't have much time," Deckard told the leader of the group. "You need to know that you and the other resistance groups are being set up. Turned against each other by propaganda and lies. They are trying to make it look like Wafiq, Wafa, and Wa'ad have all turned on each other. Do not believe the lies."

"I don't understand."

"You will. Call your contacts in Wafa and warn them that we will be coming to kill them next. Warn them so they can get away. You can continue to work with them against the Royal family."

"I don't believe this," the older man said.

"I understand. Just run. Make that phone call when you get to a safe place, just to be sure."

"I will."

With a wave of his hand, he motioned his Wa'ad brothers forward. They ran past him and down the side street.

"I don't believe you Amriki," the old man said. "But if it turns out that you are telling me the truth, then God be with you."

"And with you," Deckard said. "But I think God has left me to my own devices this time."

The arab looked at Deckard long and hard. Finally, he turned and ran to catch up with his comrades.

Deckard wasn't looking forward to what was coming next. Reaching into his kit, he palmed a hand grenade. Pulling the pin he held down the spoon and carefully placed himself just outside the blast radius of the grenade from where he would throw it next to Zach's body.

Holding his breath, Deckard tossed the grenade as the spoon flew into the air. Rolling into the fetal position, he lay on the ground facing away from the grenade and jammed his fingers in his ears while slightly opening his mouth to help equalize the pressure.

It didn't help him any when the blast rolled over him and everything went black.

Deckard opened his eyes.

He felt like he had been hit by a truck. Lifting his head up off the ground, his mind struggled to make sense of what was happening. He heard someone calling his name. The voice sounded distant and faint. Then it was suddenly right in his ear as someone was trying to lift him up.

"Deckard!"

Nadeesha cradled his head in her hands. His eyes focused and he realized he was laying in the street. Men dressed in para-military gear were standing over him. Deckard managed to get out a single word.

"Zach."

The big man standing over him shook his head. It was Bill.

"You guys got hit with a grenade. You're lucky to be alive."

Paul pushed Nadeesha out of the way. Bending over, he grabbed Deckard under the armpits and helped him to his feet.

Deckard found that he could stand but was shaky on his feet. Rick picked up Deckard's AK-47 and looked it over before handing it over to him.

"Looks like the magazine got blown out but the receiver is still good."

Bill and Paul watched him try to reload the AK. He was sloppy as hell. It felt like he was wearing Hamburger Helper mittens.

Bill leaned down and picked up Zach. Dead weight, wearing body armor, was completely different than carrying a live person, but Bill didn't even flinch as he flopped the body over his shoulder.

"Let's go," the Liquid Sky leader said.

Paul placed a palm in the small of Deckard's back and pushed him forward toward the vehicles. They navigated the streets to the black SUVs and got inside. Deckard found that his head was beginning to clear. He was still alive. Still alive, still a member of Liquid Sky. For now. The grenade blast had covered up the fact that he had executed Zach. The body was mangled enough by fragmentation that Bill could not tell that he had been killed by a shot to the back of the head.

Deckard's state when the team arrived at the scene of the killing had alleviated him from suspicion.

With Zach's body loaded in the back of the truck, Bill took the wheel and led out, heading for their third target of the night. It was the Wafa political party headquarters to the north of the island on Muharraq.

"Deckard," Bill said as he drove. "I know you just got blown up but you can pick your weeping vagina off the ground when we get back home. Put in a TBI claim with VA or some shit, I don't care, but don't puss out on us."

"I'm good," Deckard said even though he only half believed it. "Just tell me where you need me."

Bill made a phone call to Nerve while he drove.

"We're en route to the third objective," he said to someone on the other end of the line. "Is the bridge to Muharraq open?"

He paused while someone talked.

"Okay, I'm pulling over."

Bill pulled on to the shoulder of the road, the second SUV pulling up behind them.

"The military has road blocks up on both bridges," Bill informed them. "We have to wait a minute for Nerve to get commo through to make a hole for us. Otherwise those Pakistani monkeys will open fire on us."

The cell phone rang two minutes later.

"Yeah?" Bill said as he picked up.

A few seconds passed while he listened.

"Got it."

Terminating the call, Bill pulled back onto the road. A half mile later they were at the bridge. An armored personnel carrier manned by Pakistani mercenaries chugged to life and blasted out a plume of black smoke as it drove forward on its treads to clear the road for the two Liquid Sky vehicles. The camouflaged soldiers stood guard with rifles at the ready, dressed in full battle rattle for when the rioters showed up.

Liquid Sky shot across the bridge. The water between the two islands looked like glass in the night. Golden light from the tall buildings near the shore bounced off the sea. Another Pakistani road block moved out of the way on the other side of the bridge, allowing them to pass onto Muharraq.

Unlike Manama, the streets of Muharraq did not follow a grid pattern but wound around neighborhoods in a haphazard manner. Some of the main streets were absolutely flooded with rioters. Cars were tipped over, storefronts smashed. Pakistani riot-control police moved forward with shields, batons, and face shields as they attempted to control the Shia majority that had gotten fed up with being second-class citizens. With the Royal family of Bahrain now gunning them down, the protest had taken on a new, and violent, flavor.

Bill avoided the large crowds, again staying on the side streets as much as possible. After making a couple hard turns through the urban sprawl, the streets simply became too narrow for them to drive down. According to the Garmin GPS on the dashboard they were only a block away from the Wafa headquarters so they again locked up the vehicles and moved out on foot.

Liquid Sky was now one gun short. With the team in disarray, Bill took the lead. Losing a team member always mind-fucked the survivors mid-mission even if they tried to pretend otherwise. Nadeesha seemed relieved to see Deckard walking without assistance, his rifle held at the low ready. The team weaved through the streets for the third time that night. It was getting late, maybe another three hours of night left before dawn.

Approaching the target building, there was clearly a Wafa party banner hung up outside. Officially they were a banned political party, but in the last twenty-four hours, the law no longer carried the weight it once had. There was a movement under way, one that turned into a riot after hundreds of them were mowed down by security forces, and now it threatened to spiral into a full-blown civil war.

Deckard still felt like he was walking on jello, his senses a little dulled from the explosion. Still, he had to wonder if the Royal family, Al-Khalifa, wasn't shoving their trunks and suitcases onto a Gulfstream private jet to fly into exile in Qatar or the UAE right about now.

Paul and Ramon used the hoolie tool and battering ram to breach the door. Entering and clearing the structure, Deckard came in behind Bill and cleared his corners. The alcove at the door was empty. They flowed into the adjoining room. The lights were on, but nobody was home. Bill and Ramon took the kitchen while Nadeesha followed Deckard upstairs. They cleared two more rooms on the second floor. Paul and Rick came up behind them and leapfrogged to the last room. Not a single person in sight.

Shuffling back downstairs, Rick shook his head at Bill.

"Dry hole," Rick said.

Bill walked back into the kitchen. There was a tea kettle on the stove. He pulled off his glove and placed a hand on it.

"Still warm."

"Got a bad feeling," Paul said.

Deckard leaned up against a wall to support himself.

"Place could be rigged to blow," he whispered almost to himself.

Nadeesha's eyes went wide.

The cell phone in Bill's pocket began to vibrate.

"Yeah," he answered.

A pause.

"Who is coming?"

Another quick pause.

"What direction?"

Hardly any pause.

"What do you mean *ALL* directions?"

Bill put the phone back in his pocket.

"We're out of here, now. Wafa put out a call on all their social media networks that agents of the Royal family have raided their headquarters."

"Holy shit," Rick said as they ran for the back door. "They baited us in."

"How the hell did they even know we were coming?" Ramon said.

Deckard kept quiet. He was glad that the leaders of Wa'ad had placed that call to Wafa, but now there was still the matter of him escaping Bahrain with his life intact.

Liquid Sky escaped out the back way and scrambled over a low wall. Rioters were already pouring down the street they had entered from, heading for the Wafa party headquarters. The alley was so narrow that they had to turn sideways to scoot through it, stepping over empty plastic bottles and crumpled newspapers.

Bill peered around the corner to see what was going on in the street.

"It's clear."

They punched across the street and into another alley, circling around to find their vehicles. Behind them, another mob surged down the street they had just crossed. Liquid Sky was getting boxed in. When they got to the end of the alley, Bill could see the SUVs parked where the street got too narrow to drive.

The rioters had squeezed between the vehicles to get to the Wafa headquarters building, or simply climbed right over the top of the trucks. One was banging on a window with a rock to try to break inside. A couple others loitered around with crowbars or axe handles. Stepping into the street, Bill serviced each of the three targets with a burst from his Kalashnikov.

Bill again took the wheel of the first vehicle. Deckard climbed into the back seat. Once the Liquid Sky team was loaded up, they put it in reverse and started backing up. Having heard the gunfire, the rioters down the street turned to see what was happening. When the black SUVs began to make their escape, they knew these had to be the government agents they were looking for.

Bill gunned it. Ramon drove the other SUV, and they

accelerated down the narrow street, Bill's rear bumper only four feet from Ramon's front bumper. The trucks moved in unison as the rioters charged forward. Several rocks pounded the windshield as Bill drove looking over his shoulder. The glass spider-webbed on impact. Deckard recoiled further inside the vehicle as Bill side swiped a garbage can and a nearby wall which shaved off the side-view mirror.

As he drove, Bill kept one hand on the wheel at the twelve o' clock position. This way, as he swerved through the twisting streets in reverse, he always knew that bringing his hand back to that same position would straighten out the wheels.

Another rock flew, this one landing short. They had cleared off the X.

Pulling out on the highway, Ramon and Bill turned their vehicles around and started back for the causeway to the main island.

Green tracer fire flashed across the street in front of them.

"Fuck!"

Bill cursed as he jerked the wheel. A Pakistani convoy down the road hammered away at both vehicles. Automatic gunfire from a PKM machine gun skipped off the pavement. The upholstery and plastic siding in the SUV popped and hissed around Deckard as the truck was turned into a sieve. A piece of plastic housing around the arm rest blasted off and spun through the truck.

"That's one way to enforce curfew," Paul said from the passenger seat.

Bill snapped them around in a u-turn and cut off their headlights to drive blacked out. The second SUV did the same.

"I'm not driving back through that bullshit," Bill said as he got back on the phone with Nerve.

"Arrange transportation for us at Bahrain International," Bill said over the phone. Unlike Isa Air Base which was at the southern tip of the island, Bahrain International was only a kilometer away. It was the right call. The riots were getting more intense and it seemed less likely they would be able to navigate the roads. Now they were having close calls with the Pakistani soldiers that the government had deployed to control the riot as well. The more Paks that the rioters killed, the more trigger happy the soldiers would become, firing on anything that moved.

As the SUVs screamed north, Bill spotted a pile of burning tires in the middle of the street so he cut the wheel and shot into the opposing lane. Rioters threw more rocks and a few fired gunshots as they whizzed by. Bill jerked the wheel in time to body check one rioter who went flying through the air like a rag doll.

A few minutes later, they arrived at the airport. Bill called it in to Nerve, and the soldiers guarding the entrance let them drive through. Cruising onto the tarmac, their coordinator at Nerve directed them to link up with a Gulf Air pilot and crew.

Bill killed the call as he found the aircraft, a massive Airbus 330. The ground crew scrambled around to get it refueled and prepped for takeoff.

Deckard knew that, by now, the Royal family must be shitting bricks. The riots were out of control and Liquid Sky's mission had turned into a shit show. They would want the American hit squad out of their country as soon as possible.

Stepping out of the pockmarked SUVs, the team was better able to inspect the damage. It was a miracle that none of them had been killed when the Pakistanis opened up on them on the highway.

The ground crew wheeled the stairs up to the side of the aircraft and motioned to the team to get on board. Rick managed to find a tarp next to the terminal and with Paul's help, used it to wrap Zach's body in. They were not concerned with getting him back home for a proper burial, his body would have to be ditched at sea somewhere along the line. He could not be left behind in order to protect their operational security.

Manhandling Zach's remains on board the aircraft, the team took seats apart from each other and sat down. The interior of the aircraft was brightly lit and felt strange to the commandos who sat wearing their body armor, covered in sweat and blood. The airplane would normally seat hundreds of passengers but they had it all to themselves. The plane was empty and they were alone.

It was a long trip back.

27

"I always made it clear that once I broke one of you, I would have to go out and buy a new one. Now I have to blast out a help wanted. Shooter with nothing to lose. Now hiring."

Bill paused for a moment to down a gulp of beer.

"On the plus side, we get to split up his share of the contract."

Liquid Sky sat around Bill's living room, listening to him chide them. Rick turned and looked out of the corner of his eye. Ramon sat with his arms crossed. Deckard held a half-empty bottle of beer resting on his lap. He looked drunk, but it had nothing to do with the beer. He had just gotten released from the hospital in St. Louis. The doctors said he had a slight concussion. He'd be fine once the swelling of his brain went down in a day or two.

Bill's widescreen TV was on but muted. Deckard was familiar with the story that BBC was reporting on though. Some eccentric billionaire was building an artificial island off the coast of India in international waters. It was called sea steading, and the platforms were being joined together to form the floating island, but it would be a few more years until the project was complete. With the amount of enemies he had made around the world, maybe he would have to retire there.

"That mission was a total goat fuck," Rick said.

"Yeah, I picked up on that," Bill replied. "I'm going to get to the bottom of how we were compromised. After Henderson ate it in Pakistan, we knew we were being shadowed. Maybe this was them showing their hand a second time. First Henderson, then-"

"Then they got Zach," Rick finished.

Deckard took a swig from his beer.

"By putting us in a situation that would get us killed," Paul said, thankfully relieving some of the pressure Deckard felt.

"It could be a leak inside Nerve. We thought it was Perry's people but seeing how intel got leaked to Wafa before we got there and then they called down the monkeys on us, even after we cut Perry out of the loop, you have to see that two plus two equals four," Bill said.

"You're making it sound like it is separate players," Ramon said. "Rather than being the same player behind both Pakistan and Bahrain."

"If you think you can dig something up, let me know," Bill said. "Until then, I'll put my feelers out and see what turns up. I should be able to get some people working counter-intelligence on this issue full time considering the substantial investment that the client has sunk into this outfit."

"I'll make some phone calls," Ramon said. "Discreet phone calls."

"Have at it. In the meantime, I am laying on a training block for us. A couple weeks R&R wherever each of you wants. Then, we do a one-month training workup Stateside."

"What kind of training?" Nadi asked.

"Back to the basics," Bill said. "We need to continue to hone our skills. I bought us a driving and off-road package at Tier One Group in Memphis, followed by a CQB package at the same facility. Then, just because I like to torture all of you, I signed us up for the Lone Operator course at DARC," Bill said pronouncing the acronym as *dar-cee*.

"Oh shit," Ramon said as he tried to stifle a laugh.

"What is that?" Paul asked.

"Full-contact hand to hand combat," Bill said nonchalantly. "They teach you how to make improvised weapons, stun guns, shanks, shit like that."

"Sounds like a gas," Deckard said with his eyes only half open.

With that the meeting was over. Zach was at the bottom of the Indian Ocean, and they had beers to drink. Bahrain was just another bad dream.

Deckard rolled over in bed as the smartphone on his nightstand began to vibrate.

"Shit."

Nadi let out a low purr next to him. They had finally been getting some sleep. She had kept him up most of the night. Something about the job and facing death on a regular basis tended to give shooters a crazy sex drive. Deckard couldn't complain.

Reaching for the phone, he picked up.

"Hello?"

"It's Bill. Come over here right now. I'm in my office."

What was this about?

"Okay, I'll be there in a minute."

The line went dead.

Nadi was sound asleep as Deckard pulled on some clothes and walked over to Bill's pad. He walked over to the office he had set up. The one Aghassi had been unable to penetrate. Knocking on the door, he stepped inside.

Bill spun around in his chair to face him with his head cocked to the side.

"We're going to Syria."

"Jesus," Deckard said. "That place is a fucking war zone."

"Exactly."

"We're a man short."

"Not for long. I already picked someone up. The PMC he was working with wants to unload him. Tough for them to handle. HR had issues. Should fit right in with us. You and I are flying out to meet him tomorrow in a third country that we have business in. The client wants us to secure a package and get it shipped to Turkey."

"I take it vacation is canceled?"

"We can sleep when we're dead."

"That's what I'm afraid of."

"Training is off as well. The world is on fire Deckard. Be ready to roll in the early afternoon."

Deckard looked around Bill's home office. Sure enough, the walls had motion and thermal sensors on them. There were several computers in the office and the security looked to be custom.

"Sweet set up," Deckard said. "Looks like the secret hideout for the Thundercats."

"Had to bring in a professional to get it all set up. Expensive, but worth it. The client is very particular about commo arrangements. These laptops are just toys, it is that thing over there that makes the magic happen," Bill pointed to a black hardcase at the end of his desk.

Scooting across the floor on his swivel chair, Bill opened up the case. The black case had a computer built inside of it. There was a screen, a keyboard, and some other switches. There were also input and output plugs.

"Which button launches the nukes?" Deckard said.

"This baby is a cold war relic," Bill said with a hint of pride in his voice. "It was made as a redundant communications system in case of nuclear war. It bounces signals off the atmosphere rather than satellites, or so that is what I'm told."

"Continuity of Government?"

"Right, so that the military and the government can still talk to each other after the Soviets push our shit in. Really no need for this system until the nukes fly, except when certain players want to talk behind the scenes without the NSA or others tapping the line and listening in. Those players call it the Pirate's Net."

"They hijacked an official communications platform for their own purposes, turning it into a pirate net."

"That's how you get shit done," Bill said as he shut the case. "If you want to protect America, you set aside all this sheepdog bullshit. To hunt a wolf you send a wolf."

"See you in the afternoon then."

"Be here by one. Have fun with that little sex kitten

231

until then."

"Sex kitten?"

"Everybody knows Deckard. The way she ran over to you when we found you and Zach in that alley. Zach's blood was fucking everywhere and you're doing a faceplant. We all thought you were dead. Nadeesha lost her shit for a second there."

"Must be my high cheekbones."

"Enjoy it while it lasts brother, because it never does."

"Never?"

"Not in this line of work," Bill said as he turned back to his laptop. "Never."

Things were moving fast.

After attending to Nadi a few more times in the morning, Deckard told her he was going for a run. He quickly arranged the meeting using a burner phone and threw it as far as he could into the ocean.

"You look like I feel," a voice said from behind him as he jogged along the beach.

Deckard turned to Aghassi.

"Ate a frag grenade in Bahrain. I'll be back to normal in a day."

"Sure?"

"That's what the doctors say."

The two walked up stone steps to a well-manicured lawn at a French hotel. Aghassi led him inside.

"We're going to Syria," Deckard informed him. "Mobilize the other platoon. I want to hit their base of operations here in Mauritius with the platoon you pre-positioned in Madagascar. Once we arrive in Syria I will get comms with Pat and walk the other platoon in to eliminate Liquid Sky. I'll try to soften them up for you as well."

"What's in Syria other than a graveyard?"

"Don't know. We are going to a third country to pick something up and have it shipped to Turkey. I imagine that we will be smuggling it into Syria."

"That doesn't sound good."

"No, it doesn't. I'm leaving for the third country to pick up the package this afternoon. Start putting everything into place. We can't afford to fuck this up. This is my last mission with Liquid Sky. Rick is already suspicious, I had to kill Zach in Bahrain, and nearly kill myself just to maintain my cover."

"Want me to have Pat put his name out there and see if he can get picked up the same way you did?"

"No, I don't think lightning will strike the same place twice. Besides, he is more valuable to me on the outside working with the assault force that will drop the hammer on Liquid Sky. I want both Samruk platoons ready to go."

"I'll make it happen."

Together, they walked to the hotel room. Using his key card, Aghassi opened the door.

"Listen," the former ISA operator said. "I found out about Bill, found out what all this is really about."

"What do you mean?"

"I made contact with Dusty and Flakjacket. They are wrapping up their deployment to the horn of Africa with Dev Group. I have the number for the Iridium phone they have been using. They want to talk to you directly."

Aghassi handed Deckard his cellphone and showed him the number to call. Deckard hit send and held the phone to his ear. He listened as the phone began to ring. Aghassi opened the sliding door and sat out on the balcony.

"Hello?"

"Dusty? It's Deckard."

"I was told you might be calling."

"I have some questions for you if you have a minute."

"I have a minute and I already know what you're going to ask. Your buddy already told me. You want to know about Bill Geddes."

"Correct."

"You sure?"

"Positive."

"Bill Geddes is a fucking cancer."

Deckard was caught off guard by such a candid comment from one of Bill's former teammates in Dev Group.

"What do you mean?"

"I mean that there is a cancer that has grown within Dev Group and Bill is right at the center of it. He is responsible for the spread of this cancer. You know about the scalpings and shit?"

"I've become familiar."

"It gets worse."

"How the hell did all of this happen?" Deckard asked. "I mean, I'm aware of a few incidents, some things that happened in the heat of the moment, sometimes honest mistakes being made in combat. But things that none of us would be proud of."

"This is different, dude. Way different. This is pervasive throughout the unit and Bill takes it with him wherever he goes having left the cancer behind with us. You remember early on in the war when we lost Chief McAtee?"

"I wasn't there. I heard he was on an OP in Afghanistan that got overrun or something."

"Yeah, and there is a whole lot more. Stuff that never made it to the press. Stuff that got scrubbed even out of official debriefs."

"Like what?"

"When the other Dev Group element in that AO got there to rescue those guys they found McAtee. He was still technically alive when our guys found him."

"Shit."

"They had been in the process of cutting his head off but the knives were not sharp enough to fully do the job. He was in deep shock, there was nothing that could be done to save him. The enemy also ass-raped him."

"God damn."

"Bill Geddes was the team leader that led the rescue effort. It was bad, Deckard, real bad. They got denied extract, got denied air support for political reasons. They left those two recce teams out there flapping. Bill blatantly disregarded orders and left his position to go save his team. No one was surprised, Bill was always an operator's operator. Shit, he was one of my instructors when I was in Green Platoon. He was the real deal.

"After McAtee, Bill changed. A lot of us did. Bill made it clear to everyone in Dev that from here on out it was an eye for an eye. Scorched earth. He started going out on objectives and taking scalps. The unofficial insignia of his squadron has a couple of hatchets on it anyway so they started carrying hatchets out on missions. The younger guys that Bill mentored got into it as well.

"He brought up a whole generation of Dev Group operators and corrupted them, turned them into war criminals. There have been some beheadings, and cleaning out entire compounds, man, woman, and children. Executions too."

"No one tried to stop it?"

"Yeah, one of our officers went up to JSOC to try to shut this shit down. Guess what?"

"JSOC wanted to paper over it."

"You got it. When that officer went to blow the whistle internally, JSOC immediately threatened to yank his security clearance."

"These days it seems like Top Secret clearances are used as a *de facto* gag order and have little to do with keeping national security secrets."

"There have been others. OGA guys have spoken out. Rangers have tried to drop dime. It is the same shit every time. Dev Group gets shut down in Afghanistan for a month so that JSOC has time to conduct an official investigation, the real purpose of which is to paper over the war crimes. Then, they are right back in business. They make sure that a SEAL gets assigned as the investigative officer and he goes in and briefs the witnesses on what he wants them to say they saw as opposed to what they actually saw."

"What about Admiral Corbett, the JSOC commander? He was one of yours."

"Dev is too far gone, man. I'm just trying to ride out my time to retirement and hoping I don't get killed in the process."

"Corbett is covering it up?"

"He knows a little about it, but isn't doing anything to stop it. It is more of a see-no-evil deal for him. Deep down, he doesn't want to know. If this shit ever went public it would lead to Dev Group getting disbanded. Dude, I've seen these guys call in airstrikes on entire families just for shits and giggles. This war has been big money, lots of deployment funding rolling it and no one wants to see that go away.

"So I don't know what you are into Deckard, but if you are asking around about Bill, you need to stay the fuck away from him. Like I said, the guy is a fucking cancer on the Special Operations community. There is a conspiracy of silence about the war crimes and it goes straight to the top."

Deckard was silent for a moment.

"I appreciate you filling me in on all of this, Dusty."

"No problem man. And hey?"

"Yeah?"

"Be fucking careful."

"I won't."

"Yeah, I was afraid you would say that. In that case, good luck."

"Thanks."

"Hit me up when we are both back in the world. I'll buy you a drink."

"I'm going to need it."

28

Deckard squinted his eyes against the dust kicked up by the spinning props of the plane as he and Bill jumped off the back and hit the ground at Benina Airport. They had just arrived in Benghazi, Libya. The two Liquid Sky men stepped through the haze and out of the dust cloud.

Thirty feet in front of them at the edge of the runway, a lone figure stood with his arms crossed. Waiting. He wore khaki 5.11 pants, a black polo, Army-issue desert boots, and mirrored Oakley M-Frames. His hair cut was both high and tight.

"There he is," Bill said.

Deckard took one look and instantly regretted not having had Pat try to get recruited by Liquid Sky to replace Zach.

"The Operator."

"A real life fucking legend," Bill said. "And available on short notice."

"I wonder why," Deckard said out of the corner of his mouth.

The two Liquid Sky shooters approached The Operator. He was almost as big as Bill. Almost. Up close Deckard could see that his short-cropped hair was salt and pepper throughout.

"I'm Bill," the team leader said as he shook hands with The Operator. "This is Deckard."

The Operator took Deckard's hand.

"I do not know you, but I know of you," he said, his words stunted as if there was a period after each one.

"Thanks, I guess."

"My squadron Sergeant Major said you were a smart aleck."

"Listen," Bill cut in. "I'm making you the same deal I made Deckard when we picked him up a month ago. You are hired on a provisional basis. You're on probation until I say otherwise."

The Operator nodded his head confidently.

"I will perform to standard."

"Jesus, you look like a real-life action figure," Bill commented.

The Operator said nothing.

"Have you found us a ride?"

"I have secured transportation," the new Liquid Sky member said. "I have changed the oil, test-driven the vehicle, and added improvised armor using rubber conveyer-belt material I recovered from a nearby scrapyard."

"That's what I call service," Bill said with satisfaction.

The three got into the Toyota Hilux that The Operator had procured and Bill drove them away from the airport. Benina Airport was just one more in a long procession of run down third world airports that they had all visited. Customs had gotten word to leave them alone and so they drove by the roundabout outside the airport and headed towards the Mediterranean coast.

Deckard noticed that Bill was driving the route by memory. He didn't use a map or GPS. Half an hour later they arrived at an oceanside compound.

"This is Yezza's place," Bill informed them. "An old friend. All we have to do is take possession of the package and make sure it gets on a plane for Turkey."

"What's the package?" Deckard asked.

"You'll see."

Soon they arrived at yet another walled compound of the type that was ubiquitous across the Middle East. Two guards stood by the front gate armed with SIG 553 sub-machine guns. Bill leaned out the open window of the pickup and waved at them. Recognizing the former SEAL, the Libyans opened the gate and let them in.

Bill parked in the driveway next to a well-tended garden and the three Americans walked towards the door. The walls looked like they were scrubbed with lyme on a regular basis. The ocean waves could be heard crashing gently on the nearby shore. A maid answered the door as they walked onto the front steps but was brushed aside as a severely overweight Libyan pushed her away. He wore Western clothes: blue jeans and a collared shirt with gold Ray Ban sunglasses but somehow he still managed to look like he was rocking a Gaddafi starter set.

"Bill, my friend!"

"What's happening Yezza?" Bill asked as they embraced each other. "These two are part of my new crew," he said pointing to the other Liquid Sky members.

"Welcome, welcome," Yezza said as he stood aside and let them into his home. Turning to the maid, he motioned for her to get to the kitchen and fetch some drinks.

"Yezza is one of my boys going way back," Bill said. "Good for action and logistics."

"I could find a Russian hooker in the Vatican," Yezza said with a confident smile.

"Did I teach you that?"

"Does a hobby horse have a wooden dick?"

Even Deckard laughed at that one as Yezza cracked the joke in broken English. The Operator remained expressionless.

Yezza walked them through his living room. Paintings of seascapes were hung on the walls. Otherwise, it was all velvet pillows and golden curtain rods. Out on the back deck they had a brilliant view of the ocean and a cloudless blue sky.

"Damn, this place is pretty nice when you guys are not killing each other," Bill chuckled.

"I know, I know," Yezza said as if he were stating the obvious. "Please sit," he said pointing to the metal chairs he had around a table.

"Like I was saying," Bill began. "Yezza can get you anything. This guy knows guns."

"I am the man," Yezza confirmed.

As they took their seats, the maid set out bottles of beer for them.

"Talk to me, Yezza," Bill said. "You know what I'm here for."

"Yes, well, this is something quite special. It exists, of course, or you wouldn't be here. I've located what you are interested in."

"But?" Deckard saw it coming from a mile away.

"But it is held by another militia."

"For fucks sake, I should have known this couldn't be simple," Bill said.

Yezza swallowed a gulp of beer. Upon closer inspection, Deckard noted that he wasn't just wearing Ray Bans. No, those were Ray Bahns. Those bad boys really closed the deal.

"It is the Green Mountain militia boys," Yezza said with a sigh. "They've been a thorn in my side ever since the Americans peeled out of Benghazi. The Agency came back after a month but I don't have protection the way I once did, you know? Anyway, the militia is holding on to the weapons stockpile as a bargaining chip."

"What do they plan to do with it?" Bill asked.

"Trade it to the CIA in exchange for a security contract that will be routed through the State Department."

"Some people never learn."

"Tell me about it. First Gaddafi was public enemy number one for the United States, then you were friends, then you flipped the switch on him and here we are. I stopped trying to figure out what your President is thinking. Now I'm just hoping to still be standing when the smoke clears."

"We did not elect the usurper," The Operator said. "We serve the people."

Deckard bit his tongue. After all, he was the team smartass.

"Fucking undercover Muslim," Bill snorted. "No offense."

Yezza held up a hand.

"None taken my friend. Surely there must be another member of the Bush family that can run for office, no?"

"I hope so," Bill said. "I'm trying to run a business here after all."

They sat in silence for one long moment, looking at each other.

"Can you take us there?" Bill asked.

"Yes, tonight," Yezza answered. "I have a private collection of weapons in the house that you can choose from."

"And shipment on to the destination?"

"I ship weapons from here to Turkey. Where they go after that I do not know," Yezza said, his fat face split wide open as he smiled. "Everyone knows this."

Yezza's private armory was impressive to say the least. It was all top of the line along, with special rare weapons he had cherry picked from the stockpiles the arms dealer had taken control of during and after the civil war.

The wall hangers were something else. Deckard even spotted an ultra-rare Nazi STG-44 submachine gun. In some ways it was the predecessor to Mikhail Kalashnikov's famous AK-47 rifle.

Deckard claimed an HK 416 for himself. It seemed that Yezza also got a load of weapons that had flowed into the country from the European powers during the 2011 Libyan Civil War. Next he found a Glock 17 and a holster for it.

"The Glock," The Operator surprised Deckard as he came up from behind. "A reliable pistol. I prefer the 1911. That is what I carried in the desert."

"God's gun?"

"The Creator has no need for open carry," The Operator deadpanned.

"What's that over there?" Deckard asked pointing to the 1911 pistol on the wall.

"Yes, that is what I will use."

The Operator picked up the pistol and immediately blew through a complete functions check, his hands moving in a blur of motion as he completed checking the safety, trigger, and trigger reset in a fraction of a second as he worked the gun as he had so many others, doing it out of pure muscle memory.

"Perfect. A Rock Island Armory .45 caliber 1911. It is not a five thousand dollar pistol, nor need it be." The Operator nodded. "There are show horses and there are work horses. This is a work horse and will perform to my standards."

"Yeah," Deckard said. "Cool."

He was pretty gear queer himself, but this guy was over the top.

Bill walked in, grabbed up the other 416 hanging on the wall, blew dust off a Beretta 92F pistol and walked out.

"Hurry the fuck up you two, we need to get on the road."

The Operator looked at the STG-44 on the wall for a moment, seriously considering carrying a World War Two era gun into combat and then changed his mind and opted for a SIG MP-X sub-machine gun with a suppressor.

Deckard followed him out the door, shuddering to think of what was coming next.

Yezza pointed to the bright lights coming from above the desert ridge. Night had come fast in the desert.

"That is where you will find what you are looking for," he said. "You can take my fighters."

They had driven an hour outside of Benghazi into the desert to an old ammunition bunker complex that had been built by the Gaddafi regime. It had changed hands a few times over the last couple years from Gaddafi, to an American private military company that had been hired to secure WMD sites in Libya, then to Yezza who was hired to watch over the depot until it could be destroyed; then, the Green Mountain militia shot their way in and captured it from him about a month ago.

Now, the Green Mountain militia was working a backroom deal with the U.S. government to turn over the arms depot and everything inside in exchange for a hefty security contract paid for by the State Department. Liquid Sky had to get what they needed out of the depot before that happened.

The three Liquid Sky members stood in the desert with Yezza and a dozen of his gunfighters.

"You can stay in the low ground here and sneak right up to the perimeter," the Libyan gun runner said.

"I appreciate the help," Bill said. "I'll take however many fighters you are willing to lend me."

"Take them all. I want this depot back in my hands."

"So you can sell the weapons to the Syrian rebels?"

"So I can sell the weapons to the Syrians and then trade

in the scraps to the Americans for that big time security contract," Yezza said with a smile.

"We'll see what we can do."

Deckard took point as the others filed in behind him. He kept in the defilade, creeping his way up the ridge towards the arms depot. When the top of the concrete bunkers came into view, he hunched over to avoid skylining himself against the horizon. Finally, he got down on his stomach and leopard crawled forward to a depression that kept him out of the bright stadium lighting that surrounded the bunkers.

Bill snorted behind him, not even bothering to crawl, he just bent over and stayed as low as possible then laid down alongside Deckard. The Operator conducted a perfect high crawl straight out of the field manual. Yezza's fighters followed Bill's lead, and then plopped down next to them facing the armory.

"What do you think?" Bill asked Deckard while they waited for The Operator to catch up.

Deckard took one look at the bunkers and sized them up in an instant. He was an expert tactician if nothing else. He wished he had a whole company of Rangers to do this right, but from working in unconventional warfare environments, he knew how to work with what he had on hand. The compound was lightly guarded considering there were over ten bunkers, presumably filled with weaponry.

"Move to contact on the closest bunker to establish a foothold while flexing four of Yezza's fighters and one of us on the right flank of the objective to knock out that technical," Deckard said pointing to a pickup truck with a ZPU-2 anti-aircraft gun mounted on its bed. "Use the ZPU to suppress the other bunkers and enemy troops while we initiate our movement to the next bunker. Leapfrog forward in alternating bounds from bunker to bunker while we have a driver cheat forward with the ZPU to keep suppressive fire on the enemy."

"That's a pretty good plan, Deckard."

"I'd like to think so," Deckard said with a hint of feigned arrogance in his voice.

"But I've got a better one," Bill said.

"I left my wingsuit at home."

"Delta Dan, get up here," Bill said giving The Operator another nickname. "You're up."

The Operator crawled up to their position and looked

over the compound.

"Where do you want me?"

"I want you to take down this compound."

"Solo?"

"Make it happen."

"Roger."

The Operator checked the loads in his 1911 and MP-X sub-machine gun one final time before crawling off towards the compound.

"You can't be fucking serious?" Deckard said. "We're going to back him up right?"

"Maybe. First let's see what he can do. I've heard some stories about this dude."

"You and me both."

"Word on the street is that The Operator is a legend in the unit. Embassy take downs, raiding drug labs in the jungle, low-vis hostage rescue ops in denied areas, blowing up SCUD launchers out in the desert, shoot outs with the Russian mob on ops to recover nuclear material, calling in airstrikes until there is nothing left but armpits hanging from tree limbs. Bat shit crazy stuff."

"He is a legend. Been there, done that. Got the t-shirt, then went back and got t-shirts for all his ex-wives and estranged children."

"You're a hater, Deckard."

"The Operator is unstable. They fucked that dude in the head so many ways that it isn't even funny. He ran combat operations forever, many of them pumped full of issued Modafinil to keep him awake for long-duration high-stress missions. That and pseudo-ephedrine which the guys call 'ranger speed.' When he started showing signs of PTSD, they didn't want to let him go out to pasture, so they prescribed him a half-dozen different medications, none of them cleared by the FDA by the way, to deal with depression, anxiety, and paranoia, not to mention drugs for anti-psychosis purposes and others to help him sleep at night. They ran him like that for years until he finally burned out and snapped."

"Snapped?"

"Yeah, down in Basra. The Operator lost his fucking mind and started murdering civilians during operations, killing them and torturing them in the worst kinds of ways. He was a senior-ranking guy and couldn't be reined in, but everyone avoided going outside the wire with him."

"Sounds like he is the right man for the job," Bill said approvingly. "Is that all?"

"That and the steroids, but I guess that goes without saying."

The Operator was now three quarters of the way to the technical with the ZPU machine gun mounted on it. He high-crawled silently, sticking to the shadows.

"Besides," Bill said. "This is all I could get on short notice."

"Did you check the personal ads in the back of Soldier of Fortune magazine?"

"I put it out over the secret squirrel net and this was the first experienced guy that could be on a plane in a few hours. I tried my guys from Dev, but they are all mixed up in this South America deal."

"Training Colombia's Counter-Terrorist unit?"

"Way better," Bill said as they watched The Operator slowly crawl towards the technical. A Green Mountain militia man was leaning against the back of the truck smoking a cigarette. Two others stood near the truck smoking and joking with each other.

"A couple of our boys got out of the Navy and went to work with the real pirates, those fucks on Wall Street. Once these large brokerage firms saw SEAL Team Six on their resumes, they got earmarked to go straight to the top. Every one of those yuppies wants a Bin Laden killer on their staff just for bragging rights.

"So my guys, Alek and Stew, they get a line on some investments off the coast of Colombia and Venezuela. They buy in low, then convince the top guys at these brokerage firms to buy in as well. The reason why it is so low to invest is because the company is underwater, financially speaking, so Alek and Stew round up the boys and do some extracurricular activity putting the competition underwater literally."

"The ultimate insider trading."

"Who is better at underwater demolition than we are? Fly them down there on Teeny Weeny, sabotage the competing oil company's hardware, and get back home in time for hot sandwiches. All the evidence is at the bottom of the ocean. Who is going to go down there and do forensics and link it back to Alek and Stew?"

"These guys are contractors like we are?"

"Some. Others are just active-duty operators on leave from Dam Neck."

"Holy shit."

"Hey, here we go," Bill said as he started turkey-necking towards the objective. "Our boy is ready to go."

Deckard looked over in time to see The Operator stand up and stay low as he moved forward. He got the first Libyan in a choke hold before dragging him behind the technical and breaking his neck. Leaving the body concealed behind the truck, The Operator crouched down and moved along the tailgate, inching closer to the two militia men who were talking to each other.

Everyone knew about The Operator. He had been a Golden Gloves semi-pro boxer at one point. Practiced Thai kickboxing at a gym in Fayetteville for years. Then, his skills had been further refined. There was an old school Special Forces soldier who could be contacted for private lessons, provided you had been vetted and knew what number to call. He was one of those scary dudes who did work from Laos to Nicaragua. Specialized in silent takedowns of sentries and other esoteric skills.

Deckard had heard the stories, but now he would see it for himself.

Breaking from cover, The Operator confronted the two militia men.

His boot was a blur of motion that connected with the closest Libyan's temple. The Muay Thai kick sent the militia man spinning. He collapsed against the side of the truck and then crumpled to the ground. The second militia man went for the pistol on his hip but never made it. The Operator, moved and a second later his opponent had an ear torn off and one of his eyes gouged. Before the Libyan could even feel the pain, The Operator finished him off with a vicious right hook, dropping him.

"What do you think?" Bill asked.

"Someone has studied the martial art of ripping and tearing. Not something they teach at the Special Operations Combatives Program."

"No, it isn't."

The Operator was looking over the ZPU-2 heavy machine gun on the back of the pickup when two more Libyans came walking out of the nearest bunker on a security patrol. They glanced over at the technical.

The MP-X sub-machine gun materialized in The Operator's hands as he popped into a perfect shooting stance. The sub-gun burped out two stunted bursts through the suppressor with hardly a gap between each trigger squeeze. Both of the militiamen went down with bursts placed center mass in their chests.

Without missing a beat, The Operator climbed on to the back of the pickup truck and sat down on the thin metal seat behind the twin barreled ZPU-2 Anti-Aircraft gun. Spinning the traverse and elevation wheels on the weapon system, he used the metal bullseye sight on the gun to aim at a group of Green Mountain militiamen a hundred and fifty meters away near another bunker.

With the sites aligned on target, The Operator set his size 11.5 desert boot down on the foot peddle which acted as the trigger for the firing mechanism.

The,n the night lit up with orange flame from the twin-barreled weapon. The 14.5mm rounds went downrange to devastating effect. Flesh was separated from bone as red ribbons shot into the air. Then, the bullets churned into the concrete surface of the arms depot and kicked up a thick gray dust.

Spinning the traverse wheel, The Operator walked his gunfire into another technical on the other side of the bunker complex. Sparks blasted around the pickup like angry fireflies and in seconds it was reduced to scrap metal.

"Let's go," Bill said as he stood up.

Deckard ran forward with a dozen of Yezza's fighters. Several of them began firing their AK-47's at absolutely nothing as they jogged towards the closest bunker. Deckard yelled at them in Arabic to hold their fire.

"*Kif! Kif,* you assholes!"

They took cover next to the heavy steel doors of the bunker just as The Operator abandoned the ZPU-2. He had burned through the entire box of ammunition. Reaching down, he recovered an FN FAL rifle from one of the militia men he had killed with his hands and feet before joining them at the bunker.

A few pop shots still echoed throughout the arms depot. Someone shouted in Arabic.

Bill looked back to The Operator.

"Go take care of that while we secure the package."

"Roger that."

The Operator turned and ran into the night.

"I like him," Bill said with a smile.

"Suffice to say that I have my reservations," Deckard said dryly.

"Don't worry. He'll be dead after a mission or two and we'll just hire someone new."

By now, Yezza had come waddling over the ridge and made his way towards them.

"What did I tell you!" Yezza shouted to Bill. "Did my fighters not fight bravely in the re-capturing of my bunkers?"

"Oh, yeah," Bill confirmed. "Every one of them is a hero."

This made Yezza smile.

"Now do me a favor and show me which bunker has our stuff in it."

"Come with me," Yezza said. He was panting, out of breath from his arduous journey from their trucks.

The Libyan arms dealer led them across the way to another bunker. Off in the distance, they heard Kalashnikov fire. The heavier 7.62x51 FN FAL rounds answered back. As they approached the bunker, Deckard thought he heard the rapid fire of a pistol, probably God's gun, the 1911 doing its thing.

The sliding door was secured with nothing more than a bicycle chain and a padlock. Bill shot the lock off and Yezza ordered his men to slide open the steel door. With no small degree of bitching and moaning about it, the Libyans man handled the bunker door open.

Bill clicked on a Surefire flashlight he had brought along and used the light to cut through the darkness inside. There were metal racks loaded with conventional dumb bombs that could be dropped from airplanes. There were wooden crates, some empty, some full. As they walked inside, Deckard could also see 130mm artillery rounds stacked against one wall.

Their footsteps made hallow echoes inside the bunker. Everything was covered in dust. Deckard used his own pen light to find his way.

"Bingo," Bill said from deeper in the bunker. "Come over here."

Deckard joined Bill to see what he was looking at.

"Know what that is?"

From the tail fins and markings Deckard made a determination.

"Russian dumb bombs," he said as he looked over the long green bombs in the metal rack. "The mounting lugs on the sides mean they are designed to be dropped from an aircraft."

"And the payload."

Deckard noted the yellow band around each of the bombs in the rack.

"I'm not sure."

"Inside is a small tube that acts as a burster when the nose fuse is touched off on impact. Packed around the burster are a series of larger tubes which can hold up thirty liters."

"Thirty liters of what?" Deckard asked, fearing he already knew the answer.

"Each one of these puppies is a giant mustard dispenser, and not the kind you find at a hot dog stand."

Deckard clenched his teeth. It was nasty stuff. When deployed against humans, the gas acted as a blister agent against any exposed skin and in the lungs when inhaled. The first and second degree burns the gas caused could take up to a week to kill those who were exposed. The chemical warfare agent had killed thousands of troops during the first world war.

Yezza barged in between them, looking at the bombs that Bill had found.

"This is what you are looking for my friend?"

"It sure is," Bill said, clapping Yezza on the shoulder. "Have your boys load two up on the trucks. You can sell the rest to the CIA for destruction."

"And a big fat security contract."

"And a big fat security contract," Bill confirmed. "C'mon Deckard. Let's go flip the off switch on our pal outside before he fights all the way to Tehran."

"Good idea."

Bill brushed passed them and walked toward the exit.

"Gotta get back to the home station so I can get comms with higher and find out the rest of the game plan."

Deckard followed behind him, his rifle held by the pistol

249

grip at his side.

"Then what?"

"We got a war waiting for us in Syria, that's what."

29

The two chemical weapons, along with a cache of guns went on a plane from Benghazi, Libya to Antakya, Turkey while Bill, Deckard, and The Operator got on another plane back to Mauritius. Bill needed to get his high-side access on the Pirate Net in his office before continuing on to whatever their final objective was in Syria.

Once plugged into his secure commo system, Bill got the rest of the Operations Order from their client and called a team pow wow in his bungalow. Nadeesha had been playing with Deckard in the shower when they got the call. Getting dressed, they walked over to Bill's place in intervals. Nadi still didn't want anyone to know even though Deckard was pretty sure that everyone noticed when she looked at him with those bedroom eyes.

Once they had gathered around, Bill gave them the low down. Rick sat on the couch, hung over from the party the previous night. Nadeesha sat on a chair in the corner of the room with her back to the wall. Paul sat down on a stool next to the billiard table next to Ramon. The Operator stood towards the back with his arms crossed.

"We will link up with Yezza's people in Turkey and take possession of the device. Because of the amount of road blocks and choke points that both the rebels and the Syrian military have established, we are going to have to parachute in behind enemy lines and link up with the locals. We are going to handle the dispersal of the mustard gas, but these clowns will be acting as bullet traps for us on the way into the target area."

"Who are these guys?" Ramon asked. "The Free Syrian Army?"

"It gets better," Bill insisted. "Al-Nusra."

"Fuck me," Ramon snorted.

"Who else is crazy enough to launch a chemical attack on this target?"

"Wait, what's the fucking target?"

"I just got it from the client. The target is the Umayyad Mosque in Damascus."

"Holy shit," Deckard whispered.

"What the fuck is that?" Rick said.

"Yeah, what's the big fucking deal with some mosque? These people blow their own holy sites up all the time," Paul said.

"Not like this," Deckard said. "Shia Muslims consider this mosque to be maybe the fourth most holy site in the world. It is one of the largest and oldest mosques in the world. If it goes up in a cloud of poison gas that gets blamed on the Sunni Al-Nusra extremists, it will cause a sectarian shit storm that will engulf the entire region."

"What he said," Bill confirmed. "It seems the client feels it is time the United States gets decisively involved in this Syrian Civil War deal. Hezbollah is calling a lot of the shots for the Assad regime at this point, not to mention that they are providing security around the target itself and in some Shia neighborhoods in the capital. Back in D.C., the President has said that the use of chemical weapons in this war would be a red line. Detonating the package in Damascus guarantees that the President will get off his ass and push Syria's shit in."

"And strike a fatal blow to Hezbollah," The Operator spoke to everyone's surprise. They turned around to look at the new Liquid Sky member. "Once Hezbollah is defeated, we move on to Iran."

"Well, since you guys put it that way..." Rick said absently.

Deckard was grinding his teeth without realizing it. Gassing innocent civilians in the middle of Syria's capital city. Whoever the client was, they had some fucking balls. Pat had better have Samruk International in position somewhere near if not inside Syria by the time he got there. One way or the other, this would be Liquid Sky's last mission, it was just a question of whether or not Deckard went down with the ship.

They were going to launch a chemical attack in order to provoke what could very well become World War Three.

That can't happen.

"From Turkey we will fly nap of the earth during the night and pop up at altitude, dropping in to a drop zone Al-Nusra has secured for our arrival just outside of Homs. We'll HALO in from 18,000 feet with the package in secured bundles, along with an arms cache to help grease the skids with Nusra. From there, we'll stage out of Homs-"

Bill's words were cut off as rustling sounded on the back deck where the work out equipment was set up. Looking through the sliding screen doors, Deckard saw the private security team that kept watch on Liquid Sky's bungalows manhandling someone onto the deck.

The head guard was Alan, a former Royal Marine, and the other three were local off-duty policemen. The man they had captured was handcuffed and his feet duct taped together. The Operator opened the screen door as the prisoner was dragged inside.

Deckard's heart sank.

Because things can always get just a little bit worse.

"We found him poking around behind Deckard's place," the former British Marine hissed.

The guards deposited their prisoner on the floor where he landed with a hollow thud.

With his mouth duct-taped shut, the prisoner looked up at Deckard.

It was Aghassi.

Liquid Sky took turns slapping Aghassi around. Within minutes his face was bloodied and bruised. Rick picked him up and tied him to a chair. The former ISA operator's head hung down as blood dripped from his mouth. There was little Deckard could do for him without breaking cover. He would only intervene if they were going to kill him. On the other hand, they might put Aghassi under so much duress that he might blow Deckard's cover anyway. They weren't to that point yet, but Deckard knew that no one could hold out forever.

Pushing Rick aside, Deckard decided to get some face time in.

He backhanded Aghassi, sending a spray of blood across one of Bill's billiard tables.

Bill had told them that they were leaving for Turkey today. If Frank and Sergeant Major Korgan were ready to go, Deckard could call them in to rescue Aghassi just as they were flying out. He just had to keep Aghassi alive until then.

Deckard grabbed him by the shirt and out of the chair, right up to his face.

"Where are they?" he whispered.

Aghassi looked at him through the black and blue bruises around his eyes.

"Call. Under your sink."

Deckard released him and the chair clanked on the floor.

"We need to keep him alive," Deckard said just as Paul was about to step in for his turn. "You guys said you had another team shadowing you in Pakistan. We can't take it for granted that this guy was just here to break in and steal our flatscreens or something."

"You're right," Bill said as he stomped down into the living room from the staircase. "I informed the client and they are sending a couple specialists from Serbia. They will be on a plane heading here in a matter of hours. Our contracted security people can keep this guy detained here until they arrive. We have work to do.

"We're compromised," Ramon complained.

"Mauritius is compromised for us, but not our mission. We stick to the timeline. Pack what you need and we will be out of here tonight. Don't plan on coming back, because the client may shut down our entire Mauritius operation. Whatever you leave will be destroyed or mailed to you by a freight forwarding company. Let's get moving, we're wheels-up in three hours."

Paul grunted as he unclenched his fists.

Aghassi was motionless with his head down. It was on Deckard to come through for him now, even if there was a larger objective at hand.

He left Bill's place and walked across the beach to his bungalow. Nadeesha came running up behind him.

"I hope they torture that fuck like a couple kids burning ants with a magnifying glass," she said.

254

"I'm sure they will. Serbs are good at that."

"Hey," Nadi reached out and grabbed him by the arm as they walked. "Want to get another quickie in before we leave?"

She had an impossible sex drive. Finding an infiltrator in their midst didn't put her off much.

"I've got to take care of a few things before we leave. Maybe we can join the mile-high club on the way over there?" Deckard offered as a compromise.

Nadi now had a wide smile.

"You got it mister."

She spun around, her black hair blowing in the sea wind as she walked off.

Climbing the back steps to his bungalow, Deckard went inside. Aghassi's words made it sound like he had left a cache behind for him.

Sure enough, when he opened the cupboard under his kitchen sink and felt around, there was a phone taped up underneath the porcelain. It was an Apple iPhone inside a Thuraya Sat-Sleeve, which enabled the smartphone to make calls by satellite from pretty much anywhere in the world. There was one phone number saved in the address book.

Deckard took one more look around to make sure he was alone before dialing.

Holding the iPhone to his ear, Deckard listened as it began to ring on the other end.

"YES?"

Deckard recoiled from the loud voice.

"Cody?"

"YES."

No wonder, it was the hacker he had hired during Samruk International's last mission down in Mexico. He was a genius behind a keyboard but had a bit of an abrasive personality.

"I just picked up this phone. Did the guys set you up as a gateway between me and the two field teams?"

"Correct. I am to facilitate any and all calls you have between the Madagascar team and the Syria team."

"Patch me through to the Madagascar team."

"Okay."

The line began to ring again.

"Hello?"

"Hey Frank, it's me. Don't have much time. How far out are you guys?"

"About an hour. We're just off the coast in a fishing vessel waiting for the word."

"Push off in another hour and hit the targets here on the coast. Bill's place needs to be your priority target."

"You all right?"

"I'm fine, but they got Aghassi. He is alive for now, but they are flying in a couple interrogators from Serbia."

"Holy shit."

"Exactly. We're about to take off for Turkey so you can hit the targets along the shore as soon as we leave. Any updates from Pat's team?"

"They bought off some folks in Egypt and have secured some transportation by ship."

"Less than ideal," Deckard's guts turned in knots. The stress was getting to him. "Cody?"

"I'm here," the computer hacker answered.

"Get in touch with Pat and tell them to initiate movement for Syria. I will probably be in Homs within 48 hours and will re-establish comms with Pat to guide him and the boys into a position where they can ambush Liquid Sky."

Looking at his watch, Deckard quickly read on Cody and Frank to the mission brief he had just received on their plan of action in Syria.

"The balls on these guys," Frank said in response.

"Yeah," Deckard said. "This one is for all the marbles."

30

A black-clad man strode up to his captive with a hammer in one hand. With the prisoner strapped to the chair, he swung the hammer in an arc, bringing it down on his big toe. It split open like a bloody grape.

The prisoner screamed, and screamed, and screamed as he pulled against his restraints. The prisoner wasn't a Samruk International mercenary but rather a former informant of theirs. His name was Kenny Rodriguez.

The man in black was a CISEN agent. Mexican intelligence.

"We know you helped the gringos," the CISEN agent said to Kenny. The leather restraints held his head firmly against the back of the chair. He was stripped naked. The snitch began having the dry heaves as the pain overwhelmed him.

"That was just to show you that we mean business," he said as he waved the hammer at Kenny.

CISEN had rolled into Oaxaca, Mexico with the Mexican military just as the Samruk mercenaries had left. The Mexican intelligence service had a field office in Oaxaca but it went up in flames. Once the intelligence agents began prowling the streets they began to uncover details about the mercenary operation and how the gringos had taken down a number of drug lords in the space of just a few weeks. Following one lead after the next, they eventually heard about Kenny.

He was in a barroom drinking tequila when the Mexican soldiers arrested him.

After finishing up in Oaxaca, a small contingent of the foreign mercenaries had blitzed to the north, infiltrating Mexican military bases and blowing one sky high. Now CISEN's paymasters wanted answers. With Kenny under the bright lights of an underground interrogation room which had more in common with a dungeon, those answers would be forthcoming.

"The leader of the mercenaries," The CISEN agent began. "What was his name?"

"They- they- they- called him-"

"I'm listening," the Mexican interrogator said as he spun the hammer in his hand by the handle, the pry bar at the end spinning around.

"Deckard. They called him Deckard."

Another CISEN agent materialized out of the shadows in a corner of the interrogation cell. He handed the hammer-wielding agent a set of photographs. One by one, he began to hold the pictures in front of Kenny's face.

"Is this him?"

The first picture showed a Northern European looking soldier. Like the other photographs, it was a close up shot taken from a high resolution camera that had been running at a highly secure and classified Department of Energy site in Nevada. At least it had been until the men shown in the photographs crashed the party.

"No, I never saw him."

"What about this guy?" He said flipping to the next picture.

"They called him Pat. He was out there the night they took apart the Jimenez cartel."

"With your help?"

Kenny swallowed.

"Yes."

"What about this next guy?"

The next picture showed an Arab looking soldier, kitted out like the others.

"No, that's not Deckard. I don't think he was in Oaxaca either. Not with the others."

The interrogator was getting frustrated. Kenny could see the frown even under the ski mask he wore. He flipped to the next picture. It showed a thin man with high cheekbones and Asian eyes.

"They called him Nikita. He was their sniper."

The interrogator held up the last picture.

"That's him," Kenny said with a gasp as if he was about to pass out. "That's Deckard."

The interrogator stood up straight and looked at the surveillance camera in the corner of the room.

Ted Snyder looked away from the black and white surveillance footage that was streaming live to the screen of his laptop. After weeks of living in fear with round the clock security men patrolling his property and following him everywhere, he had finally identified the active threat against him.

"Deckard," he said the name to himself.

As the CEO of G3 Communications, it wouldn't be hard for him to make some phone calls and find out who the hell this cowboy was. Deckard had shot up southern Mexico and then turned his sights on a G3 Communications covert operation that ran a ratline of weapons, and bodies, into and through Mexico.

The security people at G3, all of them former CIA, SEALs, or Green Berets, had to admit that they were amazed by how fast the mercenaries had taken apart G3's operation. What Deckard had done was completely unprecedented. G3 had built a covert and clandestine infrastructure that ran down the spine of Mexico for them to fly in weapons and assassins. Deckard had identified that infrastructure, hijacked it, and rode it all the way north to its source in the Nevada desert.

Then he, and a couple other mercenaries, had dropped into Area 14, where G3 had been running the MEK terrorist organization, and burned the place to the ground. Deckard had sent a message in more ways than one, including a personal threat leveled against Ted.

G3 Communication ran covert operations for the United States government and other entities all over the world. Because of Deckard's actions, many of those operations were interrupted; others had to be closed down altogether. There was no question when it came to MEK, Deckard and his boys had killed all of them. It wasn't just Ted who was afraid, powerful people in some of the world's most influential places now had this Deckard character on their mind before even knowing his name.

Now Ted had that name.

With the MEK operation blown, Ted had transferred operational control of several other programs to other players. He had no idea how many of those programs were now blown or otherwise compromised. One of those programs was called Liquid Sky. High-end killers. Americans. They did the job right when proxies like MEK couldn't cut it.

Ted had handed Liquid Sky off to a retired General, a former JSOC commander.

The G3 Communications CEO realized that the CISEN agents in Mexico were waiting on his approval. He typed out a non-committal reply and sent it to them via instant messenger. The gist of it was that he was satisfied with the information they had obtained and he no longer needed Kenny Rodriguez. The Mexicans would know what to do with him.

Reaching for his cell phone, he entered into an encrypted phone-call app called Silent Circle and dialed General McCoy. It was time to put Liquid Sky on this target and paint a bullseye on the back of Deckard's head.

31

Two dark forms swam their way to shore.

Taking a knee in the gentle waves they carefully inspected the shoreline with their Night Optical Devices. A row of bungalows was laid out in front of them, some with lights on inside, others blacked out. Everything appeared normal, so they turned around and used a red-lens flashlight to signal the Zodiac rubber rafts that bobbed up and down in the ocean out past the breakers in the night.

With the all-clear signal confirmed, the mercenaries on the Zodiacs began paddling to shore. The Zodiacs came in with PKM machine gunners posted at the nose of each boat to pull frontal security. Three Zodiacs in total came to shore, the PKM gunners immediately jumping off and running up the beach before settling into firing positions with the Russian-made machine guns resting on their bipods.

The other mercenaries dismounted and pulled the Zodiacs up onto the beach. Samruk International's senior Non-Commissioned Officer, Sergeant Major Korgan, oversaw the entire operation. This platoon had seen their Platoon Sergeant killed by an IED in Mexico. Not that they needed the supervision. Their movements were smooth and rehearsed.

Two Squads moved up to the primary objective. Frank, the senior Samruk operative on the ground indicated the target house with an infrared laser that the other mercenaries could see through the green tint of their night vision.

The Kazakh mercenaries noted the sliding glass door. It had been left unlocked, so the point man simply slid the door open and slipped inside. The other mercenaries followed him in. Other squads were moving out to clear the other bungalows that Deckard had indicated as belonging to Liquid Sky.

Frank and Sergeant Major Koran were standing on the back deck in the middle of an impressive array of bench presses, free weights, kettlebells, and other exercise equipment when the first shot rang out from inside. Then another. Then another. A half dozen gunshots then blasted all at the same time before everything went quiet.

Inside, they found four security guards bleeding out on

the floor. Three looked to be locals from Mauritius. The fourth was an import, probably a Brit. All had been armed. The Kazakh mercenaries had efficiently eliminated each threat.

Frank rushed over to his old friend who was tied to a chair in the center of the room.

"C'mon, c'mon," he said urgently as he patted the side of his head.

He could barely recognize Aghassi after the beating he had taken. Finally, Aghassi coughed himself awake. He looked at Frank through bloodshot eyes.

"We're here to get you home," Frank told him. They went way back to when they had served in ISA together. In fact, it was Frank who recommended that Deckard hire Aghassi to work with them at Samruk International.

Aghassi nodded but was unable to talk.

He was banged up good but would live.

Sergeant Major Korgan motioned over one of the Kazakhs who carried breaching equipment. Using a pair of bolt cutters, he cut through the chain on the handcuffs and Frank slashed through the duct tape holding his feet together with his knife.

The men would make a search of the bungalow, conducting a sensitive site exploitation sweep for anything of intelligence value that could be used to help them take down Liquid Sky.

The Kazakhs had reported in to Sergeant Major Korgan by radio that they had secured each objective and were beginning their search. A medic came forward to get an IV into Aghassi so they could start pushing fluids into his system.

Everything was going exactly according to plan, which should have tipped them off.

That was about when one of the Kazakhs searching Bill's office upstairs stepped on a pressure plate. The explosion killed the Samruk mercenary instantly and destroyed everything in the office along with it.

With the office now in flames, the sea winds quickly helped the fire spread.

"Landslide, landslide," Frank called over the radio net. It was the codeword to evacuate the objective immediately and return to their last rally point.

They had hit a boobytrap and if the local authorities had

not been called due to the sound of their gunshots, they certainly would be after the explosion.

As silently as they had arrived, the Samruk International mercenaries flowed back outside, filed down the beach, and slid the Zodiacs back into the ocean. Aghassi was packaged up inside a field stretcher, the medic now pushing pain killers into him through the IV. He was loaded into the center of one of the Zodiacs.

The red flashes of fire trucks could be seen approaching, the sound of the sirens carrying on the wind as the mercenaries disappeared into the dark waters, heading back to their mothership.

32

The airfield in Turkey was buzzing.

White Land Cruisers sped around the runway, ferrying Westerners around the immediate area. Were they working for relief organizations, intelligence services, or corporations? Deckard watched another group of middle aged men depart a third airplane that had landed that morning and decided that probably they were working for all three at the same time.

Syria was now a global conflict that had pulled in actors from far and wide. Russia backed Assad as the Russian Navy had a warm water port in Syria, their last in the Mediterranean, as well as over a billion dollars in defense contracts a year sunk with the Syrian regime. The House of Saud supported the Sunni extremists such as the Al-Nusra front in order to hedge their bets against a strong Shia presence in the Middle East. Qatar supported the same simply because they wanted to be an influential player in Middle Eastern politics, and international influence meant assuming an Islamist bent these days.

America supported the rebel movement, the so-called Free Syrian Army with covert assistance but so little that even the moderates in the movement had defected to Al-Nusra as they were the best support, drawing cash and weapons from the Saudis and Qataris. With the FSA gutted, America was left with few options by the time they began to overtly assist the rebels. Meanwhile, China supported whatever players in the region were not aligned with America.

Long story short, Syria was fucked. Corrupt elites in the Assad regime fought tooth and nail knowing that the Baath party would sink or swim together. If they lost, there would be no negotiated peace. That time had long since passed. Now it was total war until one side annihilated the other. The civilians paid the price as Islamists and Alawite death squads executed entire families in their terror campaigns.

The country would hollow itself out of human life until there simply were not enough fighters left to carry the rifles.

Deckard watched the foreigners load up and drive off, no doubt heading to the converted military garrison in nearby Antakya where the FSA command center was housed along with the headquarters for other Western-sponsored rebel groups. It was also where the rebels met with American, British, Turkish, and Qatari intelligence officers.

What a shit show.

The satellite phone in his pocket buzzed.

Deckard took it out and looked at the screen.

Hostage extracted. One friendly KIA. Negative SSE.

Aghassi was alive but at the cost of another of his men and they were back to square one.

Walking back into the hangar, one of those Westerners he had seen fly in earlier was crouched over one of the two mustard gas bombs they had recovered from Libya. The technician was removing the impact fuse and replacing it with a custom electronic trigger mechanism. The plan called for the bombs to be detonated on the ground with Al-Nusra taking the rap for it, thus providing an excuse for the Western world to invade Syria because no one wanted Islamic radicals trotting around with weapons of mass destruction.

Deckard knew that whoever cooked up this plan was a quack. They were going to end up triggering World War Three.

The technician replaced the nose cap with one of his own design. It had a keypad and digital display. The client may have been a quack, but whoever he was, he wasn't crazy enough to let Al-Nusra finger the trigger. Liquid Sky would have to input a code to arm the chemical weapons. The nose cap also included a GPS so that its movement could be tracked by satellite. Otherwise, Nusra might flip the switch and ship the bombs to New York or London.

The mustard gas bombs weighed in at eighty pounds each. For them to be parachuted into Syria with the Liquid Sky team, they would both be carefully packed into a Tandem Offset Resupply Delivery System or TORDS, which consisted of a giant cylinder rigged to one of the freefall jumpers by a tether. TORDS could be loaded up with 500 pounds of gear and was designed for a parachutist to jump in a combat resupply for long range reconnaissance teams that operated deep behind enemy lines. The system was awkward to say the least and the U.S. military hardly even used it anymore.

Arriving by plane from Libya was not only the twin

mustard gas bombs but also a weapons cache the team was to infiltrate into Syria with, all courtesy of their friend Yezza. Extra weapons, ammunition, explosives, and other mission-essential gear would be loaded up in the TORDS along with the bombs. There were also extra weapons to give to Nusra to help grease the wheels and get them into the rebels' good graces.

The Liquid Sky team was on the other side of the hangar, laying out their kit and packing their MC-5 parachutes. They had Crye precision jumpable plate carriers and an AK-47 rifle for each team member. They would also jump with rucksacks filled with food, some water, ammunition, and other gear in addition to what would be going off the ramp in the TORDS.

Deckard checked over his kit again. He had considered sabotaging at least one Liquid Sky member's parachute. Probably Bill's, or maybe The Operator's, but he didn't have time to do a thorough job. There were too many fail-safes on a MC-5 between the main chute, reserve, and CYPRES system, and he would have to defeat all of them without being noticed.

The Operator sat next to him on the concrete floor, cleaning his rifle for the eighth time that day. Of course his weapon was already immaculate, as was the 1911 pistol he had shipped along with it from Libya. He had on his ever-present mirrored Oakley sunglasses, despite being indoors.

"If you need a sling, there is a box full of them around here somewhere," Deckard said as he noticed that The Operator's Kalashnikov was lacking something.

"You had your way of doing things at Range 37 and we had our way of doing things on Range 19," The Operator said curtly.

"Huh?"

The Operator took a deep breath.

"One of the things you quickly learn as an operator as opposed to being in another unit is that you don't use slings. Your weapon goes where you go and aims wherever your eyes look. If you lose your weapon you lose it; you can always get a new one."

That was an interesting theory. Deckard opted not to follow up on that.

Across the hangar, the technician finished working on the first bomb and moved on to the second. Once he was done with his work, they would load up the TORDS for airborne operations. Deckard decided to wipe down and lube up his AK rifle as well.

They had air laid on to insert them that night.

"Bring it in," Bill said, his voice echoing as he walked into the hangar. He had an Iridium satellite phone in his hand which he had been using to talk to the client. With an encryption sleeve their commo would be relatively secure, but it was clear that Bill really only talked shop over the Pirate Net he had set up in Mauritius. Over the Iridium phone they would use encryption and only use pro-words, which were pre-determined codewords.

Deckard and The Operator set their rifles down and stood up. Paul and Ramon walked away from their half-packed parachutes. Rick and Nadeesha joined them a few moments later.

"We're cleared hot for tonight," Bill informed them. "We are jumping at 18,000 feet. The only question left is who here has ever jumped the TORDS before?"

Everyone looked at each other and then up in the air or down at their feet.

"I'm qualified on the TORDS system, but not current," The Operator volunteered.

"Well nobody is checking to make sure that your online safety worksheets have been completed out here. You got the job."

"Roger that."

"Also, each of you needs to know how to work the keypad destruction sequence for the bombs," Bill told them. "In case I get killed, I expect the rest of you to carry out the mission. Not a big deal since I will never die but you never know.

Bill then walked them through how to enter the activation code into the keypads, set the timer, and how to deactivate the bombs if necessary.

"One more order of business before I cut you all lose to get some sleep before we roll."

Bill reached into his pocket and pulled out a handful of little white pills wrapped inside squares of cellophane. He held them in the palm of his hand, one for each Liquid Sky member.

"Fuck, not this again," Rick complained.

"If I wanted to hear you bitch and moan I would take my dick out of your mouth," Bill hissed.

One by one they took a pill packet out of Bill's hand.

"What are they?" Deckard asked.

"Your go-to-hell plan."

The Operator looked down at his pill pack in the palm of his hand, then made a fist and placed it in his pocket.

"I haven't seen these since Dagestan," The Operator said.

"Technically I should be making you guys carry them on every mission, I just haven't been enforcing it because I figure each of you has the good god damn common sense to do yourself if it comes to that. This time the client insisted. There is too much riding on this mission and the results are too high profile. If you are going to be captured, take the pill. It works the same way as a morphine overdose, puts you to sleep and then stops your heart. It's painless."

"How would you know? Have you ever taken one before?" Paul said.

"Yeah, what is the quality assurance on these things?" Ramon started in. "I would hate to have it only be half effective."

"And walk around like the fucking window-licker for the rest of your life," Rick added.

"Knock it the fuck off and keep those pill packs on you at all times. You won't be fucking laughing if they grab you and *Jackie the fucking Iraqi* is sawing your still-beating heart out," Bill yelled.

Turning, he stormed away from the group.

"Fuck," Rick cursed.

"Stress must be getting to him," Ramon said.

"When the time comes, I will take this pill," The Operator said flatly.

Everyone turned to look at him for a moment and then went back to doing whatever they had been doing before Bill's team huddle.

33

The interior of the Casa 235 was cramped, claustrophobic, and hot.

The passengers rocked around the inside of the plane as it skirted low over the surface of the earth to avoid surface-to-air missiles. They flew blacked-out, in the dark, the free fall jumpers sitting on the cold metal floor while their bodies quickly heated up the Casa's innards. Sweat beaded and then ran down their faces. After a few hours their stomachs churned and their heads swam. Burdened by the rucksacks clipped into their parachute harnesses, weapons, and other gear, it got really humid really fast.

Deckard closed his eyes as he began to get dizzy. This was the most dangerous part of the mission, the part where you have time to think. Time to doubt your preparations, your training, your mission. Time to doubt yourself. And when you blew off all your very rational fears, you just doubted in general because you had nothing else to busy yourself with. But like all good soldiers, Deckard possessed that psychopathic part of his brain that allowed him to arrogantly push on, figuring he could somehow survive.

Fuck it.

It wasn't like he planned to live forever.

The loadmaster standing near the ramp of the aircraft indicated that they were twenty minutes out. They could already feel the aircraft gaining altitude. This would be a straight high altitude low opening jump. No high-speed HAHO sky-pirate business, no wing suits. Just pop your chute and get to the ground without dying.

Liquid Sky snapped their Ops-Core helmets on; then, flipped on their oxygen tanks before securing the rubber oxygen masks over their faces. Then, they began the long, slow, and painful process of dragging themselves to their feet. It was then that another feeling washed over Deckard. He stood on shaky feet but the ghost of a smile was on his face behind the oxygen mask. He was going to war. Not with the Syrians, but with his own kind. He had witnessed the scalpings, the murders first hand. He had two options, join Liquid Sky and fully commit, or complete his mission.

Deckard would complete his mission.

War was the only time that life made sense to him.

Everything was finally starting to come back into focus.

The Operator was at the rear of the plane, standing next to the ramp alongside the TORDs bundle that he was tethered to. The bundle sat on rollers right next to the edge of the ramp. The freefall jumpers did one last check of their own and their teammates' equipment to make sure everything was in place. As they reached altitude, the loadmaster lowered the ramp. He was a contractor, working for who only knew what company.

When the green light came on, Rick helped roll the TORDs off the ramp, The Operator chasing it into the night. Bill held the drogue chute that would help stabilize The Operator in free fall. He released it into the night as the bundle jumper disappeared off the back of the ramp. The rest of the team waddled out the door right behind him, nearly on top of each other as they leaned forward and fell off the back of the Casa.

Deckard was the last one out.

At night, you intellectually knew that you were jumping off a plane, thousands of feet up in the sky. You knew a thousand things could go wrong and you could die. But in the dark, with your hearing restricted by ear plugs and only a single dim light to show you the way off the plane you got tunnel vision. You focused on what you had to do, your equipment, the actions you were required to do one step at a time. The night helped you focus, your brain not really registering the gravity of what you were doing.

Deckard was still smiling when he went off the end of the ramp, knowing that this would be a one-way trip.

He could smell the fuel and feel the heat from the engines as he fell. Riding the hill of air off the back of the plane, he pivoted his hips forward, kept his arms out at his sides, and made sure his knees were bent, but out. With the rucksack hanging between his legs, he wouldn't need to have his legs as outstretched as normal in order to get into a stable body position.

A light stick was rubber-banded to the altimeter on his wrist. A small slit was cut in the wrapper so that just enough green light escaped to light up the dial. He looked at it briefly as his body seesawed in the air. At 17,500 feet, he was having a hard time getting stable in the air. The other jumpers were out there, somewhere, but he couldn't see them in the dark.

Deckard continued to wobble in the air. He tried to sink his hips lower and get his arms and legs out in the most symmetrical pattern possible. Nothing seemed to be working and he knew that at this point he was just going to have to ride it out. Keeping his eyes on where he thought the horizon was, Deckard glanced again at his altimeter.

Suddenly, he dipped down. Trying to compensate in free fall was difficult and now the wind resistance against his body spun him right around onto his back. Deckard was now falling at 6,000 feet above the surface of the earth, on his back and looking up at the stars. He made one attempt to do some sort of situp in the air and get himself turned back around, but with all the kit he wore, that simply wasn't happening. He was frozen in position.

Gathering his wits, Deckard brought in one arm and held his hand against his chest. With the other arm still out, it acted like a giant rudder in the wind and propelled him back over onto his stomach. Deckard turned his wrist towards him and looked again at the altimeter from the corner of his eye.

4,200 feet.

Careful not to accidentally grab the hose running to his oxygen mask, he pulled his ripcord grip. The MC-5 parachute deployed above his head, the leg straps biting into his thighs as it felt like he was being dragged upward. In reality, he was just slowing down, losing descent speed as the parachute grabbed some air for him.

Once he had a canopy above his head, Deckard checked for the three S's. Square, stable, and yanking down on the parachute toggles he found that, yeah, it was steerable too. With a starry sky and a sliver of moon showing through the clouds, the freefall jumpers were able to get into a file formation as they glided towards the ground.

A few hundred feet above the drop zone, Deckard pulled the release tab and dropped his rucksack on a nylon tether beneath him. When he heard his rucksack hit the ground, Deckard pulled his toggles half way down to put the parachute at half breaks. Keeping his feet and knees together, he impacted the rocky ground and flopped over on one side.

He came down hard, same as every jump, but was alive. He pulled one brake line in hand over hand, collapsing the parachute. Deckard was more than happy to free himself from the parachute harness and get his AK-47 into operation. Next he balled up his parachute and packed it inside an OD green kit bag he had brought along with him.

A few other silhouettes could be seen walking against the skyline so it didn't take long for Liquid Sky to link up. Their drop zone was right next to a river so the team loaded large rocks into their kit bags with the parachutes and then one by one they hurled the parachutes into the river to sink them to the bottom. The last thing they wanted was to leave a bunch of military parachutes laying around to telegraph their presence in Syria.

The Operator had no problem landing the TORDs. Inside the cylinder were the two mustard gas bombs along with stretchers that they would lay the weapons in to help carry during transport. It would take at least two men to carry each one of the bombs. The others would walk point and pull security for them.

Deckard hefted the weight of the metal poles up onto his shoulders as he took the rear of one stretchers and Paul took the front as they walked. They had a couple of kilometers to move through what had been viable farmland before the war broke out. Their next task was perhaps the most risky part of their mission and the part that none of them were looking forward to.

The link up.

Their client had a line of communications with them and assured Liquid Sky that the road had been paved for them, but the bottom line was that they were about to link up with the most dangerous and ruthless fighting group in Syria. Al-Nusra. They were Syria's version of Al Qaeda, Islamic extremists, terrorists who killed anyone who didn't buy into their version of Islam. Many of them were foreign fighters. They came from Iraq, Pakistan, Libya, Saudi Arabia, Afghanistan, Chechnya, and even from American, Canada, and Germany. They came to fight. They came to die.

Liquid Sky came to fight as well, but there were only seven of them with nothing but the weapons and equipment on their bodies to defend themselves in a denied area with thousands of enemies around them, both rebels and regime forces.

As they neared a road intersection, Bill told them to halt. Those carrying the two packages postmarked from Libya were happy to set their load down. Bill got out his red-lens flashlight. This was where they were supposed to meet with Nusra. A bunch of former American soldiers joining forces with hardcore Jihadi terrorists who beheaded Shias, Christians, Jews, and Alawites alike in village squares just for shits and giggles.

Fuck me, Deckard cursed himself internally.

Bill flashed the *bonefidis*. Three red flashes of his light directed towards the road.

A pause.

Two red flashes answered in return from the road.

Deckard drew the bolt back with the charging handle on his AK and did a press check to make sure he had a round chambered.

Here we go again.

34

Pat cursed as machine gun fire rattled his vehicle.

It was the third time that night and they had only been in Syria a matter of hours. Tartus had been an obvious no-go to make port in so they had to come in at a much smaller port to the north. The logistics themselves were an absolute nightmare. With such a time crunch there was no way he was going to be able to get Samruk International's gun trucks into country. That alone put them at a major disadvantage. They had to use their operational funds to buy four two and half ton trucks in Egypt and travel with them by boat to Cyprus and then on to Syria. He didn't even like to think about how much he had to bribe the ship's captain to run a Han Solo style pirate run on the Syrian coast to drop them off.

They were gunning it through their third ambush. In addition, they had bribed their way through one checkpoint on the road and shot through another. This was the fight to get to the fight. The only good news was that he had a platoon of trained and battle-hardened Kazakh mercenaries. From the beds of the transport trucks, they returned fire on enemy positions up in the cliffs to their side. Led by Western advisers like Kurt Jager of Germany's GSG-9 and Leszek of Polish GROM, Samruk International definitely had their shit wired tighter than the regime thugs or the rabble that passed for a rebellion that they had encountered thus far.

The problem was that they could still be nickled and dimed until they were a bloody mess by the time they rolled into Homs in the morning. Out here they had no support, no back up, no resupply.

Another thing they didn't have was an update from Deckard. The last text he had gotten from the cell phone Aghassi had left for him was that the mission had the green light and they would be jumping in tonight on a drop zone near Homs.

By daylight, they would need to have something from him. Driving into Homs blind was a death sentence with the city divided down the middle by rebels and regime forces who were slugging it out block by block. The pictures that had emerged from the war torn city looked like Stalingrad in World War Two.

The only thing they had going in their favor, and it wasn't much, was a local fixer named Ali. Pat had called a friend in the intelligence community to get a recommendation for someone local. They picked Ali up on the side of the road in Tartus after wiring him half of his fee. He lived just outside Homs and could help guide them into their targets. So far, he hadn't been much good at helping them avoid ambushes and checkpoints.

All they needed was to cross the rest of the war-torn landscape to Homs, get comms with Deckard, and then shoot their way in to secure two chemicals weapons, destroy them, and then shoot their way out.

"Fuck," Pat cursed as a RPG streaked through the night to their front. The rocket blasted deeper into the valley and exploded harmlessly against the rocks on the other side. One RPG, one well-placed IED, and they could be put out of business. At least the enemy didn't have much night-vision capability, giving them the advantage at night. Samruk's driver drove blacked-out while looking through NODs.

The *pop-pop-pop* of AK-103's sounded in the back of Pat's truck as his men returned fire.

Cupping a hand over the screen, Pat looked at his handheld GPS. They were about to cruise past Masyaf. It was a medium-sized town but at least they were clearing out of the valleys and into the flatlands. Soon they would be halfway to Homs.

Another round of AK fire vibrated the truck.

Pat knew that the night was far from over.

"Get up front and take the lead, Deckard," Bill said.

"Why me?"

"Because you speak Arabic, and so that you can absorb the first couple bullets."

"Nice."

"Go up ahead and make nice with the jihadists. We haven't got all night."

Deckard took the lead, shuffling forward with the weight of his rucksack on his back. He held his Kalashnikov at the ready. Liquid Sky followed at an uncomfortable distance from him, hauling the two chemical weapons with them.

As he got closer to the road, he could see some movement. Some of the jihadists were standing and others looked to be popping a squat. Deckard intentionally made noise as he approached so that they knew he was coming. The last thing he wanted was a surprised jihadist pointing a weapon at him.

"*As-salamu alaykum*," Deckard greeted them when he noticed several of the dark forms turn towards him.

"*Ilnash sharaf intuu wiyaana*," someone answered in Iraqi dialect.

Deckard knew he was entering a world of shit. The Iraqi brand of Al Qaeda, The Islamic State of Iraq, had massive bounties out on the heads of people just like him.

The jihadists gathered around Deckard. There were about two dozen of them. To his surprise, they held their AK-47s at the ready, weapons on safe, with their fingers off the triggers. These guys had combat training. The war had been going on for a few years though, so maybe it had more to do with military Darwinism: only the hardcores were still left standing.

One of them, this one with a North African accent, asked him about his trip. Deckard told a joke about falling from the sky and to his relief the Islamic extremists chuckled. All except one. He was a little bigger than the others, light skinned, and with a massive black beard. Chechen. He was eye-raping Deckard up and down.

After the exchange of pleasantries, Deckard waved for Liquid Sky to come in and meet the Nusra fighters. The Liquid Sky mercenaries set down the bombs and Deckard introduced them by first names only. There was a sudden grumble amongst

276

the Nusra fighters when he introduced Nadi. They hadn't realized that there was a woman in the group.

They should have anticipated this. In the world the Nusra fighters fought for, strict Islamic law called Sharia would be the law of the land. This Bronze-Age mentality dictated that women were baby factories and domestic slaves. He had to think fast.

"Nadi and I are bound by contractual marriage," Deckard said. "She belongs to me. She is our technician who went to university to learn how to build and detonate the bombs we brought with us."

This brought on another series of strained groans.

The Chechen interrupted the Nusra complaints.

"This is acceptable," he said in nearly perfect English. "But you are responsible. She goes no where without you."

"I understand," Deckard assured him, but he knew that he hadn't heard the last of this. He decided to change the subject.

"I want to you to take a look at the gifts we have brought Nusra," Deckard told the group. "This gift comes down to you from the eyes of Allah. These weapons will strike terror into the hearts of your enemyies, destroy their will to fight."

"*Allah akbar,*" several Nusra fighters said in unison. God is great.

The two chemical weapons were presented to the Nusra fighters along with a small haul of exotic high end pistols and sub-machine guns that they had packed in their rucks after having them shipped in from Libya. Each Nusra fighter present got a party favor.

Deckard pointed to the two Mazda flatbed trucks parked alongside the road.

"Can we load the weapons on your trucks and drive to your camp?" Deckard asked.

The Chechen fighter wagged his finger at Deckard. Bill and the Liquid Sky team stood by and watched as the Nusra fighters began talking over each other in rapid-fire Arabic. Nadi was the only other team member who could even begin to keep up with the conversation. Deckard had to ask them to slow down several times.

Bill, Ramon, Rick, and Paul began to get twitchy, their thumbs slowly rotating the selector switches on their rifles from safe to semi. This mission looked to them like it was about to go south in a bad way. The Operator stood facing the Nusra fighters stoically.

"Deckard," Bill said, trying to interrupt the frantic conversation. They continued talking back and forth in Arabic.

"Deckard!"

"Yeah?"

"What the fuck is going on?"

"We have a problem."

"No shit."

"They want us to hit a Republican Guard outpost on the way to Homs with them."

"Tell them that's not what we're here for Deckard."

"I did. The soldiers working out of that outpost are making their lives miserable but the real reason they want to take it out is to capture the four T-72 tanks there. They say that they need those tanks if we plan to go to Damascus. There are just too many military checkpoints on the road between there and Homs. We need heavy firepower to clear the way for us."

"The rebels are taking out dozens and dozens of enemy armor every day," Ramon complained. "What the fuck is this about?"

"Our intel supports what they are saying about the road to Damascus though," Nadi said. "We are going to have a hell of a time getting there."

"No."

The Operator's single word cut through the night.

"They are testing us. They want to see firsthand if we have what it takes before they commit their fighters to a virtual suicide mission in Damascus."

"Fuck me," Rick said.

Bill grunted.

"So be it. We'll show them we have what it takes and then some," Bill said. "Deckard, tell them that we just need them to show us where the target is."

When Deckard translated several more shouts of *Allah akbar* went up.

After loading up the mustard gas bombs on the back of one of the flatbeds, Liquid Sky piled on along with the Nusra fighters. The drivers didn't dare turn on their headlights, not with MIG fighter jets somewhere overhead, so they just drove slowly in the dark.

The fight to get to the fight, Deckard thought. *What could go wrong?*

He wondered if Pat and his Samruk International mercenaries were doing any better.

The rocky hillside almost looked translucent under the moonlight. The jihadists may have been fundamentalist nutcases, but they knew war. This wasn't their first rodeo. They had seen combat from Libya to Iraq to Afghanistan, just like the Special Operations units that hunted them. Nusra was now the most effective fighting force in Syria. They wisely decided upon an offset infiltration. Parking their trucks, they left them under guard while the assault forces stalked up to the Syrian military outpost.

The chemical weapons were safe for the time being. They could not be detonated without the eight digit number combination and even if the Nusra guards tried to disappear with the bombs the GPS built into them would guarantee that it would only be a matter of time before an American or Israeli airstrike rained death down upon them.

The fighters snaked their way up the hill, the Chechen leading the way. Deckard found out that he was called Tiger by the other Nusra fighters, a war name he had been given by them for his bravery under fire. It was clear by now that Tiger was familiar with the terrain and that he had reconned the area previously. The Operator had been correct, this was a test. Nusra could have raided the outpost anytime they wanted.

Nearing the top of the hill, Deckard climbed hand over hand as he and the Chechen slowly crept their way to the crest.

As he looked down on the military outpost he nearly choked. They were right on top of the hard site. The Chechen had got them within ten meters of the nearest T-72 tank. There were three other tanks arrayed within a perimeter protected by a circular dirt berm. Several OD green canvas tents housed the soldiers, and there was even a small cooking fire.

"Ghosts," the Chechen told him in Arabic. His curly black beard bounced as he spoke each word. "They often sneak into Homs under the cover of dark to do their dirty work. Tonight we use the cover of dark to strike back against these devils."

Deckard had heard of the Ghosts before. Scattered reports had hit the Western media, but the real horror story was unknown to those living back in the States. Assad was an Alawite, a Muslim minority group seen as heretical by both Sunni and Shia. In Syria, the Alawites made up a large portion of the political elite. It was one more reason why they fought the civil war with such vigor. There could be no negotiated peace as their religious group would be wiped out if they lost the war.

When the protests in Syria had really turned into an armed rebellion, some of these political elites organized Alawite death squads. Their job was to literally terrify the Syrian people into compliance. They would go into villages and execute entire families with shots to the back of the head. Saw the heads off little girls. Rape wives and daughters. Send a message.

The death squads were called *Shabeeha*. Apparitions. Ghosts.

Deckard was warming to this idea of attacking the outpost. This might be some good target practice after all, provided it didn't get them all killed. One by one, the Nusra fighters and Liquid Sky mercenaries edged up to the assault line. A few soldiers below seemed to be milling around, having a smoke or taking a piss. He didn't hear any motors so the tanks were clearly not running, probably in order to save fuel. Syria's logistics lines were stretched pretty thin this late in the game.

"All we need to do is ambush from here," Tiger whispered.

The Liquid Sky members caught one word even in Arabic. *Amboush.*

"I have already assigned teams to secure the tanks. We have the high ground and will fight down to them before the

280

infidels can get in their tanks."

"Then let's do this," Deckard replied.

Tiger shouldered his AK-47. The others queued off of the Nusra leader. Two of them had carried PKM machine guns up to the assault line. A few others had RPKs with 40 round magazines. Dropping the selector on his AK one click down, Tiger opened fire on auto. He raked the nearest tent with 7.62 rounds as the entire assault line suddenly lit up the camp with green tracer fire. The rocks around them blinked in and out with orange light as their muzzle flashes flickered like strobe lights.

The machine guns fired down into the camp. Sparking off the tanks, blasting into the tents, kicking up dirt everywhere else. Mostly kicking up dirt. Deckard had too much target fixation to notice that as he focused in on the individual soldiers he could see below and pumped two shots into each. One by one they crumpled to the ground.

A single Syrian soldier scrambled to his tank. He made it as far as the hatch before Rick put a bullet in his face. The would-be tank gunner rolled off the side of the tank and took a dirt nap. The PKM gunners both went empty at the same time, an amateur move that happened because they didn't stagger their fire. Slapping in fresh belts of ammunition, the riflemen cracked off a few shots here and there as signs of life were spotted below but the camp was pretty quiet.

"What the fuck Deckard?" Bill asked. "Get these hodjis moving."

Deckard turned to the Chechen but he was already jumping to his feet.

"*Allah akbar!*" he yelled and charged down into the camp. Without missing a beat, the Nusra fighters followed their leader, descending down the rocks to the outpost.

When they got to the bottom the jihadists scattered, breaking off into their pre-assigned teams and taking control of the four tanks. Others went into the tents searching for survivors. Bodies were scattered around the camp. Most of them had been attempting to flee.

"The ghosts are not here," Tiger said to Deckard. "They must be out. This isn't good."

"We can catch up with them later. At least we got the tanks. Now we can complete our mission," Deckard reassured him.

"If God wills it."

Suddenly, voices began shouting in the night. Turning, Deckard saw Rick pushing a Nusra fighter away from one of the corpses. He had been attempting to rifle through his belongings for some war booty. As he shoved him, the Arab tripped and landed on his back.

"These are our kills," Rick yelled. "Fuck off."

The Jihadist cursed as he got to his feet. He looked like he was ready to fight the American until Rick reached for his belt and yanked out a hatchet. Even though they were all carrying guns, the sight of an edged weapons elicited a special kind of fear from the arab. Deckard held his breath. If Rick swung that hatchet on the Nusra fighter they would have a catastrophic loss of rapport, to put it mildly.

Rick did swing the hatchet. Right down on the head of the dead Syrian soldier. He chopped and cut until he reached down and grabbed a fist full of hair. Planting his boot on the corpse's back, he yanked the scalp right off the skull.

"*Allah akbar!*" the Chechen shouted.

"*Allah akbar!*" the jihadists echoed.

Nadi found another Syrian soldier who was still breathing. She fired a couple shots into his groin causing him to jump. Then she put her AK on full auto and blasted off the top of his skull.

"You guys are dragging ass tonight," Bill said as he came up behind Deckard and walked towards Nadi and Rick. He had a scalp in each hand. Looking over his shoulder, Deckard could see that Paul was also busy chopping away with a hatchet. It was a senseless orgy of violence.

"Forgive me, my brother," the Chechen said as he leaned towards Deckard. "I had no idea that Americans could be such fierce fighters."

That was about the worst thing that he possibly could have said to Deckard at that moment. Just witnessing the war crimes was enough to make his skin crawl, being complimented on them was too much.

One by one the T-72 tanks roared the life as the Nusra fighters got them started. They even had ground guides who helped them exit the razor wire switchbacks at the entrance to the outpost. The tanks took off down the road as the Chechen turned on his walkie talkie and informed their base in Homs that four friendly tanks were coming their way.

Deckard reached into his pocket and palmed the satellite enabled cellphone that he had picked up in Mauritius. He knew he was taking a risk every time he turned it on that some eyes or ears in the sky might pick him up. Now was the time to take that risk. He thumbed the power button while keeping the phone in his pocket.

"Now we head back to Homs," the Chechen told him. "You Americans have proven to be very tough fighters. I am sorry my friend, I never should have doubted you. But God willed it and now we have these tanks to help clear our way to Damascus!"

"No need to apologize," Deckard said. "I would have done the same."

It was true, the outpost had been a confidence target.

"Once we get to our staging area in Homs we will prepare the vehicles and your weapons. Let's hurry. We should get back into the city and under overhead cover before dawn. We own the night, but not the skies."

The sounds of a Syrian fighter jet somewhere off in the distance seemed to confirm that fact, almost as if on queue. Tracer fire crisscrossed the sky as someone tried to shoot it down.

"Let me tell my team and we can head back to the trucks."

"Tomorrow is a big day, the night even more so," the Chechen said, hardly able to contain his glee.

Deckard walked to the edge of the camp and pretended to take a piss. Pulling out the cellphone he quickly typed out a message and texted Pat:

In country, heading to Homs w/ package.

A few seconds later he got a reply.

About an hour out from your loc.

Deckard sent one final message before signing off.

Stand by for grid to tgt. Short timeline. Tmmrw night.

283

Turning off the phone, he strode off to find Bill and the other Liquid Sky members.

They were on a short time line, even shorter than Liquid Sky realized.

35

The staging area was a bombed-out crater, the ruins of what had once been a series of family housing units on the outskirts of Homs. Now, it was Al-Nusra's command center for their Homs offensive. The city looked even more bombed out then Beirut had been back in the 80s. Buildings were now hollowed out skeletons, walls partially collapsed, floors pancaked on top of each other. Bullet holes were blasted everywhere. Larger holes signified tank or anti-tank fire. Homs had pretty much seen it all at this point.

The odd crack of gunfire could be heard as Nusra and the Syrian Army took pot shots at each other, but for the most part it was quiet in the early morning hours. The two forces were at a stalemate. They each held their lines throughout the city and only occasionally pushed forward, making small offensives here and there where they thought they saw an opening in the enemy's defenses and could gain some ground.

As for the civilians still living in the city, they were shit out of luck. If they didn't get killed in the crossfire, the ghosts from the Alawite death squad would probably ensure that they met a fate that was much worse.

Deckard watched as the Nusra fighters prepared for battle. Nearly one hundred of the terrorists were operating out of the base. They ran around like excited little bumble bees, some as giddy as a school girl at the prospect of being able to use chemical weapons on civilians in Damascus. The tanks were being fueled up and the flatbed trucks, which would carry the weapons, were being armored with metal plating welded onto the sides. They would be taking the Mad Max convoy south during the next period of darkness.

The sun was still coming up, but Nusra could not wait. They were also preparing weapons and ammunition. Several SA-7 anti-aircraft launchers were made ready. They had the control units and multiple missiles for each. Since the battery life on the SA-7 was only about thirty seconds once it was screwed into place, they had improvised wire leads that went from the control unit to a car battery to keep them powered for the duration. The Syrian Air Force could not count on air superiority as they crashed their way into the capital city.

Deckard took a seat between the two mustard gas bombs, which had been set down under the remains of the second story of a building, now serving as more of an awning. For now, he had been placed on guard duty while the rest of the Liquid Sky team got a few hours of sleep in shifts. Paul would relieve him in an hour. Powering his satellite phone back up, Deckard used an app to get a grid location to the Nusra staging area and texted it to Pat. He also gave a brief estimate of the enemy's size, strength, and disposition.

With the phone concealed behind the bomb, he continued to type with his thumbs.

14.5 AA gun, NW corner bld.
Package centrally located
LiqSky element N bld bombed out
SA-7's in compound

He kept typing until he saw a couple jihadists approaching. They were lugging a SPG-9 recoilless rifle towards one of the trucks. Deckard pressed *send* and slipped the phone in his pocket. He would try to feed Pat as much real-time intelligence as possible. The tricky part was going to be slipping away himself in the chaos and confusion that would occur once Samruk International attacked. He had to make sure he didn't get killed by Nusra, Liquid Sky, or his own people who wouldn't recognize him in the local garb he wore at a distance.

The phone vibrated in his pocket. He waited until the jihadists had busied themselves loading the recoilless rifle on the back of the truck before looking to see what Pat had texted.

Holy fuck.

Deckard texted back:

Hold off 1 more hr. Going to soften them up for you.

Deckard waited until Paul came to relieve him on guard duty. He was still rubbing the sleep out of his eyes.

"Don't forget to wake up the family of birds that have been nesting in your beard," Deckard joked.

Paul grunted something in response. Walking through the Nusra compound, Deckard surveyed the enemy positions one more time. Guards were lazily standing up on the second and third stories of the bombed-out buildings surrounding the central area. It was really just a crater that Nusra had cleaned out to create a small courtyard. The guards were mostly looking inwards, watching their comrades prepare for their holy war, rather than facing out and looking for intruders. That would play well in Samruk's favor.

Deckard pretended to walk towards the building where the Liquid Sky team was getting some rest, but then ducked behind the flatbed trucks and tanks in the Nusra motorpool. Turning sideways, he side stepped his way between two of the tanks and then rolled under one of the Mazda flatbed trucks. He wanted to disable them first so the chemical weapons could not be driven away when the attack kicked off.

Laying on his back, he wormed his way forward until he was under the engine compartment. Finding the firewall, he was able to trace his way up and find the wires, that ran from the transmission to the computer. He carried a Grayman Duo folder knife on his kit that would do the job. Opening the knife silently with his thumb and forefinger, he locked the blade open and began slashing the wires which would prevent the engine from starting.

He froze as a pair of boots kicked up dust alongside the

truck. One of the Nusra fighters stopped next to the flatbed and was loading something on the back. While he was busy, Deckard rolled over onto his stomach and crawled hand over hand until he was under the second flatbed. He repeated the same procedure once he was under the engine, and then slashed the serpentine belt just to make sure.

Making sure the coast was clear, he crawled out from under the truck and walked over to the closest T-72 tank. At one point in time, it had been the fiercest main battle tank in the Soviet arsenal. Today, variants and surplus T-72's were sold all over the world, including countries like Syria and Iraq. Crawling up the front of the tank, he lowered himself into the driver's seat and went to work on the wiring behind the panels. None of his impromptu sabotage would take long for a mechanic to fix, but that was fine. He just had to disable the vehicles for the duration of Samruk's attack on the compound.

Another Nusra fighter came walking by with a crate of AK-47 ammunition slung on his shoulder. Deckard ducked down inside the tank until he had passed. Climbing off the now-disabled T-72, he moved on to the next tank and repeated the procedure. He was about to sabotage the third tank when four Nusra fighters heaved two crates over to the motor pool. The crates were filled with tank shells, which they began loading on the vehicles.

Playing it off, Deckard just faded away as if nothing was out of place. There wasn't much else he could do without exposing himself. Still, taking out two tanks and ensuring that the chemical weapons could not be easily moved was adequate. It was unlikely that the remaining two T-72's would play any role in the close-in urban fighting that was about occur.

Now he just had to go find a quiet corner of the compound to go hunker down in and wait until the attack commenced. He would feed real-time intel back to Pat until then.

Climbing through the rubble, Deckard skipped up a half-demolished concrete staircase and onto the second floor. Metal rebar poked through the walls where the damage was bad; cracks sheared their way down the walls as if the building had been through an earthquake.

Looking out the empty window, he watched the Nusra fighters continuing to prepare for their latest martyr operation, one that in this case would include the use of weapons of mass destruction.

Deckard took a deep breath.

He was now operating on an accelerated failure time model and his time was almost up.

Heads up, the text message read.

Deckard ducked down behind the window sill.

He heard metal meet flesh with a thwack. The sound of the body hitting the ground was muffled as the gunshot rang out like a thunder clap. It was a sniper initiated raid. Firing the .300 Win Mag, a closed bolt weapon, Nikita would be working over the guards posted around the perimeter of the staging area.

A narrow street had been barricaded over with scrap wood, sheet metal, and razor wire. It was the back door into the Nusra fortress. Samruk International opened it by firing several TP rounds into the barricade with the Carl Gustav recoilless rifle. The 84mm Training Purpose rounds were inert: they were filled with concrete instead of high explosives. For that reason, they were great for breaching an objective from a stand-off position when you didn't necessarily want to kill everyone inside, like Deckard for instance. Or maybe Pat just didn't want to blast open a couple bombs filled with mustard gas.

The first TP round sent wooden splinters flying and scrap metal spinning through the air. Before the Gustav gunner could reload and fire his second round, Nikita had taken out two more guards with his sniper rifle and Samruk's support by fire line had opened up. Deckard couldn't see outside the compound and could only visualize how it was all playing out in his mind's eye.

When the second TP round slammed into the barricade, Deckard stole a glance out the window. The barricade was demolished to the point that the Samruk commandos would be able to start putting men through the fatal funnel once they bounded up. Deckard decided to help them out a little and stayed low as he moved towards the sound of Nusra gunmen who were returning fire.

Pausing to peer through a crack in the wall, Deckard saw the Nusra fighters trying to start up the flatbeds to no avail. Two of the four tank drivers were also frustrated. Just then the Liquid Sky mercenaries burst out of the building they had been racked out in.

The Operator manhandled one of the Nusra fighters out of the cab of the truck and got behind the wheel but he wasn't getting any love either. Deckard could hear Bill cursing a storm even in the middle of the firefight.

Deckard moved like a ghost through the compound, slipping over debris and sticking to the walls as he went looking for the Nusra fighters that had run to the walls to join the fight. He found the first one leaning out one of the windows and firing down on the Samruk positions outside. Deckard took a knee, aimed, and put a bullet in the back of his head from ten feet away. The terrorist slumped forward and rolled right out the window.

Turning a corner, Deckard found two more terrorists attempting to beat back the Samruk mercenaries. He shot both of them in the back with his AK. War was an ugly thing, and this was probably the ugliest he had seen. Chivalry would get him and a lot of other good people killed.

He continued to move at a crouch, staying low and not even daring to glance outside to see where his men were. That was all it would take for Nikita to mistake him for the enemy and take his head off.

Another Nusra fighter leaped up from the stairwell with a RPG-7 launcher over his shoulder. He held the rocket launcher canted upwards so that the anti-tank rocket didn't slide out and blow up at his feet. Moving to a window, he began aiming through the iron sights until Deckard cut him down.

Back inside the compound the two operational T-72 tanks had rumbled to life. The Samruk mercenaries had to get inside and disable them before Nusra could get them into action. Heading downstairs, Deckard was just in time to see the treads on one of the tanks start spinning as it blasted through what was left of the barricade. Two seconds later, an anti-tank round fired from the Carl Gustav slammed into it. Fire belched out of the open hatch on the top and then curled into a plume of oily black smoke.

The driver in the second tank stopped near where the barricade had been as he watched his buddy get wasted. Throwing the tank into reverse, he backed right into a wall which partially collapsed onto the turret. The treads began to spin until they gain purchase and yanked the vehicle out of the debris.

"Fucking god damn pole smoking-!"

Bill was still irate at the turn of events.

Peeking around a corner, he saw the Liquid Sky team with the two mustard gas bombs up on the stretchers again. With the flatbeds disabled, they were running them back out the way they had come in. Several Nusra fighters were already opening the gate. It was clear that whoever was attacking them knew what the fuck they were doing and that Nusra would not be able to hold onto the compound.

It was Deckard's turn to curse.

With only one platoon at his disposal, Pat was unable to have Samruk contain the objective. There would be no black side security element to cut off the enemy's escape. They had relied on speed, surprise, and violence of action. The shock and awe would have worked on the Nusra fighters but Liquid Sky was composed of former Special Operations soldiers who had seen countless battles.

Even with Deckard's sabotage slowing them down, Bill had quickly sized up the situation and made a decision. He was going to squirt off the objective and live to fight another day.

He looked back at the tank, which was partially blocking the back entrance that Samruk was suppressing with automatic gunfire, then back towards Liquid Sky as they heaved the two weapons of mass destruction onto their shoulders and marched toward the gate.

"Where the fuck is Deckard?" he heard Paul ask between gunshots.

"Probably dead," Rick answered without a shred of remorse in his voice.

291

"Deckard!" Bill yelled.

Fuck.

He had to stay with those weapons.

Breaking cover, he ran over to the Liquid Sky mercenaries as the remaining T-72 fired its main gun. The blast shook the entire compound.

"Where the fuck have you been?" Nadi screamed over the noise.

"Laying down some fire," he answered. "Those fucks are right on top of us."

"Who are they?" The Operator asked as they cleared the gate.

Deckard shook his head.

"No idea."

"Coordinated. Must be Syrian Army."

"15th Special Forces," Ramon grunted as they moved out. As the short man on bomb duty, he was getting the short end of the stick. "Hardcore regime loyalists."

Tiger, the Chechen Nusra leader was up front and attempting to wave down a passing car. The Chechen wasn't going to be separated from the bombs either. They were his one way ticket to entering the Jihad Hall of Fame with Bin Laden and Zarqawi. Maybe glorious martyrdom as well.

A burst from his Kalashnikov stopped a passing car. He flung open the door and dragged the driver out. His wife started screaming so he fired another long burst into the air to shut her up. Liquid Sky quickly loaded one bomb into the trunk and the other in the back seat. A second car rolled up behind the first just in time for Rick to commandeer it as well. Tiger and the Liquid Sky mercenaries piled inside the two cars, leaving Deckard as the odd man out.

Bill slammed the passenger side door on Deckard.

"Jump on the roof and hang on."

Suddenly Tiger stepped out from behind the driver's seat and let off a few more rounds from his AK. The bullets plunged into a passing civilian riding a motor scooter. The limp body tumbled off the back and rolled on the pavement.

Tiger looked at Deckard while pointing to the scooter with a smile on his face. Murdered for a Vespa. The Chechen got back into the sedan and took the wheel. Stepping on the gas, he led the two car convoy deeper into Homs.

Deckard looked at the corpse. He had been a young kid, callously gunned down by a foreign fighter looking to make a name for himself in some kind of bogus holy war. He lifted the scooter back onto its wheels and started it as he took a seat, knowing full well that there wasn't enough soap in the world to wash off the blood that was on his hands.

All he could do was hope to hide the blood stains under a dirty pair of shooting gloves.

Peeling off after the two cars, Deckard looked over his shoulder back at the compound. Clouds of thick black smoke rose above the Nusra staging ground. They were out of business, but Samruk had been unable to close the net fast enough. All Deckard could do was try to keep up with Liquid Sky and try to walk Samruk back into the target.

Deep down, he knew that he couldn't take down Liquid Sky on his own.

Tiger led the convoy through the streets of Homs, crisscrossing through the maze of streets and navigating toward the Nusra frontlines where they battled the Syrian Army. With their rear area being overrun by Samruk International, they now had to push deeper into the city to join forces with the frontline jihadist troops.

Deckard sped after the cars, the whine of the engine sounding like a lawn mower as he buzzed down the street. Shattered car hulks sat on the sides of the road covered in a layer of cement dust created by the crumbling buildings. They were mostly four or five story structures, once apartment buildings, now hollowed out lifeless shells. This was what the world would look like after all the human beings finished killing each other and no one was left.

Cruising through the apocalypse on a Vespa was not one of Deckard's career highlights.

The cars took some sniper fire at one of the cross streets. A bullet slammed into the roof of Tiger's sedan and chipped the paint away around the hole it left. Deckard ducked as he gunned it across the intersection, knowing he was one of those yellow ducks that kids shot at with bb guns at a carnival game. But the shot never came and he continued on.

They took another turn and passed through a Nusra checkpoint. Pops and cracks sounded somewhere up ahead, the shots echoing between the buildings. A SA-7 anti-aircraft rocket whooshed off into the sky, its heat-seeking warhead tracking something up in the sky that Deckard never caught sight of.

Before long they had snaked through so many streets and back alleys that Deckard wasn't even sure where in the city they were. They stopped alongside a Toyota pickup truck that had been modified in someone's garage to fire rocket artillery. Metal pipes had been fitted to the bed of the truck on a rack, the pipes propped up at an angle so the rockets would be hurled like giant spitballs over the roofs of the buildings and into the positions held by the Syrian Army. Or at least somewhere in the same neighborhood.

The cars stopped and Tiger got out to haggle with the vehicle's owner. Meanwhile two other Nusra fighters came running down the street. They were both bloodied and one looked like he had lost his weapon. When they got near they started yelling at the Chechen. Deckard rode his scooter closer to listen to what was being said.

The Nusra fighters were telling Tiger that they couldn't go down that street. The Syrian Army was on the offensive and had just taken several buildings that allowed them to cut off that avenue. Nusra was being beat back in Homs and the frontlines were shifting minute to minute.

"What the hell is going on Deckard?" Bill asked as he stepped out of the car.

"Syrian Army up ahead. It's a no-go."

"So we got the Army to our rear and to the front?"

Deckard continued to listen to the Nusra fighters.

"And our flanks. This neighborhood is a major pocket of resistance that is holding out as the Syrians encircle them," Deckard said knowing full well that it was his own men who held the rear area and prevented their escape.

"Motherfucker," Bill said. "We will have to hard point in one of these buildings and wait for night before attempting a break out."

Four more fighters came running down the street, each one lifting a wounded fighter by an arm or a leg. They arrived panting and struggling to catch their breath. Behind them, an artillery barrage slammed into a building, probably the one they had just left. The arty barrage completely collapsed one of the exterior walls which slid apart like a Jacob's Ladder and blocked off half of the street.

294

Now a full-blown shouting match had erupted between Liquid Sky's Chechen escort and the other jihadists. Deckard was struggling to keep up with all the different accents and dialects. Everyone was losing their composure as they came to realize that they were now boxed in by the enemy.

"This is bullshit," Bill said. "I want a hard point secured for the night."

He pointed to the nearest building.

"Get in there and empty it. We own this place now."

Rick and Paul took the lead, kicking in the flimsy metal door and entering the ground level. The Operator and Ramon followed them inside. Deckard left the scooter on its kickstand and went towards the door. He was prevented from entering as several civilians came pouring out of the door screaming. Armed foreigners were now breaking into their home and forcing them out.

Several women were crying, one holding a little girl at her side. A man came stumbling out of the house, and then a teenage boy. Inside, Rick was barking orders. Nadi came up alongside Deckard and started yelling at the civilians in Arabic, attempting to get them to shut up and move along.

Another man was pushed out of the front door. He stumbled before he caught himself and then began calling back inside. A boy who Deckard took to be his son ran around Ramon as he stood in the hallway and joined his father outside.

Paul stepped around the shattered door and back outside.

"It's empty," Paul said to Bill. "We can move the weapons in."

Just then, the man broke away from his son and ran up to Paul. The Syrian got right up in his face, screaming in Arabic. Deckard knew he was saying that they were wrong for kicking them out of their own home and that they had no right. Paul didn't speak Arabic and had no idea what he was carrying on about. The Liquid Sky member reached out and pushed the civilian back.

"Get the fuck out of here guy."

Deckard spoke up in Arabic to try to get him to calm down but to no avail.

The Syrian was waving his finger in the air and shouting at Paul. He stepped forward, closing the distance again.

Paul snapped into a ready-up drill and pumped two shots

from his AK-47 into the man's chest. He fell like a marionette with its string cut. The civilian was dead before he hit the ground, lights out. Deckard stopped in his tracks.

The little boy ran to his father's corpse and threw himself on top of him as tears streamed down his cheeks. As he cried, he began sobbing for his father to wake up. The kid couldn't have been older than eight or nine.

Paul stepped forward and put the barrel of his AK to the boy's head.

Deckard never remembered reaching for his weapon.

No matter how hard he tried, he was never able to remember his fist closing on the pistol grip of the Kalashnikov, or his thumb sliding off the safety level, or bringing the stock into his shoulder. The rifle was just there, the front sight post gently bobbing as it aligned with the rear sight.

He did remember squeezing the trigger and watching the back of Paul's scalp tear off and fly through the air with a lump of hair still attached.

36

Deckard ran.

The kid disappeared through the door to his house.

Deckard jetted down the road that was getting shelled by the Syrian Army. Gunfire chased after him. Voices yelled behind him. His boots beat the street. His heart was beating right out of his chest as he did the only thing he could do.

He ran.

Deckard swerved down a side street as another burst of AK fire skipped off the pavement behind him. He was vaguely aware of the black bars closing in on either side of his vision as he sprinted for an open doorway. He was getting tunnel vision, target fixation. Flight was his only option. Fight would be like a suicide mission but worse.

Deckard ran.

His legs powered him up the stairs. He could hear footsteps beating up the steps after him. On the second landing, he pivoted and fired off a ten round burst with his rifle into the shadows below him before charging back up the stairs.

Where was he going?

A Syrian fighter jet screamed overhead and dropped its ordnance somewhere in the Nusra-controlled neighborhood. The building shook on its foundation as the bombs detonated. Deckard didn't give it much thought, but simply steadied himself and continued on.

His heart rate had to be close to 120 beats per minute at this point. Deckard kept moving, unable to process the fact that he was operating at sub-optimal levels, unable to make the most rational decisions. The little reptile brain in the back of his head was threatening to take the wheels from him. Deckard's legs were burning when he reached the fifth floor and burst out onto the roof.

Where was he going?

Deckard ran.

He sprinted hard.

Holding the Kalashnikov in one hand, he pushed off into a long jump that ate up the distance between the rooftop and that of the adjacent building. He landed on the balls of his feet and kept moving. Half of the building had imploded on itself, the roof having collapsed but still hanging on by the metal rebar inside it. The cement slab created a ramp. Another gunshot snapped from behind him as he slid across the final few feet off the remaining rooftop like a baseball player and then skidded right down the collapsed roof that sloped down at an angle.

He slid down to the fourth floor surrounded by a cloud of dust. Bouncing to his feet, he scrambled through what was left of someone's kitchen and down a hallway with cracking stucco on the walls and ceiling. Behind him, he heard the Liquid Sky members who had slid down behind him and were now shouting at each other as they looked around for him.

Finding an open door in the hallway, Deckard took it and ran into another apartment. This one still had civilians in it. An old woman wearing a scarf over her head pushed two grandchildren into a bedroom as Deckard ran through the living room. There was a small balcony that looked over a narrow side street. Deckard quickly judged the distance. A squad of soldiers was moving down below, several of them smoking cigarettes. There was no way to immediately tell if they were Nusra fighters or Syrian Army.

Deckard planted one foot on the railing and propelled himself into mid-air, to the balcony across the street. He barely cleared the ten-foot gap, stumbling over the railing and tripping over himself. The wooden doors that led inside were locked, but had some give to them. He was about to kick them in when he heard a burst of gunfire. Ducking down below the railing, AK fire chopped through the wood and sprayed him with splinters.

Down on his hands and knees, he saw a loose panel on the door and pushed it in. Tossing his rifle ahead of him, Deckard slithered through the hole like a worm while the door continued to be reduced to toothpicks. Staying low to avoid the hail of gunfire, he rolled into the next room just as a grenade went off on the balcony he had just left, blowing both doors off their hinges. He didn't bother to look back.

Arriving at the apartment door, Deckard twisted all three of the locks open and was back outside in another hallway. He still didn't know who the armed men were below and in a moment of clarity he realized that he had moved far enough through the urban sprawl that he had no idea where he was. Was he still in Nusra territory or had he crossed into a neighborhood held by the Syrian Army? Maybe he was in the no-man's land in between.

The hall was lit by a column of sunlight cutting down through a gaping hole in the roof. Finding the stairwell, Deckard took it up figuring he would be safer moving across rooftops then risking it with the roving patrols on the ground level. It was a calculated risk; there would still be snipers, indirect fire, and airstrikes to contend with.

This was no surgical raid he was on now. This wasn't Special Operations, it was straight-up combat that had more in common with Hue City, Fallujah, or Stalingrad.

Half of the staircase had crumbled away along with the exterior wall. Deckard turned sideways and moved foot over foot, carefully edging his way up to the roof as he looked out over the city. Black smoke rose from a dozen places in Homs. Another surface-to-air missile rose from a street up into the sky. The boom of the main guns on former Soviet tanks sounded. In between the cannon fire, Deckard thought he heard footsteps in the hallway behind him and hurried up the stairs.

The sun beat down from the morning sky, causing him to squint. He continued to stay low. Approaching the lip of the building, he turned his head sideways and slowly lifted it high enough to see across the way. There was a full street between the building he was on and the next so he moved to another side of the roof, looking for a way to cross. This time there was only a narrow alley between the two buildings. Deckard quickly vaulted to the other side. Once across, he breathed a sigh of relief. If there were any snipers out there, they hadn't bothered shooting at him.

He was able to move down the city block by crossing from rooftop to rooftop. Deckard heard a few shots crack, but none of them felt close enough to be meant for him. Eventually, he got to the end of the block. There wasn't a stairway that led below, so he had to drop down to the balcony on the top story and push inside. Down on the street, another T-72 tank rumbled towards the front lines. Did it belong to the Army, or was it one of the Nusra-captured tanks? The battlefield was a confusing zigzagging patchwork of terrorists, soldiers, and para-military forces.

Moving down to the ground level, Deckard waited in the alcove where the front door lay ajar. It was basic infantry training taking over. Stop, look, listen, and smell. He opened up his senses, alert for sounds of the enemy. A few voices sounded from outside, but then they passed and moved on. Deckard slowly inched to the door to take a look outside. It was a ghost town out there. A breeze carried the smell of diesel fuel and burning trash but nothing much was moving.

Deckard knew he had to press on. He had to put some distance between himself and Liquid Sky. That was his immediate concern; then, he could regroup and figure out his next move. Across the street he saw a garage. It had one of those metal roll up doors which had been crinkled and ripped away by an explosion sometime in the recent past.

Watching and listening for a few more seconds, he decided the coast was clear and sprinted out of the alcove and across the street. This time someone did shoot at him. A lone gunshot snapped behind Deckard as he ran. Whoever fired needed to learn how to lead a moving target. Deckard ignored it and continued running, then ducked, and glided right through the gap between the garage door and the concrete wall. He was glad to be back behind solid cover, even though he tripped over debris on the floor as his eyes adjusted to the darkness.

Picking his way through the rubble, he emerged from the garage and into several empty rooms that looked like they might have been used for storage at one time. The back door wouldn't budge an inch despite Deckard putting his weight into it several times. Something was blocking the way on the other side. Looking for another way out, he found a small window covered in brown dust and grit. Turning a metal handle, the window screeched open on its hinges. He crawled out and into some more collapsed rubble.

The door did indeed have a cement pillar collapsed on top of it. In fact, the first floor of the adjacent building had collapsed and made a wall that led up to the second story. An overhang was created by the ceiling of the second story. Somehow, a glass chandelier was intact and swinging from a chain on the ceiling. It had been a dining room up until the war kicked off.

Deckard slung his Kalashnikov and ran at the collapsed floor. Planting a boot on the wall he vaulted up and out, his hands reaching out and grabbing the edge of what was left of the second story floor. He kicked his feet a few more times off the cement slab while pulling himself up into the dining room.

Walking from heel to toe, the former Special Operations soldier crept forward. On the opposite end of the building, it looked like most of the exterior wall had been blasted away. The interior was covered in pockmarks and streaks where bullets had chipped away at the walls. As he got closer, Deckard could see down into the street below. There were a couple of burnt-out cars in the street. A half-dozen dead bodies were also sprawled below with bloated stomachs and flies in their eyes.

Deckard also noticed where murder holes had been punched in what was left of the wall, giving covered positions to fire from. Everything was quiet.

That was when Deckard realized that he had just walked into the middle of an ambush line occupied by a dozen gunmen.

Bill clenched his jaw so hard, that he chipped a molar.

The Iridium phone was buzzing. Looking at the screen, he saw the number of the incoming call and knew it was one he had to take. The client.

Breathing hard, he extended the antenna and accepted the incoming call.

"This is Bill," he answered gruffly. No code names or secret-squirrel nonsense. He wasn't in the mood for the client's usual bullshit.

"Uh, yes, this is Nancy," his contact answered with her usual cover name. The Iridium phone had a crypto sleeve that scrambled their conversation to eavesdroppers but basic precautions were still taken.

"We're under the gun at the moment over here Nancy,"

Bill said, putting on a show for her. "Trying to meet the terms of our contract."

"We understand and appreciate that."

"Oh yeah?"

"We've received some additional information which we felt you would want to be informed of immediately."

"What's that?"

"You recall the incident in Nevada?"

"The one that got our contract dropped until you picked it up?"

"Right. We've been searching for the party or parties involved in a string of attacks including Nevada, and the company who worked those projects, your former client, has completed their investigation."

"And?"

"A source in Mexico confirmed who was behind it. A dangerous mercenary. He is believed to be a major stakeholder, if not the leader of, a private military company based out of Kazakhstan."

"What's this got to do with me?"

"Since pinpointing his identity we have been working this issue on our end. We have SIGINT hits on a cellular phone which we believe is in the target's possession. We realize that this target was not part of our original agreement, but we are prepared to double Liquid Sky's fee if you are able to resolve this issue for us. We have a last known location for his cell phone."

"Let me guess."

"Homs, Syria. His name is Deckard."

Bill hurled the phone through the air. The satellite phone slammed into the side of a nearby building and shattered into a dozen pieces.

"Motherfucker!"

Digging into his pocket, he pulled out a walkie-talkie. It was an off the shelf model that they had brought along with them for internal team communications in case cell phones didn't work in the city. Pressing the transmit button, the receiver beeped in his hand.

"Rick?"

A hiss of static came over the line.

"Yeah?" Rick's voice answered.

"The client just offered to double our fee if we kill

302

Deckard. I will personally match that amount for whichever of you kills him."

"A cool mil?"

"Fucking A."

"We've lost him but The Operator is working on picking up his trail."

"I want that fucker's head on a plate."

The sound of gunfire came over the walkie-talkie. He could hear both Rick and The Operator's voices. Nadeesha and Ramon were out there looking for him as well.

"Never mind," Rick came back over the line with. "That has got to be him."

"Let me know when you've got his scalp in your hand."

"You got it."

Deckard wrenched the AK-47 from the Iranian's grasp. In the awkward way he had his hands on the rifle, he was holding it upside down. Somehow he managed to depress the trigger with his pinky and sweep the barrel in a long arc that split horizontally across the ambush line that three other Iranians had occupied. They went down with gut shots and sucking chest wounds.

Pulling the Kalashnikov away, he fell to the ground as bursts of gunfire sounded throughout the hollowed out second floor of the building. He had walked right into the rear end of an ambush line manned by Quds Force foreign fighters. With Iran backing the Assad regime, Quds Force was calling much of the shots and scoring many of the victories for the Syrian military.

Although they were dressed in a mix-match of

camouflage uniforms, Deckard could tell their nationality as they yelled to each other in Farsi. Point-shooting the Iranian he had struggled with for the rifle, he yanked on the trigger over and over, adrenaline taking over. As the Iranian went down in a hail of gunfire, another peered out from behind a concrete column. Deckard fired on him, but his poor trigger control skewed the shots off target, kicking up cement dust as they streaked off the pillar.

Twisting and turning, he scrambled in the opposite direction as gunfire snapped over his head.

Putting another support column between himself and the Iranian he had failed to shoot, Deckard ran. At the end of the bomb-blasted building, he found a shattered window and dived through. There were no heroics involved, he simply fell ten feet down to the ground and landed in a heap. Thankfully, his own Kalashnikov helped break his fall when the rifle swung on its sling and butt stroked him in the chin. He felt the pain explode in his head.

Pulling himself up to his feet, he stumbled forward with one hand on the wall of the building, trailing his fingers just behind him as he hobbled on. Arriving at the mouth of the ally, he glanced across the road. His options were limited. Instead of dashing across the street, he button-hooked down the street and put a burnt out Volkswagen bus behind him in case the Iranians were looking for him on the streets.

Finding a building with the front door bashed in, Deckard walked towards it, hoping to find some refuge inside as he shook off the pain in his jaw.

"Hey!"

His head automatically snapped toward the sound.

Rick stood at the other end of the street with The Operator.

Both immediately went into a shooter ready position, rifles up. Deckard flung himself towards the door as they opened fire. Their shots cut through the air and dinged off the VW bus. As he high crawled into the doorway, a fusillade of fire responded to the two Liquid Sky members. The had street just become a two-way range. Deckard smiled.

"That's my boys."

Quds Force was engaging Liquid Sky.

Deckard crawled inside the building and then jogged

304

through a hallway strewn with garbage, everything from bicycle tires to baby diapers littered the interior of the building. It sounded like the gunfire was getting closer. He was effectively doubling back on his former position now. Or so it seemed. Things got confusing real fast in the urban labyrinth. There wasn't anywhere he could stop and ask for directions, either.

Stepping over a pile of old books and newspapers, Deckard came out into an empty lot that looked to be a real garbage dump. He held his breath and crossed it quickly. As he hopped over a wall to get to the next building, another couple shots snapped right next to him. Hitting the ground on the other side of the wall, he was hit by *deja vu*.

In their first encounter, he had pursued Liquid Sky with the same level of aggressiveness.

Naji watched the two Western mercenaries give chase after the other infidel who had attacked them. The fighters in his cell of Iranians wanted to gun the two men down as they crossed the garbage dump. Naji held up a hand, stopping them in their tracks.

The Iranian commander spoke into his radio and quickly received a response from a Syrian artillery battery on the other side of the city. He waited for the two foreigners to climb over the wall before calling in the artillery strike. He shifted from a known point, the last call for fire mission he had radioed in earlier in the morning. It was only a block away and he was fairy certain that the first shells would be on target.

Suppressing a chuckle, he leaned against the door frame to watch the show.

Deckard kicked in the back door and barged inside the abandoned building. Taking a few steps inside, he immediately jolted backwards, wobbling back towards the door. The bottom floor had been blown out sometime during the battle for Homs. The concrete slab had cracked and collapsed into the basement. With Hezbollah and Liquid Sky both on his ass, he was running out of places to go.

Then he heard the crunch of debris grinding under two pairs of combat boots. Looking over his shoulder, he saw Rick and The Operator as they dropped down over the wall. The Operator snarled, his teeth exposed as he brought his AK-47 into play.

Without missing a beat, Deckard twisted back around and threw himself into the gaping hole in front of him. He landed hard and rolled, then scrambled forward. The Liquid Sky shooters lost their line of sight on Deckard as he moved deeper into the basement and were forced to drop down behind him.

That was when the arty strike fired by the Syrian Army rained down.

Deckard was tossed into one of the retaining walls at the edge of the basement as the Syrian Army fired for effect. Both Liquid Sky shooters were also knocked off their feet. The artillery rounds never found their exact target, but the blast radius shook the entire building on its foundation. The concussion rattled Deckard's teeth as cement dust engulfed the basement.

Then, the building pancaked in on itself as the upper levels collapsed. Once one of the outer support walls collapsed, the roof of the building gave way. The weight slammed into the top story and collapsed down into the second story. The entire building came down like a house of cards, right on top of the three Americans trapped in the basement.

Deckard coughed as he pushed himself onto his hands and knees. Everything was black. Running his fingers over his face, everything felt intact. He couldn't see his hand in front of his face, but it wasn't because he had been blinded. The building had collapsed and trapped them in the basement.

He heard something shuffle in the dark. A boot slipping on a piece of debris.

"Where is he?"

Rick.

"Shut up."

The Operator.

"I can hear him breathing."

Deckard froze where he was with his hands planted in front of him. He slowed his breathing and could feel his lungs taking in the cement dust with every shallow breath. The moment he made some noise would be the moment that the two Liquid Sky shooters vectored in on him. He had lost his rifle as he fell during the artillery barrage. He dared not sweep around the ground looking for it. The Liquid Sky gunmen probably still had their weapons and would start shooting the second he made a sound.

It was quiet. Nothing moved. Deckard swore that his joints were emitting an audible groan as he shifted his body weight. Somewhere in the darkness, two rifle barrels were sweeping back and forth waiting for him to make a mistake. Slowly, carefully, he reached out with one hand. His fingertips gently brushed across the floor as he looked for something to grab hold of. A rock, a piece of rebar, anything he could use as a weapon.

Sweeping around with his right hand, he found nothing. With his weight supported by his left arm, he was growing fatigued. Dehydration, physical exertion, and the stress of combat had beaten him up. Slowly, he switched arms and began sweeping around with his left hand. A few more shells came down somewhere outside.

It was unnerving. He could also hear Rick breathing once or twice. He sounded like maybe he was to Deckard's two o' clock somewhere. The Operator was a ghost.

Finally, he found something. His hand brushed up against a broken piece of concrete. Carefully reaching for it, Deckard grabbed it in his fist. Now he had something to fight with. As he lifted the concrete block and pulled it towards him, a low grinding sound echoed in the basement. A piece of rebar had been sticking out of the end of the block. As Deckard pulled it, the metal bar scratched against the floor.

Boots pounded towards Deckard. He made it from down on his hands and knees to being up on one knee before one of the Liquid Sky mercenaries blasted into him. In the dark, there was little sense of depth perception by sound alone and the mercenary had simply charged into the dark. Deckard swung the concrete block and clipped his opponent but couldn't tell where.

"Fuck!"

Deckard recognized Rick's voice as he yelled out in pain.

But Rick still had momentum on his side and carried Deckard down to the ground. He struggled to prevent the back of his head from slamming on the floor and splitting wide open. The fall jarred him but he was still in the fight, still swinging the concrete block. This time it glanced off Rick's shoulder. But now Rick was on top of Deckard and knew where he was. Rick's fists began to rain down on Deckard.

Then, Rick was snatched off of Deckard. One second he was there, the next he was gone. A dozen feet away the fight continued, fists bashing flesh and boots scuffing around the floor. Deckard rolled over and crawled away. The Operator had gone into autopilot again, taking down Rick while thinking it was Deckard.

Deckard found a wall and began tracing it to the back of the building. Behind him, he could hear someone's head getting slammed against the ground and he was pretty sure the grunting that came with each slam belonged to The Operator.

37

Ramon herded the Nusra fighters around the collapsed building. The Quds Force fighters had been beaten back for the time being and had retreated back to Syrian Army positions elsewhere in the city. A couple of civilians who were busy looting abandoned homes had told them where they had seen the white men go; into a building just before an artillery strike hammered it.

The building was flattened with the outer walls all but collapsed, and the concrete slabs that had made up the three-story building rested one on top of the other. All three of the Liquid Sky men had to be dead, Ramon figured. He didn't much care about Rick or The Operator, but he was still trying to wrap his mind around the sell out by Deckard. He had turned traitor without any indication of why. Be that as it may, Bill was offering a huge reward for his head and he'd be damned if he wouldn't have the Nusra fighters pick through the debris until they found him.

Soon, the jihadists located a basement window and began shining a flashlight inside. The yellow beam of light seemed to reflect back as it caught on sparkles of dust in the air. The window was narrow, maybe only one foot high by two feet wide. The Nusra terrorists continued to take turns poking their heads inside while others climbed up on top of the remains of the building. Then, they heard footsteps inside followed by someone coughing.

Hands covered in white chalk dust reached up for the window. The Nusra fighters grabbed on and heaved the survivor up and through the small window. He was completely covered in dust and grime from the collapsed building.

"Watch out," the survivor said in Arabic. "The traitor is somewhere behind me."

By now Ramon was jogging over to see who they pulled out of the basement. With the survivor covered in dust, he couldn't tell if the Nusra fighters were talking to Rick or The Operator.

Suddenly, the survivor tore the AK-47 from the hands of the nearest Nusra gunmen and all hell broke loose. Gunfire sprayed into the Nusra fighters, dropping two of them instantly. A third and fourth tried to run. The survivor, covered in white dust, looked like a ghost as he shot them both in the back. Catching sight of Ramon, the survivor then turned his newly acquired rifle on the Liquid Sky mercenary.

Ramon cursed as he ducked behind the rubble while 7.62 rounds chiseled away at his cover.

"Get up there," Ramon yelled at the other Nusra fighters who were also seeking cover in the rubble. "Flank around and surround him!"

Only by making some hand and arm signals did the Nusra fighters begin to understand, but by then it was too late. A couple grenade blasts covered the survivor's withdrawal. By the time Ramon got the jihadists moving and flanked around the side of the building, the survivor had already disappeared.

Deckard.

Ramon was about to radio in to Bill and tell him what had happened when he heard a grunt behind him.

It was The Operator pulling himself out through the basement window. From close up, there was no mistaking the identity this time.

"Where is Deckard?" The Operator asked as he got to his feet and began dusting himself off.

"Broke contact," Ramon replied. "Headed south."

"Into no-man's land. Nowhere else for him to go."

"Where is Rick?"

The Operator looked straight through Ramon with piercing blue eyes. His face was completely expressionless.

"Didn't make it."

The shadows were growing long, providing a place for Deckard to hide as he crept from cover to cover. He slid from behind a pile of debris to a wrecked truck and then back to another pile of rubble. He was running on fumes and he knew it. Constant combat had taken its toll. He needed to reset and get his systems back up. First he needed a hide site for the night.

There was a row of several blocks of buildings that made up a no-man's land between the Nusra front and the Syrian Army lines. Most of the structures were blown out and partially collapsed. A few were relatively intact. Deckard was dragging his feet as he stayed low and entered the nearest building. There was no electricity in the city and using a flashlight while trapped between warring factions at night was a surefire way to get nailed with another artillery strike. He needed to get situated before the sun went down.

Both sides also seemed to know that fighting would be limited during periods of darkness since both lacked proper night vision equipment. They were getting in their final RPG and recoilless rifle shots before the sun went down.

The stench of rot invaded Deckard's nostrils as he moved into the building.

He knew what it was before he even saw it. Turning into a living room he saw the bodies lined up on the floor. Taking a step closer, he could see how they had been shot. Execution style, to the back of the head. The children had been shot through the top of their heads by adults who were pointing the guns downward at them, the exit wounds then being through their mouths or jaws. Their parents and grandparents lay beside them, murdered in the same manner.

It was the ghosts. The Alawite death squad that Tiger had told them about. For once, Deckard regretted that Liquid Sky hadn't found someone and scalped them. Having missed them at the Syrian base camp, the ghosts were prowling the city, executing civilians in a brutal attempt to coerce the civilian population into compliance with government forces.

Each apartment Deckard came to, he found a similar scene. Bodies on top of bodies. Flies feasting on the dead. Entire generations of dead piled on top of each other: parents, grandparents, and children.

The murders, the smell of death, it triggered an old familiar feeling in Deckard. It wasn't rage. He was always

311

angry. What he felt now was something he hadn't felt in a long time.

It was certainty.

His knees cracked as he grabbed on to the railing and pulled himself up the stairs. After all the disgust and all the doubt that he had felt as he infiltrated Liquid Sky, he now knew that there was no question that his mission was just. American Special Operations soldiers were the good guys. For former operators like those in Liquid Sky to sink to the depths they had was unacceptable. They could engage in whatever rationalizations they wanted, but it was still wrong. No amount of mental gymnastics would ever justify cold-blooded murder.

The death squads had to be put out of business, whether they were Syrian or American was irrelevant at this point.

Climbing to the third floor, he began looking for a place to spend the night. As he searched around, Deckard did some of the math in his head. Zach was dead in Bahrain. He had just shot and killed Paul. The Operator had killed Rick for him. That left Ramon, Nadeesha, The Operator, and Bill. He had some rapport with Ramon and Nadeesha until today, but that wouldn't get him anywhere now. Bill almost certainly had them all out hunting him down.

Finding an empty apartment, Deckard stayed away from the windows as he made a quick sweep. It was empty. Sitting on the floor, he powered up his satellite phone while he continued to run the numbers. Ramon was an intel specialist and sniper. Nadeesha was a manipulator and intel gatherer. The Operator was a lunatic. Bill was a human wrecking ball. He would be taking the fight to them while trapped between the Syrian military, Hezbollah, the ghosts, and Nusra with Samruk International in the mix somewhere. That, and a couple chemical weapons thrown in just because things were not difficult enough already.

It was a suicide mission, but then, it had been all along.

As the phone reached out and made contact with a satellite, Deckard began typing out a message:

Cover blown. On my own. Somewhere between Nusra and Army lines.

A few seconds later, Pat responded to this text:

Heavy contact. Not even sure who we are fighting. We're pushing up to the front but I need you to mark on map where you are and where last loc of wpns was.

Deckard went into the map feature and marked his current location and roughly where he had been when he shot Paul. The chemical weapons had surely been moved since then, but not far. Liquid Sky could not push forward into the Syrian Army lines and could not retreat to the rear with Samruk coming up behind them. That left them with limited maneuver room on their flanks. Deckard typed out the tactical situation to Pat as well and sent it along. Another incoming message came in half a minute later.

We'll move as far up as we can tonight. Sorry dude, can't help you until we link up.

There was nothing to be sorry for, of course. They were in an impossible situation. The sun had almost set beneath the skyline of the ruined city by the time Deckard went looking for food and water. With the electricity out, everything in the refrigerator had rotted. He managed to find some canned food and a couple warm cans of soda. In a nearby apartment he was able to scrounge up a bottle of water.

Setting his stash of supplies in the corner of one room, he scooped up an empty soup can to use to construct a booby trap. Using a cinderblock that had fallen from one of the walls, Deckard wedged the soup can under it near the stairwell. Then he pushed one of his hand grenades inside the soup can. Using a piece of string he found, he then tied a knot around the grenade and the other end of it to a pipe sticking out of the wall. Finally, he very carefully removed the pin from the grenade. The spoon of the grenade was held in place by the soup can which prevented it from detonating, at least until someone came walking up the steps and hit the trip wire.

With his early warning system in place, Deckard covered himself in a blanket to keep warm in the cool desert air. It was dark as he began tearing into the food. His mind and body were sluggish, moving in slow motion, and he knew he had to replenish himself. Tomorrow was another day. Even on his best day, he might not have enough to survive what was coming.

All he could do was hope that he had enough left in him to complete his mission.

38

Deckard was up on his feet and moving the second the grenade exploded. It was early morning and the cold night air cleared his head as he threw the blanket off. Running out the door, he turned through the smoke hanging in the air from the explosion and sprinted down the hall as he slung his Kalashnikov over his shoulder. He had done a quick route recon before drifting off to a restless sleep and now it was paying off.

Diving into another empty apartment, he made for a window and took a quick look before jumping. Vaulting out of the window, he sailed through the empty space above an alley before his combat boots made contact with the balcony of an adjacent apartment. He had quickly broken contact with the enemy but had to keep moving. Using the butt of his rifle, he cleared away some broken glass and climbed through a window.

Once inside, he carefully looked out a few windows at the building he had just escaped from. He could see the Nusra fighters taking a knee in the shadows at two corners of their target building. He had no doubt that they were on the other two corners as well. Someone had directed them to isolate the building before the assault team began clearing. They were using American tactics. It was Nusra with Liquid Sky in an advisory role. They were looking for him.

Whether they had been able to specifically track him to his bed-down site or if they were just doing a cordon and search on the entire area was irrelevant. Now they were back on his trail. Deckard couldn't run and hide. There was nowhere to run to as he was in enemy territory no matter what direction he went. A stand up fight was out of the question. He'd be gunned down in seconds as he was up against overwhelming numbers.

Mentally noting the enemy positions one last time, he turned and looked for a way down to the ground floor. What he could do was wage an unconventional battle, nickle and dime Nusra bit by bit and wear them down with a harassment campaign. Hopefully he could hold out until he could link up with Samruk.

Deckard quietly stepped down the stairs and out on to the street. There were four Nusra shooters at the nearest blocking position up ahead. Deckard stayed low with his AK in his hands as he moved forward in the dark. It would be another hour or so before the sun starting coming up. There was a burned-out car in the middle of the street and he was able to keep that between him and the enemy as he advanced towards them. When he came up alongside the car, he was less than ten meters away.

The undisciplined jihadists talked amongst themselves as they waited. They had been posted at the corner of the building to prevent anyone from escaping, specifically Deckard. They didn't seem to be taking their job all that seriously despite the booby trap that their comrades had set off. The four gunmen squatted on the street corner next to the target building.

Deckard slowly eased off the safety on his Kalashnikov. Staring down his rifle sights, he had them dead to rights. The jihadists were all facing in towards the target building with no rear security posted. Deckard quickly worked them like human e-type silhouettes at the range, shooting from left to right, two shots center mass in each one.

Crawling forward towards the bodies, he could hear shouts from the other security positions. White lights flashed from inside the building as the assault element continued to clear room to room. A walkie-talkie radio snapped inside the pocket of one of the dead jihadists crackled. Arabic voices came over the net as the other checkpoints tried to find out who was shooting.

Working quickly, Deckard stripped a couple chest rigs full of AK magazines off two of the bodies, grabbed the radio and then retreated back the way he came. The voices were getting more frantic on the radio. Depressing the push-to-talk button, Deckard began shouting in Arabic.

"He's at our position, he shot at us until we had to retreat. He's there now."

Seconds later, one of the other blocking positions opened up on the one he had just taken out. The bullets kicked up little clouds of dust around the dead bodies.

"Not that one," Deckard corrected. "The other blocking position!"

That did it. The remaining three blocking positions began opening fire on each other. In the confusion, they then returned fire on each other as well. The radio cracked and hissed as shouts and screams were garbled over the net. The jihadists were working themselves up into a confused panic as they shot their team mates.

Deckard turned the knob on the radio until it clicked off. He wasn't about to get decisively engaged with the enemy when they could just wear themselves out instead. His work was done here.

For now.

They were getting close. Pat could feel it.

The fighting had picked up in volume and intensity over the last few minutes. The jihadists had their backs up against the wall and they knew it. The Syrian Army had them stonewalled on one side and Samruk International was turning the handle on the meat grinder on the other. The boys had already run through their ammunition and were scrounging what they could off dead enemy. It was Deckard's foresight that they had to thank when he bought a 7.62 platform for the mercenaries rather than going with something cooler and more high-tech which would not be able to fire ammunition found on the battlefield.

Deckard knew that Samruk would be going into austere environments and denied areas.

Homs seemed to fit the bill.

Between a rock and a hard place, the Nusra fighters knew this was their last stand and were not budging any further. Samruk had traded fire with them off and on throughout the night. With night vision capability, their shooters were much more accurate at night fire to say the least. Nikita had been having a turkey shoot up on the rooftops. Every time a Nusra gunman poked his head out from behind a wall, the Kazakh sniper had taken it off.

But now the momentum had stalled and they were not making any further progress. Samruk needed to attempt a breakthrough to blitz forward, locate the chemical weapons, and capture them. Right now they were at a stalemate; every time they tried to push across the street they took fire from multiple heavy machine guns spread around the surrounding buildings.

Cracking this problem would require a little unconventional thinking, Pat knew. While Samruk mercenaries pulled security on the front line, others were busy at work inside the buildings they had occupied. It was dawn, and Pat wanted to wait until they had some good daylight before baiting Nusra into his trap. The men would have some more time to prepare their defenses.

Pat continued to inspect the lines and their preparation until Sergeant Fedorchenko approached him. The Sergeant had been with Samruk International since day one. As one of their first recruits, he had risen to the rank of Platoon Sergeant. Between Pat's bad Russian and Fedorchenko's bad English, they were able to communicate. The Platoon Sergeant informed him that his men were ready to go.

Everyone moved to take their places. It was a few minutes past seven in the morning when Pat gave the order. Samruk mercenaries fired RPGs at the machine gun nests they were able to locate and the riflemen and machine gunners on the ground began pouring it on with everything they had. Pat let the onslaught continue for a good half-minute before ordering the men to go from a cyclic to rapid rate of fire while they initiated a phased withdrawal plan.

One element fell back at a time as the Nusra fighters returned fire in earnest from their positions in the ruined neighborhood. The Samruk mercenaries were retreating to positions to the rear in groups of five or six while others provided cover fire. To the Nusra fighters, it looked like the Kazakh mercenaries were spent and were now beating a hasty retreat. Pat knew it was working when he heard the shouts in between bursts of gunfire as the jihadists celebrated.

"*Allah Akbar!*"

"*Takbeer!*"

From his vantage point on the second floor, Pat saw

them poking their heads out from their fighting positions. Some of the Arabs were coming out into the open to fire their weapons in the general direction of the Samruk men. Pat fired off a short burst himself and then joined the retreating mercenaries.

Bailing out the back of the building, he joined the rest of the men in the secondary positions they had scouted out the night before. They were now barricaded inside three other buildings, behind what had been the front line for them over the course of the night.

Meanwhile, Nusra fighters spilled out of their own fighting positions and surged forward to occupy the ground they had lost the previous day. They were feeling the pressure from being stuck between Samruk and the Syrian Army. Now they wanted some breathing room back.

Pat smiled when he heard the first explosion.

It was a tactic called defense in depth. There is no need to hold a defensive position until the last bullet. Why waste the resources when you can just booby trap your position and then fall back to a secondary position? With the enemy running into the buildings that Samruk had occupied, they were now getting a special surprise.

Explosives ripped through the Nusra fighters as they mindlessly walked into trip wires and stepped on pressure plates that the mercenaries had rigged overnight. Many of the doorways leading out had been blocked by tumbleweeds of razor wire that the mercenaries had found on the battlefield and improvised as obstacles by jamming the mess into the exits. Now the Nusra gunmen were panicking and running right into razor wire.

Another blast sounded, probably one of the bricks of C4 plastic explosives that they had rubber-banded pieces of scrap metal to. Dust clouds rolled out of the windows and screams filled the morning air as another detonation was triggered.

Pat turned to Fedorchenko. It was time to skirt around the booby-trapped buildings. With Nusra softened up, they were ready to drive into the hold-outs and crush what was left of them. The platoon sergeant nodded and went to gather his Squad Leaders without having to be told.

The former Delta Force operator looked at the black smoke spiraling into the sky and knew that, one way or the other, it would all be over by the end of the day.

Deckard turned and pulled the Kalashnikov's stock into his shoulder. Gaining target acquisition, the front sight post on the rifle bobbed slightly as it was superimposed over a human form approximately fifty meters away. Deckard gently squeezed the trigger. The rifle recoiled in his hands and the Nusra fighter collapsed.

A stand up fight was out of the question, so Deckard turned and beat a hasty withdrawal as more gunmen bounded forward through the rubble. For the last twenty minutes or so Nusra had been alternating between trying to outflank him and simply blitzing forward to try to overwhelm him. Each time, Deckard had managed to slip through their fingers only to be picked up and engaged again moments later.

The no-man's land they fought in was the most heavily damaged part of Homs, and more than once had they come under fire from the Syrian Army. Nusra had also taken some friendly fire from their comrades who mistook them for the Army. Deckard thrived in the chaos, letting all sides of the battle bounce against each other and wear themselves down.

The building he was in now had been reduced in place by airstrikes. All that stood were waist high outer walls that gave a rectangular outline. Realizing that he was exposed to the Syrian Army lines a few hundred meters away, he ducked down behind one of the walls not a moment too soon. A bullet zipped right through the space he had occupied a fraction of a second ago and splashed against a concrete pillar.

Deckard crawled hand over hand to the other side of the building until he heard something behind him. Looking over his shoulder, he saw two of the jihadists creeping into the remains of the building behind him.

The Syrian Army sniper took out the first one, his head exploding like an overripe melon. The second jihadist looked down at his friend's body, not registering the immediate danger he was in. The sniper put a quick end to his confusion.

Deckard continued forward through the debris. Whoever the sniper was pulling overwatch on this sector of the front lines, he wasn't playing games. He had clearly ranged out the area he was to cover ahead of time so that he could dial in the correct range as soon as a target appeared.

Moving into the next collapsed structure, he finally found some good cover. It felt like the ruins of civilization went on and on, city blocks of devastation in every direction. Whatever the Syrian civil war had been about, the one thing he knew for sure was that the country would never be the same. It would take decades for Syria to recover.

It was only mid-morning. Deckard kept moving, this time doubling back on some of his old positions to observe Nusra movements. Maybe watch that sniper take out of few more of the Arab foreign fighters who had come to partake in the fighting.

Climbing into the second story of a building, Deckard had eyes on a courtyard as Nusra fighters jogged across in ones and twos. Their black man-dresses and long beards bounced as they ran. There were only a half dozen left from the cell that had attacked him before dawn. Then, he spotted the leader of the group.

Deckard's suspicions had been correct. It was Ramon. He watched as the Special Forces veteran ran across the courtyard and continued to direct the Nusra fighters.

Leaving his perch, Deckard followed after the gunmen. The hunters were now the hunted. Every now and again he could hear sandals slipping across the ground or one of the jihadists crunching over some debris. A few muffled words in Arabic here and there. Deckard was close. When an artillery strike rained down a few blocks away, Deckard took advantage of the noise that it created to close the gap and get close to the Nusra fighters.

He found one walking down an empty hallway and quickly put him into a choke hold before breaking his neck with a dull pop. Deckard moved forward cautiously, careful not to overshoot his prey and put himself into their line of fire. Before long, he caught the others bunching up in another courtyard. They realized they had lost one of their men and were having some kind of confab to figure out who was going to go looking for him.

Deckard edged as close as he could to the open door that led to the courtyard. Very carefully, he switched the selector on his Kalashnikov to full auto, trying not to make any noise. He peeked from around the cover of the door and hosed down the Nusra fighters where they stood, cutting across them with one long burst of gunfire. Four down. That left one more plus Ramon.

They announced themselves to Deckard by firing at him from the next building over. Their muzzle flashes lighting up two windows. Deckard jerked back inside to avoid the gunfire. Outside, he spotted a RPG-7 launcher that one of the dead jihadists had propped up against the courtyard wall while they had been talking. Out in the sunlight, Deckard saw that it was loaded with a PG-7 rocket.

When the gunfire tapered off for a moment, Deckard sprinted forward and then slid through the dirt in the courtyard, right up to the wall. Snatching the RPG, he swung it over his shoulder, yanked the pin on the nose cap of the PG-7 round, pulled the cap off, and cocked the hammer on the trigger mechanism in just a few seconds. Using the iron sights, he aimed at one of the windows where the gunfire had come from and pulled the trigger. The RPG was deafening as the rocket spiraled away.

Even from up close, Deckard's aim was off. He was dehydrated and exhausted, which gave him shaky hands. The RPG rocket slammed into the wall just below the window and exploded. The blast carried into the building and seemed to take out whoever was there because the gunfire ceased.

Dropping the rocket launcher, Deckard reloaded his AK and headed towards the building. With his heart pounding in his chest, Deckard forced himself to slow down, check his corners, and be more deliberate in his actions before he got himself killed. Up on the second floor he found the bodies.

The last jihadist had been standing in the window that the RPG rocket has struck under. He was basically torn in half.

Flies were already buzzing around the pink elastic of his intestines. Deckard trained his rifle on the second casualty.

Ramon was breathing heavy. His torso was soaked in dark crimson from several chest wounds. As he saw Deckard approach, his hand fumbled with the kit strapped to his chest. Ramon's gloved hand tore at the handle of the knife mounted to his chest rig.

Deckard was about to grab Ramon by the wrist and stop him when the former Special Forces soldier suddenly flipped the knife around and held it out for him. Deckard took the black karambit from him as he knelt down beside Ramon. His breaths were sharp and short. He was critical and they both knew it.

"Finish," Ramon gulped. The blood was seeping out from under his shirt and covering his neck. "Finish it."

"I'm not going to leave you here," Deckard told him.

"No." Ramon tried to catch his breath. "Finish all of them."

Deckard looked down at the Emerson Filipino fighting knife in his hand.

"We went too far," Ramon gasped. "It has to end. This can't go on."

"It ends today."

Ramon nodded, but it was barely noticeable. He was fading fast.

"That's a promise."

"That bastard," Ramon said, his voice going soft. "The Operator. He is only a few minutes behind me."

"I'll handle him."

"You need," Ramon took another breath. "To go. Leave me. I want to die alone."

Deckard looked down at him with uncertainty. Leaving him behind like this didn't seem right. Deckard never left a fallen comrade. He would not even leave an enemy to suffer without putting a mercy bullet in him.

"It's okay," Ramon said. "It's okay."

Deckard wiped the sweat off his forehead and looked down at Ramon one more time before standing up and beginning to walk away.

"Deckard..." Ramon called, his voice going soft as he faded away.

"Yeah?" Deckard said turning to face him again.

"I always. I always knew, brother."

"When?"

"Egypt."

"Because I let that poor girl who was chained up under the bridge go free?"

"Before," Ramon wheezed. "At the docks. At the armory. You let that...security guard live. Saw him breathing. You were never one of us."

Deckard was still for a moment.

"You should have said something," Deckard said, his voice now filled with regret.

"No. Too late for me. You have," Ramon took another deep breath. "Another chance."

Deckard nodded.

"Don't screw it up," Ramon said, pleading with him.

Deckard walked away.

Bill flung open the car door and started the engine.

Tiger was going to open a corridor for them to escape, but he could only keep it open for a few minutes. Their timing had to be on the money. Ramon and The Operator were still chasing Deckard around in no-man's-land, the Syrian Army was still pounding them, and some new player was smashing them from their six o' clock. Bill had gotten an eye on them and they looked like Russian mercenaries. They lured the Nusra idiots into a kill zone and killed nearly half the force that the jihadists had in this neighborhood.

Deckard's private military company.

He would deal with Deckard and his cronies, but first he

had a job to complete. If he couldn't make it to Damascus, he would just have to find some other civilian population to gas along the way.

"Get the weapons loaded," he ordered the jihadists. "Where the fuck is Nadeesha?"

He looked over at Tiger. The Chechen shrugged.

"You've gotta be fucking kidding me," Bill practically spat. He went back inside the apartment building and looked around one more time before walking back outside.

"That fucking whore cut and run."

Someone had seen the writing on the wall.

Pat reached out and slapped the muzzle of an AK-103 up in the air. The Kazakh mercenary looked at him in confusion for a moment.

"No one fires on the gray sedan," Pat said into his radio. "I repeat, do not fire on the gray car."

They had just watched a large container being loaded into the trunk of the car. There was no mistaking it. It was one of the two weapons they had come to secure. The Samruk International mercenaries had cheated forward into enemy lines. Their defense in depth had bought them some breathing room, far more than any of them had anticipated. Within minutes of bounding into what had been Nusra controlled lines they were already on top of their query.

Of course, their luck didn't hold out long enough for Pat to plan a hasty scheme of maneuver. Kalashnikovs ripped long bursts through the neighborhood as the Samruk mercenaries were spotted. The white guy who had been organizing the loading of the weapon in the car suddenly jumped into the driver's seat. From down the street, Pat had a feeling that he was looking at an American, a former soldier at that. It was one of the Liquid Sky members.

Pat had his own rifle up and trained on the vehicle as the Liquid Sky leader put it into drive and peeled off down the street.

"Fuck," he cursed in frustration. He couldn't risk shooting at the driver and inadvertently detonating the chemical weapon. In the confines of the city, it would be especially devastating. Nusra terrorists, Samruk mercenaries, and civilians on the battlefield would all die a horrible death. Once images of the bodies were broadcasted across the internet, major news services would pick them up. It would get the ball rolling towards overt international intervention in Syria, and God knew what else.

Suddenly, Pat heard a pop over his left shoulder. One of his men had blown off his order and took a shot at the fleeing vehicle. The mercenary commander was about to punch his teammate in the face for his carelessness when he spotted more movement out on the street.

Four more jihadists had walked out of the nearby building carrying a litter with the second bomb on it. Seeing the vehicle disappear, and hearing the gunfire all around them, they dropped the bomb and yelled after the getaway car. One gave chase after it with his arms flung in the air.

Pat hit the push to talk button on his radio, but their sniper was already on it. Four shots rang out from his HK 417 and four bodies hit the ground.

While the gunfire continued in spurts throughout the neighborhood, Pat looked back at the Kazakh who had fired. He was holding a Mk14 grenade launcher. The six-shot grenade launcher looked like an oversized revolver, because that was basically what it was. It was one of many weapons the private military company had scrounged off of past objectives. The Kazakh smiled.

"G-P-S," he said to his boss with a toothy grin.

Now it was Pat's turn to smile. He clicked on his satellite phone and opened the GPS app. It would take a few seconds for it to boot up. The Kazakh hadn't fired a high explosive round which was what they normally loaded in the Mk14. This time, he had shot a very specialized 40mm GPS round. The cartridge itself stuck to nearly any surface with adhesive and a GPS unit inside it would then activate and begin broadcasting.

Once the app loaded up on Pat's phone, a moving blue dot appeared in Homs. The mercenary had hit his mark. Samruk didn't do medals, but they did do pay bonuses and the Mk14 gunner had certainly earned one.

Having a tracker on the target, or rather the car, was a start but the target was mobile; Samruk was on foot and engaged with the enemy. Pat forwarded the GPS signal to Deckard's cellphone. Hitting the send button, Pat wondered whether his friend was still alive or not. The answer to that question would have to wait.

Fedorchenko was already bounding his men up to the chemical weapon laying in the street.

39

Deckard heard the screams when his hand grenade detonated.

The Operator had been driving his cell of Nusra fighters hard. They kept pushing Deckard deeper and deeper into no man's land. He had nowhere else to go. It had become a running gunfight, Deckard finding a position that offered good cover and concealment and offering an attack that would stall the enemy, if nothing else. He could nickle and dime them, but only slow the gunmen down for a few minutes at a time. Deckard never saw The Operator, but knew he was there, leading the jihadists at gunpoint.

When the grenade he had thrown exploded, he could hear the yelling of at least one Nusra gunmen caught in the blast. It was the kind of primal scream you hear from someone critically injured, from someone who is dying on a battlefield.

He turned and ran through the debris littering the streets and jumped over the twisted metal of what had once been a car before disappearing into what was left of a bombed-out apartment building. Ducking down, he shifted under a collapsed wall and kept moving.

Something slammed into Deckard's chest. The next moment he knew, he was on his back and looking up at the ceiling.

"Not bad, Johnny Rico," a voice said. "Not bad at all."

Deckard reached towards where he had dropped his rifle but a booted foot kicked it away.

"I cannot help but admire you Deckard."

It was The Operator. He'd somehow gotten behind Deckard while he was busy engaging the Nusra gunmen. He had anticipated Deckard's withdrawal route and clotheslined him, knocking the wind out of him in the process.

Deckard pushed back with his feet, backing away from The Operator as he stepped out of the shadows.

"You are strong Deckard. Resilient. I underestimated you."

Deckard continued to shuffle away on his back as The Operator stepped forward. All he had left to fight with was his

Karambit. It seemed that his foe wanted to play mind games with him before moving in for the kill. The Filipino fighting knife would do Deckard little good. The Operator could shoot him as soon as he was ready.

Continuing to back away, Deckard pushed into a couple dead bodies.

"But I have to question your resolve Deckard. In the end, we become victims of our own restraint."

He was still having trouble breathing after The Operator knocked him down but as he crawled over the bodies, Deckard realized where he was. The entire outer wall of the building was blown out.

"These bodies Deckard, these corpses. We didn't kill them. God killed them. We are merely the hand of God, carrying out his wishes."

"Keep talking," Deckard coughed.

"It isn't enough just to kill you Deckard. You are a special case. First, I have to be inside your mind."

The Operator stepped forward, cradling his AK-47 in his arms. He looked like he was barely winded, as if the combat of the last several days hadn't taken anything out of him at all. Deckard rolled and tried to scramble forward but the Operator fired two shots just inches from his face.

Deckard was trapped. The Operator stepped over the two bodies, the bodies of the two jihadists that had been killed earlier in the day when he was still chasing after Ramon.

"America is being taken over, Deckard. Someone has to act. Someone must do what must be done."

"You're a fucking wind-up toy," Deckard said.

"Patriotism means serving one's nation Deckard, not one's self. We must keep our goals in view. Would you have these Muslims install sharia law across America? That is what will happen if we fail our mission. God has delivered unto us a mission, and by God-"

The Operator's face was ripped and peeled away. It hung by a flap of skin in the air as the shot rang out, just a split second behind the bullet. The Operator collapsed to the ground. His face lay beside him like a Halloween mask.

The Syrian Army sniper had done his job.

Deckard took a couple deep breaths. Blood was surging out of The Operator's skull, the red pool quickly expanding under him. Deckard crawled forward to retrieve his rifle and beat a hasty exit. Whoever was left in the Nusra cell would probably desert without The Operator pushing them forward, but Deckard wasn't about to take that chance. He stayed low and made his way back to the courtyard where he had fired the RPG from that morning.

He felt the satellite phone vibrating in his pocket. Turning it on, he looked at the text message from Pat. Good news. Finally.

One chem wpn secure. Other tagged and on the move. Check GPS.

Sure enough, when Deckard started up his GPS app a blue dot appeared moving through the map of the city that his phone displayed. Deckard texted him back.

Who has the last wpn?

The reply came seconds later.

Not sure. Big guy. White dude.

It had to be Bill. He was the only Liquid Sky member unaccounted for aside from Nadeesha. Who knew where she had gotten to. Deckard texted Pat one more time.

I'm going after him.

Samruk International had completed half of their mission by securing one of the chemical weapons. They had three dead and a dozen walking wounded at this point. Pat had to move his element out of the city before Nusra reduced them to the point that they were no longer an effective fighting force. Samruk was composed of two rifle platoons with machine guns, sniper, and anti-tank attachments but those numbers could dwindle fast.

Mk48 gunners and Carl Gustav gunners were helping blast a path for them out of the city. Several Nusra vehicles had been hijacked. The dead and some of the wounded were loaded onboard and driven forward as Samruk cut a path out of Homs. The city was still a slaughterhouse. Practically every street welcomed the mercenaries with fresh horrors.

Pat was moving with the lead element. His Mk48 gunner suppressed an enemy machine gun while the riflemen scooted down the street. One of the Kazakhs took out the enemy position with a well-placed hand grenade.

The former Delta Force operator had seen a lot of war over the years. Sometimes he felt as though he has seen it all. Life, however, had a very unpleasant way of surprising him.

A woman ran out into the street. She was covered in blood. She held her son above her head as she screamed. The boy could not have been more than two years old. His skull had been turned into a canoe. He had been executed. The woman pushed the dead boy into the arms of one of the Kazakh riflemen. She began clawing at her face, tearing away the skin as she screamed.

Pat tried to calm her down with the limited amount of Arabic that he knew but she kept yelling at the top of her lungs the same word over and over again.

"Shabeeha, Shabeeha, Shabeeha!"

Bill watched as one of Tiger's men operated the remote control. Suicide bombers were going out of style. These days they were building remote control cars. Better for terminal guidance than human beings since you don't have to worry about them getting afraid. Better in most cases anyway. Sometimes there were people in your group you wanted to get rid of after all.

The Nusra technician finished his functions check by manipulating the joy sticks on the remote control and watching to make sure the hardware attached to the steering column responded appropriately. A bicycle chain wound around a couple of gears moved the steering column which turned the car's wheels.

Some key neighborhoods in Damascus were controlled by the rebels, but the route from there to Homs was dodgy at best with both rebels and the Syrian Army setting up snap checkpoints along the road. They were about a hundred miles from Syria's capital city and had encountered the first Army checkpoint only twenty miles into their journey.

Tiger looked at the rebel fighter and nodded. The rebel used the remote control to nudge the car forward and it gradually began to pick up speed. Bill looked at the soldiers manning the checkpoint through his binoculars. They appeared tired and lackadaisical. With the sun setting, they knew the day was almost over and were probably preparing for a shift change.

The Syrian soldiers didn't notice the car barreling down on them until it was only a hundred meters away. By the time they got their guns up, the car had closed to fifty meters. Maybe one of them got a shot off, maybe not. It was hard to tell as the entire checkpoint went up in a giant fireball. The remote control IED had been loaded with four 155mm artillery rounds. It had been overkill for taking out a half dozen Syrian soldiers, but Bill wasn't complaining.

He was done with this mission. Ready to gas some civilians and get the hell out of the country. He'd broken another Liquid Sky team. Not his first and certainly not his last. He'd get more from somewhere and start picking up contracts again within a month. It was only within the last thirty minutes that he had stopped seeing red and started to get back on task. He had over-committed to the task of chasing down Deckard. He was ultimately irrelevant to Bill's goals, just a loose end to tie up when it was all over.

That was one scalp that Bill relished the thought of taking. He would add it to his collection.

When the smoke cleared, there was nothing left of the car that the IED had been in or the Syrian soldiers. They were reduced to scraps of burnt flesh. Tiger looked at Bill. The Chechen smiled.

"Good!"

"Good," Bill affirmed. "Lets get moving."

Bill got behind the wheel of the car with his last chemical weapon. Tiger got in a second car with the rebel who had piloted the remote control car and a third Nusra fighter. Between Deckard, the mercenaries, and the Syrian Army, it was all they had left.

The former SEAL Team Six operator started down the road towards Damascus. They might be light on manpower, but he knew damn well that he had the ultimate equalizer riding in the backseat. They would push hard for the capitol through the night and by early morning it would all be over.

333

Deckard looked down at his satellite phone as the battery continued to dwindle.

Pat had gotten him on the line and forwarded the GPS tracker information to Deckard so he could follow the last weapon, assuming they hadn't changed cars. Deckard could feel his entire mission slipping through his fingertips. If Bill was able to detonate that weapon in the middle of Damascus, it was likely that the entire Middle East would explode. More so if the rebels coupled the attack with an effective propaganda campaign.

Thirty minutes prior, he had driven through the smoking remains of what was probably a roadside checkpoint. The stench of smoke and burning flesh had seeped in through the crack in the window of his hotwired car.

Looking down at the blue dot moving across the map on his satellite phone, Deckard saw that the vehicle he was after was nearly half way to the capitol already. They were tearing down the highway, pushing for Damascus before dawn. Deckard was already driving recklessly fast through the night in an attempt to catch up with them. He only had one more replacement battery for the satellite phone. If he had to improvise a recharger with some copper wiring to the car's internal electrical system, it would only waste more of his time.

He was gradually gaining on the blue dot. For now, anyway.

One way or another, he knew that it would all be over soon. If Bill had his way, he would murder thousands of civilians with mustard gas and drag the Middle East into a massive war, all because his mysterious employers had designs on the region.

Deckard floored the gas.
He couldn't let that happen.

40

Bill tugged on the black canister stuck to the back of his car. Whatever adhesive it used was powerful stuff, as even a physical specimen like him had a hard time yanking the tracker off the car. Locking the canister in a vice grip, it wasn't the glue that gave way but rather the canister itself when it shattered in Bill's hands. The exposed guts of the device were left in Bill's hands. At just a glance, it was clear that it was a GPS device. His car had a tag, track, and locate device stuck to it, probably since Homs.

Deckard.

The former SEAL Team Six operator smiled. So much the better. It would save him the trouble of tracking the traitor down. Instead, Deckard would come to him.

With Tiger's help, they lifted the chemical weapon out of the back of his car.

It was morning by the time Deckard rolled into central Damascus.

He had killed way too much time skirting around several city checkpoints, and now the blue dot on his map had been stationary for half an hour. They would be preparing the weapon for deployment. At least now he knew the target area. The vehicle had stopped smack dab in the middle of the city. That told Deckard that Bill was still on track for hitting their original target, Umayyad mosque.

The Al-Hamidiyeh market was also nearby, and the deployment of a chemical weapon was likely to kill people in the nearby market as well. Both targets were central features of life in Damascus with high visibility. Either target would ensure a high body count, but Deckard was putting his money on Umayyad Mosque since it also carried the religious significance of being the holiest site in Syria and perhaps the fourth holiest site in all of Islam. Destroying the great mosque of Damascus would almost certainly drag the entire Middle East into a conflagration of death and destruction.

Deckard parked his car several blocks away from where the tracker stopped and moved out on foot. The streets were already growing busy with people setting out for work in the morning. While the war raged outside and even within Damascus, the people of the city still had to get up everyday and find a way to earn a living. He blended in with many of the morning workers as he was still wearing his native garb, even if the clothes were now dirty and torn. The AK-47, on the other hand had to be concealed. He folded the buttstock and wrapped the weapon in a towel he found in the backseat. Extra magazines went into his pockets.

Deckard shook his head as he closed the car door behind him. This operation was so half-assed that it was a miracle he had even gotten this far. He was shooting from the hip and making it up as he went along at this point. His only consolation was that Bill was doing the same, as his initial mission plan was now lying in ruins. If Bill was making as many mistakes as Deckard was, there might be margin of error for him to exploit and get the drop on his opposition.

This was the oldest part of the city, where narrow streets twisted through ancient buildings. Many of the walls and pillars dated from far into antiquity. Untold numbers of conquerors and empires had occupied the city over the course of human history. The remains of Roman temples stood side by side with mosques. The scenery all blended into the background for Deckard, however. He was focused on dodging between the locals on the streets as he made his way to the tracker, looking down at the screen on his phone occasionally to make sure he was heading in the right direction.

Deckard kept the concealed Kalashnikov in the crook of his arm, holding it low and hoping to go unnoticed. The entire city was on a war footing and all it would take was for one police officer or soldier in the street to get a hint of suspicion, and it would all be over for him.

Moving several blocks deeper into the city, Deckard slipped down another narrow side street until he was almost on top of the signal coming from the GPS tracker. The blue dot looked to be broadcasting from inside the squat, two-story apartment building he was standing in front of. He tried to remain in the shadows cast by the walls and keep well away while doing a quick visual reconnaissance. A metal gate blocked ingress through the front door. After his hasty assessment, Deckard decided that there was no way he was going in through the front, even if he could force the door open.

The side street was quiet, just a few merchants shifting around and opening their shops. The whole thing felt like a trap.

Finding another alleyway, Deckard looked for an appropriate place to scale a wall. He would climb onto the roof of the adjacent building and then creep over to the target building. His arms strained as he found hand and footholds on the stone wall as he climbed up. The wall was on a slight incline, which made it easier, but his joints felt like they were about to pop out of their sockets. He had enough urban climbing in the last few days to last him a lifetime, however much longer that might be.

Up on the roof, he loaded the Kalashnikov and extended the buttstock, making the weapon ready before hitting the target building. Over on the next rooftop, Deckard was able to look down into an open courtyard in the center of the building. A carpet hung over a railing. There was a small pool of water on the ground level where a few birds were having a drink.

The GPS was accurate enough to pinpoint what building it was in, but not enough to tell exactly where it was without doing some searching around. If Samruk had TTLed the car then the GPS tracker must be on the ground level somewhere in a garage. He could only hope that the weapon was still nearby. A gap in the roof was covered over with a piece of plywood with an old car tire used to weight it down. Deckard carefully removed the covering to find a stairwell, and descended into the apartments below.

On the second level, Deckard followed a set of marble steps down to the courtyard. His eyes swept around for an entrance to a garage or basement where the car could have been stashed. Spotting another narrow doorway, he walked towards it.

Suddenly, the sound of a rifle's bolt being racked startled him. As Deckard spun around, the sound of the bolt slamming home into the chamber echoed through the courtyard. A young Nusra fighter on the terrace of the second floor stared down at him. Several more rifles also clacked as bullets were chambered. More Nusra fighters appeared on the balconies and terraces above him.

Deckard was boxed in. It had been a trap and he walked right into it.

He was about to make a mad dash for the door, see if he could smash through it before hundreds of 7.62 bullets tore through him. It was a pointless gesture, but better than being taken alive.

"Deckard."

His name was said like a curse.

Bill came walking down the steps. Tiger, the Chechen rebel leader walked alongside him.

"Go ahead and drop the weapon."

"I'll take my chances," Deckard said.

"You have no chance dumbass, open your fucking eyes," Bill told him as he waved towards the gunmen standing above them. "You're a dead man walking."

"That's nothing new," Deckard replied. "For either of us."

"I have to say though, this really is a first for me."

Bill stood just in front of him with the bearded Chechen at his side. Both of them appeared unarmed.

"My time with Dev. My Liquid Sky teams. I've seen operators come and go, believe me. Some of them were more talented than you, but it's like I told you back in Mauritius. You've got something extra that none of them had. You challenged the odds just because you could. You like having nowhere to run, don't you?"

"Whoever can make the biggest grandstand play. Guess my luck finally ran out."

"You had a good run, Deckard. You got this far, after all. Where the fuck is Ramon and The Operator?"

Deckard said nothing.

"Exactly. You cut right through them. I'm beginning to

think that the fucking cunt is the only smart one of us. Nadeesha pulled a fade. She's probably sipping a Mai Tai and having herself a good ride with a Cabana boy on some island by now."

"Sounds like a plan."

"I don't get you Deckard, I really don't," Bill said with a frown. "You had a seat at the table. It's like everywhere you go you piss everyone off and burn all your bridges. I'm not even going to ask why because the truth is I don't even care."

"So what are we doing here?"

"I'm going to take your scalp, Deckard. I'm even going to tell you exactly what we are doing so that it will motivate you to cut the shit and hand over that AK of yours. Tiger is about to leave with the bomb. He is going to detonate it once he gets near the Umayyad mosque. The moose limbs are finishing up their morning prayer, so now we're going to help them go and find Allah."

Tiger had a shit-eating grin on his face as Bill patted him on the back. The Chechen was joined by several other Nusra fighters who came down the steps behind them. Bill gave him the thumbs up.

"Make it happen Tiger."

"*Insha'Allah*," the Chechen commander replied. With that, he disappeared with three gunmen out the side door that Deckard had spotted.

"So here is the deal Deckard," Bill told him. "You get to square off with me. Bone to bone to see who is bigger. First, you drop that weapon; then, I call off the dogs and it will be just you and me. If you somehow get past me, maybe you've got a fifty-fifty shot of catching up with Tiger before he detonates the weapon. Then maybe you've got a slim chance at stopping him. Who knows, crazier shit has happened. So which is it? Me or the firing squad?"

Deckard depressed the magazine release on his AK with his thumb and rocked the magazine forward. Dropping the magazine, he racked the charging handle, ejecting the round from the chamber. Finally, he dropped the rifle and let it clatter to the stone floor at his feet.

"That's my boy," Bill said with a wicked smile. Reaching under his shirt, he removed his hatchet from the holster on his waist. "Been carrying this since my third trip to A-stan. I made a promise up in them mountains. Been carrying it out every day since. Going to carry your scalp out in a few minutes, Deckard."

Deckard looked down at the hatchet. It was the same one that Bill has used on their mission in Afghanistan and then again at the military outpost they had hit the night they infilled into Syria. The hatchet was more like a miniature battle axe. He had heard of other Dev Group operators carrying them. They were handmade by a world-famous edged weapons specialist and custom engraved with SEAL Team Six squadron insignia.

The hatchet was designed for close-in combat. Under a foot long, it was coated in black no-glare finish and had a nasty looking spike on the back side of the head. How many ears, scalps, dicks, and fingers had been taken by this particular hatchet was impossible to know.

Bill smiled at Deckard as his fist tightened around the hatchet and waved away the gunmen standing above them. True to his word, the gunmen faded back inside.

Reaching for his own edged weapon, Deckard yanked free Ramon's karambit from its Klydex sheath at his hip.

"Nice. You looted that off Ramon's body? You are a cold fucker, Deckard. I can't figure out your hangups. You're just like us. My initial assessment was correct, you're a perfect fit for Liquid Sky. Too bad you sold out."

Now it was Deckard's turn to smile. Bill thought that someone was cutting him a paycheck. Money was the only terms that he could understand.

"I hope they paid you well."

"Tired of listening to you talk."

With that, Bill surged forward. Deckard kicked the Kalashnikov laying at his feet into the air. Dropping the rifle in front of his feet had been a deliberate maneuver. The metal receiver spun into the air, distracting Bill as he charged toward Deckard like a rhinoceros. The rifle hit Bill in the face. With his nose bloodied, Bill reached out to grab Deckard while the other brought the hatchet up to swing down on him.

Deckard's hands moved in a blur of motion. The razor sharp edge of the karambit ended up clawing into Bill's inner wrist. Pulling up with his knife hand drew the hook of the karambit's blade, and Bill's wrist towards him. Meanwhile, he grabbed hold of Bill's hand and bent it towards his opponent, trapping Bill in a bloody wrist lock.

Bill was nearly driven down to his knees by Deckard's surprise counter. His flailed with the hatchet, Deckard pivoting away at the last moment, the blade passing an inch from his head. Then the hatchet came flailing back towards him again; this time he was unable to avoid it, and the metal spike on the reverse side of the weapon slammed into Deckard's ribs.

Knocked off his feet by the blast to his abdomen, Deckard rolled across the courtyard. Bill managed to struggle back to his feet, one bloody hand hanging at his side. Deckard was struggling to breath as he held on to the side of the water fountain and pulled himself up. He didn't have a punctured lung, but the hatchet had left a ragged tear in his side and probably cracked a rib.

"Deckard, you cocksucker."

The two combatants tightened their grip on their weapons. There was no doubt in either of their minds that one of them wasn't walking away from this fight. They circled each other, looking for an opening to strike. Bill had an oil leak; he was trailing blood across the courtyard from his wrist. Deckard took several deep breaths, wincing at the pain while trying to force oxygen into his system.

Bill swung first. The hatchet came at him in a blur, the trajectory aimed right at Deckard's face. Deckard sidestepped the attack, then immediately had to backpedal to avoid Bill's follow-up attack. The evil looking black hatchet came at him again and again. More blood sprayed from Bill's wrist with each swing, splattering across Deckard's chest.

The former SEAL Team Six operator was fast, faster than someone his size should be. He had training and knew how to use his weight to his advantage. Experience in martial arts and military hand-to-hand combat made his every movement seem smooth and rehearsed, because they were. Deckard was avoiding his attacks, but only because his opening gambit had injured Bill and left him at a disadvantage.

Like The Operator, Bill was someone that Deckard could not let get ahold of him, or he would be taken apart in short order. One more screw up, like the blow he already took from the hatchet, and this fight was over. Bill would be walking out the door with Deckard's scalp in his hand.

The Umayyad mosque was only three city blocks away and Tiger was already on the way with the chemical weapon in tow. Deckard knew he had to bypass this fight somehow, or otherwise defeat Bill in the next sixty seconds, or it would be impossible for him to catch up with the Chechen and prevent him from gassing thousands of Muslims on their way home from their morning *salat*.

Bill swung the hatchet again, backing Deckard closer to the wall behind them. The former SEAL grunted in anger; then, came at him again, slashing the hatchet diagonally one way and then the next. Deckard moved in to stab Bill in the forearm with his fighting knife, but he was a fraction of a second too slow. Bill brought the spike on the axe behind Deckard's knee and forced him down, his knee smashing into the stone floor. He was now looking up at Bill as the hatchet came swinging down towards his throat.

Deckard rolled away at the last moment, the hatchet cutting through empty space instead of his neck. Before he could fully get to his feet, Bill came at him again. Instead of trying to parry or dodge the attack, Deckard stepped into it.

The fight was over one second later.

As the hatchet came towards him, Deckard blocked the attack with his forearm and brought the Karambit straight up in a vertical slashing motion. The claw of the knife cut through Bill's bicep like a hot knife through butter. Ducking under the hatchet, Deckard then slid the knife across Bill's stomach. The knife separated skin and abdominal muscles, partially disemboweling him.

Without missing a beat, Deckard dashed towards the door and blasted right through it, the wooden panels smashing on the wall as he flung himself through. Bill was out of the fight and irrelevant to his objective. He couldn't spare a single second on him now. The passageway was so tight that he had to turn sideways at times as he fought his way towards the streets. Finally, he came to another door, booted it open and was back outside in the sunlight.

Now the streets were bustling with people. He still held the karambit in his fist, having forgotten it was there as his eyes swept the street for the Nusra goons. The entrance to the Al-Hamidiyeh market was right in front of him. From scanning the map on his phone earlier, he knew that the market was a commercial ribbon of shops on both sides of the street.

Once inside the market, it was a straight shot for five-hundred meters, right to the mosque.

Deckard forced his way through the throngs of people and into the entrance of the market. Several saw the blood splattered across his shirt and stepped aside of their own volition. Inside the market, Deckard turned right. With the arched roof reaching across the market, it basically formed a long tunnel all the way to the exit where the mosque was. The corrugated metal roof was held up by an iron support structure. Deckard could literally see the light at the end of the tunnel, some five-hundred meters away. He took off at a dead sprint.

His legs felt wobbly, his arms slightly out of tune with his body as they reciprocated with his legs. He was over twenty-four hours without sleep and had been in combat off and on for days. His body would charge with adrenaline for a fight and then dump it, leaving him drained. Now he steeled himself for one final push to the finish line.

Shops filled with spices, produce, and clothing passed on both sides and became a blur as Deckard's long strides ate up the ground in front of him. The daylight at the end of the tunnel was growing as he got closer, his lungs struggling to fill with air because of the throbbing pain in his side.

Suddenly a police officer blew his whistle and jumped out in front of Deckard. His body reacted before his mind even fully processed what was happening. The karambit was still in his fist. Deckard had his trigger finger looped through the hole at the end of the karambit's handle, and used it like a set of brass knuckles to plow the policemen in the jaw with. The cop went down and stayed down. He would wake up in the hospital, but at least he would wake up.

Deckard had barely even slowed down and vaulted over a fruit stand as he continued to run towards the mosque. He dodged several more pedestrians as he reached the end of the market. Suddenly, he stood in the remains of the Temple of Jupiter. The Roman ruin had columns and arches that formed colonnades on both sides of the walkway. There on the walkway was four merchants pushing a wooden cart covered in children's toys on display and for sale. One of the merchants had a long black beard.

Tiger.

The four Nusra fighters turned towards the sound of the commotion as Deckard dashed towards them. Civilians scattered in all directions. About fifty meters from the Jupiter temple was the Umayyad mosque.

As Deckard crashed into the nearest Nusra fighter, the jihadist held up his arm to try to defend against the attack. Deckard reached over the arm and snaked the karambit under his jaw on the far side of his neck. He then used his forearm to push against the side of the jihadist's face while simultaneously drawing the hook of the karambit across his throat. The Filipino fighting knife cut across the jihadist's neck at a depth of about two inches. He dropped to the ground, clutching his throat.

His buddy saw what was going on and jumped into the fray, grabbing Deckard by the wrist to try to prevent him from doing any more damage with his knife hand. Deckard simply reversed the knife around and hooked the blade over his opponents wrist, slashing through the flesh and breaking his grip. He maintained pressure on the forearm and locked it in with his weak hand while slashing the jihadist's triceps muscle and finishing by slashing one of his eyeballs.

By this time, Tiger had backed away from the cart and began reaching for a pistol he kept in concealment under his shirt. The remaining Nusra fighter was doing the same. Deckard's knife hand shot out and hooked the karambit into Tiger's elbow, getting him in a vicious arm-lock that tore through his skin and the ligaments underneath. The other Nusra fighter almost had his pistol out by now, so Deckard punched Tiger in the forehead with the metal loop at the end of his knife and quickly diverted his attention to the other would-be gunman.

The pistol had barely cleared leather when Deckard stepped into the attack, coming up under what would have been the gun arm, forced the Nusra fighter into a bent over position, and slashed his fingers. The pistol dropped to the ground, and Deckard slashed his throat.

Tiger had recovered enough to wipe some of the blood flowing down his face away and grab his own pistol. Deckard went for a grab while pivoting sideways. Tiger squeezed off a shot with the Glock that chiseled into one of the Roman pillars behind Deckard. Before he could get off another shot, Deckard slammed the hook edge of the Karambit into his inner elbow and forced him down, then used it to slash through his fingers and pry the gun out of his grasp. Finally, Deckard went in low, sinking the Karambit into Tiger's groin and ripping upwards.

The Filipino blade carved the Chechen open from groin all the way up to his chest, opening him like a Christmas turkey.

All four of the terrorists were now dead or dying.

Deckard turned his attention to the cart they had been pushing. Ripping through the stuffed animals and plastic toys, the facade on the top of the cart easily came away and crashed to the ground. Inside was what Deckard had been looking for. The bomb that they had pulled out of a bunker in Libya; the chemical weapon was laying in the bottom of the cart.

He cursed as he looked down at the LED screen attached to the side of the weapon. There was 29 seconds left on the clock. The Nusra fighters had intended to martyr themselves. The market and the area just outside the mosque were now filled with people. The results of deploying a chemical weapon here would kill thousands of people.

Leaning over the cart, Deckard reached inside and quickly began punching in the activation/deactivation code that Bill had briefed them on before they left Turkey. He could already hear police whistles behind him. He hit the enter button, then the eight digit code number, and finally pressed enter a second time.

The red numbers on the display screen froze at twelve seconds.

41

Pat watched as a car approached in the distance.

It was late afternoon. The city of Homs was burning. Again.

The mercenaries had managed to fight their way out of the city and find a defendable position to bunker down in until they were extracted. Pat had also sent out a few scouting parties to try to find a place where they could safely dispose of chemical weapons. Relatively safe at least, where they wouldn't kill anyone. There would be environmental damage, but that was the least of Syria's worries right now.

At the moment, they had sent out a reception party to take control of the second chemical weapon. Pat and a half dozen Kazakh mercenaries were in fixed security positions watching their perimeter while Nikita was in overwatch, using the scope on his sniper rifle to watch for enemy movements. Pat watched as the approaching vehicle swerved a few times and drove a little erratically.

Pat stood up and flashed a red-lens flashlight. It was their agreed upon far recognition signal. The driver flashed his headlights three times in response. The car slowed down before coming to a stop in a cloud of dust. The driver's side door creaked open. Deckard looked like he was struggling just to get out of the vehicle. Finally, he stood while bracing himself against the side of the car.

"You okay?" Pat asked.

Deckard looked at him like he was a total asshole.

"I've been better." His voice was low and dry.

"The weapon?"

Deckard shook his head.

"But it's disarmed and out of terrorist hands. I had to escape and evade after deactivating it. The Syrian police were right on top of me. I did see them take possession of the bomb though. Now it is on them if they want to cover the whole thing up or exploit it for propaganda purposes."

"That could get ugly."

"Real ugly, but not as ugly as thousands of dead civilians would have been. If the regime puts footage of the bomb in TV news, it would be a huge propaganda victory for them, but mostly just an embarrassment for the international community rather than World War Three. Besides, the bomb was made by the Russians rather than America, so I doubt they will go that route."

"The 50% solution. I'm impressed that we even managed that."

"You and me both."

"We found a cave nearby. Are you sure you want to do this?"

"Detonating the second bomb is the only way to be sure that it won't be recycled for use by the rebels down the line. Technically, even the bomb that the government now has could have the electronics torn out of it and be re-used, but they already have a chemical weapons stockpile. If they want to use weapons of mass destruction, then one mustard gas bomb isn't going to change anything. Setting off the other bomb in a controlled manner ensures that it can never be used again."

Pat noticed that Deckard was slurring some of his words. He was obviously exhausted and winced a little each time he took a deep breath.

"We need to have one of our medics take a look at you. You're pretty beat up. But there is something else I want you to see. We captured handful of government loyalists who have been running around the battlefield murdering civilians. Death squad shit designed to intimidate the locals into aligning with government forces."

"*Shabeeha*. Ghosts. I'm glad you caught up with them. Liquid Sky just missed them."

"We killed a couple and the others immediately surrendered. They're not soldiers, just thugs who were in over their heads the second they were up against anyone who wasn't a four year old kid."

"Good. Stick them down in the hole with the mustard gas bomb when we blow it."

"Serious?"

"Better fucking believe it."

Just then, a thud sounded in the back of Deckard's car. Something banging around inside the trunk.

"What the hell is that?" Pat asked curiously.

"Another addition to go into the pit with our *Shabeeha*

348

pals."

The cave was located in the outskirts of Homs, its existence only evident by a small gap in the side of a cliff. Inside, the rock floor was worn smooth as if it had been polished. The cave had served as a hideout, redoubt, and clandestine meeting place for soldiers, thieves, and bandits since before the time of the Romans.

The latest occupants were four sullen-faced young men in their twenties. They had been restrained with flexcuffs around their hands and ankles. A dozen green glow sticks illuminated the interior of the cave as the Kazakh mercenaries lifted and carried the chemical weapon they had captured inside.

Once the bomb was set down, the four Syrians looked at it and then at each other nervously knowing that nothing good could come from this. Then there was a shuffling at the mouth of the cave as someone was dragged inside by the mercenaries. He was a human giant but walked all hunched over. He was set down in front of the bomb.

Another silhouette was crouched in the opening to the cave, looking inside. He said something in Russian and the foreign mercenaries turned and exited the cave.

Deckard moved aside to let the Kazakhs leave and then stepped inside. He walked into the center of the circle of green chem sticks surrounding the weapon and his five prisoners. Bill didn't even make eye contact with him. Samruk International medics had patched him up, got his blood pressure back up with an IV bag of HexTend solution, and injected him with some stimulants to keep him conscious. Deckard's karambit had sliced one of his biceps in half, slashed the veins in his wrist, and disemboweled him. His guts had been balled up on his stomach and stuck in place with gauze and medical tape.

Deckard drew the karambit and knelt down next to him. The Syrian death squad members looked on in dreadful anticipation.

"End of the line."

Bill continued to look straight down at the ground.

"Get it over with," he mumbled. "It's what I would have done to you."

"It isn't that simple. I need names. I need to know who you talk to on that encryption system in Mauritius. Who is your client?"

"We've changed hands a few times. Multiple Liquid Sky teams, multiple employers."

"When was the last time you changed hands?"

"A couple months ago when there was a major compromise in Nevada. We were working for Ted Snyder at G3 Communications, but after the compromise everything they were doing came under scrutiny. They moved Liquid Sky off to another handler for security reasons, but since you were the guy in Nevada who made that mess, I guess you already put most of that together."

"What makes you think I was the guy in Nevada?"

"Got a phone call from the new client. They're starting to put it all together. They knew you were in Syria but not that you were with us. They asked me to find you and take you out while we were here."

"Who is the new client?"

Bill looked up at him.

"McCoy."

Deckard was silent for a moment.

"A bold claim."

Bill shrugged.

"It is what it is. This fight is over and I have no loyalty to him."

"I'm going to need some details."

"I only know my part of the operation. If you want to know about colored pins stuck in a map of the world then you'll have to ask McCoy yourself."

Deckard spent the next hour debriefing Bill, writing

350

things down on a notepad as needed. Bill went over how they communicated with the client, what their arrangements were, how payments were handled, where targeting and intelligence information came from, and the personalities involved in handling Liquid Sky, at least the ones he knew of.

Finally, Deckard stood up and walked over to the bomb.

"That was you in Pakistan, wasn't it?" Bill asked Deckard as he punched the activation code into the keypad on the bomb.

"Yeah. We did compromise Liquid Sky. Found periphery information in documents in Nevada and traced it to your operations. I would have taken out your whole team right there if possible, but after you slipped through our hands, I had to try something different."

"I guess we really are two sides of the same coin, then. Letting clients tell us where to go and who to kill."

"You don't get it Bill. I don't have a client. This was a mission that I chose."

"Why?"

"Because," Deckard told him as he activated the bomb and set thirty minutes on the timer. "It isn't enough to just throw on a scroll, a tab, or a trident. We have to earn it. Every day."

"What a boy scout."

"I don't know what happened to you Bill, not sure I want to know, but defaulting to the level of the enemy is unacceptable. You had to have known that what you were doing was sick, even by the standards of war. It couldn't go on forever. It was vain and self-indulgent. Nothing more."

Bill leaned forward to try to relieve some of the pain in his abdomen.

"What the fuck ever," he grunted. "Just leave me the fuck alone."

Deckard turned and walked away, leaving Bill with the confused death squad members. Unable to understand English, they had no idea what was going on. As Deckard climbed up out of the hole in the ground, he didn't even think of looking back.

Deckard finished reviewing his notes and put them in his pocket.

"Did you get what you were looking for?" Pat asked him.

"Enough to finish this."

"Satisfied with the answers?"

Deckard frowned.

"No, never."

The mercenaries looked on as the bomb exploded and a wisp of mustard gas slowly plumed out of the opening of the cave. They had made sure they were upwind before detonation.

"How are we getting out of here?" Deckard asked without taking his eyes off the cloud of mustard gas.

"Unimproved airstrip an hour or so from here. You'll like what you see."

Samruk International piled onto a flatbed truck and a van

they had procured on the battlefield and drove across a series of back roads to an unmaintained airstrip in the middle of nowhere. From there, they set up a security perimeter and waited. It was too risky to extract during the day with so many surface-to-air missiles floating around.

After having the medics look at his wounds again, Deckard slept like a stone. With the sun going down, the mercenaries measured out some distances and set out infrared strobe lights to mark the landing zone. The pilots would be flying blacked out and under night vision. Pat got on his satellite phone and made contact with the pilots. Encrypted cellular and satellite phones like he and Deckard had been using were really the future of military communications, not just tactical comms but for covert and clandestine operations as well.

Tactics, techniques, and procedures changed fast, and they were all just struggling to keep up.

Deckard woke as the first airplane screamed into the desert airstrip. He hugged himself, trying to get warm. The night air was cold against his skin. He stood and rubbed the sleep out of his eyes, but still felt like he was moving in molasses as his body was no where near recovered.

"Take a look," Pat said, handing him a PVS-14 night vision monocle.

Deckard looked through the night vision device at the plane turning itself around at the end of the landing zone. He whistled.

"C-27J. Samruk International now owns two of them. I figured that if we are going to be a smaller force then we need a tactical air capability. Those Antonovs are great, but these C-27s can conduct short take off and landing on unimproved airfields."

"Did you bankrupt the company while I was gone?"

"Nah, I got these babies at bargain basement rates. The U.S. government mothballed them the second they came off the assembly line. Budget cuts."

"Their loss is our gain," Deckard said as he continued to watch the aircraft.

He watched as the second C-27J landed and dropped its ramp to begin loading the mercenaries onboard.

"Pat?"

"Yeah?"

"I don't think I can do this job anymore."

Pat was silent for a moment before replying.
"Deckard, I think this is the only job that you can do."

42

Nadeesha smiled and the young NGO worker responded in kind.

He was a young kid with one of the save-the-children type non-governmental organizations that scooted back and forth across the border everyday. She had told him that she was a freelance journalist who had gotten trapped behind enemy lines for several days. She had linked up with the western NGO and their two security contractors after coming across them doing a medical detail for children. She immediately struck up a rapport with the boy who was now sitting next to her in the car. Chet was one of their medics.

She was filthy as everyone else in the third world hell hole, but a little field improvisation and showing some cleavage went a long way. Chet wouldn't shut up now and talked to her constantly. She could put up with it if it got her a ride, a bottle of water, and helped her escape back into Turkey.

The overland route had been rough, but far better than staying in Homs. When everything went pear-shaped she knew when to cut her losses. Without a doubt, her team had been encircled and killed. When she left they were trapped between some foreign mercenaries and the Syrian Army. She knew the men would be executed, but as a woman her fate would be far worse.

Too bad about Deckard, she thought as she tried to ignore Chet's blabber mouth. He had been a nice ride, but now it was time to move on.

They drove into the village of Jarabulus near the border with Turkey. While Chet couldn't shut up about his graduate-school program, she had elicited some information from one of the NGO's security men, a middle aged Australian SAS veteran. The relatively moderate Free Syrian Army controlled the border checkpoints on the Syrian side. Whenever the Nusra jihadist fighters took over a border checkpoint the Turkish military would push into Syria and kill them or chase them off, then the military would withdraw back into their own territory. At least the Turks were not letting the crazies control the border, which made life easier for the NGOs to cross.

At the checkpoint, the former SASR soldier handled the FSA members standing guard. The NGO had a fairly good reputation and had built some strong rapport with the FSA. After a cursory inspection of the vehicle, which was really just a formality, they were then waved through the checkpoint. The procedure was repeated on the Turkish side of the border, and then they were ushered forward.

Nadeesha breathed a sigh of relief. They were in Karkamış, Turkey. It was a small, quaint village where the NGO worked out of.

She stared out the window as houses passed by.

There was one thing that Nadeesha knew about herself if nothing else.

She was a survivor.

43

Two weeks later:

McCoy turned over in bed as his wife grumbled next to him. The phone on the nightstand was ringing. The red numbers on the clock said that it was three in the morning. Rubbing his eyes, the retired General knew that only a handful of people had the number to the landline in his home. If he was being called at this time of night, it was for a good reason. Probably someone needing him to fix a problem in another time zone.

"Hello," he said answering the phone.

"Come downstairs," a voice whispered over the phone.

"What?"

"Don't bother trying to call the police. You won't be able too."

"Who is this?"

The line went dead. McCoy fiddled with the phone but there was no dial tone.

"What is it?" His wife asked as she turned to him.

"Nothing, just some problem in another timezone that work needs me to fix," the lie came off the tip of his tongue without even thinking about it. Occupational hazard.

Walking across the bedroom he retrieved his cell phone from its charger and turned it on. No bars. Was the signal jammed? WiFi was out too. The voice on the phone said to come downstairs. It had to be a prank call. No way was anyone getting through the layers of security around his house. Just in case, he grabbed his HK USP pistol from the safe in the closet before heading downstairs.

At the bottom of the steps, he saw that the kitchen light was on. Frowning, he moved forward, holding the pistol out in front of him. He never heard the sounds of the man coming up from behind him. He was driven down to his knees and the pistol wrenched from his hands.

"If you want to leave your wife out of this I suggest not screaming for help."

McCoy looked up at his attacker.

"What do you want?"

"I want you. I want Ted Snyder. I want anyone else involved."

"Deckard," the old General hissed his name.

Deckard helped McCoy to his feet and shoved him into one of the dining room chairs.

"How did you even get in here?"

"I've got a guy who does breaking and entering. I'm not half bad myself. Your two security guards are tied up in the backyard."

"Everyone thought you died in Syria."

"Me too."

"Bill?"

"Sorry for your loss."

"Look, not in here. My wife designed the kitchen. I don't want her to find my brains plastered on the wall."

"Have it your way. Outside," Deckard motioned towards the door.

He followed McCoy out into the yard. Still wearing his pajamas, he was freezing cold and began to shiver.

"I know it isn't just you and Ted in this little cabal," Deckard said. "You guys don't self task. Not without top cover. You don't make a move without protection from powerful people, everyone knows that about you."

McCoy spilled three names.

Deckard snorted.

"What the fuck?"

"You want Ted too? I'm as sick of these fucking weasels as you are. The four of them are meeting in New York in a couple days. The Others Club. Their favorite place, for brunch. I'm supposed to be there as well."

"Sorry you can't make it."

"Feel free to tell those fucks that I sent you."

"I will."

Deckard flicked the USP's selector to safe and tucked it under his jacket.

"What are you doing?"

Reaching in his pocket, he pulled out a small cellophane packet and tossed it to McCoy. The retired General looked down at the package with a small white pill inside and then back up at

358

Deckard. The mercenary tapped the face of his wristwatch.
"On you."

44

New York City:

Ted Snyder nervously tapped his foot against the floor.

"Relax," the younger of the two Biermann brothers told him, seeing the worried expression on his face. "The medical examiner confirmed that it was a heart attack."

"Maybe they weren't looking for the right thing in the tox screen."

"Wait until the old man gets here and then we'll get this all sorted out," the older Biermann brother said, dismissively waving his hand.

They were seated for brunch just a few minutes ago and the waitress was now bringing their drink orders. Ted was the CEO of a major defense company and knew his share of heavy drinkers in his industry, but the fact that the Biermann brothers routinely drank bourbon for breakfast was something that he could never quite figure out. The waitress set down the Bloody Mary he ordered in front of him.

They sat in the old man's favorite room, which had been reserved for their private meeting ahead of time. The walls were painted in pastels and long, tall windows let the morning light in, giving the Upper East Side club a very warm feeling inside. As one of Manhattan's most exclusive clubs, the décor was strongly in contrast to the other stuffy formal clubs, some of which dated back to the Revolutionary War.

The Biermann brothers clinked glasses and drank up, but Ted wasn't in the mood. He'd spent a week holed up in a safe room eating military rations after Area 14 in Nevada got hit and then lived under unbearable amounts of security while still trying to run G3 Communications. Only recently had he identified who was behind the strike in Nevada. They believed that he had been killed in Syria. Then General McCoy turned up dead in his backyard. The coroner said it was a heart attack, but Ted wasn't taking anything for granted at this point.

There was a knock at the door and then a body guard opened it for the old man.

George Szabo had arrived.

Having just celebrated his 90th birthday, he looked none the worse for wear. The three men stood to shake hands with Szabo, which was nothing if not appropriate considering that he was the owner of The Others Club, not to mention a self-made billionaire.

Together, the Biermann brothers and Szabo occupied an interesting political space. They were all billionaires with vast financial empires. The brothers and Szabo also pulled political puppet strings through foundations, think tanks, and lobby groups both domestically and internationally. Szabo was notionally on the left and the Biermann brothers notionally on the right, but as Ted watched them shake hands there was no doubt in his mind that they were all drinking bourbon together at the end of the day. No matter who won, Wall Street won. It was a fixed game if ever there was one.

With the three of them combined, the oligarchs controlled an entire political dialectic in America. Through their media holdings and lobbyist firms, the left and the right ends of the spectrum were routinely played off each other for the gain of the three oligarchs. Ted, on the other hand, was firmly inside the defense establishment and had spent his entire professional life there since retiring as a commander in the Navy.

But you couldn't run a fixed game in a free market, so these titans of the finance sector had to employ various tools to maintain their oligarchy. One of those tools was espionage. Another was direct action by mercenary soldiers. Lately, their hobby had been assassinating pro-democracy advocates in certain parts of the world. They encouraged the Arab Spring in places where they wanted regime change, like in Egypt or Libya, and suppressed it to maintain the status quo in Saudi Arabia and Bahrain.

"I just heard back from my people," Szabo said as he took his seat. "I had them test for some specific chemical markers."

The Biermann brothers looked on with identical expressions. Ted swallowed.

"McCoy took a suicide pill. The type we issue to spies and assassins for deniable operations."

"Fuck me," Ted gasped.

Szabo ignored the foul language.

"We'll just let the media continue to run with the story

about the heart attack. Worked with Bill Colby back when. Might as well leave well enough alone."

"Was it Deckard?" Ted asked.

"We don't know for sure. Our analysts are combing through some interesting metadata though. Nothing definitive yet but..."

"But?" the older Biermann spoke up.

"They are ninety percent sure that he survived Syria."

"Fuck," Ted cursed again.

Szabo looked at him disapprovingly.

"The mission in Syria was an abject failure. As near as we can tell, Deckard was the only survivor. Somehow, he actually infiltrated Liquid Sky before Ted discovered that he was the one who did Area 14."

"We've also heard from our contacts," the younger Biermann said.

"In the Pentagon," the older brother said finishing the other's sentence. "Chemical sensors picked up the detonation of one of the weapons. They think it was sub-surface and mostly contained."

"The other weapon is in possession of the Syrian government," the younger brother picked up. "They are asking for some serious collateral if we want it back. This embarrassment is seriously limiting our kinetic options with the regime right now."

"This has the potential to turn into a real shit show," Ted said. "We barely contained G3's role in Nevada and Mexico. Now we've got to contend with the Assad regime and Deckard on the loose."

"Not to mention controlled leaks from foreign intelligence services trying to thwart our plans," The younger Biermann said.

"A few nihilistic young people being manipulated by the FSB and MSS. Nothing we haven't handled in the past," Szabo said as the server brought him his own bourbon. The young woman took all of their brunch orders. Once she left the room, Szabo continued the conversation.

"Liquid Sky no longer exists. I want Cobra Gold pulled off the sabotage operation in Pakistan and Green Light taken off standby for Iran. Both teams need to be on Deckard full time until he is eliminated. The CIA has had him on a target deck for a while, but I know he has his fans at the Agency. That ends now. We start putting pressure on this issue from all sides."

"He also has an operation in Kazakhstan, with tacit approval from the country's government," Ted said.

Szabo looked at the Biermann brothers.

"We'll handle it," they said in unison. It was an annoying habit that the twins had.

"I don't know how he has managed it and I don't care, but Deckard has compromised huge portions of our ongoing operations. The amount of damage he can still do is impossible to calculate," Szabo lectured. "I want all resources re-tasked and dedicated to destroying him immediately."

"We're on the same page," the older Biermann said.

"Same here," Ted confirmed.

"Tomorrow morning I have a meeting with the director-"

Szabo's words were cut off as they heard a loud thud outside in the hall.

The four men turned as the door swung open. Deckard stood in the doorway. Walking inside, he pulled a chair from one of the other tables and sat himself with the oligarchs. None of them said a word. The Biermann brothers were literally speechless. Ted may or may not have defecated in his pants judging from the expression on his face. Szabo remained stoic.

Deckard reached into the pocket of the black leather jacket he wore and pulled out four cellophane wrappers, each containing a tiny white pill inside. He tossed one onto each of their plates.

"Same deal I gave McCoy. It is far better than any of you deserve."

"If we refuse?" Szabo taunted.

Deckard shrugged.

"Ask your bodyguards outside, if any of them can still talk."

Ted looked down at his suicide pill.

"You've run out of moves. It's over," Deckard said as he looked at the old man. "Take the pills. Go out with what ever sorry fucking excuse for dignity you have left. You're still pieces of shit, but your legacies are secure. Like McCoy, no one will ever know of the crimes that have been done in your names."

"Hey, listen," Ted began. "You've got it all wrong-"

"Shut up," Szabo ordered.

363

"Exactly," Deckard agreed. "I'm sick of looking at your goddamn faces. Let's get this over with."

One by one the men sitting around the table opened the plastic wrapper, put the pills in their mouth, and then washed them down with their drinks.

Deckard sat back in his chair and waited for them to die.

Epilogue:

The twin rotor blades on the CH-47 helicopter slowly, almost lazily, began to turn as the pilots cranked the engine.

The forward operating base at Tarin Kot, Afghanistan was stirring, slowly at first, but more and more Multi-Cam clad Special Operations soldiers began to arrive at the airfield. They carried an assortment of weapons and kit but all Special Operations soldiers basically looked the same at this stage in the war. They had all worked together, shared tactics, shared experiences, and even shared grief when they lost their own.

Although they wore almost identical uniforms and equipment, the tribes of Special Operations often spoke different languages. From Polish, to Italian, to Danish, they hailed from across the Western world. Perhaps the one thing they had in common was the belief that they were the only thing holding their societies together. Although they were not American, the tribe arriving at the airfield spoke English.

One of the operators set his M4 carbine on the hood of the white land cruiser he had driven to the airfield while he readjusted the plate carrier he wore. His helmet also went on the hood. He wouldn't bother putting it on until they were ready to board the CH-47 Chinook. The Americans were prone to sarcastically calling it the shit-hook. His unit just called it the heli.

The Special Operations soldier then snapped on his belt which had his pistol, extra magazines, and a few other tools of the trade on it. He slapped at the pouches, brushing off the fine layer of dust that was still there from the last mission. As he moved the belt around until it was comfortable, one of the younger soldiers in his unit approached.

"Hey, mate," the other operator began. "What's that on your belt there?"

"Oh that?" he said, looking down at his hip.

"Yeah, is that a hatchet?"

"Yes, it is," the older soldier responded. The hatchet was mounted horizontally on the side of his belt in a special sheath.

"Why in the hell are you carrying a hatchet?"

The operator shrugged. The rotor blades on the CH-47

365

were beginning to pick up speed. Soon they would get the call from the flight crew and they could then climb up the ramp and find a place to sit down inside. It was going to be another long night.

"Did a rotation last year with the guys from Dam Neck," he told the younger troop. They were both in the same squadron but did not know each other very well, not yet anyway. "Most of those boys carry hatchets. They have them specially made with their unit insignia on them and such."

"It looks pretty wicked mate."

"It does. They gave me this one as a parting gift at the end of the rotation. They are specially made for Dev Group. Do you want me to look into getting one for you?"

"Yeah, I'd really appreciate that."

"Stick with me when we get out there then. I'll show you the right way to use one."

The younger Special Operations soldier nodded his head approvingly.

"Will do," he said. "Will do."

A Final note from the author:

Thanks for reading Direct Action. I'm sure that the graphic content in this book offended many readers, but I assure you that I did not write the book for shock value. I had reasons for writing the previous two Deckard novels, like wanting to write the ultimate action-adventure novel, or writing a novel that depicts modern day counter-terrorism operations. This book was different. I wrote this book as a message to a very specific group of people and to those who know what is going on but have been running top cover instead of putting a stop to it. I hope this book begins a dialog because not talking about the problem is not helping to solve it.

Please consider reviewing this novel on Amazon.com if you have a moment. Your feedback is very helpful. Also, you can connect with me and my other work by following the links below.

Website: www.Reflexivefire.com
Facebook: www.facebook.com/JackMurphyAuthor
Twitter: @JackMurphyRGR
E-mail: Reflexivefire@yahoo.com

Acknowledgments:

Direct Action was by far the most exhausting of the three Deckard novels I've written thus far. Like the previous two books, I hammered it out while being a full time student, having a job, and everything else that life throws at you. However, I did it with a lot of help. Special thanks to my wife for understanding why I wrote this book.

Again, I must thank Marc Lee for the amazing cover art that he did for this project. This is the third novel we've worked on together and we are pretty much reading each other's minds at this point. He designed the cover on his own as a side project for his own amusement. I quickly offered to buy it from him because I knew it was perfect for Direct Action. Thanks for your hard work and constant support Marc.

I also want to thank Nate Granzow and Laura K. for the edits and proof reading. This book is ten times better because of your help. Thanks for spotting all my mental hiccups. I'd also like to thank Laura Walker for helping me with some of the technical details when it comes to computers and physical security.

At least ten people beta read this book prior to publication and gave me their notes. Thanks so much Paul Ciolino, Emil, Fredrick, Lawrence, and all the others for your feedback. Direct Action is a stronger novel because of you. I also want to thank Kerry Patton, Brandon Webb, Charlie Jackman, and everyone else who has been a part of the SOFREP team.

Most importantly, I have to thank those who can never be named. You took a stand against those who chose the easy wrong over the hard right. Maybe one day things will change and this mess will get cleaned up. All the soldiers who served, and died, honorably deserve nothing less.

Until that day.

Glossary:

160th SOAR: Special Operations Aviation Regiment. Army helicopter unit which flies Special Operations missions, often delivering Special Operations soldiers to their targets.

AAR: After Action Review. Soldiers typically conduct an AAR post-mission to evaluate what was done wrong and how to improve performance for the next mission.

AK-103: An updated form of the AK-47 rifle that can be fitted with a variety of different optics.

AK-47: Avtomat Kalashnikova-1947, following the standard Soviet weapons naming convention. Avtomat meaning the type of rifle: automatic. Kalashnikov comes from the last name of the inventor, Mikhail Kalashnikov and the year 1947 is when the rifle went into production. The AK-47 is the world's most ubiquitous battle rifle, having been used in virtually every conflict since the Cold War.

An-125: Large Russian-made cargo airplane.

AO: Area of Operations.

APC: Armored Personnel Carrier.

AQ: Al Qaeda.

BW: Blackwater. A now defunct private security company.

C-27J: Medium-sized military transport aircraft.

C4: Composition Four plastic explosives.

Carl Gustav: Recoiless rifle.

CH-47: Twin rotor military transport helicopter.

CI: Counter-Intelligence.

SOP:Standard Operating Procedure

CIA: Central Intelligence Agency

CIF: Commander's In-Extremis Force

CISEN: Mexican Intelligence Agency

Commo: Communications

CQB: Close Quarter Battle

CYPRES: Emergency device on a Military parachute.

DARPA: Defense Advanced Research Projects Agency.

Delta Force: US Army Counter-Terrorism unit. Also known as Combat Applications Group, Task Force Green, or simply The Unit.

Dev Group: US Navy SEAL Counter-Terrorism unit. Also known as Task Force Blue, Naval Special Warfare Development Group, and more recently, TACDEVRON.

DUI: Driving While Intoxicated.

E&E: Escape and Evasion.

ECT: Explosive Cutting Tape. A type of explosive used for breaching targets.

EMP: Electro-Magnetic Pulse.

EOD: Explosive Ordinance Disposal.

Exfil: Exfiltrate.

FDA: Food and Drug Administration

FN-FAL: Belgium 7.62 rifle.

FRP: Final Reference Point, used as a known point that can be paced off to help find a previously hidden cache.

FSA: Free Syrian Army.

FSB: Russian intelligence agency.

G3 Communications: Fictional security firm.

GPS: Global Positioning System.

GROM: Polish Counter-Terrorism unit.

Ground Branch: CIA para-military unit.

GRS: Global Response Staff, CIA contractor that often escort and protect case officers in dangerous parts of the world.

GSG-9: German police unit that conducts counter-terrorist operations.

HAHO: High Altitude, High Opening.

HALO: High Altitude, Low Opening.

HERF: High-Energy Radio Frequency.

HK 417: Heckler and Koch 7.62 gas piston operated rifle.

HK USP: Series of Heckler and Koch pistols.

HME: Home Made Explosives.

HQ: Headquarters.

HUMINT: Human Intelligence.

IED: Improvised Explosive Device.

Infil: Infiltrate.

ISA: Intelligence Support Activity. A classified Army unit which collects intelligence information, often to support SEAL Team Six and Delta Force operations.

ISU-90: US military enclosed pallet for transporting equipment.

J2: Joint Staff Intelligence.

JCET: Joint Combined Exchange Training.

JPL: Jet Propulsion Laboratory.

JSOC: Joint Special Operations Command.

LED: light-emitting diode.

Liquid Sky: Fictional mercenary strike force.

LPC: Leather Personnel Carriers (ie: boots).

M4: Standard issue US military rifle.

MAC-10: Sub-Machine Gun.

MC-5: HALO/HAHO military parachute.

MEK: Iranian terrorist organization sponsored by the United States.

MFF: Military Free Fall.

Mk 48: A 7.62 machine gun that is smaller and lighter than the M240B.

MO: Method of operation.

MSS: Chinese intelligence agency.

NASA: National Air and Space Association.

NGO: Non-Governmental Organization.

NODS: Night Optical Device.

NPA: New People's Army.

NSA: National Security Agency.

OD: Olive Drab.

OGA: Other Governmental Organizations such as Ground Branch or Global Response Staff.

ONI: Office of Naval Intelligence.

OP: Observation Point. A vantage point for snipers of reconnaissance troops to use to over watch enemy movements.

OPB: Operational Preparation of the Battlefield.

Operator: Soldier assigned to SEAL Team Six or Delta Force.

OPSEC: Operational Security.

PIN: Personal Identification Number.

PKM: Belt fed Russian made machine gun.

PMC: Private Military Company.

PT: Physical Training.

PTSD: Post Traumatic Stress Disorder.

PVS-14: Night vision monocle.

QRF: Quick Reaction Force.

R&R: Rest and Relaxation.

Rangers: US Army elite airborne light infantry unit.

Raufoss: Armor piercing explosive incendiary rounds.

RDX: Research Development Explosives.

RFID:Radio-frequency identification.

RPG: Rocket Propelled Grenade.

RPK: 7.62 light machine gun.

RUMINT: A non-official humorous term meaning Rumor Intelligence.

SA-7: Russian shoulder fired anti-aircraft missile.

Samruk International: A fictional Private Military Company based out of Kazakhstan.

SCUBA: Self Contained Underwater Breathing Apparatus.

SEAL: SEa, Air, and Land. US Navy maritime commando unit.

SEAL Team Six: US Navy SEAL Counter-Terrorism unit. Also known as Task Force Blue, Naval Special Warfare Development Group, and more recently, TACDEVRON.

SIGINT: Signals Intelligence.

SIM: Subscriber Identity Module.

SOF: Special Operations Forces.

SOTIC: Special Operations Target Interdiction Course, now knows as the Special Forces Sniper Course.

Special Forces: Also known as Green Berets, specialize in training indigenous forces. A separate unit from SEALs, Rangers, and Delta Force

SPG-9: 73mm recoiless rifle.

SSE: Sensitive Site Exploitation.

T-72: Russian main battle tank.

TACDEVRON: US Navy SEAL Counter-Terrorism unit. Also known as Task Force Blue, Naval Special Warfare Development Group, and more recently, TACDEVRON.

TF Blue: See Dev Group.

TF Green: See Delta Force.

TORDS: Tandem Offset Resupply Delivery System.

TTL: Tag, Track, and Locate.

UAE: United Arab Emirates.

VBIED: Vehicular Borne Improvised Explosive Device.

VDO: Vehicle Drop Off.

WMD: Weapon of Mass Destruction.

ZPU: Russian anti-aircraft machine gun.

Jack Murphy is a Army Special Operations veteran who served as a Sniper and Team Leader in 3rd Ranger Battalion and as a Senior Weapons Sergeant on a Military Free Fall team in 5th Special Forces Group.

Murphy is the New York Times Bestselling author of REFLEXIVE FIRE, TARGET DECK, and DIRECT ACTION. He also co-authored the non-fiction work, BENGHAZI: THE DEFINITIVE REPORT which exploded the true story behind what really happened when the US consulate in Libya came under attack.

Having left the military in 2010 after serving three combat deployments to Afghanistan and Iraq, he is now working towards a degree in Political Science at Columbia University. He has penned numerous non-fiction articles about Weapons, Tactics, Special Operations, Terrorism, and Counter-Terrorism. He has appeared in documentaries, on national television, and on syndicated radio.